Behind The Curtain

Anita D Hunt

SpellBound Books

Published in 2024 by SpellBound Books

To Ben, Michael and David.
Never give up on your dreams.

Prologue

Penny-May

Sunday June 26th 2016

It was a gradual descent. I slid so slowly into the abyss I didn't know it was happening. Didn't realise I was falling because he made me feel as if I was flying. Flying so high above the rest, I didn't need anybody else. I only needed him. He did everything for me. He became my best friend, my family and my soul mate all rolled into one. He was the one who caught me when I fell.

And when I did?

He beat me while I lay at his feet, cowering and begging him for mercy.

'I'm sorry,' I cried, time after time. 'I won't do it again, I promise.' I hid my face behind my hands, peering between taut fingers to see his face, puce with anger, fists clenched with rage. He would draw his foot back and I would wait for the sharp sting of pain when he finally launched it into the soft mass of my stomach. I would listen to him berating me for my bad behaviour all the while.

I tried so hard to be the perfect wife. The wife he deserved and demanded me to be. I tried not to cry out, I knew he didn't like it when I was that weak, it made him angrier.

But it hurt so much I couldn't help it.

I tried so hard to be just like Lucy. I was her replacement after all. I used to envy her, but now all I feel is sympathy for her weakness. For having to be the perfect woman; the perfect wife.

It was such a high pedestal upon which we teetered.

It was such a long way for us to fall.

Chapter One

Penny-May
Monday August 4th 2014.

The bedroom was a mess.

A mixture of clothes grew taller on the unmade double bed as I tried more on before throwing them away in frustration. The towels from my shower were lying in a soggy heap on the floor.

Standing in the middle of the disaster zone in my mismatched underwear, I ran my fingers through my still damp hair. If I didn't dry it soon it would turn into its usual frizzy mess, the curls were already forming their spaghetti of ringlets over my shoulders. Damn, I needed it straight today, business-like and professional was the look I was going for, not cutesy Playboy bunny girl.

'Em!' I yelled down the corridor as I turned on the straighteners, 'what do I wear? This is such a bad idea!'

Emma came into my room, breaking into a smile, long brown ponytail bobbing in time with her movements as she took in the turmoil around me.

'Because this job paid more and you wanted the extra cash to take Daniel for a holiday, remember?'

Even the thought of my brother and how much he would enjoy going away with me couldn't stop my inner panic.

'Yes, but I could do that next year, go somewhere cheaper. Daniel's happy in his home and they spoil him. I could wear jeans before, it was so much easier wearing jeans.'

'Calm down, what've you tried?' Emma walked over to the bed and started sorting through my discarded clothing. Shaking her head at the jeans and jumpers, discarding the miniskirts, holding up the plain and pinstripe trousers and placing them in a separate pile on the bed she found a few blouses that were still on hangers in my wardrobe 'What about these?' she asked, holding up the plain black pegleg trousers and a soft pink short-sleeve blouse.

'It's too cold for short sleeves and my bum looks massive in those peglegs.'

'It's August, it's not cold and you can wear a long cardi to cover your backside, which isn't too big by the way. I wish mine was just as good.' She pointed at my legs, 'In those trousers you're going to have every man in that office going gaga over your rear view.'

'Well, I'm cold,' I said, folding my arms and scowling. I knew how big my bum was and it wasn't pretty.

'That's because you're standing in your underwear with wet hair.'

I grabbed the trousers from her and started to yank them over my feet, pulling them up to cover the offending article. I'd show her what was big, she was the one with the pert bum, not me. 'See!' I said, once I had breathed in and forced the button and zip to close, 'big fat bum' I pointed to my rear and became more annoyed as Em just laughed out loud, a real guttural laugh that came from the depths of her diaphragm and spilled out, echoing around the room. Her ponytail looked as if it was in danger of falling off it was bouncing so hard.

'Don't be so daft; those trousers are a size ten. You're a right skinny bint,' she said, raising her hand to wipe her eyes. 'Now, put the shirt on over the top and don't tuck it in.'

I did as I was told, making a big show of forcing the buttons to close over my breasts. 'It's too tight, what if it gapes? I can't have my shirt gaping on my first day,' I wailed.

'It's not going to gape, just stick a sleeveless top underneath.'

With a sigh, I undressed and redressed again. As usual, Emma was right. The shirt tapered in at my waist flaring over my hips and making me look taller than my 5ft 6inches.

'That's why I love you,' I said, smiling for the first time in over an hour, 'you are the perfect best friend!'

Twirling in front of the mirror I caught sight of my hair. 'Oh my God! Look at me!' I cried, hands already trying to pull out the curls that were stubbornly forming their dense unruly waves. Emma resumed her laughter as she walked into the corridor.

'You're on your own there, I'm not going anywhere near your hair.'

The office of Mistral Architectural Designs was as impressive looking as its name sounded. A four-story glass box surrounded by landscaped gardens, strategically placed benches in half-hidden arbours dotted around the outside space. Elegant women with their hair in chignons glided effortlessly across the grass in their three inch heels. How did they do that? My heels always got stuck, I looked like a baby horse taking its first steps. The men strode confidently forward, briefcases in hand, umbrellas at the ready as they glared at the brooding grey cloud, almost daring it to split open before they could enter the building. I clutched my own umbrella tightly, hoping I wouldn't have to use it. Maybe grabbing the closest one on the way out of the door wasn't such a good idea. I'd taken a closer look whilst sitting on the bus and realised it was the bright yellow one with monkeys on it bearing the phrase *'I'm the King of the Swingers'* around the edge when it was fully unfurled. A Christmas gift from Emma last year. I loved it, but it certainly wasn't the image I was looking for today.

Glancing at my watch I saw it was 8.40am. No more dilly-dawdling. Squaring my shoulders and adjusting my new beige Top Shop handbag, I made my way through the revolving door. Hesitating slightly to gauge the speed it was turning at so I didn't fall flat on my face as I was spat out on the other side. *Result! Made it!*

Confident and business-like, that's me. Always professional and I always know what I'm doing. In front of me was the reception desk. All marbled top and gloss black front, this whole building oozed intimidation.

'Excuse me,' I said as I approached it.

The receptionist glanced up and walked around the desk towards me. Peering over her half-moon glasses, sweeping from my sensible one-inch heels up my legs and over my torso until eventually looking in my eyes. I swear she could read my fear.

'Yes, can I help you?'

'Um, yes. I'm the new secretary, Penny-May Meares. The agency sent me. Mr Lambert's office?'

'Ah, yes, of course. Sign in here please,' she replied, thrusting a leather-bound book and a fountain pen towards me across the desk. *A fountain pen? Who on earth uses a fountain pen these days? Oh my God, what if it blotches, I'm going to look so stupid if it blotches, Gee, look at that, no blotches, written like a proper pro...*

'...and then you turn left and the office is right in front of you.'

Bugger. Concentrate Penny May, now you're going to look like a right div.

'Sorry, um, would you mind repeating that again?'

She fixed me with her steely glare and glanced over my shoulder. 'Mrs Alton, I think this is the new temp you were expecting today?'

I turned and saw a woman in her mid-forties approaching the desk. Dressed in similar office attire to everyone else milling about the entrance hall, her hair neatly coiffed, face made up to perfection. She dropped her phone into her Hermes handbag and I felt the sweep of judgement descend over me again. This time though, she smiled. She really smiled.

'You must be Penny,' she said holding her hand out towards me.

Please don't let me have a sweaty palm, please don't be a sweaty palm. And don't limp shake, a proper firm grip that's what I need to do. I grabbed her hand, squeezed it firmly and let go. *Well, she's not wiping it on her coat, must have been ok.* 'Welcome to Mistral. I'm Kate Alton and I'm senior PA to Mr Lambert. You'll be working under me until Michelle comes back from her maternity leave.'

'Yes, I'm Penny-May.'

'Oh, that's pretty,' she replied, still smiling, but I'm sure there was a subtle change to the set of her lips. A hardening of the outside lines. It always happens when I use my full name. 'Follow me.' She swept towards the lift, pressing the button for up and the doors slid open with surprising speed. I'm guessing Mrs Kate Alton waits for nothing.

She pressed for floor three as I jumped in beside her. Catching my reflection in the surrounding floor to ceiling mirror, I winced. The hair straightening had not gone well.

'Mr Lambert has the third floor; Mr Reece is on the fourth

floor. You know that Mistral is made up of the names Misters Reece And Lambert.' This was said more as a statement than a question. I didn't know, but I nodded anyway.

'The ground floor is the reception and individual meeting rooms. Security are also down there. The second floor houses the three full time architects, two apprentices and two secretaries. Old Mr Reece is the senior partner so he has the penthouse suite of offices. Mr Lambert is second partner so he gets this whole floor.'

As she spoke, the doors slid open to reveal a large open plan office with four desks, two either side of a wide walkway in front of us. At the far end of the room was a full height, frosted glass partition wall with two doors embedded into it. The one on the right said Board Room whilst the one on the left said Samuel Lambert.

'Your desk is over there.' She pointed to the empty desk next to the lift door. In between it and its neighbour was another door which was slightly ajar. 'I'll show you around quickly before Mr Lambert arrives,' she said.

She strode through the door, pointing as she went, 'here are the toilets, Mr Lambert has his own shower room in his suite so it's just us staff that use these. This is the kitchen area, please clean up after yourself, there's a small lounge area over there.' She indicated another room before turning back to the office. I really wanted to have a look into the lounge, I wondered if it had really cosy armchairs I could have a lunchtime nap in, but figured I'd better not ask. 'Mr Lambert usually arrives about 9:30. I deal with him directly. You don't need to. Anything you want to ask, come to me. Don't bother him, he's a very busy man.'

We were back in the main office; I was nodding again and remembered the nodding dog in the back of my parents Austin Metro. My cosy little job as secretary in Littletons Estate Agency didn't seem so bad after all. I was so out of my comfort zone it was unreal.

'Yes Mrs Alton, where do you want me to start?'

She stopped in her tracks, turning to face me. 'Call me Kate. Mrs Alton makes me sound like a Matron in a mental institution, although sometimes that could be quite apt for here.' She laughed. A warm tinkly laugh that reminded me of my late Mother. Maybe, this was going to be OK.

Chapter Two

Penny-May
Monday August 4th 2014

'Jeez, what a day.' I pushed the apartment door closed behind me and flopped into an armchair in the lounge we shared, kicking my shoes off and folding one foot underneath me.

'You shouldn't do that you know,' Emma said, pointing at my leg, 'you'll get varicose veins. How'd it go then?'

I unfolded my leg again and pulled the coffee table closer, resting both feet on the edge. Emma harrumphed and brought over the footstool, knocking my feet off the table in the process. 'What are you like?' she asked crossly.

'Ah, but you love me really,' I bantered back. It was an old exchange; she would get exasperated with me and I would charm her out of her cantankerous mood. It usually worked, today was no exception.

'I don't know why. You're an annoying pain in the neck!' Emma smiled and I knew that I had won her around. 'So? How was it?'

She sat on the sofa opposite me and turned the tv down.

'I was so scared! This just walking in and being efficient isn't as easy as it looks you know.'

'But you did ok, didn't you?' She leaned forward, resting her chin on her hands, elbows on her knees.

'I think so. Kate, the senior PA, was scary at first. I thought she was going to have a fit when I corrected her about my name.'

'She called you Penny then?' Emma and I went back a long way, she knew about the troubles I had with my name.

'Yep. Turns out she was fine about it and was at great pains to introduce me to everyone else as Penny-May. She was alright really. A bit strict, but fair I guess. She doesn't like anyone else talking to Mr Lambert though, she's really possessive about him.'

'Who's he?'

'Who's he? He is the partner that I'm working for.'

'Bit of an old fuddy duddy then?'

'Oh no, far from it. He is hot with a capital H O T!' I waved my hand in front of my face as if I were holding a fan, 'I only saw him briefly but, phew, if only!' I replied as I pretended to faint in my chair.

'Oh, I'll bet that's why Kate wants to keep him all to herself then, it's a secret office romance.' Emma loved illicit rendezvous. Her Mills + Boon collection was threatening to take over her room.

'No, I don't think so. I think Kate is married. She wears a wedding ring.'

'Even better, an extra-marital secret office affair. They don't want to create a scandal so they have to sneak around in the stationery cupboards.'

'I don't think they'd need to hide in a cupboard, he's got his own bathroom suite in his office,' I replied, starting to laugh as I got caught up in Emma's overactive imagination. 'But no, according to the other secretary, Charlotte, Mr Lambert's wife committed suicide last year. He was devastated.'

'Really? That's so sad.'

'I know, I was so taken aback when she told me. She was young as well, only thirty-two.'

Emma leaned back in her chair and tugged at the elastic band holding her ponytail in place, allowing her hair to cascade over her shoulders.

'I can't imagine how anyone could do that.'

'Me neither. Apparently, he didn't come in for months and that's why he only talks to Kate. He doesn't want to be around anyone else.'

'That's shocking. So how did she do it?

'Charlotte said she jumped off the cliff over at Trecase. I mean, that's not a cry for help is it? That's a pretty final way to go.'

'Poor woman,' Emma said as she raised herself back up out of the chair and walked into the kitchen. 'Wine or a cup of tea?'

'Damn stupid question Em, what do you think?'

'Wine it is then.'

I settled back into my chair and turned the volume back up on the TV. 'Quick,

Emmerdale's starting!'

Chapter Three

PENNY-MAY
Tuesday August 5th 2014

The office was quiet when I walked in. I was first, which was amazing, even my hair behaved today. Sometimes, you just know you are onto a winner. The sun was shining, the bus into town was on time and I didn't have to sit next to anybody else on the usually crowded rush hour commute. A whole seat to myself and no need for a coat was heaven. It was a shame that I couldn't show off my new umbrella though. I nipped into New Look yesterday and bought a plain black one which is much more appropriate than the monkey swingers one is. Bloody typical the sun comes out now.

Looking out of the window I wondered if the cliff that Sam's (Mr Lambert's, but I like to call him Sam) wife had jumped from was visible from here. I hope it wasn't, that must be terrible to have to see it every day from your office window. I hope it was around the coast a bit more. There are a lot of places that are quite infamous for suicide jumps but I think they're hidden around the other side of the Cornish headland.

Charlotte told me his wife's name was Lucy.

She was beautiful she said. Tall, blonde and picture perfect and they were very much in love. She was a physiotherapist and that was how they met. She worked in the very posh Silverwell health club he went to and she sorted out his damaged shoulder. It was love at first sight apparently, or maybe that should be love at first rub? Charlotte is such a gossip, I wouldn't tell her any of my secrets but she's quite handy for finding out stuff about everyone else, especially the delicious Sam Lambert.

She said you could see just how much they were in love with each other when they were together. Whenever she was here the atmosphere was electric. He was always touching or holding her and she would always be looking at him, like she was drinking in his beauty and he would drop a light kiss on her forehead. Charlotte's eyes had that dreamy look in them when she was talking.

'She was so lucky,' she said, 'I'd have killed for it to be me; that he treated that way. That's the kind of relationship I want to have. Sam is my perfect man.'

I smiled when I heard this, keep dreaming, I thought. Charlotte was lovely, but from what she had said, she was hardly the type that Sam would go for. Not that I had even been brave enough to utter one word to him in the week that I had been here. He walked straight past my desk in the mornings, head facing forward and glancing at no-one. Five minutes later Kate would follow him into his office with a pot of coffee and a notepad, closing the door behind her. Ten minutes after that she would re-emerge, close the door firmly behind and give Charlotte and I our work for the next few hours. Sam rarely left the office again for the rest of the day. Meetings were held in the board room which had an inter-connecting door into his office. Kate would keep him supplied with hot and cold drinks, either going out to get his lunch herself or sending one of us if she was tied up. We were never allowed to take it into him though. That was her job, she protected him like a tiger over her newborn kitten.

Emma would be having a field day if she could see it.

But Charlotte? Poor Charlotte was not Sam's perfect woman at all. She was only twenty-three and had a penchant for wearing her trousers too tight and her tops too small. She wasn't worried about possible gaping issues, oh no, quite the opposite, the more gape the better by the looks of it. No, from what she had said, Charlotte wasn't Sam's type at all, I think I fitted the bill better. In my dreams anyway, but they were really good dreams. The kind you never want to wake up from.

Tearing myself away from the view, I headed over to my desk as the lift opened and Kate tumbled through the doors. Her hair was a mess, the perfectly coiffed image I was greeted with last week had certainly not been managed this morning.

'Kate? Are you ok? You look a bit...ah...flustered?'

'No, I'm obviously not ok. Mr Lambert texted me this morning, the ten am meeting has been brought forward to nine thirty, he's on his way and I haven't set the board room up yet or got his coffee on.'

She picked up a pile of folders from her desk. 'Here,' she said, dumping them in my arms, 'take these into the board room and put them, one in front of each chair. You also need a couple of jugs of water and fresh lemon in the middle of each table and a glass at each seat. Make sure they're placed upside down so no dust falls into them.'

Personally, I didn't think that a couple of dust motes in the next half an hour would make much difference but what did I know?

'Make sure you put them on placemats,' Kate continued, 'that's a very expensive walnut table and Mr Lambert will get really mad if there are any water marks left on it. I'll get his coffee ready, he's very particular about his coffee.'

I hadn't been in the boardroom before and I was surprised at how impersonal it was. The walnut table was flanked by eight walnut carver chairs and I could see a matching walnut dresser where the glasses and placemats were neatly stacked. A projector hung from the centre of the ceiling, pointing towards an expanse of blank wall next to the open doorway which led into Sam's office. Looking in I saw that one whole wall of his office was the same glass window that we had, but the views of the coastline were totally uninterrupted by desks and plastic plants that were designed to make our office look more exotic and welcoming. Another walnut desk was at the back of the room, angled to make the most of the view, and a further drawing desk behind it which gained the most natural light from the windows. A two-seater sofa and two armchairs were positioned opposite each other with a low coffee table separating them.

The door opened behind me, assuming it was Kate with the coffee, I turned and then jumped when I saw it was Mr Lambert standing there.

The files became slippery in my hands and the top two began sliding off the top, landing on the floor at his feet.

'Oh, Mr Lambert, I...I...I'm so sorry' I said as more started to slide and I tried to catch the falling files. Unfortunately, I only succeeded in dropping two more and knocking the water jug off the table. I never was much good at juggling and although I managed to stop the water from spilling all down his trouser leg, I didn't manage to stop it from soaking the files.

'What are you doing in here? Where's Kate?' Mr Lambert asked, staccato style. No chance of a smile on his face, I'd certainly failed in my attempts to make a good impression. Not even a twinkle in those deep brown eyes. Oh, I could drown in those eyes. They were smouldering in their darkness and they turned my legs into an even greater mound of quivering jelly than they already were.

'Uh...I think Kate's in the kitchen making your coffee, she asked me to put these on the table.' Putting the rest of the files down, I scrabbled around at his feet, trying to mop up the spilt water with the scarf I'd taken off from around my neck. Picking up the pieces of paper that had fallen out of one of them, I tried scramming them back together. Yes, great first impression Penny-May, you're certainly winning so far.

'Well, you're not doing a very good job of it are you?'

'Uh, no, I'm afraid not. I'm really sorry Mr Lambert, I'll do it now.' Yep, great first impression Penny-May, you are unbelievably amazing at your job.

I stood up and started placing the folders onto the table as he turned, walked into his office and firmly shut the door behind him.

Damn! I am so screwed now.

Chapter Four

SAM

Tuesday August 5th 2014

'Kate, what's the new girl's name?'

'The new girl? That's Penny-May. She's from the agency. Is everything alright?' Kate put his tray of coffee on the table in front of him. Double espresso shot followed by a more leisurely cappuccino, no sugar. So hot it would scald his throat on the way down.

'I was surprised to see her in the boardroom earlier. She made a mess when I walked in. Dropped a couple of files onto the floor and then knocked the jug of water over them.'

'Oh, I'm so sorry. Usually I would organise the room but with the meeting being brought forward, there was so much to do. I thought she would be ok with such a simple job. I'll get onto the agency and get a replacement.' She started heading towards the door.

'No, don't do that,' Sam replied, 'it was probably my fault, I think I startled her a bit, made her jump.'

'If you're sure?'

'Yes. For now anyway. Give her the benefit of the doubt.' Sam picked up the espresso and drank it in one fast gulp. 'Perfect. That will be all.' He waved the cup in the general direction of the door and turned his attention to the papers on his desk. As the door closed behind her, he put them down again and walked to the window, searching the sea for answers. It was a calm day today, restful and beguiling. He preferred the sea when it was more turbulent and angry; when he could use its mood to match his. Imagine he was that churning, boiling body of water crashing against the shore.

The woman in the boardroom intrigued him. There was something about her that had taken his mind away from the impending meeting about the new housing development. She reminded him of another time. Another person.

Lucy.

It was when the girl was on her knees. She'd revealed a glimpse of milk white breast as she'd removed her scarf and started to mop up the spilt water. The tip of her tongue showed through those cherry-coloured lips in that sexy self-conscious way that Lucy always did. It had always turned him on and he was surprised to feel a low spark of fire igniting inside him. It had been a long and frustrating year since Lucy had gone. Maybe it was time to have some fun.

Sam opened the door a few inches. He could watch her if he sat on his sofa to do his work. Picking up his papers in one hand and holding his cappuccino in the other, sipping it slowly so he could savour the taste, he set to work, glancing up occasionally to watch the new recruit.

Chapter Five

Penny-May

Tuesday August 5th 2014

The afternoon stretched ahead. I couldn't believe I had made such a complete idiot of myself in front of Sam. Charlotte laughed when I told her what happened, but inside I'd cringed. I sat there, waiting for Kate to come and send me packing because of my incompetence. The panic began to set in. I mean, I'm not on the permanent staff team; I can't make stupid mistakes and the agency would get annoyed because it was my first posting and I'd already cocked it up in the first week and they wouldn't want to send me anywhere else so I wouldn't get any work and I might not even get paid because they'd have to find another temp to replace me. I wouldn't be able to pay my half of the rent to Emma and she would get angry and we could lose the flat because she didn't earn enough to pay the full rent herself and what about Daniel?

My palms began to feel sweaty and I wiped them on my trousers. I wouldn't have the money to pay for the bus ticket to go and see him and then he'd be upset wondering where I was. I took a deep breath and exhaled slowly. At least the home fees were paid for by the social. He wouldn't lose his home, but I need this job.

I was over-reacting again; I knew I was but it's so hard to stop. *Calm down Pen. Daniel's fine, you'll go and see him on Saturday as usual and nothing has happened here yet. Save the panicking for if something does happen. You're smart, business-like and professional. See, you can do it.* I sat up straighter in my chair, hands hovering over the keyboard. *You're poised and working at the top of the secretarial tree.* Visions of my monkey umbrella came unbidden but I rapidly banished it again as a not very useful thought. Pressing my fingers down onto the keyboard, they started to sweep over the keys as I began typing up the minutes of yesterday's meeting.

The office door was still open, just a bit; I could see Sam sitting on the sofa facing me. I thought I saw him looking at me when I glanced up, but when I looked properly his head was bowed towards the piece of paper he was holding. He looked relaxed as he flipped through the pages, his black hair flopping forward over his eyes as he worked. He shook it away as I watched him lift his coffee cup to his mouth, pressing it gently against those gloriously supple lips. *Oh, if only I could reach up and sweep it away. See those deep brown eyes soften as they gazed into mine... bugger, he's looking up again, get busy Penny-May.* I quickly looked at the computer screen, making my fingers fly faster than they ever had before. Out of the corner of my eye I saw him stand up, walk forwards and gently close the door. I sighed as I realised I was not quite the quickest typist on the block if I actually wanted the words to make sense —

I pressed delete.

This was going to be a really long afternoon.

Chapter Six

Penny-May
Saturday August 9th 2014

'Penny-May, Penny-May!' Daniel shouted, running towards me in his loping, lopsided way.

I opened my arms and gave my younger brother a hug as he barrelled into me, reaching his arms around my waist and squeezing me tight.

'Careful Danny, you'll break me if you squeeze any harder.' Pulling gently on his arms, I freed myself from his embrace.

Danny let go, 'Won't break Penny-May, Penny-May strong like me.' He let me go and flexed his arms into a champion pose. I obligingly gave his biceps a prod with my fingers, 'me Hulk,' he said.

'Big muscles,' I replied, 'I wouldn't like to see you get angry.'

'No,' Danny put on his gruffest voice, 'you wouldn't like me when I'm angry. Me turn big and green.'

I laughed, 'Come on then Hulk, come and show me what your green fingers have done.'

Danny grabbed my hand, pulling me down the hallway and out into the garden. There were raised beds filled with herbs and edible flowers lining a paved pathway leading to a wooden gate. I swept my hand through the flowering purple haze of lavender to release the scent into the air, picking one flower and raising it to my nose. I loved this fragrance. Memories of mum making potpourri came back to me every time I inhaled it. Pushing the gate open, Daniel told me the names of all the vegetables we passed that would be used in the home's kitchen. They called it their '*Garden to Plate Project*' and all five residents would be involved in either the planting or the cooking of them.

Approaching the walk-in greenhouse at the back of the garden, Danny dropped my hand and ran ahead to open the door. To the left were some tomato plants; cucumber plants on the right and in front of us were two shelves full of chilli and pepper plants. As I watched, Danny started to lift leaves to check for pests, tenderly checking the fruit for ripeness before picking up a small wicker bowl from the floor. He carefully picked the ripe chillies and placed them inside it. Dad used to be so patient with him. He would sit for hours with Danny in the greenhouse, showing him how to grow plants from seeds and enter them into the Grand Cottage Garden Show. Danny loved it when they won a certificate and a little golden cup.

I was seven years old when Mum brought him home from the hospital. He was tightly swaddled in a pure white, hand crocheted blanket she had spent weeks making for him. I would cuddle up beside her as she worked, safe and snug under the snowy fluffiness of it.

I peeped inside, gently pulling on the scalloped woollen edge and inhaling the waft of Johnson's baby powder that floated up to me. I heard a sniff and looked up to see my mother crying.

'We have to take extra special care of Daniel,' mum said, wiping the tear from her cheek, 'he's going to need a lot of help.'

'Why?'

'He's different to the rest of us. He's not going to think the same way we do.' I took another peek inside.

'But he looks the same?'

'He looks a bit different, and he's going to change more as he gets older. The Doctors said he has something called Down's Syndrome.'

'Down's Syndrome,' I repeated, trying to commit this new phrase into my memory. 'Does it hurt?'

Mum smiled, 'no honey, it doesn't hurt. He's just a bit different and we have to look after him to keep him safe. Can you help us to do that?'

I nodded, leaning over and pressing a tiny kiss on his forehead. I felt so grown up with all this responsibility. 'Yes, he's my extra special baby brother.'

As he grew I kept my promise. When the children at school started to push him around in the local park, I walked right up to the ringleader and punched him in the face, knocking him over and making him cry. Word got around not to mess with Daniel Meares or Penny-May Meares would be after them. In return, Danny followed me around and always made me laugh with his antics.

When our parents died in a car crash six years ago, I took over as Power of Attorney for him. I had no idea what I was doing. I knew I had always looked out for him, but this? This wasn't supposed to happen. Mum and Dad always figured out his day-to-day stuff. What did I know about the finances for his day care, and the respite provision? And I had to work. I couldn't look after him on my own, I didn't even have my own house and the landlord wouldn't switch my parents lease to me. He wanted the house for his own son. It was the social worker who found Danny a place in

Oak Tree Lodge, a residential home for adults with learning disabilities. We bought a pear tree and together we planted it in the garden so he had somewhere to sit and remember them. I was only twenty-nine and my world was broken, but at least having him to focus on gave me a reason to continue. I may no longer have had a safety net, but I was damn sure that Danny always would.

'Got any ripe pears yet Dan?'

'We picked some today. Martha's making crumble for tea. Yummy, yummy, crumbly pie,' he added in his sing-song voice.

'Yummy crumbly pie?,' I repeated after him. 'I'm so jealous.'

'Penny-May stay. You have some crumbly pie?'

'I wish I could Danny boy, but I have to go home soon. I'll be back next Saturday and you can tell me what it's like.'

'When's Saturday?'

'Let's go and put it on your calendar and then you can count down the days again.'

Carrying the bowl inside and giving it to Martha in the kitchen with a cheery high five as he passed her, he took me to his room where his calendar was hung up on his wall. Every previous Saturday I had written 'Penny-May' on it in red ink pen and every morning when he woke up he would cross the day off so he knew how long he had to wait until he could see me again. The red felt tip pen was attached to the side of the calendar with a big blob of blue tack so he would know where it was.

'There,' I said, when I'd written myself in for the following week and placed the pen back where it belonged, 'it's a date. Seven sleeps and I'll be here again.'

As far as I was concerned, nothing would stop my Saturday afternoon with my little brother.

Chapter Seven

Penny-May
Tuesday August 12th 2014

'I'm so tired,' I kicked off my stiletto shoes and flopped onto the aging sofa. 'I don't know how on earth people can wear these damn things all day. My feet are killing me.' I started to massage my dead toes through the sheer black stockings I had worn today and let out a long sigh of pleasure. 'Oh, that's heaven. Any chance of a foot rub?'

Emma gave me the look she normally reserves for only the stupidest of questions.

'Get lost, you need to do what the rest of us do and take them off when you are at your desk. No-one sees your feet under there.'

'I can't do that. What if I have to stand up quick and do something officey like get an important document from the filing cabinet? I'd waste too much time putting them back on again.'

Emma shook her head, 'sometimes you're just too dense for words.' She had a smile playing around her lips so I knew she was joking, but really? Dense? Me? I am the epitome of a successful working woman. With very sore feet.

'Why are you wearing them anyway? You always used to wear flats at your old job. And while we're at it, what's with the stockings and the tight pencil skirt?'

'No reason,' I replied, refusing to look her in the eye, 'I just thought it would look smart, that's all.

'Oh, just look smart eh? That's why you're doing that twirly thing with your finger in your hair is it?'

Damn. I quickly pulled my hand down from where I had been making those tell-tale ringlets on the right-hand side.

'You're trying to impress a bloke aren't you!' She continued.

'No!' I replied, a touch too quickly.

'Oh yes you are, come on Missus, spill the beans. And I want all the gory details.' I could feel the blush rising up and spilling out across my cheeks.

'This is getting better and better. Look at your face! I could fry an egg on that!' Now. You haven't talked about any men in your office, so, is this all about hot lurve over the water cooler with someone from another office then?'

'Don't be so stupid Em, they're all old and fuddy duddy apart fr— ' I stopped speaking, realising that I was about to give myself away, '— anyway, how's your day been? Given any of the little darlings a clip around the ear yet?'

'I've been tempted, but no. Stop trying to change the subject. Apart from who?'

I really should know by now that once Emma gets wind of a juicy piece of gossip she is harder to shake off than a dog on a bitch in heat. Which is something I'm not; I'm just mildly interested, that's all.

'No-one, I told you they're all fuddy duddy. I'm just trying to make a good impression in a new workplace, that's all. Do you want a coffee?' I stood up and walked towards the door.

'No, I don't want a coffee and I think you're definitely hiding something.'

'Well, I'm going to make one, are you sure?'

'Yes, I'm sure, and you don't normally drink coffee this late, it keeps you awake.' 'I'll drink decaf.'

'We don't have any decaf.'

I swear she was being annoying on purpose. 'Then I'll go to the shop and get some. I really fancy a coffee.' I walked back to the sofa and started to squeeze my toes back into my stiletto shoes. 'As soon as I have changed into my jeans and trainers.'

'I think you fancy something different from a coffee. Or someone.' Emma called as I left the room, closing the door behind me. I could hear her smirk. 'And don't you worry,' she continued, raising her voice slightly, 'I'll get to the bottom of it!'

It was weird that I was so reluctant to talk to her about my feelings. We had been best friends since college over fifteen years ago and flat mates for the last ten years. We usually shared everything, but this was different. I knew I was being stupid. I mean, who has a crush on their recently widowed and grieving boss and actually expects it to become real? I had been at Mistral for three weeks and, except for that disastrous meeting in the board room, he hasn't said a single word to me. I'm an idiot. I'm going to wear my Vans in again tomorrow, stuff the heels. Throwing my stilettos into the bottom of the wardrobe I pulled out my favourite flatties and placed them ready to wear the next day.

'I know who it is!' I heard Emma yell from the lounge. 'It's that sexy boss of yours isn't it? What's his name again? Ah...yes, Sam wasn't it?' She had used her '*I'm in lurve*' voice when she said his name. I grimaced as I shut the bedroom door behind me and slipped my skirt and stockings off.

'Penny loves Sam! Sam loves Penny!' Emma continued to banter and then laughed. Actually, I think it was more of a cackle, just like the witch that she really is.

'I wish,' I said quietly to myself as I took my jeans from the back of the bedroom chair and jammed my leg into them. 'I should be so lucky.'

Chapter Eight

Penny-May

Wednesday September 17th 2014

Today is a new day and I am going to show them what I'm made of and I'm not going to pander to anyone. I'm a strong, independent woman and I am good at my job.

I won't be nervous.
I won't fuck anything up.
I will be the perfect PA.

I won't be nervous.
I won't fuck anything up.
I will be the perfect PA.

I won't be nervous.

I won't fuck—

Oh, who am I trying to kid. I let out a big sigh and stared at my reflection. Em had left one of her self-help books on the coffee table in the lounge and I had started to flick through it last night. The author was adamant that you could make yourself into the woman you wanted to be by using positive thought and actions.

Step one in her '*think yourself successful*' to do list was to look at yourself in the mirror first thing in the morning and recite a mantra ten times to yourself. You had to stare intently into your own eyes and will the words into them.

'Let them seep deep into the subconscious that lies behind the windows to your soul'

It had sounded such a good idea when coupled with the glass or two of rosé wine I had found in the fridge. That had belonged to Emma too, but she was out and the bottle was already open. I couldn't let it go sour could I? I was doing her a favour really. I hate to see money wasted, it's too hard to come by. I was listening to 'The Best of The Beautiful South' on the CD player, turned down low so the old lady downstairs wouldn't complain, a couple of tea lights flickering in the darkness. It had all seemed so easy. I could turn myself into a poised, confident professional in no time.

This morning, all I could see when I stared deep into my eyes were bloodshot hell holes leering back at me rimmed with the remains of yesterday's mascara that I hadn't removed properly before I fell into bed. The dull throb of the headache from hell doesn't help either.

Oh, this is ridiculous. What sort of a wuss am I? I can't even get through a mantra without giving up.

I am a Wuss.
I am doomed to fail.
I'm never going to win.

I am a Wuss.
I am doomed to fail.
I'm never going to win.

Yep, that sounds much more like me.

'Penny-May? Helloo? Anybody in there?'

I looked up from my computer screen to see Charlotte standing beside me. She looked weird. She always had a bit of a strange look about her, but this was different. Normally she was just plain kooky, but this was kooky with attitude. I'm not sure I want to know what the glint in her eye is all about but I had a feeling I wasn't going to get a choice in the matter.

'Uh, yeah, where else would I be? What's up?'

'This is my big chance.'

'Big chance for what?'

'Duh! With Sam!' She whispered with a glance over her shoulder towards his office.

My fingers stilled on the keyboard as I looked over her shoulder towards the closed door.

'What do you mean? Your big chance? What's happened.' I found myself copying her stage whisper although I had no idea why I was doing it. There was nobody else around that could hear us.

'Kate's just phoned me from her car. She went out to get his lunch, but she's got

a migraine started. She's going home but she asked me to nip down to the car park and get his lunch from her and then take it into him.'

'She's gone home because she's got a headache?'

'I guess you've never had a migraine?'

'Well, no, but it's just a headache isn't it?'

'Oh, when Kate gets them, she gets them really bad. Her face turns green and she throws up and everything!' Whilst I was reminded of Daniel doing his Hulk impression, Charlotte made the appropriate gagging gestures which immediately put me off any thoughts of going for my own lunch.

'It's the only time she's ever away when Sam's here. She even takes her holidays at the same time as him.'

'Really?' Maybe they were in a clandestine relationship after all. Em was going to be so pleased with this piece of gossip. And it would throw her off the scent of my stupid crush.

'You don't suppose there's anything between them do you?'

Charlotte looked horrified as she raised her hand to her mouth, 'What, Sam and Kate? Are you kidding?'

'Well, they do spend a fair bit of time locked away in that office.'

'Surely not. Oh, but that's so gross. She's married and Clive is such a great guy. He bought me flowers for my birthday, even waited outside work to give them to me.'

Now that really would give Emma something to fantasise about. I was going to carry on teasing Charlotte but she looked so upset that I decided to stop. I swear that girl is just too gullible for her own good sometimes.

'I'm sure they're not,' I said, 'I'm just teasing. Aren't you keeping Kate waiting downstairs?'

'Oh yes, I've got to go.'

Charlotte turned and ran for the lift, pressing the button furiously as if that would make it hurry up and get to our floor. When it did arrive and the doors opened, I could see Charlotte doing the same on the inside.

'It's probably quicker to use the stairs!' I called as the doors slid shut and hid her from view.

No more than five minutes later, Charlotte came rushing through the door that led to the stairwell. She was breathing heavily and bent over to catch her breath.

'I think I've got a stitch,' she said as she held her hand to her side to try and ease the pain. 'It might be quicker, but it's one helluva lot more knackering.'

I giggled as I saw the slight sheen of sweat on her forehead and her rose coloured cheeks. The paper bag in her other hand looking slightly crushed at the top where she had gripped it too hard while running up the stairs.

'I don't think you're going to be any great threat to Usain Bolt are you?' I said, 'I hope whatever is in there isn't squashable?'

Charlotte looked at the bedraggled bag she was holding. 'I can't take it in like that,' she wailed.

'Go in the kitchen and put it on a plate, make it all pretty and he'll never know. Take him a coffee as well, that'll help.'

Just as Charlotte disappeared through to the staff room, Sam's door opened and he filled the doorway. Pale grey shirt stretched taut across his chest, top button undone. He had a slightly darker grey tie, loose around the neck. Black suit trousers fitted snugly around his upper thighs and I knew they were even more snug around his backside. It was a pleasure to sit at my desk and watch him stride past me every morning as he walked to h office.

'Penny-May isn't it? Kate said she'd send my lunch up. Is there any sign of it yet? I have a meeting in half an hour.'

'Oh yes, Mr Lambert, Charlotte is just in the kitchen doing it now.'

'Good, tell her to hurry up please.'

He turned and went back into his office, but he left the door ajar and I could see him sit down onto the sofa and reach his arm across the back as he looked out of the window.

I tore myself away from my own private view and poked my head around the kitchen door. 'What are you doing in here, he has a meeting in thirty minutes and he's waiting for his lunch.'

Charlotte turned around, she had a plate in one hand on which was perched a sandwich and salad from the deli across the road. She had a steaming mug of coffee in the other.

'I'm on it,' she said heading for the door.

'Get a tray, Kate always walks through the office with his food on a tray. You've been here longer than me, surely you've seen that?'

'Oh, uh, yeah, right,' she said, I put the tray on the table and she put the lunch on it, picked it up with one hand and flicked her hair over her shoulder with the other. The purple highlights flashed in the autumn sunlight that came in through the window.

'Wish me luck,' she said as she sashayed her way out of the room. She gave me the fingers crossed sign behind her back just as she went out of my sight.

I smiled. She was funny in her kooky way, but I really didn't think she stood a chance with someone as confident and self-assured as Sam. He would go for someone much more like he was, someone confident and beautiful.

Like Lucy.

Neither Charlotte nor I would be able to snag him.

Chapter Nine

Sam

Wednesday September 17th 2014

Sam looked at his watch and tutted loudly. It was half twelve already, and he liked to have his lunch at midday. That way, he could eat it slowly and make sure that it was fully digested before his round of afternoon meetings. It really wasn't good enough for it to be this late. Even if Kate did have to go home sick, she should have sorted this properly before she went. He stood up from his desk and walked to the office door. Looking out into the room he could only see the new girl sat typing at her desk. There was nobody else around.

'Penny-May isn't it? Kate said she'd send my lunch up. Is there any sign of it yet? I have a meeting in half an hour.'

'Oh yes, Mr Lambert, Charlotte is just in the kitchen doing it now.'

'Good, tell her to hurry up please.'

He turned and pushed the door behind him, but leaving it

open just a little bit so he could still see into the room. Sitting down onto the sofa and relaxing back into it, he stretched, placing his arm across the cushion next to him and looked out of the window. He knew the girl was watching him. The girls always watched him. Always wanted him.

He was fussy about the girls he went for though. They had to have that certain something that set them apart from the rest of the crowd. The ones that were gagging for it. No, he didn't want them, they were far too easy. He wanted the chase, and he wanted them to make him chase them.

From the corner of his eye he saw her stand and walk towards the kitchen, closing the door behind her.

She did as she was told. That was good.

Charlotte came into the room bearing a tray with his lunch and a mug of coffee on it, approached the table and put the tray down.

'Take it off the tray please, where's the espresso?'

'The espresso?' Charlotte replied, 'I'm sorry, I didn't know you had one of those as well, Kate just said coffee. I'll go and get it now.'

'Don't bother, you're so late that I won't have time to drink it by the time you've made it anyway.'

'Uh, it's no bother Mr Lambert, it won't take me two ticks.' She turned to go out of the door as a grimace flashed across his face on hearing her last words. He hated it when people used such commonplace language. This was a business and a professional manner was required at all times. There was no room for any amount of

'ticks' in his office.

He watched her retreating back as she went out of the room.

Her code of dress wasn't appropriate either. Those skin-tight trousers and DMs were certainly not professional. Although the low-cut top was quite nice. In a trashy kind of way.

He made a mental note to speak to Kate on her return. She would have to sort the girl out. It was simply not acceptable.

Chapter Ten

Penny-May
Wednesday September 17th 2014

'Penny-May, would you follow me please?'

Startled, I looked up from my computer as Sam walked past me to his office. I saw Charlotte look up as well and send me a questioning glance. I shrugged my shoulders as I slipped my shoes back onto my feet before standing up and, taking my notepad and pen, followed him into his office.

'Yes Mr Lambert.'

I had no idea why he would be asking me to go with him, he'd never done that before and surely Charlotte should be first to be called in Kate's absence? I didn't think I'd done anything wrong lately, I'd kept my head down and got on with the work.

I took a deep breath and tried to stop the shaking that had just started in my fingers.

Sam went into the office first and put his briefcase on his desk. He slipped his jacket off and hung it on the coat stand. Walking back to his desk, he pulled his tie a short way down and undid the top button of his shirt before sitting down in the chair behind his desk and wheeling it forward so that he was able to lean his arms on the walnut top.

This man really liked his walnut furniture. I thought it was too dark, I much preferred the lighter beech wood style, although this did suit his sexy, dark and brooding manner.

'I need the Davis file as well as the plans for the Pencoven development over at Trecase.'

'Trecase? You're working up there?' I asked before I could stop myself.

Sam looked up at me, 'Yes, Trecase, you know where it is I take it?' He spoke gruffly and I regretted saying anything.

'Uh, yes, of course. We used to take my dog for a walk up there when I was a child. I used to love watching the surfers down on the beach.'

'Yes, well, we are not here to reminisce. Just get me the paperwork I need would you?' He pulled his briefcase over to him and snapped open the clasps.

'Yes, I'll go right now. Sorry.'

I turned and started to walk briskly and efficiently out of the room when his voice called me back.

'Penny-May?'

'Yes,' I replied as I turned halfway towards him.

'Don't spill any water on them this time will you. They are the originals.'

I felt my face begin to flush as I replied, 'Yes, um, I mean no, I mean yes, uh I won't spill any water.' I turned and fled out of the door.

'What did he want?' asked Charlotte as I came past her desk. Her fingers stilled on the computer keyboard while she looked at me expectantly and waited for my reply.

'He just wants a file and a set of plans from the storage room,' I replied as I walked through the room, 'I'm going to get them now.'

'But why did he ask you?'

Charlotte looked petulant, like a child who had been denied an extra sweet at playtime. I stopped and turned toward her.

'I don't know. He's never done that before.'

'He must have a reason. I'm next in line when Kate's not here.' I had a vision of her stamping her foot in annoyance as she spoke.

'I know. I'm as surprised as you are. He never usually speaks to me.'

'I'll bet it was because I'd stuffed up his lunch. Why didn't you tell me he had espresso as well? That's it. You sabotaged my big chance.' She folded her arms in front of her and lowered her head, 'and now he's going to go for you instead of me.'

'Oh Charlotte, I did nothing of the sort. I honestly didn't know about him wanting an espresso with his lunch and I have no idea why he called me instead of you. Maybe he just saw me first when he opened the door? It does look straight out onto my desk area.'

Charlotte looked up from under her brown blunt cut fringe. She would be so much prettier if she had that styled around her face a bit more, but this wasn't the right time to give her fashion advice. She had stopped wearing those awful clumpy shoes though. I had said about how nice her new shoes looked and she had just shrugged and not replied at the time. 'Do you think so?'

Relieved that she seemed to be coming out of her black mood I nodded sincerely. I hoped it was coming across as sincere anyway. I didn't want her to turn against me.

'Yes, I'm sure that's it. There's no way he's going to go for me in a million years.'

'You're probably right,' she replied as she started tapping on the keys in front of her, 'Lucy was much younger and prettier than you.'

I opened my mouth to utter a response to her catty comment but then thought better of it and continued on my way to the storeroom. I mentally fist punched the air as I left the room, I was able to think before I spoke after all.

I took a deep breath before knocking on Sam's office door.

'Come.' His tone was short, abrupt, as if he had been concentrating and didn't want the interruption.

Opening the door gingerly, I peered into the room and saw him still sat at his desk with papers strewn around him. His briefcase was on the floor beside him and he was closing the top drawer of his desk.

'The files you asked for?' I indicated the folder and the rolled tube I held in my arms.

'Yes, thank you. Put them down over there,' he said as he pointed towards his drawing board and wiped his hand across his right eye.

I did as I was asked, aware that he was watching me as I passed his desk. I was glad I had taken Emma's advice and brought the stiletto's to change into when needed. My squashed toes would be in agony by now if I hadn't. I was also glad that I had decided against wearing my trainers to work. They wouldn't have given the impression I was hoping for.

'Is there anything else?' I asked as I turned to face him again and walked to the front of his desk.

'I don't think so, not for now.' He stood and turned towards his board, reaching out and picking up the cylindrical tube I had just placed there. Feeling I was dismissed I walked to the door.

With my hand on the handle, he called me again,

'Oh, hang on, there is one thing.'

I stopped and turned, but still holding the door.

'Yes Mr Lambert?'

'I have an evening appointment tonight and I need a PA there. Normally Kate would do it but she's not going to be able to because of her migraine. I don't suppose you would be free for a couple of hours tonight would you?' Perfectly straight, even white teeth shone through his smile as his cheeks crinkled and his eyes danced.

I didn't know what to say. A million things were running around in my mind and my initial impulse was to say no. There was no way I could do that. I'd cock it all up and prove myself to be the idiot I really was.

'Please? I promise I won't be an ogre. I'm only one of those in normal working hours.'

I smiled and found myself saying, 'It's fine Mr Lambert, I'm free this evening.

What time and where?'

'It's about the Pencoven development so Mr Davis will be there. We will be eating at Pareusi's in Dowrporth Bay. I'll pick you up from your house at 6:30pm and then fill you in on the details as I drive. What is your address?'

Oh my goodness, I'm going to be alone in the car with him. What will we talk about? Oh my God!

I told him where I lived and then turned and left the room, closing the door behind me.

I decided not to tell Charlotte about Sam's request. Judging by her reaction to my being asked to get a file, I didn't fancy seeing her reaction to this piece of news.

Chapter Eleven

Penny-May

Wednesday September 17th 2014

Emma jumped as I charged through the door of our flat. She was sitting curled up on the sofa reading her book with her favourite Dido cd playing softly in the background. A half-empty coffee mug sat forlornly on the table, I knew it would have gone cold already, Emma got so engrossed in her reading that she often forgot she had made it. She looked wildly around her as her book slid from her hands and landed in a heap on the floor.

'Arrgh!! You've got to help me!' I wailed as I threw my handbag onto her vacated seat and kicked my shoes under the table.

'What? What's happened?'

'He's taking me to dinner. We're going to Pareusi's! What the hell do I wear?'

Emma put one hand on her hips, the other she raised in front of her as if she was stopping traffic. Her mouth pursed and she pulled her full five feet, two inches into action as she tried to understand what I was saying. 'Hang on. You're going to need to back up a bit. Who's asking you to dinner?'

'Sam! I mean, Mr Lambert! God help me Em!' I was getting more panic stricken by the second, I didn't know how I got myself into this mess and I was totally certain there was no way I was going to be able to go through with it.

'Sam? Your boss Sam?'

'Yes!' I squeaked. 'He's taking me to Pareusi's!'

'Pareusi's? But that's mega expensive in there, how the hell did you swing a date with your boss to Pareusi's?' Her ponytail was bobbing excitedly behind her, I could see the end of it bouncing haphazardly as she started to jump up and down.

'Oh my God, that's amazing,' she continued, 'I knew you could do it.

You've only gone and bagged a date with Mr H O T Lambert! Come on, tell me how you wangled that one.'

By now she was running around the room, book forgotten, whilst Dido had moved on to sing about things changing and she was the queen of her domain. I heard her start the chorus, telling the world that the land was hers, but she would let her man in and rule beside her. Emma started belting out the tune at full volume, drowning out the singer's voice with her own, not quite so in tune version. She then grabbed both my hands and started dancing me around the room with her.

'Stop,' I said as she twirled me around, 'it's not a date. It's a business meeting. He's taking me as a PA because Kate's sick.' Emma stopped abruptly.

'A business meeting? To Pareusi's? Must be some client.' She looked crestfallen. Her ponytail stopped its dancing and hung limply from the, now loose, hairband.

'It is. He's the head of a massive new development of houses on that open land behind Trecase. But what am I going to wear?'

I looked at the clock on the mantlepiece, 'and he's going to be here in forty five minutes!'

'He's coming here?' Emma grabbed my arms.

'Right,' she said. 'Action plan. You shower and wash your hair. I'll go raid your wardrobe.'

Within half an hour Emma had found an outfit of a chic little black dress, high fronted but with a choker style neckband that left exposed shoulders and back. There were also black sheer tights and matching stiletto shoes. I felt my toes curl in agony as soon as they saw them, but I forced them in despite their cries of protest. She lent me a copper-coloured lacy pashmina to go with it and her own smart briefcase that she used for work complete with notebook, pen and a packet of mints inside.

'You can't go out with that rucksack you always use,' she said when I protested.

She blow-dried my hair so that it curled softly around my face and also put on such a thin layer of make-up that it didn't look as if I had any on, but I knew the spot on my chin which had been threatening to break through all day was hidden.

When Emma was on a mission, there was no stopping her.

'Just a touch of lip gloss,' she said as she touched her little finger into the pot and then dabbed it onto my lips and stood back to survey her handiwork.

'Perfect. You are the epitome of professionalism and he will adore you.'

'You don't think it's a bit over the top, do you?' I was starting to feel a bit self-conscious and I was really out of my depth here. Panic started to take over again.

'Oh my God Em, I really can't do it. I'm so stupid thinking I can. Maybe I'll phone Kate and if she is feeling better now, she can go instead. She's much more professional than I am. She's made for those types of places.' My voice was rising in pitch as the panic began to take hold. 'That's it, Em, you go and ring Kate. I can't do this, I really, really can't do this.'

'Don't be such a daft a'peth,' she started to laugh and held onto my hands to stop them from raking through my hair. 'You'll be fine.'

The ring of the doorbell echoed through the flat and my hands shot to my mouth.

'Oh, he's here. What do I do?'

'Well, I'll go and answer the door, and then you pick up that briefcase and follow me to the door. You hold your head high. You walk past me and say hello to Sam. Then you let him lead you to his car. If he's a gentleman, he'll open the door for you, and you sit in. Bum first. And keep your legs closed.

That skirt's a bit short for getting in and out of cars.' She moved towards the door of the room.

'Oh, and stick to water. You know what you're like when you get on the vino.'

As she vanished, I took a deep breath and did as I was told. A quick glance in the mirror told me I was looking ok. It was time to see what I could do.

I won't be nervous.

I won't fuck anything up.

I will be the perfect PA...

Chapter Twelve

Penny-May

Wednesday September 17th 2014

Sam waited for me at the door of the flat. He was dressed in a formal black suit with a grey shirt and tie, buttoned up to the neck. As he stepped aside to let me walk past him into the entrance hall, I could smell his scent. His aftershave was dark and woody and smelt so masculine, I had to stop myself from leaning in and taking a bigger whiff of his neck.

Stop it Pen. Be professional. This is a business meeting, not a date. No matter how much you would like it to be otherwise.

'Penny-May,' he said as he waved his arm in the direction of the outer door. 'My driver is waiting. After you.'

His driver? I thought he said he was driving. Oh bugger, where do I sit when I get in? I'm going to look like a right idiot.

'Aren't you driving?' I asked as he followed me out of the door. I looked back at him and saw Emma, still in the doorway to our flat, giving me a massive double thumbs up and grinning madly, waving her head from side to side and jiggling her bottom sideways in time with it. She looked so comical I was struggling not to laugh so shot her my *'stop it right now'* look which only made her jiggle even more and poke her tongue out at me.

'No, I have a driver when I go out in the evenings so that I can have something different from an orange juice. Is that ok?'

Realising he must have caught my *'stop it now'* look and thinking I was directing it at him, I flashed him a quick smile as Emma closed the door behind us. I was going to kill her when I got back home.

'Yes, that's fine, not a problem for me.' I replied, as I saw his driver standing outside the sleek black car and holding the rear passenger door open.

The sun was starting to lower in the autumn sky and as it did so, I could see the beginning of a red glow spreading through the wispy, cotton wool clouds. A cool breeze caught the edge of my pashmina, lifting it slightly so I pulled it a bit tighter, shielding my exposed shoulders from the brief chill.

I walked towards the open car door hoping that was what I was supposed to do. Nobody stopped me so, remembering Emma's bum first advice, I sat onto the cool leather seat and swung my feet into the footwell. As I was trying to decide whether I had to shufty over so Sam could slide in next to me, the driver closed the door with the softest of clicks and I watched Sam walk around to the driver's side, open his own door and sit beside me. I had placed Emma's briefcase in the middle of the seat and it now acted as a barrier between us. His aftershave slowly wafted towards me and I concentrated on watching the urban sprawl begin to change from grey brick to green hedgerow as the car gathered speed.

'The man we're meeting is Carl Davis. He's head of the Pencoven development and worth a lot of money to the company. He will have his wife with him, she's called Rhea. You'll be taking notes of the meeting,' he nodded at my case, 'I'm assuming you have an iPad in there?'

Damn! No iPad. Does he know how expensive they are?

I opened the case and pulled out a spiral bound notepad.

'Umm, sort of,' I replied, 'of the old school variety. I even remembered two pens, just in case one runs out. That's something you can't do when an iPad runs out of power.' I said, holding them up, wincing as I realised they were both pink and fluffy.

Yeah, I am so the professional PA.

He laughed so it can't have been that bad.

'It's good to be prepared,' he said, 'were you in the boy scouts when you were younger?'

'Uh, funnily enough, no. Were you in the Brownies then?' I countered, smiling right back at him.

'Touché. And no. I wasn't. Although I was in the Scouts myself for a short time.'

'Why did you leave?'

I saw Sam's face close over briefly, 'It didn't work out.'

I shouldn't have asked such a personal question. *Professional, stay professional.*

'Now, Rhea doesn't like going to the bathroom on her own.' He continued without any hesitation, 'It's a girl thing apparently, if she says she needs to use the lady's room, you go too.'

Opening the notepad, I wrote,

go to bathroom

on the top of the first page and then held the pen still, poised over the paper

waiting for the next instruction. I was tempted to start doodling a flower in the corner of the page, I could draw a pretty mean rosebush when I got going but I managed to turn the first petal into a squiggle as if I was checking the pen was working properly. It's probably not possible to do doodles on an iPad either.

The maître d' knew Sam by name. We were greeted at the door and ushered straight to our table where two people were already waiting. Carl and Rhea Davis, I assumed and, for once, I had assumed correctly. They stood as we approached, him putting his wine glass down on the table and wiping his damp hand on his napkin while she bowed her head and smoothed her already very smooth dress down.

'Carl, Rhea, this is Penny-May. I'm afraid Kate is sick today, so she's standing in.'

Carl appeared to be in his mid-forties with a hairline that was beginning to recede. Rhea looked a fair bit younger, late twenties? It was always so much harder to tell with women. Especially rich women. Her blonde hair was pinned in an elegant chignon revealing a milky white neck. Earrings that looked suspiciously like real diamonds dropped on a single silver strand from her earlobes to dust her shoulders. A midnight blue dress, tight, short and low cut; the perfect frame for the matching diamond drop that nestled into her cleavage.

'Mr Davis, Mrs Davis, pleased to meet you.' I said, as I resisted the urge to curtsy and shook their proffered hands instead.

'Oh, don't be so formal here,' Mr Davis said, shaking my hand so hard I was afraid it would fall off, 'Carl and Rhea will be fine.'

Rhea's handshake, in stark contrast, was barely a touch before being pulled back quickly, 'Pleased to meet you,' she said, so quietly I could barely hear the words.

'Let's sit, shall we?' Sam said as he pulled a chair out for me and held it while I sat. Rhea was opposite me; Carl was to my left and Sam on the right.

Oh bugger. Now do I call him Sam or Mr Lambert? Ha, I just won't address him by name all night. That'll sort it.

'Thank you,' I nodded slightly, reaching down to get the notepad and pen from my case and placing it on the table in front of me.

Pleased with myself for my brilliant plan, I picked up the menu and wondered what I should order.

Chapter Thirteen

PENNY-MAY
Wednesday September 17th 2014

'Tell me then! How'd it go?'

Emma jumped up from her chair as I walked in and ran across the room, grabbed me and plonked me into an armchair. She then sat on the edge of the coffee table in front of me and, hands clasped, rested her forearms on her knees. There was an empty wine glass beside her seat and her eyes shone with excitement.

Relaxing back into the soft and squishy cushions of the chair, I discarded my heels, leaving them in a tangle on the carpet, and tucked my feet underneath me. Emma's warning about varicose veins echoed around my head but I was too comfy to listen.

I didn't want to tell Emma about the evening yet. I would eventually, we told each other everything, but I wanted time to think about it, get it sorted in my own head. Emma would turn it into the romance of the year. She would analyse every little nuance and word that he had spoken and turn it into her own little Mills + Boon novel. I wasn't sure I wanted her to do that this time. Not yet anyway. 'Come on,' she said, 'I want to hear every tiny little detail.'

'There's not very much to say,' I replied.

'Oh, don't give me that! I know you better than anyone. Come on, what did he do?'

'It was just a business meeting. He talked business with Carl, and I took notes. I also went to the bathroom with Carl's wife Rhea because she's too scared to go on her own.'

'Too scared? Really? What kind of a wimp is she?'

That thought had occurred to me as well, especially in such a posh restaurant, I mean, it's not as if the joint was full of druggies or anything.

'She didn't say very much, I guess she was just shy.' I shrugged my shoulders as I spoke.

'Carl and Rhea eh? First name terms with the clients?'

'They asked me to call them that, I guess it seemed weird to be saying Mr and

Mrs Davis in the middle of a restaurant.'

'Hang on, Carl and Rhea Davis? Is she a lot younger than him? Blonde, medium length hair?'

'I couldn't tell how long her hair was, she was wearing it up, but it's blonde yes, and I'd say she was around fifteen years younger than him. Why?'

'They have a son at the school, he's in Mrs Lindsey's class. Lovely little boy called Joshua, very polite.'

'Oh? I can't imagine Rhea as a mother, she didn't seem strong enough somehow.'

'We don't see her very much. There's an au pair that does the school runs and looks after Josh. They only come in for parents evening and fundraising events.'

'So, what are they like? The Davis's?'

Now that I had shifted Emma's focus away from Sam, I was going to keep it away. I wasn't particularly interested in what the couple were like, I had been with them all evening and thought they were ok. He was jolly and good humoured. She was demure and a bit quiet but joined in the conversation when it was required. She hadn't eaten much of her meal. That was probably how she kept her slim figure. I felt guilty as I remembered the massive piece of double chocolate fudge cake and huge dollop of clotted cream that I had eaten. It was going to be salad for lunch for at least a week to work that off.

'They seem alright. They always pay their bills on time without any fuss and they always donate something to the fundraising events. We look forward to seeing what they give actually, because it's always something good. The last one was a fully paid 'Go Karting' party for ten kids and their parents. You wouldn't believe how many raffle books we went through for that one.'

Emma worked in the account's office at Havenmoor Preparatory School. I should have known she would focus on the finance side rather than the personal one.

I glanced at the clock on the wall, 'oh, is that the time? I'm off to bed. It's been such a long day.'

Faking a yawn, I stretched my arms above my head, uncurled my legs and stood up from the chair.

'Hang on, what about Sam?' Emma asked, standing as well and putting her hands on her hips.

'Nothing happened, it was just a business meeting. Go to bed. You've got school in the morning.'

'You're fibbing, I know you are, but I'll get it out of you one way or another.' She replied, pointing her finger at me in that schoolmarmish way she had when she went into mother mode.

I smiled in return as I leant over and kissed her on the cheek. 'You're my best friend and I tell you everything. Night night.' I turned and left her standing in the middle of the lounge.

. . .

As I slipped out of my dress I relived the slight touch of his hand on my bare shoulder as he helped me with my pashmina at the end of the meal. It had been soft and delicate as he stood behind me, wrapping the lace around my neck and smoothing it out. I was burnt by his touch. A jolt of electricity flashing through my skin and into the very depths of me, lingering long after he had removed his hand and opened the restaurant door to let me walk through before him and into the waiting car.

With a smile, I tumbled between the sheets and hugged my secrets tight as I closed my eyes and dreamt of what I wished to happen.

Chapter Fourteen

SAM

Wednesday September 17th 2014

Sam flicked open his top button and pulled off his tie, dropping it on the arm of the sofa as he walked through the lounge. He would pick it up again later when he went to the bedroom and put it away in his wardrobe. His shoes were already stacked neatly on the shoe rack in the front vestibule. He never wore shoes in the house, not even to run in and pick up something he had forgotten after he had left the house. That didn't happen very often though, he was far too much of a perfectionist to forget anything he needed before he went anywhere. In his view, it was only sloppy, disorganised people who forgot things. If they were focussed and put items where they belonged, then they wouldn't have any problems with forgetfulness. It was just a matter of priorities and forward planning.

The evening had gone better than he'd expected. It had been quite refreshing having Penny-May there instead of Kate. Not that there was ever anything wrong with Kate, she was always professional and always calm and collected, the perfect PA.

And she had an iPad.

Sam smiled as he remembered Penny-May proudly showing him her notebook and two pens. There was something about her naivety that appealed to him. She didn't have the gloss that the women he usually rubbed shoulders within his social circle had and he'd enjoyed seeing her looking around the restaurant, taking in the elaborate detail of the decor, the fussing of the waiters all under the ever watchful eye of the maître d'. She had been quite shocked as one waiter was called to the front desk and discreetly spoken to. His face had flamed red as he had muttered an apology to his senior and scuttled into the kitchen. He didn't reappear again for the rest of the evening and Penny-May had been quite disconcerted that he might have been upset, or worse, lost his job. Carl laughed when she voiced her concerns,

'Oh, don't worry about him. He's probably just paying penance and being sent to wash the dishes for the rest of the night.'

She'd smiled and agreed with him, looking down at her plate whilst twisting her napkin that was resting on her lap. He'd watched her wrapping the corner of it around and around her forefinger until she had glanced up and seen him looking at her. She had smiled shyly at him before dropping the napkin back onto her knees and picking up her pink fluffy pen as Carl returned to the subject of the Pencoven development.

'Nice bit of skirt you've brought tonight mate.' Carl said, as the ladies went to the bathroom before the dessert, 'better looking than Kate, and more available eh?

Where did you find her?'

Sam gave his friend a grin, 'well, she is quite easy on the eye.

She's covering for Michelle in the office while she's off having another ankle biter. I've lost count of how many she's got now, she's like a bloody breeding factory.'

Carl nodded, his smile fading, 'I guess it can't be easy for you to see pregnant women all the time. Yours would be about two years old now, wouldn't he?'

'Yeah, or there abouts. I try not to think about it too much.'

'Sorry, it's just when I think of how Lucy lost the baby, you were both so excited about it. I guess she couldn't move on again afterwards.'

'No.' Sam looked across the restaurant and took a mouthful of his wine. 'The ladies are on their way back.'

Carl followed his gaze and watched the two women walking towards their table, they were chatting and Penny-May laughed at something Rhea had said, 'I can think of worse ways to get back into the saddle you know, she's actually quite hot.'

Sam smiled and declined to answer, taking another sip from his glass as he watched them get closer. *Maybe*, he thought, *just maybe.*

Chapter Fifteen

Penny-May

Saturday September 20th 2014

'Hey Dan, you got your bus pass ready?' I asked as I walked into his bedroom.

Daniel jumped off his bed, knocking his colouring pens on the floor where they scattered, threatening to trip him up as he started running towards me,

'Penny-May early!' He stopped and held back from his usual greeting of nearly bowling me over, looking at me suspiciously instead. 'Where we going?'

He's not always a fan of surprises and sometimes can be stroppy and uncooperative, so I would normally phone in advance if we have an appointment anywhere to give him time to prepare for it. This time though, I knew he would be happy once he knew what I was up to.

'I thought it might be fun to go and watch the penguins being fed at the zoo.' His face beaming, he started jumping up and down on the spot.

'Me love penguins!' He clamped his arms to his sides and started waddling around the room making loud honking noises. I couldn't help but laugh at my funny little brother.

'Come on Happy Feet, you're gonna have to be quicker than that if we're going to catch the next bus.'

'I'll be right there Penny-May.' He started picking his pens up from where they had fallen and stuffing them into his backpack. I knew we weren't going anywhere until we had his bag filled with all of the items he thought were important and wouldn't leave the house without so I knelt down and picked up the rest of them, handing them to him so he would know they were in there safely. This ritual could go on all day if he thought even one of them was missing as he would have to take them all out again and check each one. Next to go in was his colouring book and then his mobile phone. It was an old one of mine that had broken a long time ago, but when he saw other people talking on theirs, he would pull his out and make conversations on it as well. I had thought about getting him a working one of his own but when I'd tried to teach him on mine, he couldn't understand how to work it. Even with the numbers pre-programmed in for him, he couldn't get into the menu to find them and if he got there by accident, he couldn't read the names to know who he was calling. He got angry and frustrated so it was easier to give him back the broken one. He was happy, that was all that mattered.

I'd already spoken to Martha and she had a packed lunch ready to go when we finally clattered down the stairs, his coat half on where he had got his arms in but not pulled it over his shoulders, leaving the collar tucked underneath which stopped him from pulling it up properly. His backpack was dangling from his hand dragging behind him.

'We going to the Zoo, Martha!'

'I know Hun, look what I've made for you.' She handed him the box and a drinks bottle with apple squash in it.

'Is that my beer?'

'Of course it's not beer, silly,' I said, 'it's apple juice, but you can make cider with apple juice.'

He took the box and the bottle and started jamming it into his bag, 'Got cider! Danny get drunk!'

'Ok dude,' I said. 'Shall I help you out with that?'

He nodded and passed me the bag so I could repack it in order for his lunch to fit without breaking the zip. 'There you go.' I handed it back to him and he tried to get it over his shoulders, struggling because of the bulky coat.

'Come here, lets sort you out, shall we?'

Eventually, coat on and zipped up, bag in place with a final check to make sure he had his bus pass and some spending money, we were out of the door, waving at Martha as we walked down the drive.

I loved this time of year. The kids had all gone back to school which meant that the tourists had mostly gone home leaving the Newquay streets and holiday destinations to us locals. It was still autumn, so the weather was not too cold to go out either. It was a beautiful place to be. We caught the bus and Daniel chattered all the way to the zoo. Not all the time to me, he would chatter to anyone he saw and while sometimes I could tell that the other person didn't want to speak, or didn't know how to, meaning I would have to intervene, most of the time they would answer his questions and join in his conversations without any problems. It only ever annoyed me when they started to patronise and talk down to him. Or worse, over him to me or the carer like he couldn't answer for himself. He was twenty-five, not two and he deserved to be treated like it, even if he sometimes struggled to understand.

Today wasn't one of those days though, the lady he was talking to was asking him all about his day and where we were going and he was answering her, telling her all about the penguins. How they honked and waddled around the pool and how much he loved it when they jumped in and started swimming around.

'Have you got a girlfriend yet?' I asked as we ate our lunch on the bench tables set outside the penguin arena.

Daniel held up his hand and started to point to each finger as if ticking them off, 'I got lots of girlfriends, there's Zoe and Paula and Lisa and—'

'Ok Casanova, I get the picture! You're gonna to get a reputation if you have that many girlfriends. Who's your favourite?'

'Umm, I think it's Zoe, she lets me have her chocolate cake at lunchtime.'

'And the others don't?'

'No, they always eat theirs, so I dump them.'

'Well, that's not very nice, do you give them any of your lunch?

'No, I eat all my lunch.' He patted his stomach.

'Maybe that's where I'm going wrong then Danny Boy, maybe I need to start giving my lunch away.'

'Penny-May got girlfriend?'

I smiled at his simple understanding of the world around him and wondered how to best put him straight, 'No, I have many friends that are girls, just like you do, but I wouldn't have a special girlfriend like you do with Zoe. I would have a boyfriend because I fancy boys not girls.'

Daniel cocked his head to one side. 'Danny Penny-May's boyfriend.'

'Not quite, you're my brother, not my boyfriend. A boyfriend is someone that you love but isn't in your family.'

'Penny-May got boyfriend then?'

'Not at the moment, but there is someone I like, and I think he likes me.'

'Will he give you his chocolate cake?'

'I haven't asked him, but he did take me for a meal last night in a restaurant.'

'Was there chocolate cake?'

'There was, and it had clotted cream with it. It was yummy.'

Daniel screwed up his nose, 'Didn't bring Danny any.' He pushed his empty lunch box towards me so I could put the lid back on for him.

'I'm sorry, maybe if we go out again, I will bring some home.' Not that I would dare ask for a doggy bag from somewhere like Pareusi's, but I could always get a slice from the bakery instead. 'It was really nice, and so was he.'

Daniel picked up his backpack from the bench beside him and crammed the lunchbox back inside it. 'Monkeys now?'

'What, so we can spot which one you are?'

'No silly, we find Penny-May's monkey, and her boyfriend's.'

Chapter Sixteen

Penny-May

Monday September 22nd 2014

Catching the bus into work I had a hello for everyone, and everyone smiled back. I'd really enjoyed the zoo on Saturday with Daniel and I made the decision that I must do things like that more often. It was far too easy to pop into Oak Tree Lodge on a Saturday afternoon and spend some time with him there, but we really needed to spend some more quality time together. I enjoy being with him. He's funny and brings all of life's little problems down to the innocence of a child. I mean, why couldn't getting a boyfriend to love you be as simple as letting them have your

chocolate cake? Emma mentioned something about them having their cake and

eating it when I'd told her last night, but I think that's ok. As I long as I get to eat their chocolate cake too.

Sam was already in when I got to the office. His door was ajar and I could see him sat on his sofa, a manuscript in one hand and a coffee mug in the other. He looked up as I walked around my desk and he lifted his mug in kind of salute. I smiled back. There was a package on my desk, a plain box with my name on it.

Lifting the lid, I gasped as I saw what was inside.

I pulled out the white box and broke the seal to find a brand spanking new iPad nestled inside.

'You'll need to charge it and set it all up, but it will be much easier for you to take notes on for next time.' Sam's voice made me turn to see him now stood in his doorway. I swear I could see a twinkle in his eye as he half smiled. I didn't dare look at Charlotte, I could feel the darts she was throwing at my back without helping them to make contact.

'Thank you, Mr Lambert, but you didn't need to do this.'

'I know I didn't need to, but it made sense for me to get it. You need to be able to make notes more efficiently and with that you can send them direct to the computer. Saves you writing them twice. If it makes you more proficient, it helps me to run my business better.'

'Oh, ok. That makes sense.' I felt so stupid as I realised that it was a business decision and not a personal one. He hadn't bought me a gift, an expensive gift at that, he was just upgrading his office computer system.

'And in case you've never used one before, I bought this as well.'

He handed me a black and yellow book with *iPad for Dummies* written on the cover.

'Not that I think you are a dummy,' he said as I obviously must have looked horrified at the implication of the cover title, 'but I thought you might need a little bit of help finding your way around one of these. They've not been around for very long and Kate doesn't have time to teach you.'

I smiled and thanked him again as I took the book. This time I did look at Charlotte and she was smirking; a big cheesy smirk and her shoulders were starting to shake. His office door closed behind me and I sat down on my chair, reaching to switch on my computer.

'So, what else did you two get up to on your *"business meeting",'* Charlotte asked. She even did the air quote thing with her fingers as she said it. Either Kate or Sam must have told her that I had gone because I certainly hadn't.

I could feel my face going red, 'Nothing else, I was taking notes by hand and I must have embarrassed him in front of his clients.'

Kate walked to her own desk with a mug of steaming coffee.

'Don't worry about it,' she said, 'men are idiots sometimes. You must have done ok if he got you that, it means he wants you to accompany him another time when I'm not available.'

'Really?'

'Yes, he doesn't get iPads for all the members of staff here.'

I saw the scowl return to Charlotte's face as she buried her head behind her own computer and started tapping furiously on the keys.

I guessed he'd never bought her one.

Chapter Seventeen

Penny-May

Monday September 22nd 2014

'He bought you what? Do you know how expensive they are?' Emma was squealing at me as I showed her the iPad. I had taken it home so I could figure out how the hell it worked without everyone sniggering at me when I got it wrong. I was determined to be an expert by tomorrow morning.

'You still haven't told me what happened at that meal. It must have been more than '*just business*' if he got you that.' I was getting bored of people doing the air quote thing at me, that was twice today, two times too many when I was already confused and feeling stupid about being so naive.

'I did tell you and it was just business. He doesn't want to be embarrassed by me sitting there with a notebook and a fluffy pen the next time we go out.'

'Ooooo, get her, the next time we go out eh? Something must have happened.'

'It was nothing. It didn't mean anything and he has proven

today exactly what he thinks of me. I mean, have you seen the title of this book?'

'Yes, there are lots of those books around, it's just a brand name, it doesn't mean anything apart from the fact that you don't know anything about that particular subject. So, what was nothing?'

'Nothing, I said it was nothing.'

'Well, that nothing has to be something if you've been thinking about it and thought it was enough of a something to be so disappointed that it has turned out to be a nothing.'

Once I'd got my head around what she had said I figured I had no way out. Emma would never let this drop so I may as well reveal my stupidity and give her something else to laugh at me for.

'As we were leaving the restaurant, he put my pashmina over my shoulders for me. I said it was nothing.'

'And then?'

'And then, nothing. I was just being silly, desperate as I am for a man to love me before I turn into an old spinster.'

'I don't believe you, there must have been something else. What exactly did he do?' She raised her hand in front of her, 'hang on, just wait there.'

She ran out of the room, ponytail streaming behind her as if afraid it was going to be left behind. When she came back, she had the pashmina in her hands.

'Now, do it to me. Exactly what he did to you.'

'Oh, don't be so silly.'

'Yes, I need to know exactly what he did that might have made you misread the situation. Just do it.'

I took the scarf from her hands and opened it out, stood behind her and started to put it on her shoulders.

'Is that where he was stood, you're nearly throwing it at me you're so far away.'

'I guess he was a bit closer.' I said as I moved forward to stand behind her, barely a couple of inches between us.

'Oh, that close eh?'

I carried on, slowly lowering the pashmina into place and smoothing it out across her shoulders with the flat of my hand, gently, as a caress. Then lifting one corner of it and taking it around the front, my arm leaning across her body from behind as I placed it across her other shoulder, my face just an inch from her neck. Before letting go and stepping back to allow her to turn in my direction.

'Whoa! He did it like that?'

'I think so, it felt like that anyway, he was so close I could feel his breath on the side of my neck as he leant around me. I thought he was going to kiss my neck at one point.'

'Did he?' Emma was agog now, her eyes wide open and her mouth forming a perfect 'O' shape.

'No, he moved away and showed me to the car. He talked about the meeting all the way home then, said goodbye to me in the car and got his chauffeur to walk me up the pathway.'

'Oh, you didn't misread anything girl, he was about to make a move on you and then, for whatever reason, he changed his mind.'

'You think?'

'Of course, no bloke gets that close and is that tender if he's not attracted to the woman. I'm telling you; he's got the hots for you.'

'So why did he stop? I wouldn't have stopped him if he had tried anything. Well, not kissing anyway.'

'I don't know, maybe he was unsure about how you would react? He's your boss after all, he doesn't want a sexual harassment charge put on him does he? You keep saying it was a business meeting.'

'I guess.' I still wasn't sure though, 'it just doesn't seem normal for a bloke to pull himself back like that. All the guys I've been out with before have been so desperate to get a quick shag they would never have stopped if they thought I was up for it.'

'But Sam isn't any of those blokes, is he? Sam is a gentleman, and he knows how to treat a lady. I'm telling you; you didn't misread any signals. If you play your cards right, I'm guessing you could get to know a helluva lot more about Mr Lambert.'

'You really think so?'

'Yep, and I want to know every juicy detail, right down to his inside leg measurement.'

I laughed. I could always rely on Emma to bring the conversation down to a sexual level. If I did ever find out that piece of information, I was going to keep it to myself.

Chapter Eighteen

Penny-May

Tuesday September 23rd 2014

'Have you sorted out how to use the iPad yet then?'

'Argh!' My hand flew to my chest and I jumped when Sam materialised beside me. I had been so engrossed in what I was typing that I didn't hear him approach my desk. 'You nearly gave me a heart attack!'

'I'm sorry, I didn't mean to scare you,' he said, but I could see he thought it was funny. The twinkle in his eyes and the slight upturn of the corner of his mouth gave him away.

'I think I'm getting there; Emma helped me a bit with it last night and I've got the email thing set up and downloaded a few apps and got them to work. I even managed to send myself an email which I picked up here this morning when I first came in. It's an amazing piece of kit!' I realised I was gabbling. I always prattle on when I'm nervous and make myself look stupid because of it. I stopped abruptly when I saw him looking me. Probably thinking I was as stupid as I felt and wondering what he ever saw in me. If he did see anything. My jury was still out on that one regardless of what Emma said.

'Well, if you want some practice with it, I'm in need of a PA to go with me to the Pencoven development. Kate is too busy sorting out some meetings for me for next week and I only need someone to take notes. She's more useful to me here and I thought you would like to give that machine a proper workout.'

That was me pushed back into my secretarial hole then. He just wanted someone who could take notes. Yes, that's me. Although at least I get to spend some time alone with him again, even if it didn't mean anything.

'Ok, I'll get my coat.'

'No rush, I'll be going in about fifteen minutes so you've plenty of time to get yourself sorted.'

I almost ran to the bathroom to check my make-up and reapply my lipstick. Had a quick wee while I was in there as well as I didn't want to have to ask him while we were out where the female bathroom was. I would have made a brilliant boy scout.

I was back at my desk, coat on and iPad in my handbag (along with a notepad as well, just in case the battery died) within ten minutes. I resisted the urge to put my fluffy pen in, thought I'd better go with the good old reliable Bic special. Charlotte was throwing her invisible daggers my way again and I avoided looking at her so they didn't hit their target.

Sam came out of the office, he looked so handsome with his long woollen coat over his suit and his briefcase clasped in his hand. Almost made me swoon at the sight of him, if we had been in Victorian times that's just what I would have done. Raised my hand up to my forehead and swooned at his feet so he would have to drop his briefcase and catch me in his arms. He would then revive me with a gentle kiss on my delicate lips and the feel of my soft skin against his would bind him to me forever—

'Ah, you're ready, that's good. Shall we go then?' Sam asked. He swept right past me and pressed the button on the lift.

'Yes, I'm right behind you,' I said catching up with him as the lift doors slid open. As they closed on us, I just caught a glimpse of the scowl lining Charlotte's face.

Ok, turn it on with this button and then swipe right to open the screen. I was mentally going through the procedure as we were being driven to the site by his driver, Brian.

'Do you want to practice before we get there?' Sam asked. I had been fiddling with my bag, my hand folded around the iPad, starting to lift it out and then put it back in again and zipped the bag shut.

I looked at him, I knew I'd been caught out and I hoped he wasn't annoyed by my fidgeting and fumbling. He was smiling though, that had to be a good sign, surely?

'Oh, I don't need to. I've got it sorted now.'

'I don't mind helping you out a bit if you want me to, take you through the basics.'

Oh, he can so take me through the basics! Concentrate Penny-May, get your smutty mind out of the gutter! I gave myself a mental shake and tried to stop the blush from blooming across my cheeks.

'Uh, well, uh, oh, I'll be alright. I've heard so much about the development, so I'm really excited to see it.' I knew I was gushing, as usual my mouth was running away with me. I decided to shut up.

'Ok, well, I'm quite a whizz at those things so if you get stuck just ask me and I'll point you in the right direction.'

My smutty mind was threatening to take over again, so I just nodded politely and kept my head bowed.

. . .

Carl was waiting for us when we arrived. The site was huge, there were builders in yellow hard hats and hi-viz jackets everywhere. Carl was sporting a white hard hat with a red stripe around it. He ushered us straight into the portakabin where he gave us a hat each too. Ours were plain white and had *Visitor* emblazoned on it.

It felt weird when I put it on. It wobbled alarmingly and both the men laughed at me as it flopped forward over my eyes. Sam picked it off my head and pulled at a plastic tab at the back.

'It's adjustable,' he said, 'you need to make it smaller.'

'Oh, I've never worn one before, I didn't realise that.' I replied.

I turned to the desk and put my bag down on the only corner that didn't have any paper piled up on it. While my back was turned to them, I took the opportunity to take a few deep breaths, a couple of seconds to calm the nerves that were threatening to take over and make my hands shake.

'Shall we start the tour?' Carl asked, leading the way out of the cabin. Sam held the door open for me and followed me out to join the property developer.

Carl led us all around the site, stopping to point out the different buildings and the stage of development that each one was at. I fiddled with the iPad, quite pleased when I found the writing app and when the keyboard came on screen I was well impressed with myself. Flitting over the keys with one hand, taking notes on all the details Sam asked me to put down, the sizes of the plots, the next stage for each section that needed to be worked on, I felt like a real whizz kid. This was so much easier than trying to write it all down on a floppy notepad and turn pages.

Back at the cabin, Carl made us coffee in white mugs with *The Future is Pencoven* written on them. After what I had just seen, I believed the slogan and I could see why this company was so important to Sam. I pressed the save icon to make sure I didn't lose the notes I'd made. Then I pressed it again, just to make sure.

Then I pressed it again before turning it off. Third time lucky and all that. I was tempted to reopen it again, just to check that it had saved, that it hadn't deleted itself when I'd turned it off, but I resisted the urge. I caught Sam looking at me though. I know he was laughing at me, even though he didn't make a sound. The twinkle in his eyes and the twitch of his mouth gave him away again.

I took a sip of my still too hot coffee. I couldn't spit it out, so I tried not to draw attention to myself as I swallowed it far too quickly to stop it burning my tongue.

Carl had been talking about Rhea and Josh and looked up when he heard Sam laughing, no doubt wondering if it was something he had said.

'Sorry,' Sam said, 'It's not you, it's that ridiculous hat on Penny-May's head.'

I hadn't realised I was still wearing it until it had flopped forwards again as I had tried to hide the inferno in my mouth. I reached up to take it off as Sam leant over and took it from my hand, I'm sure he held it there, a fraction longer than was necessary. It felt good, that little touch of reassurance that all was well. My secrets were safe with him.

As we walked towards the car, his hand gently touched my shoulder, steering me protectively towards the car where Brian was waiting with the door open.

Maybe Emma was right.

Maybe there was more to it than him just being a gentleman.

Or maybe she's talking twaddle and I need to get my head read.

Chapter Nineteen

SAM

Wednesday September 24th 2014

Sam sat in his office staring out of the window at the sea. It was calm today, the tide was coming in and the waves lapped over the golden sand, the white crests echoing his thoughts as they rose and then fell back, gaining more strength for another attempt.

Penny-May intrigued him that was for sure. She was definitely his type to look at, blonde hair, deep brown eyes that he could fall into and never be able to climb out of. Drowning eyes they were, when he was allowed deep into their depths, but so often they were guarded, a form of protection from seeing the inner person. The real Penny-May. He would bet there was a perfect soul in there that she was protecting and he wanted to know why. He wanted to remove the shadows and make her gaze at him with her eyes wide open.

He had left the office door ajar again. He was doing that more and more often when he knew she would be at her desk. He liked watching her while she worked without realising he was there.

Yesterday had been just as interesting as the evening meeting had been. She was funny in her naive way and he enjoyed her company, enjoyed seeing her determination to succeed with the new technology and trying her best not to let him know she didn't know what she was doing. He admired that in a woman. He liked them to be trying to better themselves, to try to be perfect.

That was where it went wrong with Lucy.

She gave up too easily and she let her perfectionist streak be overshadowed by her laziness. The amount of time she spent at home doing nothing was such a waste and it had infuriated him.

He looked through the door again, sipping his coffee and watching Penny-May as she typed. After a few minutes she stopped and he saw her sit back and stretch her arms above her head. He saw the material of her blouse start to strain against the pressure of her breasts as her arms moved back and he felt that stirring in his loins again. The one that had been dormant since Lucy died.

Penny-May looked up and saw him watching her, he smiled as she brought her hands back down on the keyboard and he saw that faint blush begin to spread across her cheeks again. That was so cute. She always seemed to be so embarrassed when he caught her blushing but there was no need, she looked beautiful when she did that. He wanted to see her blush more often.

That wouldn't be enough. It wasn't just seeing her every day that he wanted. He wanted all of her.

Chapter Twenty

Penny-May

Thursday October 9th 2014

I was surprised to see Sam sitting on a bench outside Mistral as I left. He had been in a meeting all afternoon and I assumed he had gone straight home afterwards. I smiled and he beckoned me over to him.

'Please, take a seat.' He said, gesturing to the empty space beside him, 'If you have a couple of minutes to spare that is.'

I made a show of checking my watch, didn't want to seem too eager, shrugged my shoulders and sat down next to him. The wind caught my hair and flipped it across my eyes. He reached up to sweep it out of the way for me. It was such a gentle gesture, almost a caress as he tucked the errant strands behind my ear before pulling his hand away.

'Sorry,' he said, 'that was very forward of me. I shouldn't have done that.'

Shouldn't he? Why not? I wanted to scream at him to do it

some more, but I remained all calm and serene. I was quite proud of myself actually,

'Oh, no, that's ok, I'm not worried.'

'I have to be so careful. I don't want you to think that I am overstepping the mark here. I am your boss after all.'

'My temporary boss,' I replied, 'and I don't think you've done anything to be worried about. You've been the perfect gentleman whenever we've been out for work.'

'That's just it though, it's always been work. You intrigue me Penny-May, I like you a lot and I would be honoured if you would come out with me tonight. Not for work. Just me and you. To Pareusi's?'

He looked so vulnerable sitting there, like he was waiting to be scolded for being a naughty boy. But I couldn't believe he was actually asking me out! I mean, me! Little Penny-May! I wanted to run around and scream and shout, but I didn't think that would be appropriate, and I couldn't scare him off now, he might not ask me again, but I didn't want him to think I was desperate either.

But I am almost desperate. And he is such a hot hunk of eye candy.

'Oh, it's a bit unexpected but yes, I'd really like to go out with you tonight.' He looked at me and a grin started to spread across his face.

'That's brilliant, I'll pick you up at 7:30 then, is that ok? Brian will be driving.'

'Yes, that's fine.' I replied. I checked my watch, it was already half past five, there was no way I was going to be ready on time. 'I'd better go now though. I'll miss my bus.'

'See you later then.' He raised his hand and I cursed myself as I realised he was going to hold mine, but I'd already moved forwards and started waving at him.

I blushed, 'Yes, can't wait.'

Damn! I thought I wasn't going to look desperate!

. . .

'Oh my God, oh my God, oh my God! It's really happened? He's asked you out? Not for a business meeting?' Emma stopped running around the room with her hands threatening to pull her hair out of its ponytail.

'Yes, he really asked me out on a date. A proper, proper date.' I wasn't as excited as Emma was. I was struggling to stop the nausea that was fluttering in my stomach from spilling out of me while mildly panicking that I had got it wrong. That it wasn't a date at all and it was all a joke. He had to be having me on surely? There's no way a man like that would be asking me out on a date.

'Well, he said it wasn't for work. It was going to be just the two of us and we are going to Pareusi's. I mean, that's a date isn't it? He could just be wanting a friend to go out for a meal with him. Couldn't he?'

'Oh, Penny-May, you have such a lot to learn about men. There is no way on this planet that he is asking you out just to keep him company for a meal. That man will have lots of friends to go out with and could ask any woman he meets.'

'So, it is a date? I've not got it wrong?'

'No honey, you have most definitely not got it wrong, and if you play your cards right, you'll be singing all the way there, back and beyond. Now, get in the shower, I'll find you something to wear.'

The doorbell rang and I turned to Emma who threw her arms around me and gave me a massive hug. I needed that, my hands were shaking and I was regretting saying yes to him. It was a moment of madness even thinking that I could do this.

'I'll get the door, you stay here, count to twenty, take a deep breath and then come out to us.' She stopped at the door and turned round to me again, 'and don't panic, you look gorgeous and you are the most amazing woman I know. He'd be a mug not to see that.'

I won't be nervous,
I won't fuck anything up,
I will be the perfect date.

I won't be nervous,
I won't fuck anything up,
I will be the perfect date.

I took a deep breath, repeated my mantra once more and walked out of the room.

Sam was stood just inside the door.

'I hope you like roses,' he said as he took a couple of steps towards me and held out a huge bouquet of the deepest red buds I had ever seen.'

'Of course I do, they're beautiful,' I said, burying my nose into them and inhaling their scent, giving myself a few seconds thinking time. I had not been expecting these, it really did mean that it was a date.

'I'll put them in some water, shall I? Let you two get off?' Emma took the flowers out of my hands and shooed me towards the door, and Sam. 'Have fun,' she said.

Sam put his arm around my back and led me out of the flat. 'We will,' he replied with a wink at me, 'Brian's waiting; shall we?'

I let him lead me to his car, his arm felt comforting and secure around my back and I was sorry when he dropped it down so he could get in the other side of the car. Brian closed the door behind me and slid into the driver's seat. Sam sat in the back with me. I didn't have a big bag on the seat between us this time. There was no barrier and I could almost feel the heat of his thighs on the seat next to me. The little black clutch bag in my hands began to feel clammy as I gripped it too tightly on my lap and the lump in my throat felt like it was going to choke me. I swallowed, trying to make it go down, but it didn't work. It lodged like a golf ball teetering on the edge and refusing to score the hole in one.

Sam reached across and put his hand on mine, 'That bag doesn't look big enough to hold your notebook and fluffy pen today?'

'No, no pad and pen today, Can't even fit an iPad in this thing,' I said, 'just big enough for the essentials - purse and lipstick.'

And armour I thought, something to cling onto while I drowned quietly with my stupid, boring comments. Why did I tell him the contents of my bag? I'm sure there are many more interesting things I could be saying. Come on brain, wake up and be witty and charming!

'Well,' he replied, 'you don't need your purse as I am paying but I know how important a lipstick is to a lady.'

He called me a lady! Me! A lady. Wow! I felt the blush begin to creep up my face again and I was glad of the darkness of the car to hide it.

The maître d' was as attentive as ever and there was a bottle of champagne already chilling in the ice bucket when we were shown to our table. As we sat, the waiter lifted it and popped the cork, pouring it into a glass and handing it to Sam to taste. He nodded after his quick swig and the waiter then poured both glasses out for us.

'I hope you don't mind me choosing,' Sam said, 'I phoned

ahead and ordered so that it would be chilled and ready when we got here.'

I couldn't believe he could be so thoughtful and boy, was I ready for some alcohol.

'No, of course not, it's a lovely thing to do.' I picked up my glass.

'Here's to a charming evening with a beautiful companion,' he said, chinking his glass against mine.

I took a sip, managed to get it past the golf ball and into my swirling stomach without spilling a drop. I felt so proud of myself.

Sam made me laugh so much throughout the meal. I didn't even realise when the golf ball vanished and I was able to swallow normally again. We just connected and it seemed so natural when he reached over and covered my hand with his on the table. We never stopped talking either, none of those awkward silences where you wonder what on earth you are going to say next and all your brain can think of is really not worth uttering out loud. It just flowed, one subject into another. He was so attentive, so interested in my life and what was important to me. I found that I told him everything, my parents car crash, my disabled brother, the struggle I'd had since mum and dad died to learn how to advocate for Daniel, be his spokesperson and make sure he had everything he needed. I also told him of my guilt at not being able to provide a home for him, how I had to get him into a residential home because there wasn't enough room in the flat I shared with Emma. Sam made me feel so good about that, he asked if Daniel was happy where he was and when I said that yes, he was, he said I shouldn't feel guilty about it. I had done everything right and Daniel was where he could receive the best life he could with people around him who could do all the things that I couldn't.

Sam was right of course, and deep down I knew that, but it felt so lovely to be talking to someone who understood my feelings, who cared enough to help me to make sense of them.

The end of the evening came far too soon. He helped me on with my coat and I felt the burn of his fingers on my neck again. I found myself leaning back into him and began to turn around, inhaling the masculine scent of his aftershave and wanting so much for his arms to fold around me, to pull me to him but his hand slid down my back instead, steering me towards the door which was being held open by the maître d' and into the waiting car at the kerbside.

We sat in the back, hips almost touching, his arm slung casually across the back of my seat. His hand resting on my shoulder as we carried on talking and talking. I was so sad when we pulled up outside the flat. I glanced up and saw the curtain twitch back into position. Emma was still up, waiting to hear all about it. I didn't blame her; I would have been the same if it had been the other way around.

Sam walked me up to the front door and into the hallway, all the way to my own front door.

'Emma's still up so I can't really offer you a coffee,' I said, the disappointment making my voice crackle.

He placed his forefinger under my chin and tipped my face towards his.

'That's ok,' he replied, 'there will be other times. I hope?'

'Really?' I said, realising I was blushing again and the glaring light in the hallway wasn't going to do anything to hide it, 'you want us to go out again?'

He laughed, 'Of course I do, I've had a wonderful time. Would you mind?'

'No, I mean, yes, I mean—' I stopped, realising that I was gabbling and composed myself, 'I mean, I'd love for us to go out again.'

He lowered his head and gave me the softest kiss on the lips. Just a second long, barely a graze before they were whisked away, my own lips desperate for more.

'That's alright then.' He released me and started walking to the front door, turning back as he reached to open it.

'Just one thing?' he asked, 'Can we not let them know at work about this, it might make things a bit awkward with Kate and Charlotte if they know you are seeing me.

Let's keep it to ourselves for a while. Is that ok?'

Ok? Of course it was ok, Charlotte was going to kill me if she ever found out about this so there was no way I was going to broadcast it.

'Yes, that's fine with me.'

'Good, I'll phone you.'

The door closed behind him with its usual ceremonial clatter and bang. I leant back against my own door, just as it was opened and Emma caught me as I started to fall backwards into the room.

'Christ,' she said, 'I've been there for ages! I thought he was never going to leave!

Come on and tell me all about it. And I want every little detail. And I don't want anything about nothing happened either, that look on your face tells me that lots of things have happened.'

Chapter Twenty-One

Penny-May
Monday October 13th 2014

I couldn't stop smiling as I sat at my desk, I was even humming as the lift opened and Kate walked past my desk.

'Crikey,' she said, 'humming on a Monday morning? Somebody must have had fun at the weekend?'

I stopped humming and felt the blush begin to rise up my cheeks. Damn that blushing, it gave me away every time.

I had enjoyed my weekend. Sam had been texting me, saying how much he had enjoyed himself and how he hoped I hadn't changed my mind and still wanted to see him again. He wanted to know what I was doing, how Daniel was, what we had both been up to on our Saturday afternoon together. He was just so considerate, I was the luckiest girl in the world and wanted to shout out to everyone that I had been on a date with Sam Lambert, and that he wanted another one! I couldn't though. I didn't want to blow my chances of another date and, after he said he didn't want anyone else in the office to know, I had to keep my big mouth shut.

'Oh, uh, no, just the usual really, went and saw my brother, nothing different happened.'

I bent my head and carried on typing, getting all the letters in the wrong places again. I'd have to redo it when Kate left me be.

'I don't believe that for one second,' she said, 'I know that glow, there's a new man in your life isn't there?'

'It could be a woman you know,' chimed in Charlotte from across the room, 'she could be gay and fancy women.'

'It's not a woman,' I retorted too quickly.

The lift door opened and Sam walked in, making his way past my desk and towards his office.

'Ha,' said Charlotte, 'caught you out, so there is a man! Come on, tell us about him then.'

'There really is nothing to tell,' I replied, the blush now a flaming red across my cheeks, 'I just spent Saturday with my brother and it was good to be with him, He's in a really happy place right now.'

'Good morning Mr Lambert,' said Kate, 'I'll be right in with your morning coffee.'

'Good morning ladies, thank you Kate.' He stopped by his door and turned to face us, 'so you have a new man do you Penny-May?'

I swear there was a twinkle in his eye and I saw the slightest twitch at the corner of his mouth as if he was holding in the laughter.

'Uh, no, Mr Lambert, I'm just happy today and these two think that can't happen without a man being involved.'

'Well, if there isn't, then I'm very glad to see you so happy. If there is then I hope he's the right one for you and treats you well. I can see why he would like you so much. The Pencoven file as well please Kate.'

He turned, went into his office and closed the door behind him.

I didn't have a clue what to think now. Was he joking with me? Trying to deflect the attention? Was he annoyed with me? Bugger, I hoped I hadn't wrecked everything.

'I should start again if I were you,' Kate said as she went into the kitchen.

I looked at her, I thought she had cottoned on to what I was thinking but then I realised she had been looking at my computer screen.

I sighed and pressed delete, again.

Chapter Twenty-Two

Penny-May
Saturday October 18th 2014

Daniel was in the greenhouse when I arrived. Bundled up in his gardening coat that he kept for the colder days. It was covered in dirt and had a rip in one arm where he'd caught it on a shelving rack last year, but he didn't care. Neither did I, it did the job and he was happy with it. Besides, trying to change it would cause a lot of arguments and it wasn't worth the bother. He'd get rid of it when he wanted to.

Even though it wasn't the growing season, he still spent a lot of time in there, pottering around, tidying up, making sure everything was ready for when February came round and he could start planting his seeds again. On one shelf he had a plastic box where he kept all the seeds he'd harvested from this year's plants, all neatly labelled with the picture of the plant it would become. Dan couldn't read or write so the home helped him out by putting pictures on everything so he could be as independent as possible. He always knew when to plant each type of seed though, I had no idea how he knew that. I guess Dad had taught him.

'How's it going Hulk?'

'Penny-May!' he ran over and engulfed me in his biggest bear hug. I was too slow to ward him off, so his muddy handprints were left on my coat. Just as well it was washable, I thought, benefits of buying cheap clothes. I hugged him back. It was worth the little bit of dirt.

'What are you planting?'

'Silly Penny-May, nothing to plant now. It's winter!'

'Silly me, you know I'm rubbish in the garden, not half as clever as you. So, what are you doing out here?'

'Planning,' he said with such a serious look on his face.

'Oh? Planning for what?'

'What we plant next year, of course.'

'Oh, of course. And what are you going to plant for next year?'

He lifted down the box and showed me the envelopes that contained the seeds, flicking through them and telling me their contents. 'Carrots, peas, cabbage, lettuce, tomatoes, cucumber, chillies, leeks—'

'You're gonna be busy after Christmas then aren't you?' I cut in, as it was going to be a long conversation and I was starting to get cold.

'Shall we go indoors and get a nice mug of hot chocolate to warm us up?'

Dan quickly put the lid back on the box and put it back in its place, took off his coat and hung it up on the hook by the door. He was far tidier than me.

'Brrr, tis sum cold Penny-May, let's go put the kettle on.'

He blew into his hands just like Dad used to when he came into the kitchen from the garden before walking over to the fire-place and warming his hands in front of the blazing coal fire.

He ran out of the greenhouse and up the path. I swallowed

the lump in my throat at the unbidden memory and followed him at a more leisurely pace.

'How's Penny-May's boyfriend?'

Dan surprised me with his question, but he had a habit of coming out with questions you didn't think he would know.

'Boyfriend? What, Sam?'

'The man Penny-May likes, is he your boyfriend? Like me and Zoe?'

'Not yet, but I'm still hoping he will be. We're going out later tonight. Well, he's cooking me a meal at his house, so I'm going out anyway.'

Daniel was quiet, his hands cupped around his mug as he sat cross legged on his bed.

'Hey, what's up champ?'

'Penny-May not love Dan no more. Dan not Penny-May's boyfriend.'

I was shocked that he might have thought this, it hadn't even occurred to me that he could have mixed this all up. I thought I'd explained it all when we were at the zoo.

'No, of course I love you! I will always love you!' Sitting on the bed beside him I took the mug from his hand and placed it onto the bedside cabinet. Putting my arms around him, he curled into my chest, 'you're not my boyfriend, you're my brother and that makes you very special in my life. Nothing is going to change that, do you hear me?'

'You sure?' He sounded so lost; it made me hug him tighter.

'Of course I'm sure, and guess what?'

He pulled his head out of my embrace and looked up at me, 'What?'

'If Sam does become my boyfriend, a real and proper boyfriend, then he's going to love you just as much as I do so you'll get two of us coming to visit and taking you out. Wouldn't that be great?'

'Dunno,' he said, as he snuggled back into my arms. 'Danny wait and see.'

I knew I couldn't ask anything else of him. He wouldn't understand and he needed to get used to new situations gradually. I was sure he would see though, and we would make a brilliant family. He would love Sam just as much as I already did.

Chapter Twenty-Three

Penny-May

Saturday October 18th 2014

Brian picked me up at seven pm just like Sam said he would. I was nervous sat in the back on my own, but Sam had said he needed to stay at home to make sure the food didn't spoil. When I asked if he was a good cook or should I bring my own he had grinned and told me a local caterer had made the food for us so all he had to do was serve it once they left. I was glad the caterers weren't staying; it would have been so weird to have people hanging around in the kitchen while we ate. I would be self-conscious and want to finish eating quickly so they could go home.

He came and met me at the door, gave me a kiss on the cheek, then took my coat and hung it in a cupboard. I saw there was a shoe rack and he was wearing socks, so I took my shoes off as well. I suddenly felt a lot shorter and a bit vulnerable, but he smiled, took my hand and led me into the dining area.

'I hope you're hungry?' He pulled the dining chair out and

encouraged me to take a seat, 'I might have ordered a bit too much.'

'It smells divine.' The aroma filling the room was heavenly and I couldn't wait to tuck in, although my dress was quite tight dress so I would have to restrain myself a bit.

'We have melon to start, fresh locally caught lobster and then a pavlova for dessert. Is that ok?'

I've never had lobster before so I wasn't totally sure, 'Oh yes,' I said, 'It sounds perfect.' I hoped I liked lobster; I was sure I would.

I was right, the lobster was delicious along with the wine and the rest of the meal. The lights were kept low and there was soft music playing in the background. It was so romantic.

Sam made us Irish coffees to finish and suggested we went into the lounge to drink them where it would be cosier. The sofa was soft and squishy. I sat in one corner and Sam sat next to me, the coffees on the table in front of us, the log fire burning itself down so that just the glow of embers could be seen, the occasional spark fizzing up the chimney. He put his arm around me and I couldn't help but snuggle in close, the scent of him mingling with that of the woodsmoke. It was so perfect and so natural.

I lifted my head to speak to him, but he put his finger over my mouth, gently running it around my lips as they started to part and then he lowered his head, grazing my mouth with his, asking permission to kiss me. As I responded, joining with him, his kiss got harder and more insistent. Our tongues connected and I raised my hand to his head, pulling him down to me. I didn't ever want that kiss to end. I felt his arm fold around my waist, feeling its way around my body, his thumb tentatively flicking over my erect nipple and then jolting away, back to my waist as if testing the water, testing my reaction.

I heard myself sigh into his mouth and I wiggled closer to him, my hands more insistent as he leaned into me, his hands reaching behind me to open the zipper on my dress.

'Is this ok?' he asked, his lips barely lifting an inch from my own.

'Yes,' I breathed back, I could barely think of anything else to say, all I wanted was him.

I tugged his shirt out of his trousers and ran my hands over his taut chest. It felt so smooth and muscled under my fingers, his own nipples springing to attention in response to my touch.

We wrestled each other out of our clothes and lay down on the rug in front of the fire. Our passion increasing our haste to feel our bodies next to each other, skin on skin, feeling, touching, tasting everywhere. When he released me to put the condom on I felt bereft, the cold space where his body had been hitting me with a blast that made me tingle with anticipation. I reached out to stroke his penis, and then pulled him on top of me, guiding him into the depths of my body where he started to move, slowly at first and, as I joined him, we were moving as one, faster and faster until he held still, forcing himself into the very heart of me and making me shout as every nerve in my body answered his pulsating cock. Sparks flew through my brain, ricocheting from each other and causing more to flicker. I didn't think it was ever going to end. I didn't want it to ever end.

As his body relaxed, he kissed me again, slowly and tenderly. His thumb caressed my cheek and I ran my hands over his back, keeping him where he was. I wasn't ready to release him yet.

'Your coffee's gone cold,' he said as he eased his way to lay beside me.

'I think I'm quite happy with the alternative after dinner entertainment.'

'Mmm, so am I,' he replied as he reached up to pull a cushion from the sofa and placed it under my head before resting his hand back onto my breast. The lightest of touches sending another jolt through me.

'Are you staying tonight?' He asked me as he stroked my nipple, 'I'd like you to.'

'Oh yes, definitely,' I replied, probably a bit too eagerly, but I was not ready to go home, I didn't want to leave this bubble we had created and if there was any chance of a follow up performance, there was no way I was going to say no.

'I'll just message Brian, tell him he's not needed after all.'

Bugger, I'd forgotten all about Brian. And Emma would still be up as well. I reached for my phone and tapped out a message.

'Don't wait up, staying here, all good.'

Just as I was putting the phone back down a reply came through,

'Oh my God, really? Yay!! You go girl!!!'

I didn't reply again, Sam was back and we made our way upstairs to his bed, where we didn't get very much sleep.

Chapter Twenty-Four

Sam

Sunday October 19th 2014

Sam woke and watched Penny-May as she lay beside him. She was curled into his body and he could feel her naked heat as she slept.

He had really enjoyed last night. She had taken him by surprise with just how forward she had been throughout their lovemaking. She was so quiet and reserved in the office, but she was such a little firecracker in bed. So horny, and she made him horny too. They had made love throughout the night, exploring each other's bodies and seeing what turned each other on. It seemed everything turned her on, everywhere he touched made her quiver with excitement and had her reaching for him again and again. Who would have thought such a harlot would be hidden behind that quiet, shy exterior. He was one lucky guy to find that again, and now that he had it, he was going to keep it.

She stirred beside him, rolling onto her back and he gently lifted the sheet to gaze at her body. She was certainly in good nick.

Her breasts were pert and she was a perfect size ten. She had even shaved her pussy so he could see her in all her beauty and taste her too. She had tasted really nice last night. As he looked at her, he felt himself beginning to get hard again, the stirring in his loins too much to resist and he moved in closer to her, rubbed his penis against her side and bent his head down to suck on her nipple. He felt her stir and he moved his hand to cup her pussy, gently stroking her as she woke. Her hips started moving against his hand, pushing against him, letting go of her nipple, grazing it with a little nip as he did so, he moved up to kiss her on the mouth,

'Good morning beautiful,' he said as she opened her eyes and gazed at him.

'Good morning,' she replied, wiggling under his hand and manoeuvring him on top of her, 'this is a nice way to wake up.'

'Isn't it just?' He slipped inside her and they began moving as one, she was so tight and wet it took his breath away and he pushed as far as he could inside of her, her legs wrapping around him and her hands on his buttocks, pulling him in again and again.

When he came, it felt incredible.

Arching her pelvis into his he felt her body begin to tremble and stiffen as her own orgasm tore through her body.

Oh yes, this was the one. Penny-May was definitely a keeper.

Chapter Twenty-Five

Penny-May

Monday October 20th 2014

I was still floating on a cloud of multiple orgasms when I walked into Mistral. There was absolutely nothing that was going to remove the grin from my face today.

The wind and rain that was lashing down as I stood at the bus stop had only been a bit of a nuisance and I didn't even mind that the bus was late. Sam wasn't going to tell me off for bad timekeeping. Even if I had slept in, I could blame him for my all but sleepless night on Saturday.

Oh, but it had been good waking up next to him, making love and then he made us breakfast to eat in bed. It was the afternoon when he called Brian and asked him to take me home. I didn't want to go, but I could hardly turn up to work in what I had been wearing.

I felt a bit embarrassed when I walked out to the car, knowing that Brian would know what we had been up to. Sam stayed at

Karadow, said he needed to get some work done by today, but he kissed me goodbye and waved until the car was out of sight.

'Good morning,' I said to Charlotte as I dropped my bag on my desk, 'did you have a good weekend?'

'The usual,' she replied, 'a gang of us went to *The Notoriety,* got bladdered and Scott ended up puking at the taxi rank so the driver wouldn't take us home. The walk sobered us all up a bit. How about you? You certainly look as if you did?'

'Oh, you know, the usual, spent Saturday with my brother and then lazed around at home yesterday.' Sam had said that we still needed to keep our relationship secret, he didn't want the gossip mill to start their tongues wagging and ruining what we had together. I was happy with that. I didn't want Charlotte to start shooting me daggers again. If she knew what had really happened they might even be real ones.

'I'm going to make a coffee, do you want one?' I asked.

'Yes please, I need the caffeine.'

Sam walked through the office just as I was coming back in with the drinks.

'Good morning Penny-May, Charlotte. You've both had a good weekend I trust?'

'Oh yes, Mr Lambert,' replied Charlotte before I could get anywhere near answering his question. 'I've had a lovely, relaxed weekend, how was yours?'

'It was enjoyable,' he said, 'very enjoyable. Any chance you could bring me a coffee as well please Penny-May?'

'Yes, Mr Lambert, I'll bring it right in.' I turned and went back out to the kitchen again before he could see me blush. Only when I got there did I realise that I was still carrying the original cups of coffee. I felt so silly as I put them on the worktop.

Charlotte came in the room behind me and picked up her mug.

'Well, he's quite chipper this morning, do you think he actually got some this weekend? It's been a long time since he's been like that. Not since Lucy was around in fact.'

'Really? I wouldn't know, he does seem quite happy but that could be because of anything. Maybe he just got out of bed on a good side? Maybe he's finally getting over Lucy? What was she like?'

'Oh, she was beautiful, and funny. She didn't come in very often, but she was always laughing. She was a stunner. You could see how much in love they were. It's no wonder her dying the way she did hit him so hard.'

'How could you tell?'

'She used to hang on his every word and they were always looking at each other or looking out for each other. His eyes would follow her around the room as if he couldn't get enough of looking at her. I don't think he could believe that she was truly his, or he was hers. I wish someone would love me like that.' Charlotte's eyes started to glaze over and I felt a hollow pit begin to open in the centre of my stomach. How could I ever compete with a love like that?

'I'd better get this to him, and keep him in a good mood on a Monday,' I said, lifting the tray with his double espresso and separate cappuccino and walking out of the room.

Sam's door was open, but I still knocked and waited for him to beckon me in.

'Close the door behind you,' he said quietly so no-one in the outer office could hear him. I did as he bid, after placing the tray on the coffee table he reached up and grabbed my hand. Pulling me to sit on his lap and wrapping his arms around me he kissed me as I began to squeal with laughter.

'Ssshh,' he said, 'we don't want them wondering what I'm

doing to you in here. It will ruin my reputation as an upstanding member of the community.'

I reached down and felt the hardness that was beginning to develop in his trousers, 'looks like you're more than ready to be upstanding,' I whispered into his mouth.

'You little minx, wait until I get you into bed later, then you'll see what upstanding is.'

With another quick kiss, he let me go. As I sashayed towards the door, my stilettos helping my bum to wiggle in its tight black pencil skirt, I heard him moan from the sofa.

'Oh God, today is going to be torture with you looking like that.'

I giggled, turned towards him and blew him a perfect Marilyn Monroe kiss.

'Likewise, but it will be worth it when no-one else is around.'

I closed the door behind me and walked to my desk. How I did that with the fire that was burning inside me I didn't know. Sitting down and turning the computer on I forgot my fears about how I was going to compare to Lucy. Sam was definitely interested in me. He was definitely not pining for her in there and I was having fun. Her ghost wouldn't come between us.

Chapter Twenty-Six

Penny-May
Wednesday November 12th 2014

'Penny-May, would you come in here a minute please?'

Sam stood in the open doorway of his office, one arm holding the door open as he looked over to my desk. He'd taken his jacket off so I could see his muscled chest and arms through his white cotton shirt. His tie was slightly pulled down and the top button undone.

'Yes Mr Lambert,' I stood and walked past him into the office. He closed the door behind me and I heard the lock click into place.

His arm reached out and snaked around my back, pulling me into him and both of his hands settled on my buttocks holding me tight against his groin. I could feel the hardness there and felt myself quiver as he began to gyrate against me.

'It's torture having you sat out there where I can see you all the time.'

His hand moved to tug my blouse out of my skirt, the touch of his hand on my bare skin sent shivers through me as he unhooked my bra so my breasts fell free. I began to pull at his shirt, feeling his muscled chest go taut under my fingers.

'Me too,' I replied, stretching my arms up and sliding them around his neck, pulling his head down to mine and kissing him deeply. He groaned into my mouth, I could feel his penis getting harder and I reached down to flick open his fly, 'poor thing must be quite squashed in there, think he needs a bit of fresh air.'

Sam groaned again, 'not here,' he said, taking my arm and steering me towards the back of the office and into his ensuite bathroom. He closed the door behind us and pulled me to him again, our clothes rapidly being tossed across the floor.

Within seconds he was inside me, held against the wall I wrapped my legs around him as he pushed against me, into me and I onto him. The coldness of the tiles felt good against the sweat of my back as he brought me to orgasm, his mouth clamping down onto mine as I came, swallowing my scream of ecstasy as he ejaculated into me. Wave after wave of electricity jolted through my veins until he was spent. His head coming to rest on mine as our breathing lessened.

'You need to work on quieter orgasms if we are going to do this in here more often,' he said as I unwound my legs from his waist.

'It's all your fault for making me so damn horny all the time,' I countered, the same level of mirth in my voice as he had used, 'and for being so damn good at sex!' He laughed, 'I guess we make a great pair then?'

'Definitely.'

Releasing me, we gathered our clothes and began getting dressed. Looking at the shower I thought how nice it would be to be able to have a quick rinse before going back out into the office, but Sam shook his head.

'Sorry, no time, I've got a meeting in half an hour which I have to prepare for. Damn good way of releasing tension before it though. We should do this before every meeting.'

'Well, I'm not complaining,' I said, 'although maybe if you could get a hairdryer in here I could have a very quick one next time?'

'We are going to have lots of quick ones,' he winked at me and reached out to pat my bottom as I tucked my blouse in and slid the zip of my skirt back into place.

'Cheeky, you know what I mean.'

'Yes, and I like to think of you sat at your desk afterwards, smelling of our lovemaking and still able to feel my hands all over your body. It's like pheromones, my scent to keep all those other suiters away.'

As I hadn't had even a sniff of a suiter for ages, I didn't think this was the way it worked, but it felt good that he wanted to own me in this way. To mark me out as his territory. It made me feel wanted in a way that I hadn't been for far too long.

'So, I'm yours am I?' I asked. I thought I might have gone too far. We've only been together for a few weeks and most of that time has been spent in the bedroom.

Was it too early to ask such a question?

'Oh yes, you are definitely mine.' He replied, kissing me to seal his words.

I did a final check of my make-up and hair in his mirror, thankful that I'd chosen a lip stain this morning. As I walked to the door, he grabbed me again and went to kiss me but I put my finger on his lips, 'Uh uh, you don't have time for a second course, you'll have to save it until later.'

'You're such a tease,' he said, letting me go and picking up his jacket from the back of the chair on which it was hung.

'Unlock the door quietly, we don't want them out there hearing it and wondering why it was locked.'

'If they tried it, they would already know,' I replied.

'Smart arse! Let's assume they didn't eh?'

I blew him a kiss across the room, slowly turned the key in the lock and walked back to my desk.

'You were gone a while, what did he want?' Charlotte asked from across the room.

'Oh, just needed me to take down some dictation for him about the Pencoven Development. The builders are getting teasy because they reckon some of the dimensions are wrong on the Gannel Wing. He just wanted to set the record straight and put some things to bed.'

I heard a snigger coming from the direction of Sam's office where the door was still open. I daren't look across because I knew that he would make me blush again and that would really give us away.

'Well, I could have done that for him. Why didn't he ask me? I'm more senior than you are.' Charlotte sounded annoyed and I knew she would be more than annoyed if she found out what we were really doing.

'I don't know, maybe he thought you were a bit busy with what you were doing. I don't have much on at the moment.'

Another snigger and then Sam was walking briskly through the room towards the lift.

'Very good dictation-taking Penny-May. You can take things down for me again another time if you like. Seeing as you don't have much on at the moment.'

He turned his back on Charlotte and gave me a wink, then vanished into the lift and I watched the downwards arrow light up as the lift moved.

'Are you ok? That sounded a bit harsh,' Charlotte asked.

'Uh, yes, I think so. I didn't realise he was listening. He's probably harder on me because I'm the temp.' I knew I was going to burst out laughing at any minute. 'I need a coffee, can I get you one?'

'No, I'm fine. You're not going to cry about it or anything are you?' she looked as if she was going to stand up and come over to comfort me and there was no way I was going to be able to cope with that, it would only make me want to laugh even more, I knew I was being really cruel.

'No, I'm not going to cry, I just need a few minutes to myself ok?'

'Oh, ok, no worries,' she said as she lowered herself back down into her seat again.

I hurried out into the kitchen area, taking care to close the door so she wouldn't hear me.

Chapter Twenty-Seven

Penny-May

Monday November 24th 2014

'Hi there stranger, you actually spending a night at home are you?' Emma asked when she came into the lounge and saw me sprawled out on the sofa in my joggers and comfy jumper watching Emmerdale on the telly. I would never let Sam see me wearing these, they were quite unglamorous and definitely verging on ugly, but they were also really comfortable.

'Yes, he has to be away on business for the next few days and he's taken Kate as she always accompanies him on his away meetings. It would raise too much suspicion for him to take me instead.

'So, now I get to hear all the gossip about the two of you properly can I?' She put on a mock pout, 'I've hardly seen my bestie for ages!'

'I'm sorry,' I said, 'I know I've neglected you, but he's just so delicious.'

'And sexy.'

'Yes, and sexy.' I agreed.

'And good in bed.'

'Oh yes, and very good in bed. Actually, he's the very best in bed. And out of it,' I started to laugh.

'I'm surprised you can still walk straight you little hussy! No, don't get up, you get your rest, I'll go get the wine out of the fridge and you can tell Aunty Em all about it. And I want to know every tiny little detail.'

I reached over to the coffee table and grabbed the remote control to turn the volume down. I had no idea what was going on anyway as I had missed so many episodes through being with Sam.

Emma came back in with the bottle of wine and two glasses.

'Shift your feet then, I need somewhere to sit to pour this out.'

'Thought you said I could relax?' I raised myself to a half sitting position and curled my feet underneath me, giving her room to sit at the end of the settee. Once she was settled, she passed me my glass and I took a sip.

'So, he's bonking you senseless every night and you are both pretending nothing is going on in work? How can that even happen, are your workmates blind or something? You never used to be that good an actress.'

'I think they must be, we even had sex in his bathroom the other day while they were in the office. That was such a turn on, knowing we could be found out any minute.'

'That's incredible, how on earth did you get away with that? Surely they saw you go in and wondered why you were so long?'

'That's just it, he asked me to take some notes for him, locked the door behind me and we just couldn't keep our hands off each other. When we'd finished, I came out first, told Charlotte that I'd just been taking some stuff down for him and then he went out to a meeting. He said a bit of a snide comment on his way out which made Charlotte actually feel sorry for me and asked if I was alright. It was hilarious!' Emma took a sip of her wine.

'Are you sure he's not using you? You hear of these bosses who take advantage of their secretaries. And if he doesn't want anyone else to know about the two of you? It sounds a bit suspect to me.'

'No, definitely not. He just doesn't want to cause an atmosphere in the office with the other women and he knows the dynamics would change if they knew we are a couple. He wants to protect me from any teasing from them, or jealousy. Charlotte would be evil if she knew what we are up to all the time.'

'I don't know, if it were me I'd want the whole world to know and to hell with the jealous cows who would never stand a chance with him anyway.'

'I know, but it's different for me and Sam. He's the boss and I'm just the temp. He doesn't want to upset anyone working there. I'm sure once we've been together for a while, he'll make it official.'

I didn't like this conversation. I wanted to float along on the tide of love that I had built up around our relationship, but Emma was threatening to poke pins into my bubble and it was far too soon for it to burst. I was having too much fun and I felt loved for the first time in many years.

The text alert on my mobile went off and I glanced at the screen, glad of the opportunity to focus on something else for a minute. When I saw Sam's name come up I quickly punched the buttons to get to the message:

Hey Sexy! Missing you! Kate isn't half as much fun as you are, although she's not so distracting either so getting some work done! Can't wait to see you. Xxx

I smiled and quickly typed out a reply:

. . .

Hi Handsome! Missing you too! I should hope she's not lol!!!!

'That was him I take it? You've got your soppy face on.' Emma asked, nodding towards the phone.

'Yes, he's missing me and not having so much fun with Kate as he would be with me. See, he wouldn't be texting me now if he was just using me, would he?'

Emma reached out and patted my knee, 'No, of course not, I'm just being overprotective that's all. And maybe just a tad jealous myself.'

I closed her hand in mine and gave it a squeeze, 'I'm sorry, I know you're only looking out for me and I've neglected you over the last month or so. We can make it up now though can't we? And you can be happy for me?'

'Only if I can be maid of honour at your wedding!'

'I think you're way ahead of yourself there, but who else would I pick anyway?

You're the only one I'd ever want. And Daniel to give me away of course.'

'Oh, of course, and then there are the dresses to consider. You'll be in white of course, not that you can lay any claim to being virginal but as your bestie I'll keep your secret. I want to be in purple, you know, that deep Cadbury purple that is in right now. Daniel will love to be in a deep purple waistcoat, although you might want to weave in something green somewhere so he can do his Hulk impression.'

Planning my perfect wedding day while we made our way through the whole bottle of wine and then started on another was so much fun that it only seemed fitting to watch *Four Weddings and a Funeral,* followed by *Pretty Woman.* I had asked if she was insinuating anything when she chose that one, but we were very drunk by that time and she said that it was the most romantic film she had ever seen and, taking the prostitute out of it, she could see it totally as our love story. Rich man and working-class girl meet and fall in love.

I let her off, I knew I was in love, and so did she. I just hoped that he was too.

Chapter Twenty-Eight

PENNY-MAY

Saturday December 6th 2014

'Are you sure you're ok with this?' I asked Sam as we sat in his car outside Oak Tree

Lodge. 'Dan's really excited to meet you. He's been asking for weeks.'

'Of course it's ok, I can't wait to meet the little guy.'

I wondered what he would think when he saw that Dan wasn't quite so little but I let it go. People that didn't know Dan always thought that, but they soon realised he wasn't a child. I was a bit worried though, I mean, what if they didn't hit it off? That would be so difficult, I really wanted them to love each other as much as I loved both of them.

'Hey, take that worried look off your face,' Sam said as he plonked a kiss on my forehead. 'Come on, lead me to the dragon's den!'

He opened his door and got out of the car while I did the same on my side. Sam had driven himself today, I liked it when we were able to get out and about on our own. I always felt that Brian was watching and it stopped me from being myself.

'More like the Hulk's hideout, although don't give him ideas. The image of Hulk with a dragon in tow is a pretty scary one, even for me.'

Sam put his arm around me and we walked up the path, just as we got to the door, it burst open and Daniel came bowling out and into my arms.

'Penny-May! Penny-May! Me checked calendar and been looking for you out the window!'

'Hey Hulk! Careful or you'll knock me over.' I returned his hug and then let go,

'this is Sam, the man I told you about.'

'You Penny-May's boyfriend.' Dan put his right hand out ready to shake Sam's. A second later, Sam held his own out and Dan grasped it and started pumping it up and down enthusiastically.

'Pleased to meet you Daniel,' Sam said. Wincing at the unexpected grip. 'Yes, I'm Penny-May's friend.'

I noticed that Sam didn't say boyfriend. Maybe he didn't want to appear too familiar in front of my brother.

'Dan, you can let his hand go now,' I said. 'Shall we go and get a drink? You can show Sam your house.'

Sam massaged his hand, 'Uh, yes, I'd love that. Mine's a coffee.'

'Dan like cider, Martha makes me loads. Come on Penny-May's boyfriend.'

'He drinks cider?' He asked me as Dan shot off and we followed, 'Is that

allowed?'

'Actually, Martha makes him apple squash and he always calls it cider but yes, if he goes to the pub he usually has a cider or two. He's over 18.'

'Oh, yes, I guess. I hadn't really thought about it like that. Doesn't it affect his medication? I mean, can he drink alcohol with his condition?'

I laughed, 'You really haven't ever been with a Down's person have you? He's actually really healthy and doesn't take any medication. His condition is just as normal to him as ours is to you and me. He can eat and drink whatever he chooses.'

'Is my ignorance that obvious?' He replied with a grin. 'I guess I have a lot to learn if I want to be with you.'

'What, as my boyfriend?' I asked.

'Hmmm, seems a pretty good idea to me. Now, where's that coffee and the amazing Martha who can turn apple squash into cider? She could make a fortune on the black market.'

In the kitchen Dan already had the drinks made, Martha standing by to make sure he didn't burn himself on the kettle.

'Penny-May's boyfriend want sugar?' He asked as he held the sugar bowl in his hand, spoon poised to dip into it should Sam say yes.

'No thanks, just milk is fine.'

'Oh, ok,' Dan went to put the bowl back onto the work surface, then lifted it back up again, 'you sure? Sugar good in coffee.'

'I'm sure, I don't like sugar in my drink.'

'That's enough Dan,' I said. 'Sam said no didn't he? Just because you keep asking doesn't change the answer does it.'

'Ok. I sorry.'

Dan put the bowl down, and I felt bad about telling him off. His shoulders had slumped and he had stopped bouncing around.

'You gonna show us your bedroom then? We can take our drinks in there and you can tell us everything you've been doing this week.'

Daniel almost ran from the room, his mood rising again as quick as it had gone down. That was what I loved about him, no matter what made him sad, it was fleeting, he always flipped back to the happy and loving young man that I knew best.

'Me drawed picture for you,' he called as he headed for the stairs. We picked up our mugs and followed him at a more sedate pace. 'Come on Granny's,' he yelled, 'you so slow!'

'You go on, we'll catch you up speedy,' I said. 'What do you think of him so far then?' I asked Sam as we walked down the corridor.

'He seems quite a character, not at all what I was expecting.'

'What were you expecting then?'

'I don't know really, certainly not someone as active, or who would be drinking alcohol.'

'You'll get to know him, and you'll adore him.'

'I'm sure I will, he's really funny and he obviously loves you and that is as good a reason as any for me to get to know him better. Anyone who loves you has got very good taste.'

I turned to look at him, he hadn't said that he loved me yet, but that seemed to

come pretty damn close.

'Come on, Grannies. What you doing down there? I turn big and green if you don't hurry up!'

'Oh no,' I called, 'not the Hulk! Don't bring the scary Hulk out, we're on our way!' Sam looked bemused but hurried his pace to match mine anyway.

Chapter Twenty-Nine

Sam

Saturday December 6th 2014

Christ, what an idiot. What the hell does she see in him? He should have been drowned at birth. Whatever happened to those looney bins? Surely, they should lock all spastics like that up and throw away the keys?

Sam paced up and down the lounge. This was going to be a problem. He really liked Penny-May, she was funny and caring and he knew she was totally hooked. She was amazing in bed and he couldn't get enough of her. He wanted her with him all the time, she did everything he asked her to and she was in love with him. She hadn't said it, but he knew she was.

The dimwit brother though. He wasn't in the plan.

Sam stopped his pacing when he reached the kitchen, put a pod into the coffee machine and placed a cup under the spout.

Although, he'd done a pretty good show of getting to know the cabbage, even did a drawing of the three of them together at the zoo. He'd promised a day trip there during Christmas as well which pleased Penny-May. That was what mattered. As long as he pleased her then she would please him in return. He wouldn't have to get to know Daniel, just be nice to him occasionally. He didn't even have to see him very often.

The coffee made, Sam picked it up and took a tentative sip, checking it for temperature before taking a larger mouthful, feeling it scald the back of his throat and then wiped the froth from his top lip.

He was surprised at how she was with her brother though. He hadn't seen that side of her before. He'd thought her a bit naive and insecure, but she was different with Daniel. She was more confident and self-assured. She knew what to do with him, what to say to him. Her caring nature really came to the fore when she was with him.

Sam felt a stab of anger course through him, his mouth grimaced and he dropped the now empty cup into the sink so hard the handle broke. Swearing, he picked the pieces out and dumped them into the bin.

How dare she show someone else the affection that was meant for him? She needed to leave the spastic to those who were being paid to look after him, not spend every Saturday afternoon pandering to him. Doing stupid drawings and wandering aimlessly around looking at caged animals. It wasn't right. Daniel should be the one who was caged. Penny-May had her own life to lead, and she needed to do what was best for her.

That wasn't with Daniel. That was with Sam.

Chapter Thirty

Penny-May

Monday December 8th 2014

'Sam was so sweet with Daniel,' I said to Emma as she stood washing the dishes in the sink.

'Was he?'

'Yes.'

I picked up the tea towel and started to dry the pile of wet plates.

'It was quite funny at first, I could see that he wasn't used to speaking to someone with a learning disability, but after about half an hour he had it sussed.'

Emma looked at me in that questioning way she had. She should have been a teacher in that school of hers, not the accountant.

'He did!' I flicked the towel at her, 'honestly, he was brilliant. He was laughing and joking with him, calling him The Hulkman and he even drew pictures of the three of us together.'

'Oh, well, that settles it then, he's the best boyfriend ever because he can draw a fancy picture of you lot as a happy family.'

'It wasn't that fancy, it was stick people, but he said it was us and wrote our names on it. Daniel stuck it on his wall so he could see it all the time.'

'I thought he drew for a living?'

'He draws boxes, he's not an artist!' I'd finished drying the plates and started on the mugs. 'Anyway, what's made you so anti-Sam all of a sudden? You were the one pushing me to get with him in the first place when I didn't think I stood a chance.' I saw her shoulders slump and she stopped scrubbing the saucepan.

'I've had a crabby day that's all. End of month accounts blah, blah, blah.'

'I'm not buying that,' I put down the towel and turned her to face me. 'What's up?

And I want the real reason.'

'Ok,' she held her hands in the air, 'I'm just jealous, I hardly ever see you anymore because you're always at his beck and call. Even when you're sleeping here, you jump to pick up the phone every time he texts.' She returned her attention to the saucepan.

I was shocked, I hadn't realised she felt that way, or that I had been ignoring her. She was right though. I had been so wrapped up in Sam that I hadn't taken any time to be with her.

'I'm so sorry Emma, I didn't know. You should have said something. I know, how's about we go out and hit *The Notoriety* tonight. Sam's at a boring business dinner with Kate anyway and I promise I'll leave my phone at home so it'll be just me and you. What do you think?'

'I don't know, I don't want you to think that you have to. We could get a film in and a bottle of wine if you'd rather not go out. You aren't home often and I know how attached you are to those things.' She pointed down towards my legs which were currently covered by my favourite jogging trousers, complete with the coffee stain from the drink I'd spilled earlier.

'Nah, it's been ages since we had a girly night out on the town, I can slob around in these another day.'

'Really?' her smile reached her eyes and she pulled her hands out of the sink, wrenching the pink rubber gloves off as she did so.

'Really,' I replied, 'I can see you don't need very much persuasion.'

'There's a good band on at the pub tonight, maybe we could go onto a club after they finish?'

'Sounds like a plan.' I said.

We left the dishes and got changed quickly. Slapped a bit of make up on and were soon ready for our night out.

Before we left, I sent Sam a quick text, just in case he messaged while we were out.

Going out with Em, not taking phone. Will text you when I get back home. Promise I'll be a good girl! Xxx

It buzzed as I was leaving the room, snatching it up I quickly read his reply,

You'd better be a good girl, or I'll have to spank you when I see you next! Xxx

Oh, trashy sex talk! Even his texts turned me on.

Chapter Thirty-One

Penny-May

Friday December 12th 2014

'But what if she doesn't like me?' I leaned back onto the kitchen worktop and nibbled on the edge of my fingernail.

Sam walked over, gently pulled my finger from my mouth and put his arms around my shoulders, pulling me into him and kissing the top of my head.

'How on earth can she not like you?'

'Well, I don't know? I might not be her type.'

Sam laughed and held me out at arm's length, bending down slightly to look into my eyes, 'You're silly; Mum doesn't have a type. It's me that needs to be concerned whether you're my type or not. And because you most definitely are, Mum will love you.'

'Are you sure? I mean, she will definitely be ok with us being together?'

I hated being so needy, but I was really scared of meeting Sam's mum. He had it easy, Emma and Daniel were my only family and they were bound to fall in love with him. Being introduced to his mother was a huge step and I was fast running out of fingernails to chew on.

'But what if she hates me and makes you stop seeing me?'

'Is that really what's worrying you?' he said.

I gave the briefest of nods, eyes cast downwards and looked at my stockinged feet.

I felt his finger under my chin, lifting it up to look at his face.

'I'm a grown man now Pen. Mum stopped telling me what to do a long time ago.'

I smiled, 'I know, I'm being silly.'

'Yes, you are, but I love you anyway.' I did a double take.

'You love me?'

'Yes, of course I do. There's no-one else in the world I'd introduce to my Mum as

my girlfriend and that's because I'm in love with you.'

I flung my arms around his neck, 'Oh, and I love you too Sam, so much!' I kissed him hard on the mouth, searching for his tongue and felt an answering twitch from his groin as he pressed up against me.

'Oh, you little minx,' he mumbled into my mouth, 'she'll be here any minute, I'm going to have to sit through a whole meal, in front of my mother with a semi now.

How am I going to cope?'

I giggled and wiggled my hips against his growing hardness.

'Then it won't just be me that's anxious will it?'

As the lights from a car sweeping across the drive flashed through the window, he pushed me away and adjusted his trousers.

'You could always think of something that doesn't turn you on?' I added, 'Like me in a nun outfit or something.'

'That really doesn't help. I'll sort you out later, and then I'll be thinking of you in a really sexy nun's outfit.'

The front door opened and I heard the tapping of heeled shoes on the tiled hallway floor.

'Sam?'

'In here, Mum.'

She appeared around the door still with her shoes on, wearing a long camel hair coat, belted around the waist. Her hair was piled into a chignon at the back of her head and her make-up was immaculate in the '*there but not there*' variety. As Sam took the coat from her shoulders, I saw that she was dressed in a tight woollen pencil skirt with a pale blue twinset and pearls. The clichéd image of the perfect middle class woman, not a thing out of place. I immediately felt insecure again as I thought about my choice of clothing, black skirt and a white blouse. I'd thought I looked smart but casual; now I figured I looked more like a waitress.

Her gaze raked from my head to my toes and back again before turning to face the door.

'Is Penny upstairs then?' She asked Sam when he returned to the room.

'No, this is Penny-May,' he replied.

'Really? Oh, I'm so sorry.' She came over to me and held out her hand for me to shake.

'Sam said we were eating so I assumed you were with the caterers.'

'They've already delivered the food,' Sam said. 'We sent them home again.

Penny-May and I are going to serve it up.'

'Oh, well that seems a bit silly, they cost enough. You should get what you pay for and that's the full service, surely?'

'No Mum, we wanted it to be just the three of us tonight, without people walking in and out all the time. I wanted you to meet Penny-May properly. And so far, you're being very rude.'

She had the grace to look ashamed and fiddled with the strap of her handbag.

'It's not a problem,' I said, 'I can see why you got confused. Would you like a drink?'

'Yes please, a chardonnay if you have it? Are we going to be standing out here all night?'

'Let's go into the lounge, shall we? Pen can bring the drinks in for us.'

'Yes, of course,' I replied as he steered her out of the room. I reached for the wine bottle, pouring myself a quick snifter first and downing it in one before following with the tray of glasses.

'Where have Lucy's photos from mantlepiece gone?'

'I've put them away. Lucy isn't here anymore, and I thought it was time to move on,' Sam replied.

Maggie pursed her lips. 'She may be gone but she isn't forgotten you know.' She turned to me, 'She was a lovely girl, would do anything for Sam and he loved her so much. So cruel what she did to him, wasn't it dear?'

We had finished the wine and were sat in the lounge drinking coffee. I could see that Sam wasn't happy with the way the conversation was going. I had done my waitressing bit very well; hadn't spilt or spoilt anything but Maggie had been quite rude all the way through with her little digs about my appearance and that I was *just* a secretary. Not like physiotherapist extraordinaire, Lucy. Perfect little Lucy who had broken Sam's heart when she jumped off a cliff.

I was beginning to think it must have been to get away from her that made Lucy do it. Christ, I wasn't far away from doing the same.

'That's enough now Mum, I don't think Pen needs to hear any more about her tonight.'

'It's fine,' I said, 'It must have been difficult for both of you to get over her loss and it helps if you can speak about your grief.'

'Then I don't need to hear anything more about her tonight, ok?' He sounded gruff and upset. Not like the Sam that had been pressed up against me in the kitchen earlier.

Maggie stopped speaking and looked at her son.

'Are you alright?' she asked him.

'Yes. I'm fine. I'm just moving on and that's the end of it.'

I excused myself to go to the bathroom. I wasn't feeling comfortable in the room with them and couldn't figure out any other way of making myself scarce.

When I returned, Sam was helping his mother into her coat and Brian was at the front door to help her to the car.

'Mum's just leaving,' Sam said, 'She's tired and decided it's time to go home.' He went outside to talk to Brian.

'Oh, goodbye then, it was lovely to meet you,' I said to her, holding my hand out. She gripped it and pulled me in, I thought to kiss me on the cheek but instead I felt her lips close to my ear.

'Don't you dare hurt him. I know you're using him and only after his money. You're no Lucy and I won't see him broken like that again.'

I was shocked as she drew away, turned her back on me and walked to the car.

'What's up?' Sam asked as he closed the door on the retreating car, 'You don't look very happy?'

'It's nothing,' I said, shaking my head, 'I'm just tired, it's been a long night. I'll sort the kitchen out and then maybe we can go to bed?'

'Leave the kitchen. I'd rather finish what we started before the old bat came in and gave you such a hard time.'

He held my hand and pulled me towards the stairs.

'I have a miracle cure for all your aches and woes,' he said.

I let him lead me upstairs and the cure he promised was all

that and more, but I wondered what I could possibly do to be cured of Maggie.

And of Lucy's ghost.

Chapter Thirty-Two

Penny-May

Wednesday December 24th 2014.

'Ready for a hot chocolate, Dan?'

'With marshmallows?'

'And lots of squirty cream on top?'

'Yes please!' Dan clapped his mittened hands together in excitement.

'Costa's, here we come then eh?'

He grabbed my wrist and pulled me through the festive shoppers towards the coffee shop. It was always our treat. Our special time together on Christmas Eve. Shopping in Truro and then into Costa to warm our hands around a steaming hot mug.

I could never see him on Christmas Day because there were no buses running and taxis were too expensive. Oak Tree Lodge put on a lavish meal for those that stayed, and I usually went to Emma's parents with her for a couple of days. The first year after our parents died, Daniel came too, but it was too much for him to be able to handle the excitement of the season and the change of environment.

Our drinks finished, we caught the bus back to the home and played board games with a couple of the other residents. The staff popped in and out supplying us with more drinks and there were crisps, peanuts and mini crackers in bowls on the table for us all to snack on. Dan beat me at snakes and ladders of course. I've never known anyone so lucky at landing on the ladders all the time and never on the snakes. He ran around the room shouting,

'Me won! Me whooped Penny-May's ass!' I burst into laughter, it was a new phrase that I'd never heard him say before, but it was so appropriate and innocent I couldn't reprimand him for it.

Before I left I handed Dan the bag of presents I'd bought for him and he carefully lifted all the wrapped and bow tied gifts out one by one, giving each a shake and a prod before placing them under the tree where he would find them the next morning. He was copying what our Mum had always done when she was given a gift. She never could resist trying to guess what was inside and Dad always went to great lengths to try and disguise what it was. In the end, he stuck everything in shoe boxes and wrapped them up so she wouldn't be able to guess anything. All year long we wouldn't be allowed to throw any shoe boxes away, he would take them to his potting shed and store them until they were needed.

Once they were in exactly the right place, Daniel handed me mine. He'd wrapped it himself so it wasn't the neatest of presents I received, but it was always the most loved in all of its tattered beauty. He must have used almost a whole roll of Sellotape to hold all the bits together and there was a bright red bow stuck on the top, holding a home-made label on which he had written *Penny-May* followed by *love Daniel* and loads of kisses. I knew he could write his own name without any help, but the rest he would have had to have a staff member write for him on another piece of paper for him to copy. I pictured him sitting at the kitchen table with his tongue poking out of the side of his mouth, concentrating really hard to get the letters right.

'You not open it yet!' He said, as he passed it to me.

'I won't, I promise,' I'd replied, 'I'll take it to Sam's and put it under his tree so I can open it tomorrow. Then I'll phone you in the morning. Ok?'

He nodded and gave me a huge bear hug as I left.

'Merry Christmas, Mr Hulk,'

He answered in his sing-song voice, 'Merry Christmas, Penny-May! Danny love you.'

I felt a lump in my throat, 'I love you too Dan, very, very much. Now shoo, go and see if you can beat Zoe at bingo. I've put my next visit into your calendar for you and

I'll phone you tomorrow.'

He planted a kiss on my cheek, turned and ran back into the lounge leaving me to close the front door as I left. I wished my parents were here to see the man he had become. They would have been so proud. Christmas was always when I missed them the most.

I didn't need to catch the bus. Sam said Brian could pick me up from Oak Tree Lodge and take me home to pick up my stuff, then bring me straight to Karadow so I didn't have to be away from him any longer than I had to be. He's been so sweet and ever so apologetic about the horrible way his mother spoke to me.

I couldn't wait to spend Christmas with Sam. Emma was with her parents and this was the first time I wasn't going to be there. I'd felt a bit guilty when we were arranging it all, but Emma told me not to be so silly. She was going to miss me, but she had her family and she knew I really wanted to be with him. The only downer was going to be his mother. Maggie was coming over for Christmas dinner, but he'd promised to get rid of her before the evening set in. He said he'd told her not to keep talking about

Lucy again. I was grateful that he'd tried, but I was still uneasy about having to sit through another meal with her.

He must have been looking out of the kitchen window because as soon as we pulled up the drive he opened the door and came out to help Brian get my suitcase and presents out of the car. I'd brought the ones that Emma had given me as well as the ones I was giving him and his mum. I'd even bought Brian and his wife a big box of chocolates. I wasn't sure if that was the right thing to do or not, but he was always polite and friendly towards me. It seemed only right to get him something. It was on top of one of the present bags so I gave it to him before he drove the car back to the garage.

'Thank you, Miss Meares, I wasn't expecting that.' A smile broke across his face as he gently shook the package up and down. 'I think Mary and I will enjoy those with a nice bottle of wine tomorrow evening.' He gave me a wink and climbed into the driver's seat.

'That was nice of you,' Sam said as we walked into the house with my bags.

'I can be sometimes, you know.'

'Oh really? How's about you show me just how nice you can be?'

The bags were dropped on the hallway floor. His hands around my waist, his foot kicking the door shut behind us.

We didn't make it upstairs to the bedroom. We headed for the sofa and started celebrating Christmas in front of the log fire, our bodies moving in time with the hisses and the crackles, the heat from the flames matching our burning desire for each other.

Christmas morning started with Sam waking me up by his usual method of prodding his erect penis into my back and reaching around me to fondle my breasts. I loved early morning sex. That slow awakening of the mind as his hands and fingers woke my body from its place of rest and relaxation, bringing me to a climax barely before I had a chance to fully open my eyes. It was a wonderful way to start the day.

We snuggled then and said how much we loved each other. I still found it difficult to believe he could love me; I didn't know why I was so special that he should fall for me. I mean, I knew why I loved him, anyone could see why that was, but not the other way around.

'Breakfast in bed?' he asked. He pulled the covers back and swung his legs over the side. Not bothering to put anything on to cover his nakedness, he left the room and I could hear him clattering around in the kitchen. Ten minutes later, he came back bearing a tray with two glasses of Buck's Fizz and a plate of warm French pastries on it.

When we'd finished eating I couldn't wait any longer. I threw back the covers and knelt on the bed, bouncing it up and down.

'Present time! It must be present time now!'

'Presents?' He asked, 'Wasn't your wakeup call enough of a present?'

'You tease!' I said, shoving him on the shoulder, 'Come on, it's time for me to give you your gift, I can't wait any longer for you to see what it is.'

Sam relented, he was as big a kid as I was and we both bolted downstairs and plunged under the tree to divvy out the presents.

I had a bigger pile than Sam did, and most were from Sam. There was a whole new wardrobe of clothes, all smart casual and expensive. They were beautiful, and I loved all of them. There weren't any jogging trousers though, but I'd never let Sam see me wearing mine, so he probably didn't think I'd like any. The last box I unwrapped was long and thin and had the name of *Matthew Millers Jewellers* emblazoned across it. I couldn't believe he had bought me anything from there, I was usually too frightened to even window shop when I walked past because they were so expensive.

Inside, nestled on a velvet cushion was a gold necklace with a double heart pendant in the centre of the chain. The upper heart had what looked like a diamond in the centre. It couldn't be real, no one had ever bought me a real diamond necklace before.

My mouth dropped open as I first stared at it and then at Sam.

'It's our two hearts entwined together,' he said, lifting the delicate chain and placing it around my neck. The cold of the metal felt strange against the warmth of my skin and I raised my hand to clasp the heart as he kissed the back of my neck where he'd fastened the chain together. I turned to him, kissing him full on the mouth as his arms folded around me and I melted into his body.

'It's beautiful,' I managed to say when we parted, 'I love you so much.'

'It's not as beautiful as you,' he replied.

I said a courteous goodbye to Maggie as the taxi drove off. She had been better during the meal than before, but it was obvious that she really didn't approve of me dating Sam. She started a conversation about footballers' wives and how the women were only with them because of the money. I'm sure she was aiming it at me, but Sam didn't say anything, so I kept quiet.

She said I'd overcooked the turkey and the gravy was too runny. I got the feeling that nothing I could do was right.

With the door closed behind her, I heaved a sigh of relief.

'Where's the wine?' I asked Sam, 'I think I can properly relax now it's just the two of us again.'

'You go into the lounge, I'll get it,' he said, moving into the kitchen.

He returned bearing two flute glasses and a bottle of champagne which he set on the coffee table.

'Champagne?'

'Well, I thought we'd celebrate,' Sam said.

'What are we celebrating? Your mum going home?' Sam grinned and put his hand into his pocket.

'I have one more gift for you.'

He pulled out a small box and knelt down in front of me. This had to be a wind up, he couldn't be. Could he?

'I thought we'd celebrate you becoming my fiancée.'

He cracked open the box to reveal a ring set with one large, square cut, solitary diamond. My hand flew to my mouth, this had to be a joke.

'Wh... wh... what did you say?'

'I said, will you marry me?'

This really was happening. He reached out and took hold of my left hand, lifted the ring out of its box and slid it onto my ring finger. It fit perfectly and I burst into tears.

'Is that a yes then?' he asked.

I flung my arms around his neck, almost knocking him over in the process.

'Yes, oh yes, a million times yes!' I squealed before we sealed the deal with a kiss which inevitably and quickly led to the best sex ever on the fluffy cream rug in front of the fire.

Chapter Thirty-Three

Penny-May

Friday December 26th 2014

Lying in bed, I couldn't wait any longer to tell Emma my news.

'You know you wanted to be my bridesmaid,' I said when she answered my call.

'Yeah?'

'Well, I don't want you to be my bridesmaid.'

'Ok?'

'I want you to be my Maid of Honour!'

'What are you on about Penny? I know we were messing around the other day, but it was just messing around.'

'No, you don't get it! He asked me! He actually, really, truly asked me!'

'What do you mean? He asked you. Asked you what?'

'To marry him dumbhead! I've got like, a diamond ring and everything!'

'You what? Really?'

'Really, really!'

'Really, really, really? This isn't a wind up? You and Sam are getting married?'

'Yes! I'm going to be Mrs Penny-May Lambert.'

'Oh my God, oh my God, oh my God, that is the best news I've heard all day. I totally forgive you for bailing out on me and spending Christmas over there. Oh My

God! Tell me every little detail of how he proposed, I'll bet it was real romantic.'

'Oh, it so was. I couldn't believe what I was seeing when he went down on one

knee in front of me.'

'He did that?'

'He did!'

'Right, planning mode engaged. We need to sort your dress and a venue and the hen night, oh we are going to have such a fun hen night, and—'

'Hey, hold on a bit, we haven't even set a date yet!'

'Well, get a move on, you don't want to hang around in case he changes his mind.'

I knew she was only teasing but still.

'Charming! Thanks for the vote of confidence.'

'He's a lucky man to get you. He might be worried that you're going to change your mind instead!'

'I won't be changing my mind. He is amazing and perfect and so sexy. I'd be mad to change my mind.'

'I'm so pleased for you Pen; we'll have to have our own celebration when we get home again. *The Notoriety* for drinks and a pub meal?'

'It's a date. And do you mind if we invite Rhea? Josh's mum from the school? She's really nice, you'll love her when you get to know her properly. We can have it as a pre-hen night, without the hen stuff.'

'Can't see why not, I've never had a problem with her at the school.'

'Perfect!'

We said our goodbyes as Sam came upstairs with breakfast.

'Who was that?' He asked as I placed the mobile back onto the bedside table.

'Emma, I told her we were engaged. She's so excited for us.'

'Oh. That's good.' He replied.

'This is turning into a habit,' I said, nodding towards the tray in his hands, 'I could start to expect this every day.'

'You can pay me back later with a bit of stress relief,' he said. He placed the tray on the bed beside me and bent down to give me a kiss.

'I'll pay you back later with a lot of stress relief if you like?'

'That is just what I was hoping you'd say. Now eat, you're going to need the energy. I'm going for a shower.'

I poked my tongue out at him as he walked into the ensuite, 'I'll out energy you any day!'

'We'll see about that,' he called, 'we'll see who can hold out the longest eh?'

I took a bite of my croissant as the patter of high-powered water drops started to land on the glass shower screen.

Yeah, we'll see.

The familiar butterflies started their fluttering in my stomach. Putting my breakfast aside and climbing out of the bed, I went to join him in the shower.

Chapter Thirty-Four

Penny-May

Monday January 5th 2015.

I couldn't believe we were actually doing this. Sam and I walking into work together.

Our relationship was about to go public.

I was shaking as we walked through the reception and into the lift, side by side but not touching. Nobody turned or said anything. Nobody noticed. It was just two colleagues who'd happened to turn up at the front door at the same time. Nobody had seen us both stepping out of Sam's Audi and Brian driving off again. Everybody nodded at Sam of course, they all said good morning and asked if he'd had a good Christmas to which he replied good morning and yes, thank you.

Nobody noticed the temp girl walking by his side. If they did and saw my nervousness, they would have thought it was because I didn't know what to say to the big boss man. A girl out of her depth and feeling embarrassed to have ended up in the same lift with him. They were probably right, but not in the way they were thinking. I was feeling out of my depth, and I didn't know how I'd ended up with him.

But I was glad I had.

Sam must have noticed my nerves because when the lift doors were closed, he reached over and squeezed my gloved hand.

'You ok?' He asked.

I looked up at him and saw him smile, felt the pressure of his hand and his strength pulsing into me.

'Yes. With you I'm always ok.'

'Good,' he raised my hand and placed it against his mouth, then released it again just before the door opened.

We walked into the room. I was a step behind him, neither of us talking. He went straight to his office. I went to my desk and removed my gloves and my coat.

The conversation was the same as downstairs, Kate and Charlotte asking each other about Christmas, how they'd enjoyed the break and spending time with their families.

'Anyone want a coffee?' I asked.

'Yes please,' they both replied as one. I knew they would, they never turn down an offer of a drink and I figured it would give me some time to settle down.

When I returned with the tray and carried it over to Charlotte's desk she let out a squeal and grabbed my hand.

'Oh my goodness! You're engaged? You didn't even have a boyfriend before Christmas. Come on, tell us all the details.'

I felt the colour rise and heard Kate come across the room.

'That's nice,' Kate said, taking my hand from Charlotte and looking at the ring.

'That's quite a big rock, must have been expensive.'

'I don't know,' I replied, 'it was a present, and a total surprise. I really wasn't expecting it.'

'But who is he?' Asked Charlotte again, 'you weren't seeing anyone! Or were you? Was it a secret love affair?'

I knew my face was scarlet and it wasn't helped by hearing Sam's office door open and seeing him walk across the room towards us.

'What's all the noise about?' he asked, 'I know it's the first day back, but we still have work to do.'

'I'm sorry Mr Lambert,' Kate replied, 'it's just that Penny-May has got herself engaged and we're trying to find out who the lucky man is.'

'Ah, that's easy,' he said as he stood behind me and clasped his arms around my waist, 'It's me. Penny-May and I are engaged.'

Both women's mouths dropped open, but neither spoke.

Sam dropped a kiss on the top of my head and, releasing me, started walking back to his office.

'Now, back to work ladies. Pen, is there any coffee on there for me?'

'I'll go and make you a fresh one.'

His door closed and I was left with the staring, speechless figures of my colleagues.

'How the hell did you do that?' Charlotte asked, 'and how long has it been going on right in front of us?'

'A while,' I replied turning to make his morning coffee.

Chapter Thirty-Five

Sam

Tuesday January 13th 2015

'What do you mean I can't get married yet?' Sam exploded at his lawyer.

'I mean, you can't get married because, in the eyes of the law, you are still married to Lucy.'

'How the fuck can I be married to someone who's dead? "Till death us do part," is in the vows isn't it? She's dead, so we are parted, marriage ended. Kaput.'

Sam thumped the desk in front of him and, unable to sit in the chair any longer listening to this idiotic moron, he stood up and started to pace the room.

'I'm sorry mate, but it's because the body was never found.' Gareth said.

'What difference does that make? We all know she's dead.'

'The difference is that, without a body, there has to be a time lapse of at least seven years with absolutely no evidence of her being alive before your current marriage can be classified as finished.'

'But she left a suicide note, her handbag and shoes were found at the top of the cliff, her scarf was found washed up on the shore. How the hell can she not be dead?' He thumped the desk again on the final word.

'I know. We all know she did it. There's no way she could be anything but dead.

But that's the way the law in this Country works.'

'The law's an ass,' Sam replied. 'Just get on with the Pencoven paperwork, I'll see you later.'

Sam slammed the door shut behind him so hard it rattled the frosted glass window.

Staring at the sea being buffeted by the cold blustery wind, Sam walked across Arvor beach. The tide was low and, as usual, he found the ebb and flow of the waves soothing as they crashed on the shoreline, matching his mood.

There must be some way around it, he thought. Some way that he could marry Penny-May. He didn't want to just move her in. He didn't agree with it. If they were going to live together then they needed to be married. He wanted her to know that she was his, in name as well as in body. He'd promised her they'd get married and he was going to find a way to do it.

Sam stopped walking as a thought occurred to him. Gareth had said it was the way the law worked in this Country. That was it, he'd just get married in another Country. One that didn't have such cock and bull laws. Seven years was far too long to wait to make Pen his wife. He'd find somewhere else and marry her that way. And it would be on a beach, of that he was certain.

Feeling happier now he had a solution, he strode back up the sand dunes and along the road to Mistral. Locking himself in his office, he turned on the computer and began his search for the perfect wedding location.

Chapter Thirty-Six

Penny-May

Saturday February 7th 2015

'I'm not going to be able to come and see you next week Dan, but I promise I'll come and spend even longer with you the week after. I'll bring Sam as well, that will be cool won't it?'

It was raining outside so we'd stayed in and played board games all afternoon. We both hated being stuck inside.

He didn't smile. He folded his arms across his chest and moved back on his bed so he was in the corner by the headboard.

'Why Penny-May not come? It says on calendar.'

'Sam and I are going on holiday for a week. He's taking me to The Maldives for a bit of sun and to relax for a few days.'

'Danny come?'

'I'm sorry Dan, not this time. But maybe we can in the future eh? We'll go away as one big family. Will that be good?'

Daniel nodded slowly, but he didn't move forward or uncross his arms, so I knew I wasn't forgiven yet.

'I'll bring you back a present.'

He lifted his head and looked at me.

'Big present?'

'Of course, a big present, I might even get you two!'

A smile started to play at the corner of his mouth.

'Danny like presents.'

'I know you do. Now, shall we change the calendar dates?'

Daniel slid forwards and stood up from the bed, going across the room to fetch it for me. I'd never missed a Saturday, I never went on holiday, so I was going to miss him just as much as he was going to miss me.

'There. All done,' I said, replacing the pen onto the blob of sticky tack on the side of the board. 'Brian's outside now so I gotta go. You be a good man and I'll see you in two weeks, ok?'

I held my arms out for a hug and he stepped inside them, returning it slightly too tightly.

'Whoa, Hulkman, take it easy eh?'

Danny released me and I walked towards the door.

'Love you!'

'Don't forget presents.'

I laughed. He was going to be ok. 'I won't, I promise.'

I pulled up the hood of my duffle coat and ran to Brian's waiting car.

Chapter Thirty-Seven

Penny-May

Saturday February 14th 2015

'I've got a surprise for you.' Sam said as we lay in bed.

'Another one?' I asked, snuggling up beside him and running my hand across his chest.

'A different one, it's in that suitcase over there.' He pointed to a large case that he hadn't unpacked when we arrived, saying he'd get around to it later. 'It's an extra special Valentine's present.'

'For me? But this whole holiday was for our Valentine celebration wasn't it?' I got out of bed, still naked, and walked to the case.

'Yes, but that doesn't mean we can't do more does it?'

Smiling broadly, he was lying back onto the pillows, sheet casually draped across his abdomen and his arms crossed behind his head.

'Open it and tell me what you think?'

I saw that the padlock, which had kept it closed yesterday, had been removed. Opening the lid, I carefully peeled the layer of tissue paper back to reveal white fabric below. Lifting it out I found a beautiful long white dress. I looked across at Sam where he was still grinning.

'Is this a wedding dress?' I asked.

'Yes. Top marks for observation.'

I was confused. 'But who's is it? And what's it doing here?'

'It's yours, I hope you like it. I got the stylist at *Belle's Belles* to pick it out for you. Today is going to be our wedding day.'

'Today? We're getting married?'

Sam sat up in the bed.

'That's what I said. You're going to have to get a move on in the shower though, the beautician will be here in half an hour and we need to be on the beach in front of the celebrant in two hours.'

'Two hours? I only have two hours to get ready? For my wedding?'

I was starting to panic. This really couldn't be true. It must be April Fool's day, not Valentine's.

'I can't get ready in just two hours!'

Sam got out of bed and crossed the room. Reaching out, he held the tops of my arms and gazed into my eyes.

'You are beautiful anyway; two hours will just be the icing.'

'But Danny and Emma won't be here,' I wailed.

'I know, but I wanted it to be a surprise for you, and if they knew they wouldn't have been able to keep it a secret. Especially Danny.'

'No,' I smiled as I thought of my funny brother, 'Danny can't keep a secret for a minute.'

'I was also being selfish in that I wanted you all to myself. I've done the big Church wedding and it was too many people around. I love you and I wanted it to be just you and I on our day together. Is that ok?'

I nodded and leaned into him as he put his arms around me.

'Can we do something special with them when we get back?'

'Of course we can, anything you want. Now, it's twenty-five minutes until the beautician arrives, go get your butt into the shower, I'll have mine after.'

I felt amazing. The dress was a perfect sheath of ankle length white chiffon over a white lining which stopped just above the knee. The chiffon had delicate roses embroidered into the short train as well as around my waist and over one shoulder. The shoes were simple white leather sandals with diamond rhinestones that flashed in the sunlight. A headdress covered in pale roses and a matching bouquet completed the outfit.

A white horse drawn carriage carried me to the beach where I could see Sam standing with a man in a plain white suit under an arch of white tulle and red and white roses. It took my breath away.

Soft music played as I approached the flower strewn altar. Sam met me there and took my hands in his.

'You look beautiful,' he said before turning towards the celebrant.

It was so romantic and perfect. I couldn't believe it was happening. A tear slid down my cheek as I said, 'I do.'

Sam reached across and tenderly wiped it away with his thumb. I felt myself leaning into his hand, his caress saying so much that words couldn't.

When we kissed for the first time as man and wife, I felt so totally and utterly in love, and I know that Sam felt it too. The heat on our backs from the afternoon sun, the sound of the sea echoing around us and the rustle of the palm trees behind us in the gentle breeze all came together in this one perfect moment.

'I love you Mrs Lambert,' he whispered as we broke apart.

I smiled.

'Ditto Mr Lambert,' I replied.

Sam bent and picked me up in his arms, swinging us around in a circle. I shrieked with joy and flung my arm with the bouquet of white roses out to the side as we twirled around.

Setting me down onto the sandy floor again, he pulled me in for another kiss.

'Congratulations,' the celebrant said, 'I can see that you have a long and happy future ahead of you.'

'Thank you,' Sam said shaking his hand and then looking straight into my eyes, 'we certainly do.'

A wedding breakfast complete with a chilled bottle of champagne was waiting in our room. Sam poured two glasses and handed me one.

'To us,' he said.

'To us,' I replied, taking a long sip and then putting the glass back down on the table.

Sam put his down also and came over to me. He gently removed the headdress and then slid his arms around my back and began to pull down the zip.

'I've been wanting to do this all afternoon. You look so damn sexy in that and I can't wait any longer.'

He started peppering my neck with small kisses and nips as he edged the fabric from my shoulder, allowing it to fall in a cloud at my feet. I pulled at his shirt, wanting to feel his skin as his hands ran amok across mine. Within minutes we were naked on the bed, kissing and stroking, licking and biting as we came together as one, pushing each other to the most exquisite moment of release. Fireworks exploding through me while I clung tightly to him, giving him every part of me, knowing I would never want to be parted from him.

We lay together for a while afterwards. Our heartbeats slowed and our bodies cooled. We held each other, not wanting to let the other go or for this moment to be over.

His breathing shallowed and I looked up to see him sleeping. Placing a gentle kiss on his shoulder I snuggled back into the crook of his arm and let myself drift away, safe, secure and most of all, loved.

Chapter Thirty-Eight

PENNY-MAY
Monday February 16th 2015

'I can't believe you got married out there!' Emma said.

'I know, it was such a surprise. He had everything sorted, all I had to do was get dressed and turn up at the beach.'

'I thought I was going to be the Maid of Honour? I had it all planned. What I would wear and how we would have so much fun dress shopping and food tasting for the reception and stuff.'

She was sulking. I wasn't surprised, I would be too if it had happened the other way around. In some respects, I felt as cheated as she did as I couldn't do any of those things either.

'I'm sorry, Hun.'

I was packing my boxes at the flat, Emma was supposed to be helping me but how she could do that while she just sat on my bed watching me was something I hadn't figured out.

'But I'm not ready for you to move out yet,' she said.

'I'm not sure I am either. It's going to be so weird living at Karadow all the time.' I sat on the bed beside her and gave her a hug. 'It's going to be weird not having you around all the time either,' I continued. 'You're still my very best friend. You have to come around all the time and see me and we can get drunk and have girly nights when Sam is away on business. It'll be cool, you'll see.'

She sniffed and raised her hand to wipe a tear away from her eye.

'It won't be the same though will it.'

'It'll be better, we can drink better quality wine for a start instead of whatever's on special at Bargain Booze.'

Emma raised her head and looked at me, a slow smile beginning to emerge, 'I hadn't thought of that,' she said, 'and I could stay over, and we could pig out on posh canapés with caviar?'

I laughed; I could always get around her by talking about food and alcohol.

I heard the doorbell ring and went to answer it. Sam had said he was going to be late so I'd ordered a Chinese takeaway to be delivered to the flat. There was way too much, but Sam said to make it a treat as it was the last time Emma and I would be able to do it here. He said it could be our way of celebrating the marriage. He even gave me his credit card to use and told me not to worry about the cost. He's going to get me one of my own, but he said it will take a while for the name change thing to work and to use this for anything I need in the meantime.

I'd laughed at first and said that I could use my salary for my bits and pieces, but he told me not to be so silly. A wife of his didn't need to work, and especially not as his PA. That was just not fitting. Michelle was due back from her maternity leave in a few weeks anyway, Kate and Charlotte would just have to cope without me. He reckoned I would have enough to do just keeping up with him and being the perfect hostess for the business meetings we would need to go to.

'You're such a lucky bugger not having to work anymore,'

Emma said as we ate our meal, 'It's going to be amazing for you to be able to spend your time doing whatever you want.'

'I guess,' I replied, 'It's going to be strange though. It'll probably be like a long holiday at first and I'm sure Sam will keep me busy doing stuff for him.'

'Oh, the way you two are always at it, he's bound to keep you busy!'

I poked my fork in her direction, 'Well, when the sex is *sooo* good, it would be a shame not to be there to take advantage of it wouldn't it?'

Emma laughed, 'Oh, too much information, especially when I'm going through such a drought!'

'There's another Sam out there for you too, and now that I'm not here to cramp your style, you can bring him back whenever you want.'

'You know as well as I do that I have to find a new flat mate; I can't afford this place on my own.' Emma looked downcast again.

'Oh, I forgot, I've got you this.'

My fork clattered onto the almost empty plate and I rummaged in my handbag, bringing out a cheque made out to her.

'What's that?'

'Well, I said to Sam that I was feeling guilty for leaving you in the lurch with the rent and I was worried that you would have to take in the first person that was interested, and they may turn out to be horrible. He wrote that out for you. It's six months' worth of my share of the rent so you can take your time and make sure you get someone nice.'

'I...I don't know what to say,' she said as she looked at the four-figure sum on the piece of paper in her hand.

'Don't say anything, it's just the kind of man he is. He's so kind and generous to everyone.'

Emma nodded.

'And I'll even come around when you interview and help you vet them.'

I looked at the clock on the wall and then picked up the half empty bottle of red wine, 'Brian will be here to get me in two hours. I say, finish this and a chick flick for old times eh?'

Chapter Thirty-Nine

Penny-May

Sunday March 1st 2015

I rolled over in bed and stroked my fingers across Sam's bare chest. His gentle breathing began to get deeper as I lifted his arm and snuggled into his shoulder. Looking up into his face I saw his eyes flutter open and I turned his face to mine, kissing him lightly on his lips.

'Do you know how much I love you?' I asked him as his free arm snaked around my waist, pulling me even closer into him.

'I have an idea,' he replied, 'but how's about you refresh my memory just a little bit?'

'Well, I could do this,' I wiggled down and flicked my tongue over his nipples, 'or I could do this,' I moved my hand down and felt his shaft hardening under my touch, 'and I could definitely do this,' I sat up and straddled my legs across his chest, positioning myself just above his throbbing penis and held myself there. I bent forward and kissed him full on the mouth, feeling his tongue with mine and his hands grasping my hips, trying to pull me downwards.

'Oh, that is starting to work,' he said into the moistness of my mouth, a groan escaping as I hovered, my wetness just touching the tip of his shaft, his groin reaching up to meet mine until I could hold the position no longer. The need to feel him deep inside me making me slip down onto him, my own moan of pleasure meeting his as I started to slowly move up and down, his hands gripping and pulling with every downward thrust. I sat up and threw my head back, pushing my nipples forward so I could feel him deeper, feel him fill every last millimetre of my soul. Our movements increased with the rhythm, so in sync with each other that we knew instinctively when the time was right to let go. I felt his last push, his hands pulled me hard, down onto him as his body spasmed in ecstasy. His release setting off my own chain reaction, those hundreds and thousands of sparks flying across my body, holding me onto him until we were both spent.

I lay down on top of him, not ready to release him yet, still relishing in the afterglow of my orgasm.

'White rabbits,' I said as I kissed his chest.

'What?'

I lifted my head and looked at him, 'White rabbits! Pinch, punch first of the month.'

Sam looked bemused, 'What on earth are you on about?'

'It's the first of the month, the first of March. It's what you say when you see someone, it brings them good luck.'

Sam closed his eyes, 'White rabbits,' he whispered. His eyes were glistening as if he was about to start crying.

'Hey silly,' I said, 'It's not that serious. But you are so sweet. Do you want me to bring you some breakfast up? We have fresh croissants and coffee?'

Sam smiled at me, 'No, it's ok. You go on downstairs and get it all ready, I'll just grab a shower and be down in a few minutes.'

. . .

I had set the table, made the coffee and warmed the pastries just in time for him to enter the room. I had a question I wanted to ask him and I wanted him in just the right relaxed mood to ask it.

He reached out and took a sip of his drink, 'perfect,' he said, 'have you ever thought of being my wife?'

I laughed, 'I couldn't think of anything better,' I replied, taking a sip of my own and then breaking a croissant in half and putting them both back down onto the plate in front of me.

'I was just wondering though?' I paused, waiting until he looked up at me.

'Yes?'

'Well, you know the study upstairs?'

'Yes?'

'I was wondering if we could turn it into a bedroom?'

'Why do we need another bedroom? It's fine as it is isn't it? Didn't we say that Emma could sleep in the box room if she stayed over while I was away? I don't think we need to rig out a whole room for her for just the odd night.'

'Oh, no, I wasn't thinking about Emma. I was thinking about Daniel. It would be nice for Daniel to come over sometimes and have some space of his own wouldn't it?'

Sam didn't answer immediately. He took another drink of his coffee, swirled what was left around before drinking the last in one swift gulp. He stood and pushed his chair across the table.

'I don't think so,' he said. 'Daniel has a home of his own where he is looked after by people who are paid to do the job. I don't think we need to upset that do we?'

I dropped my head to look at my plate, my fingers pulling the bread to pieces. 'Yes, I guess. It was just an idea. I miss him so much.'

Sam came round behind my chair and put his hand on my shoulder, giving it a gentle squeeze. 'I know you do, but I want to be selfish and keep you all to myself for a while. We are only just starting our lives together and if he comes to stay then we wouldn't be able to be spontaneous and do what we wanted would we?'

'You're right,' I replied, 'It's far too early to be thinking of anything like that.'

He squeezed my shoulder again, 'That's right, let's just keep it as us for now. I'm going to drive into town, is there anything you want?'

'Oh, not really, but I'll come with you, just let me grab a shower and get ready.'

'No. It's fine. You stay here and relax. I have a few errands to do and you'll only be bored.'

With a kiss dropped onto the top of my head and a breeze from the opening and closing of the door he was gone. I'd really messed that one up.

'How's it going,' Rhea asked when I answered the telephone, 'I just saw Sam in town buying flowers from the garage, he didn't look very happy. But I guess he wouldn't today, would he?'

'Today? Why would today be any different?'

'He didn't tell you?'

'Uh, no? He didn't tell me anything. Just that he had a few errands to do and he wanted to do them on his own? What's wrong?'

A feeling of dread was descending on me. He was ill, or he was going to leave me, or both, he was so ill that he was going to die and the flowers were to console me when he gave me the terminal diagnosis.

'Tell me Rhea, if he's ill then I really need to know.'

'Calm down, he's not ill or anything like that. It's just the date.'

'The date? The first of March?'

'Yes, the day that Lucy committed suicide. Two years ago today.'

'Oh my God, I had no idea.' My hand shot to my mouth, 'and I chose today to ask if we could change her study into a room for Daniel. No wonder he didn't like the idea.'

'I guess you could have timed it a bit better, although having that as a shrine to her can't be easy.'

'No, it's unused most of the time, I only go in there to make sure it doesn't need cleaning. As far as I know he never goes in there. Christ, my timing is bad.'

'Don't worry about it, I'm sure it will all be fine. He looked like he was driving up to Trecase after he left the forecourt so my guess is that he's taking the flowers up there for her and didn't want you to know because he loves you as well and is trying to move his life forward.'

'He wasn't saying white rabbits to me,' I said, more to myself than to Rhea. 'What?'

I shook my head. 'Nothing, just me being silly. Thanks for the info, I'm sure it will all be fine. I'll make a big fuss of him when he gets back.'

'Just so you know,' she said before I clicked the phone off, 'the anniversary of his father's death is coming up too. A couple of weeks I think, it's going to be four years. He was really upset when his dad died, took it really bad so he might be a bit withdrawn because of that as well. Maybe be extra nice to him for a bit eh?'

'Thank you. I didn't know that either. You're a star.'

'So are you Hun, take care.'

I placed the phone back onto the table and wondered how much else I didn't know.

Chapter Forty

Sam

Sunday March 1st 2015

'Why did you do it Luce? I know I wasn't a brilliant husband, but why did you have to take that way out? We could have made it so much better. I could have been so much better.'

Sam knelt on the damp grass at the top of Trecase head. The bunch of chrysanthemums and gypsophila in his hand. He ripped the cheap cellophane wrapper and pulled the flowers free.

'Do you remember these? I bought them for you on our first date. You said they were your favourite flower. I later found out you liked lilies better but, for me, these mean more. I gave you these when I first fell in love with you. I would have put them in your coffin if I could have. I wish you were here so I could give them to you in person.'

Sam pulled one chrysanthemum away and dropped it over the cliff edge to the churning spring tide below. He watched it tumble down the jagged rocks before being swallowed by the icy grip of the sea and dragged under, forever to be held deep within its depths. One by one, each of the blooms met the same fate. As the last one fell, Sam wiped his eyes with the palm of his hand, stood up, bowed his head and then began walking back to the car.

As he walked, his thoughts turned to the conversation he'd had earlier. He was surprised that Penny-May had asked for Daniel to have his own room. Whether she meant permanently or the odd weekend, he didn't know but whichever it was, there was no way that the idiot brother was ever going to live with them. It would be over his dead body first. He kicked the straggly looking daffodil that was trying its best to defeat the clifftop wind and ground it under his heel.

He wanted Penny-May for himself, the retard had enough people dancing around after him. People who were paid to do it and who were too stupid to do anything else. To have him at Karadow, going on with his stupid Incredible Hulk impressions and pretending to talk into mobile phones was just too ridiculous an idea to contemplate. Although, maybe he could add to that? Maybe, if he paid for a personal assistant to work especially with him, then Penny-May wouldn't have to spend so much time over there and she wouldn't have to take him places either. The PA could do it instead, he'd pay for someone else to take Daniel to Newquay Zoo every day of the week if it meant that Penny-May would get off his back about needing to do stuff with him herself, and definitely if that meant dragging Sam along as well. He frowned as he thought of the couple of hours they had spent there just before the wedding. It was horrendous, all that song and dance over making sure they got to see the penguins being fed. Christ, he'd felt like chucking Daniel in there with them, maybe he could do that with the lion cage instead, that would solve the problem good and proper.

No, Penny-May would have to stop seeing so much of him, especially if she thought she was going to bring him into the house with them. There was no room for anyone else in her life apart from Sam. He'd find an agency to deal with Daniel instead and she would do as she was told.

Arriving back at his car, he clicked the central locking system and started whistling to himself as he lowered himself into the driving seat.

The bright side. He'd have to check out the film again later, Monty Python always made him laugh.

Chapter Forty-One

Penny-May

Saturday March 14th 2015

'Are you ok to come to the site with me this afternoon?' Sam asked as he came out of the ensuite shower. He had a towel wrapped around his hips and was tousling his hair dry with another while he walked over to the bed, I was wearing just my underwear and trying to choose between trousers or a skirt. The weather was getting a bit warmer and I really wanted to be able to wear my thinner summer stuff.

I shook my head, 'I'm sorry, it's Saturday, I need to go and see Daniel today. I was hoping that Brian could nip me over because the buses don't come out this way. Unless you have enough cash on you for a taxi that is?' I hated not having my own money, I always had to ask Sam for everything. I mean, he was brilliant and he never said no. I still had his second credit card which he never quibbled over paying, but it wasn't the same as having my own money. He rarely had cash either and the taxi's didn't take card payments.

'Sorry babe, I don't have any on me and I don't have time to get to a cash point. I'm going to need Brian all day as well.'

I looked down at my hands as they were clasped in my lap.

'But I promised him I would see him today, it's on his calendar. It was such a rushed visit last week and I really need to take him out somewhere, just the two of us if you can't make it as well? I know how busy you are.' I hated sounding whiney, but I needed to spend some quality time with my brother, we'd barely had any of that since the wedding and he hadn't forgiven me yet for doing that without him. He had been really looking forward to walking me down the aisle as my best man.

Sam dropped the wet towel into the linen basket and went to his wardrobe to choose his clothes for the day. A white tight fitting cotton shirt and black trousers came out and he placed them onto the bed beside me.

'I think the jeans will be best for you today, your bum looks amazing in those tight ones,' he said, giving my choices a cursory glance.

'Not the skirt?' I asked, holding it up on its hanger so he could see it better. It was fitted at the top and gradually flared out to just above the ankles. White with small pink embroidered flowers at varying heights around the hemline. It had cost more than anything I was used to wearing, and I had felt so guilty spending so much money on it, but Sam had been insistent that I go shopping with Rhea and update my wardrobe *again*. 'Only the best for my wife,' he had said.

Now he took it from me and put it back into the wardrobe. 'No, save that for another day, wear the jeans. They'll be much more suitable for walking around the site.' He started flicking through the rest of my clothes that were hanging up and selected a baby pink cotton blouse. 'This will look good with them,' he said, passing it to me. 'And that short black leather jacket, you'll look amazing.'

I took the shirt and began to dress. It wasn't what I wanted to wear but, with his father's death anniversary so close, I went with it. He didn't talk about Frank very much and I didn't want to upset him at a time when he was obviously feeling so fragile and vulnerable.

'Ok, I think you're right, it's still a bit too chilly for skirts really. How long until we leave? I'm going to need to phone Daniel and let him know I can't make it.'

'About twenty minutes, it'll take you that long to do your hair and make-up.' He smiled as he said it, and he wasn't far off, it would take me at least that before I was ready to leave the house. 'Why don't you phone him from the car? Or phone the home and leave a message? It will be a lot quicker.'

I didn't want to leave a message. I wanted to speak to him myself, to explain why I had to miss yet another Saturday. And I didn't want to do it in the car either. I wanted to talk to him in private. With Sam listening I couldn't tell Daniel that I had to be with Sam because he was missing his father, I would have to invent some other excuse.

'I'll phone him from the car then, I'll say we have to attend a very important business meeting but that I will definitely see him next week. That will be ok won't it?' Sam nodded. 'Yes, that'll be fine, I'll wait for you downstairs ok? Don't be long.'

'Ok, I'll be right down,' but he had already left the room before I had finished speaking.

Daniel wasn't very happy with me when I spoke to him on our way to Pencoven. He said he was going to get angry and turn green and he would only turn pink again when I came to see him. I told him that it was silly to do that and the daycare centre wouldn't be very happy if a Hulk turned up on Monday instead of a happy and sunny Daniel and that I would like it very much if he didn't get angry. I promised him I would buy him a big present to bring with me next week to make up for today. I spoke to Martha as well and asked if it was at all possible for the staff to get him out somewhere today to make up for his disappointment but she said it was doubtful. A staff member had phoned in sick so they were on short numbers themselves. She'd get him to help her do some baking in the kitchen though, make up the cakes and buns for the week. Sam reached over and squeezed my hand when I put the phone down into my lap with a sigh.

'He'll be fine. Give him a few minutes and Martha will have him laughing and helping her like she always does.'

'I guess. But he so looks forward to me taking him out somewhere, and I miss him as well.'

'I know you do. Let me think about it for a while. I'm sure there's something that can be done.'

I looked at him, was he going to relent on the bedroom conversion after all? That would be amazing if he did. To have Daniel move in with us would be perfect. I smiled and returned his squeeze, feeling better than I had all morning. Sam had been right about my clothing; it was perfect for the day and I knew that he was going to come through on this one for me as well. I leant across and kissed him on the mouth,

'I love you Sam Lambert.'

Sam returned the kiss, 'I love you too, Mrs Lambert.'

Carl was waiting for us in the office and we put on our protective hats before walking out to the newest part of the development. Sam had explained to me that this part was almost nearing completion and it was the final fixings now going in. Two of the townhouses had been sold and the buyers would be moving in within the next fortnight. Sam just needed to double check that everything had been fitted to his plans. I didn't think that meant it was necessary for me to be there to see it, it wasn't as if I was his secretary anymore, so I wasn't taking notes. But it's always nice to have a nose around new houses and imagine what it would be like living there, how you would decorate it and what you would put where. Sam said that he needed me to spot the things that him and Carl would miss because they were too close to it. They knew what should be there so they might scan over something important. Rhea couldn't do it apparently. It was the nanny's day off and they didn't like having Josh on the building site, it was too dangerous for him.

As we walked into the kitchen of the second house Carl's phone rang.

'Sorry mate,' he said to Sam, 'I've got to take this, you don't mind?' He was already pressing to accept the call as Sam replied,

'Yeah, no worries, tell you what, go back to the office, we'll finish up here and meet you back there.'

Carl nodded, already talking to his caller.

Sam closed the door behind him and flicked the latch.

'That was fortuitous,' he said as he walked over to me and put his arms around my waist, his hands resting on my backside, 'I've been looking at that sexy butt of yours all morning and it's making me go cross-eyed.'

He bent down and kissed me on my mouth, his hands moving round to undo the button and zip of my jeans.

'What, here?' I asked, my eyes widening in surprise as I felt his fingers moving down inside my knickers and beginning to rub my clit.

'Why not, we have the place to ourselves and nobody has made love in here before. Doesn't that turn you on?'

I was already starting to gyrate against his probing fingers, my own hands moving down his body to undo his trousers and release him, my hands slipping down his shaft and rubbing my thumb over the tip, feeling a small amount of moisture begin to break free.

'You turn me on,' I replied, 'and I can feel how horny you are.'

He undid my clothing and I left them in a heap on the floor as he lifted me onto the edge of the worktop, his hands moving up to undo my bra and fondle my nipples under the cotton shirt. He lifted the fabric, bending his head to lick and then suck on them, placing his penis into me while I moaned in ecstasy, grabbing his hips and forcing them to meet mine. Just as we were about to come, he stopped and pulled out, making me open my eyes to see what had made him withdraw and I fell deep into the black depths of his eyes. 'Turn over,' he rasped, 'I need to see that ass.'

Quickly, I did as he asked, desperate to have him inside me again, to finish what we had started. As I leant over the kitchen worktop, the cold granite making me shiver as it touched my bare skin, he entered me again, pulling me into him with his hands on my hips and we began to move as one together again, moving faster and faster until our shattering climax, his fingers digging into my skin and mine gripping the edge of the worktop as if it was the only thing keeping me on the earth.

Our breathing slowed and Sam kissed my neck as he withdrew.

'I've wanted to do that for a long time,' he said, pulling up his trousers and fastening them as I found my own discarded clothing and got dressed again.

'Really? You surprise me.'

'I have another surprise as well.'

'What, for me?'

'Of course, for you, I've figured what to do about Daniel.'

'Daniel?'

'Yes, about you feeling guilty about not being able to take him out as much as you used to. I'll pay for a personal assistant for him. That way, they can take him wherever he wants to go every weekend and you don't have to feel guilty if you can't make it because we are busy doing something else.'

I was stunned, the afterglow of good sex vanished as his words began to sink in.

Sam wasn't going to let Daniel stay after all.

'Isn't that just the perfect answer to your problem? I'll put an advert out and we can interview next week to make sure we get the right person.' He replaced a strand of my fringe to where it should be and kissed me on the nose. 'Now, hurry up and make yourself presentable, Carl will be wondering where we are.'

I finished getting dressed, picked up my handbag and quietly followed him out of the door.

Chapter Forty-Two

Penny-May

Saturday March 21st 2015.

'Daniel's in the greenhouse with Dave,' Martha said as I walked into the kitchen, 'I saw your car coming so I told him you were here but he just shrugged his shoulders and didn't reply. I don't think he's forgiven you for last week yet.'

'I thought as much when he wouldn't speak to me on the phone,' I replied, 'It's ok, I'll go and find him.'

'Here, take this,' Martha handed me a plate holding two chocolate muffins, 'it might soften the ice a bit, he's been after one of these all morning.'

'Thank you, I'll give it a go.'

There was a coolness to the air as I walked down the garden path. I could see Daniel working at the bench and he looked up as I approached. He saw me but then turned his back and carried on with what he was doing. I assumed he was potting his seeds as it was the right time of year for it, but I couldn't quite see to be sure.

'Hey Hulkman,' I said as I entered, turning to slide the door shut again behind me. The heaters were on so I didn't want to let too much of the heat out.

Daniel didn't reply, just carried on picking up the seeds and placing them carefully into the tray of soil I could now see was on the bench in front of him.

'I've got some of Martha's chocolate muffins, do you want one?'

Dave looked towards me and winked over Daniel's head, 'Oh, you've only brought two. Where's mine then? I love Martha's chocolate buns, don't you mate?'

'Dave have Penny-May's. She not staying.'

'Oh, don't say that Bud, she's your sister and she's come all this way to see you. And she managed to get some muffins out of Martha. I mean, we've been trying all morning and got absolutely nothing so that has to count for something eh?' Daniel shrugged his shoulders.

'Tell you what. You wash your hands under the tap and sit down with Penny-May.

I'll go and get a couple of mugs of hot chocolate to go with those muffins shall I?' 'With cream and marshmallows?' Daniel asked, raising his head at last.

'I'll see if I can sweet talk Martha into letting me into her secret stash. If I do that, are you going to sit and listen to your sister?'

After a moment's hesitation, Dan shrugged his shoulders again and walked over to the tap, turned the water on and stuck his hands briefly under the running stream.

'Brrr, too cold,' he said, grabbing for the towel beside the hosepipe and wiping the soil off his hands on that instead. Slowly, he looked at me and then the plate that I was holding.

'Ok,' he said, 'I'll do that.'

'Good man, I'll be back as soon as the kettle has boiled and I've disarmed Martha of the sweet cupboard keys.' replied Dave. He patted my shoulder as he left the greenhouse.

'I'm sorry about the last few weeks,' I said once we were alone. 'I just couldn't get over here, Sam needed me to be with him.' The thought of what we were doing in the kitchen of the Pencoven house crossed my mind, causing me to blush and then for that sinking feeling to begin to envelop me again. The guilt that, despite my initial upset at not coming over, I was having mind-blowing sex when my brother needed me. 'I'm really sorry that I couldn't come over and take you out. But I'm here today, and I have Brian waiting in the car outside. What do you want to do?'

Daniel reached out and took one of the muffins, carefully peeling the wrapper away before taking a bite.

'It's Zoe's birthday on Thursday,' he said between mouthfuls, 'Danny need buy present.'

'Is it? Well, you certainly do. What do you want to buy her?'

'She like chocolate,' he said, nodding, 'Danny buy chocolate for Zoe.'

'O...k..., we can do that, but do you think she would like something else besides chocolate, something she can keep? Something like a new jumper or t-shirt? And you can pick something out for yourself as well, I promised you a present remember?'

'And hot chocolate with marshmallows?'

I smiled, he was coming round, 'Definitely a hot chocolate with marshmallows.'

'Ok,' he said, finishing the muffin and running towards the door. 'We go now.'

And he was gone, running down the path and leaving me behind. As he got to the kitchen doorway he turned and shouted, 'Come on slow coach, we gotta go!'

'I'm coming.' I carried the plate back with me. Handing it to Martha as I walked through, I lifted my uneaten muffin off it.

'I'll eat mine in the car,' I said, 'there's no way I am giving back one of your delicious cakes.'

'Spoil sport,' said Dave, 'she still hasn't let me have one yet, I had my eye on that one.'

I giggled as I followed Daniel out the front door and into the waiting car. That was what I loved about this home; it was one happy family.

'How do you feel about having your own helper to take you out sometimes instead of me when I can't make it?' I asked Daniel. We were sat in Costa's again having the hot chocolate that we didn't have before we left home. Daniel was pleased with the extra marshmallows and chocolate sprinkles the barista had put on his and the tell-tale marks around his mouth showed just how much he was enjoying his treat.

'Penny-May not come no more?' his smile vanished and his head dropped.

'Of course, I will still come and see you! Don't be silly. This will be someone extra, just to make sure that you can still get out at weekends and go wherever you want to if I'm caught up with Sam.'

Daniel sat still, processing what I had just told him. He picked up his long-handled teaspoon and started prodding the last remaining marshmallow around his half empty mug.

'Is that ok?' I prompted, 'and maybe they will be able to bring you over to Karadow sometimes and we can be together then? You could see my home too.

Isn't that a great idea?'

Surely Sam would be alright with that arrangement? Daniel would probably be able to see me a lot more often if he had a helper bringing him over as well. They could go off somewhere on their own for an hour or so and I could spend some quality time with him at home. The more I thought about it, I realised this could be a brilliant idea. Not as good as having Daniel to stay or live with us but maybe that could be sorted out in a year or so's time when Sam had grown to love him just as much as I do. This situation could work out better for all of us.

Daniel scooped up the molten sweet on the spoon and popped it straight into his mouth, swallowing without needing to chew because it was so gooey.

'You promise?' He asked.

'Yep, total pinky promise,' I replied, holding my little finger up for him to link with his own.

He responded by completing the age-old ritual we had always done as children and which was as binding to him as any oath sworn on a bible in a court of law. There was no backing out now, Sam was going to have to agree to it.

Chapter Forty-Three

Penny-May

Saturday April 25th 2015

'I think you are eating far too much cake my girl,' Sam said, reaching his arms around me and squeezing my butt cheeks, 'although it's quite nice being able to grab a handful like this.'

I was horrified and swung round out of his grasp to check out my rear view in the mirror.

'Do you really think I'm getting fat? My jeans were a bit tight to pull on yesterday but I thought that was because they had just come out of the wash.' I bent over to get a better perspective, then stood up and turned to the left and the right, checking it out from all angles. It can't be that bad, they are size 10's after all and I could still do them up, eventually.

'You have put on a bit, but you still look beautiful to me. Maybe you shouldn't put on any more though.' He reached out to grab me again, but I pulled away and playfully slapped his wandering hands, 'No time for that now, your mum will be here in a minute and I need to get ready.'

'I guess, but I'll be back to see what that extra bounce-ability is like in practice later.'

He winked at me as he left the room and I turned my attention back to my reflection in the mirror, was my stomach getting bigger as well? This was certainly no good, there was no way I could put on any more weight, I would look hideous and then Sam wouldn't fancy me anymore and then he would start looking at other, much more prettier women, and he would start to hate me and then he would send me packing for his much sexier new model... Oh no, this wouldn't do at all. I would have to do something, start exercising - although I'd have thought that all the bedroom antics we do would be more than enough exercise wouldn't it?

Maggie was being her usual non-friendly, judgemental self through dinner. She still hadn't forgiven us for not inviting her to the wedding and she was putting all the blame on me.

'Was Cornwall not good enough for you to get married in then?' She said when Sam had excused himself to go to the bathroom. Stupid bat wouldn't ever say anything like that in front of him.

'Cornwall is beautiful and I would have loved to get married here, but Sam did it all as a lovely surprise. He's told you all that happened hasn't he?'

'Yes, he did, but I'm sure there must be more to it than that. And why the rush? Are you pregnant? Was it a shotgun wedding? Because if so, I would like to be informed if I am about to be a grandmother, or am I not important enough to know about that until after it's born as well?'

I was shocked by the venom that was spitting out of her mouth and willed for Sam to come back and actually hear how she was talking to me for once.

'No, I'm not pregnant. I promise we will tell you should that happen but at the moment it hasn't and we aren't planning to in the immediate future either. Would you like dessert?'

I smiled sweetly as I rose and went to take the plates to the kitchen.

'Yes please dear, but maybe you shouldn't have any, that's another reason I thought you might be pregnant, you've put on a bit of weight lately. You look like you're with child.'

Christ, was it that noticeable that even the mother-in-law from hell had felt she had to comment on it? She was hardly skinny herself! Wonder what she would say if

I commented on her midlife, menopausal spread...

'It's Eton mess tonight, would you like extra clotted cream?'

'Of course,' she replied.

Wishing I could shove the whole tub in her smarmy face, I left the table and went to fix the desserts. There was no way I was going back in that room until Sam came back.

'That was a lovely couple hours wasn't it?' Sam said as he closed the door after seeing Maggie to the waiting car. In my book, Brian was a right hero for putting up with her all the way home. I wasn't sure if Sam was being sarcastic or not so decided to play safe.

'Yes. Is there any wine left in that bottle? I wouldn't mind another glass just to see the end of a perfect night.'

'We'll open another one, I wouldn't mind a snifter as well.'

'Do you really think I've put on too much weight?' I asked as he sat down on the sofa beside me and handed me my full glass. 'Your mum made a comment about it as well, asked if I was pregnant.'

Sam laughed, 'She didn't?'

I nodded, 'She really did, I never thought I was that fat. You must think I'm getting really ugly if it's that noticeable.'

He ran his hand along my thigh and gave a slight squeeze.

'You have put a bit on, but you're not fat yet and you definitely aren't ugly. Maybe watch it a bit though, make sure you don't put any more on?' He took a sip of his drink and placed the glass on the coffee table beside him.

I took a sip of my own drink. I certainly wasn't feeling very good about myself, that was for sure. How could I have let myself go so much?

'It must be because I'm not working anymore, I'm not running around the office and burning energy so much. Sitting around here watching the telly until you come home doesn't burn up as many calories.' I omitted to add the chocolate bars I ate while I watched trashy daytime TV.

'Hmm, maybe, but you don't need to work, and I like you being here waiting for me.'

'It would be easier if I could get out more, living so isolated makes it so difficult and if Brian isn't around then I don't have a choice. What about if I learnt to drive and then I could have my own car?'

Sam looked at me, 'Do you really think that's a good idea?' he asked, 'you are so scatty, it would take you forever to do that. And look what happens whenever you get nervous. It's not the same as knocking over a water jug and mopping up the mess. In a car the mess is a lot bigger and you don't have time to make mistakes. No, I don't think that is going to work.'

'Well, what about exercise then? You go to that posh gym don't you? Maybe I could go there while you're working and do some classes or work with a personal trainer or something to help shift the weight? Only a couple of days a week maybe? When Brian can drop me off for a couple of hours and then come back for me later?'

Sam took a couple of minutes to answer, sipping more of his wine and then draining his glass, replacing it onto the table.

'I think that would be alright, I'll book you in with my trainer, Tabitha. She's the best one in there, you don't want to be bothering with any of the rest. Yes, Tabitha will take care of you and get you back to how you used to be. He stood up and took my half-empty glass out of my hand, placing it beside his. Pulling me up to stand in front of him and reaching around my waist, he grabbed my bum cheeks again.

'Before you get rid of them then, let's go upstairs and find out just how bouncy they really are shall we?'

He kissed me and the familiar embers began to glow in the pit of my stomach, the fire would soon start and I knew that it could only be doused by Sam's magic touch.

It would seem that even as fat as I obviously was, he still made me incredibly horny.

We didn't take long making it upstairs to the bedroom. We took a very long time investigating how much I could bounce.

Chapter Forty-Four

Penny-May

Wednesday April 28th 2015

I jumped in the back of the car all decked out in my brand new exercise gear. My pumps looked so shiny they screamed to everyone that I'm no exercise fanatic. I considered scuffing them across the gravel outside the house to make them look a bit worn in but Brian was early as usual and I thought he might laugh at me if he saw what I was doing.

We chatted a little bit on the way to Silverwell Health Club. He rarely spoke when both Sam and I were in the car together but when it was just me, he was a lot more sociable. I wondered what he was like with Sam when they were on their own. Whether they chatted or Sam did his phone/iPad/paperwork thing. Probably the latter, he was always so pedantic about his work, that's why he's been so successful though. Unlike me as a mere secretary. I guess I spent too much time messing about in pubs with Emma when I should have been forging my own career. It's all worked out though, if I hadn't done all of those things then I wouldn't have met Sam and I wouldn't be here now, so I shall forgive myself for my past lazy behaviour and concentrate on getting fit again so he doesn't trade me in for a better model.

Brian told me that he and Mary had a daughter who lived in Plymouth and she was pregnant with her first child. They couldn't wait to be grandparents and were having bets on whether it was a boy or a girl. I said it didn't matter what it was, as long as it was happy and healthy that was the main thing. He then asked me about when Daniel was born and how we had coped with his disability so I told him all about mum and dad making sure that he learnt all that he could, and I told him about me beating up the 'cool' kids when they tried to bully him. Brian had replied that he would bear that in mind and wouldn't ever try and cross me in a dark street. I knew he was joking of course, but it's amazing what happens when the people you love are threatened and they can't do anything about it. You go into ultra-protective mode and fight to the death for them.

'It's good that he's found you, Sam struggled so much after Lucy died,' Brian said. 'We think it's because he thought he'd never be able to have a family without her.'

'Oh, that is so sad. Sam doesn't talk about Lucy very often. I hardly know anything about her. She was beautiful looking at the pictures of her.'

'Yes, she was. They met here you know.' We were just pulling into the long driveway.

'What at Silverwell? Was she another client?'

Brian laughed, 'No, she certainly wasn't that. She was a physiotherapist based here. She fixed his shoulder one day and the rest was history. It was love at first sight for Sam.' I saw him glance at me in his rear-view mirror. 'Oh, sorry, I probably shouldn't have said that. He feels the same about you as well.'

I smiled slightly, 'I know, but I sometimes wonder whether we would have got together if Lucy hadn't...well...you know...'

'We never know what the future will bring do we. We can only embrace what we have today.' We pulled to a halt at the front entrance. 'Here you go, I'll pick you up again in a couple of hours, if that's ok.'

'Two hours? I'll likely be needing a wheelchair if I exercise for that long,' I replied.

'They have a very nice cafe inside, Sam has a tab. I'd recommend using it if I were you.' He winked at me as I got out of the car.

'Thanks, I will. See you soon, if I'm still alive!'

As he drove away, I looked up at the building in front of me. It was like my first day at Mistral all over again. I squared my shoulders, mentally pulled up my big girl pants and strode confidently up the front steps.

'Hi there, I'm Penny-May Lambert,' I said to the girl behind the reception desk. I noticed she had a silver badge on her tunic saying *Kelly, Receptionist.* 'I have an exercise session with Tabitha?'

The woman seemed to do a double take and then busied herself with the computer.

'Oh, uh, yes, I'm afraid there's a bit of a problem with your booking

Mrs...Lambert. Tabitha has had to go home early because of a personal problem, but we've arranged cover for you with one of our other trainers. He's called Will, is that ok?'

'Um, yes, that's fine,' I squeaked. Bugger! A bloke, how am I going to look sexy and gorgeous when I'm sweating and panting and looking like a ripe tomato? I'll bet he's muscle bound and gorgeous as well. This is so not going to be any fun. Not that he would be a patch on my Sam of course, nobody is better looking than him.

Although, it doesn't hurt to check out the eye candy sometimes.

'That's great, he's just finishing off with another client so if you don't mind waiting in the cafe, I'll send him to find you when he's ready.' She smiled sweetly at me and pointed me in the right direction.

'Thank you.' I nodded and followed her directions, deciding not to purchase a coffee just yet, I didn't want to throw it up over the trainer when he got me working on the machines, I was nervous enough. I decided to sit at a table and wait, pulling out my mobile and idly playing candy crush so I didn't look too out of place in my new leggings and shiny trainers.

'Good afternoon, it's Penny-May isn't it? Is it alright if I call you that? I'm Will, pleased to meet you.'

I looked up and saw a slim man of average height and bleach blonde hair which he wore in a ponytail standing in front of me holding his hand out. Slipping my phone back into my handbag, I stood and reached out to shake his proffered hand.

'Yes, that's me. Yes, that's fine.'

'Would you like to follow me? We've got some paperwork to fill in first and we'll see where you are in your fitness levels today and what you want to achieve. Then we'll work out a plan of how to get you there.' A broad grin spread across his cleanshaven face, 'I promise it won't hurt.'

I liked Will. He was funny and although gorgeous to look at, definitely not in the masculine, hunky sort of way. It wasn't long into our conversation that I found out he had a husband called Drew. Knowing he wasn't likely to be making any kind of sexual advances towards me meant that I was soon completely at ease in his company and I didn't have to worry that anything I said might be misconstrued, which would be rather embarrassing to have to rebuff if he had been heterosexual.

'So, what are your goals? What do you want to achieve by coming here?' He asked.

'Well,' I could feel my cheeks beginning to colour, 'I'm concerned about putting too much weight on now that I'm not working anymore. My husband said that I may be gaining a couple of pounds, so I want to get rid of them before they become a problem.'

'Right, I can't see any problem with your size, you look quite fit. Even to me.' He laughed after he said the last bit and I laughed alongside him, feeling the embarrassment of my admission slipping away.

'You know, working out only works if you really want it to. Not because someone else is telling you to do it because of their own warped ideals.'

I must have looked shocked because he immediately apologised.

'I'm sorry, I shouldn't have said that. It was crass of me. I didn't mean to imply anything about your relationship, I barely know you.'

'It's fine. What I said probably sounded like I didn't want it, but I do.' I suddenly realised how much I was enjoying just being in this environment, talking to somebody different and new rather than just Sam, Maggie or Brian. Or shouting at Jeremy Kyle on TV. I had missed random conversation being shut away at Karadow and now I had gained a taste of it, even with a stranger, I wanted to keep it. I was even wondering if I could persuade Emma to join and keep me company here, I could match my sessions to when she wasn't working. It would be amazing, and so easy to set up. Especially if I treated her to a pizza afterwards.

Will's voice dragged me back into the room,

'Do you want to try out the machines? And then we can go through the list of exercise classes and see which ones you might like to try?'

Will took me through a few warmup exercises first and then introduced me to the treadmill, the cross trainer and the rowing machine. He said I didn't need to worry about the weights as I wasn't trying to build muscle, just burn calories. He even said I didn't have to run on the treadmill if I didn't want to, I would do much better going at a steady pace that I could '*sustain for longer rather than running full pelt for a couple of minutes and then being too knackered to do anything else*'. A couple of minutes? Who was he trying to kid, I'd be dead after a couple of seconds if I had to run on anything. No. Walking was definitely much more my style.

'Well, if you're happy with what we've discussed, I'll write up a formal exercise plan for you to complete in the gym and, coupled with a few classes of Zumba, we should start seeing some pretty good results quite quickly. As I said, you don't really have a problem with your size so just maintaining what you have should be enough of a goal for you.'

'Thank you so much Will, I can't wait to tell Sam all about it and what we have decided.' I held out my hand to shake it as we were closing and he reached out and grasped it but didn't let go immediately.

'Ah, if you want to stay with me, you might not want to tell Sam about not seeing Tabitha today and working with me instead. He might not like it.'

'Why's that? You're great.'

It was his turn to blush, 'Thank you. But it's a bit personal and I fully understand if you want to go back to Tabitha when she gets better. I should have told you before, but I was Lucy's best friend. Sam and I have a history and he would probably prefer that you didn't work with me.'

Now I was torn. It also explained why Sam had been so definite about me being with the female instructor. I had assumed it was because he didn't want me working with another man, but I was obviously wrong. This explained everything. But Will was so nice and for all I knew, this Tabitha woman could be a whip cracking vixen who wouldn't let me get away with walking on the treadmill. I had been so nervous before I started. Will helped me feel comfortable in his company, and now he was telling me that if I wanted to stay on his books, I would have to lie to my husband.

'I see. This is difficult.' I replied, 'I would love to stay with you training me, but I'm not sure I can lie to Sam.'

'I know, and again, I'm sorry I didn't tell you when we first met. Obviously, I knew who you were. I guess I just wanted to see what Lucy's replacement was like. I miss her so much you see.' He let go of my hand and jammed his hands into the pockets of his shorts.

'I'll pass my notes onto Tab when she comes back, it might be a couple of weeks though, her mother's ill and she's looking after her.'

He turned to walk away when I found myself reaching out and grabbing his arm, turning him back towards me.

'You knew Lucy?'

'Yes, most of us here knew her, apart from Tab of course, she's only been with us for a year or so. Lucy had gone by then.'

'Well, I guess it won't hurt for the next couple of weeks, until she gets back anyway. Now that I'm here I don't want to have to wait to start all over again. I'll tell Sam that I'm working on my own on the machines, just taking it steady until she comes back. And the Zumba classes of course, but they aren't with you anyway.'

I didn't add that my real motivation was because I wanted to find out more about my predecessor. I wanted to know what was so special about her, how she had captured my husband's heart so fully that he had to give her flowers even when she had no grave.

Why Maggie was so against me taking her place and just what it was about Lucy that made Will look so upset as he remembered her.

I wanted to know just how she managed to be so damn perfect.

Chapter Forty-Five

Sam

Wednesday April 28th 2015

Sam sat at his mother's dining table while she filled the coffee machine and made him his favourite cappuccino. The gurgle of the milk being forced through the pipe filled the silence and the aroma of freshly ground coffee beans filled the air.

'So,' she said as she placed the steaming cup on the cork coaster in front of him, 'How is it going? Really.'

Sam put his hands around his drink, warming them from the spring chill he had felt outside.

'How's what going?'

'You know what I'm talking about. You and her. Are you happy together?'

Sam bit back the retort that it was none of her damn business what was happening between him and his wife.

'We're fine, of course we are. What makes you think that we aren't?'

'Well, she's no Lucy is she.'

'No. She's not. She's special and I like it that way. She's totally different.'

'Just special?'

'Mum! No, not just special. I love her. That's why I made her my wife!'

He knew he was starting to lose his temper, sometimes his mum got totally on his nerves with her stupid questions. How his dad had put up with her for so many years baffled him. He sat up straighter in his chair and took a sip of his coffee, using the time to calm his anger.

'I guess not. But does she love you as much?'

'She says she does. I'm quite sure she wouldn't have married me if she didn't.'

'Well, springing it on her like you did, she didn't have much choice did she?'

So that was it. She was still bitter about not getting a chance to wear her fancy hat again. As if he would ever give her a chance to make him look like a fool again. She had looked ridiculous at his first wedding, all those flowers and feathers all over it. She hadn't even stuck to the Cornish tartan theme. She had worn purple for God's sake.

'Penny-May does have her own voice. She could have said no if she wanted to, and we were already engaged when I took her away. She wasn't forced to do anything she didn't want to.'

'When is she going to show it then?'

'Show it? Show what? What on earth does she have to do to prove she loves me?'

'Well, give you a baby of course.'

Sam felt his anger beginning to rise again and pushed his chair back from the table, the legs scraping across the flagged stone floor. Standing, he turned his back on his mother and looked out of the window, at the sun glinting through the apple tree he had climbed so many times as a child.

'There's plenty of time for that yet. We aren't ready.'

'Tosh! If everyone waited until they were 'ready' the human race would have long died out.'

He frowned. His lips pursed as he fought to control his words. He loved his mother, he would do anything for her, but sometimes, her bigoted viewpoint would come close to destroying him. If only his father had fought harder and was still here, Frank was much better at dealing with her than he was.

'Besides, she has Daniel to think of. He takes up a lot of her time and she needs to make sure he is safe and cared for.'

'That's ridiculous.' Maggie scoffed, 'Isn't he in that special place where they look after them for you? She should forget all about him and think about creating her own family. Caring for you and providing you with an heir.'

Sam relaxed, he agreed with her about Penny-May's reluctance to leaving the spastic in the care of others and spending her time totally with him. That was the way it should be. But giving him a child? He barked out a gruff laugh and turned to face her again,

'An heir Mum? Who do you think I am, bloody Prince Charlie?'

Maggie looked hurt, 'Please don't swear. You know what I mean. Someone to leave everything to when you pass away. It happens to all of us you know. Well, you should know that more than anyone after the last few years.'

Sam felt his anger evaporate as quickly as it had erupted. How could he be so mean to her. She was just an old woman. An interfering one. An old, bitter and twisted woman who spent too much time on her own. Maybe he should think about getting her into day care somewhere. The idea of her off his hands as well pleased him as he imagined her and Daniel in a place together. Neither of them had much of a life anyway.

'Maybe in a year or so. We're having a bit of fun just being together first ok? You'll be the first to know when we change our minds.'

There will be snow in hell first though, he thought as he lifted his cup and drained the last dregs.

Chapter Forty-Six

PENNY-MAY
Wednesday April 28th 2015

'So how did it go at the gym?' Sam put down his briefcase in the hall and walked over to give me a quick kiss on the back of my head. I was standing in the kitchen preparing the evening meal. A chicken stir-fry and fresh salad with garlic bread on the side. It was all ready to go as soon as he was ready to eat. I poured him a glass of wine from the bottle I had placed in the fridge earlier to chill and removed again when I saw the car pulling up the drive.

'It went ok. It's really nice there isn't it? Tabitha wasn't there so I had a look around. There are some really cool exercise classes as well, I'm thinking of giving the Zumba class a try.'

He picked up the wine and took a drink.

'No Tabitha? I booked it with her especially, they didn't tell me she wasn't there?' 'She had an emergency at home, something to do with her mum apparently.'

I was aiming for a nonchalant air, but there was something

about the way Sam was standing, the set of his shoulders, that made me feel a bit wary, 'I don't mind, it isn't a problem.'

'It is for me,' Sam started to raise his voice, 'I'm paying for her to do her job, not run off on some errand for her mother.'

He placed the glass back down onto the counter, so hard that it sloshed over the top, making a small puddle on the granite surface. I automatically pulled some kitchen towel from the dispenser and wiped it up. I was shocked at his burst of anger. It seemed a bit strange for him to be so angry over something so little. The action of cleaning gave me a window of thinking space.

'I'm sure it wasn't just an errand and the staff were very apologetic and lovely about it. I don't mind, honestly.' It wondered if, maybe, telling Sam that I had still had a gym session after all might help calm him down, if what was upsetting him was that I hadn't had the session that I had asked for.

I opened my mouth to tell him the whole truth, but his own words cut over mine,

'It's a ridiculous situation. Tabitha is the only trainer there who is worth anything, all the others are utter incompetents. It's just a fucking shame there aren't any other decent gyms around this godforsaken dive. I'll phone them tomorrow and sort it out, when is she due back?'

I stopped framing the words I was about to utter. Will was obviously right about Sam not liking him if that comment was anything to go by.

'I don't know, they didn't say for sure. I got the impression it could only be a short while though. I'll be fine with the Zumba sessions until she's back, it will ease me into exercising a bit more gently.' I turned back to the hob, 'Shall I put dinner on? It won't take long to cook.'

'Well, I'll give it a week. If she's not back by then I'll phone them. That means my training is going to go off kilter as well doesn't it!'

'I'm sure it will all be fine. You can keep going with your morning sessions without her for a while can't you?'

'Hmmm,' Sam picked his glass up again and gestured towards the cooker with it, 'Are you going to cook that or are you waiting for it to grow feathers again?' He turned and headed for the stairs, taking the glass with him. 'I'm going for a quick shower. We'll eat when I come down.'

My mouth dropped open. He'd never been so rude to me before. I bit back the retort though, not that he would have heard it anyway, he was already in the bathroom.

With a sigh, I turned on the hob.

The silence at the table crowded in on me. Sam sat opposite me, alternately eating and then pushing his stir-fry around his plate.

'Is everything alright?' I eventually asked him, 'Did you see your mum earlier today? I know you said you were going to.'

'Everything's fine,' he replied, 'yes I did.'

'And is she ok?'

'Yes. I said everything's fine.'

The silence settled around us again like a thick woollen blanket, harsh and

scratchy, its points needling into my skin, irritating it until I could bear it no longer and had to scratch.

'You're not yourself today, are you sure there's nothing wrong?' Sam dropped his fork and pushed his plate away.

'The only thing wrong is this crap you're calling food. It's disgusting.'

His chair scraped along the tiled floor as he stood, grabbed the bottle of wine and his glass from the middle of the table and stalked into the lounge. I heard him switch on the TV and start searching for a news channel to watch.

I had been enjoying my meal but, unable to swallow because

of the lump that was suddenly choking my throat, my appetite vanished and I placed my own fork down onto my plate. I didn't know what I had done or what was upsetting him and I really didn't want to cry. I had a drink out of my own glass, trying to wash the lump away and partially succeeding. The alcohol hitting my stomach starting to ease my unhappiness.

I drained my glass and started clearing the table. After a few minutes I heard Sam come back into the kitchen and open the fridge door.

'Is there not another bottle of wine in here?' He asked.

'I think so, let me have a look.' I went over and stood by him, peering into the fridge to find the second bottle I had put in there earlier.

'Ah, here it is,' I pulled it out from the back of the shelf, 'I must have put the fruit in front of it after the shopping was delivered.'

'Why wasn't it on the rack where it should be?'

Personally, I couldn't see the difference about exactly where it was stored but I decided to let it go.

'I'm sorry, I didn't think about it when I put it in there. Look, you go and sit down, you've had a long day. I'll pour it out and bring it in for you and then I'll finish clearing up out here. Maybe we can sit and watch something together? How's about you choose something to watch?'

'Don't take too long about it then.' He walked straight past me and returned to the lounge.

When I took his drink in, he was flicking through the channels. I placed the glass on the table beside him.

'Half a million fucking channels and there's fuck all to watch,' he said, throwing the remote control onto the sofa cushion.

I left the room again and returned to clearing the kitchen.

'Haven't you finished that yet?'

With all my clattering around I hadn't heard him creep up behind me and he made me jump. My hand flew to my chest,

'Christ, you scared me. I didn't hear you coming.'

His hand sneaked around my waist and pulled me into him, thrusting his groin into mine and I could feel he was already getting hard. After the way he had behaved though, I wasn't quite as ready for his advances and started to wriggle out of his grasp, but his hand gripped tighter,

'What's the matter? You're normally desperate for it.' His groin thrust against mine again and I pushed him away.

'And you're normally much nicer than this. What's wrong Sam?'

Sam grimaced, 'I said nothing's wrong. All I want to do is fuck my wife's fat ass. What is wrong with that?'

His words hurt with every syllable that he uttered and I pushed my way out of his grip, walking towards the lounge and stopping in the doorway. I swallowed down the urge to cry again.

'I don't like you like this, that's what wrong with it. You're scaring me.'

'Ooo, you're scaring me!' He mimicked. He walked over and grabbed my wrist, squeezing it so hard I could see my fingers begin to turn white. I tried to pull it back but he was too strong. He lowered his face to within inches of my face.

'You do what I say, when I say, and I say I want to fuck your fat ass. Understand?' His spittle landed on my cheek as I turned my face away. His free hand gripped my chin and turned it back to face him again. I felt his lips press against mine, rough and hard as he pushed me back into the door frame. A searing pain shot across the back of my head as I felt it connect with the unforgiving wood and I cried out, raising my hand to protect it and, feeling wetness, pulled it away again to see a bright red streak across my palm.

On hearing my cry, Sam released my bruised mouth, 'I'm bleeding,' I cried, 'please, stop.'

My legs began to buckle underneath me as the sobs I had been holding back began to burst forth in an unstoppable flood.

He stepped back and let go of my wrist, leaving me to continue to slide to the floor where I lay in a heap at his feet.

'I'm so sorry I'm ugly,' I sobbed, 'I'll fix it, I promise.'

I saw his feet turn and walk away from me, seconds later, I heard the front door slam and he was gone.

I lay on the floor, still sobbing. Too hurt and confused to do anything else.

I was in bed when I heard the front door open and close several hours later. I huddled under the duvet, not knowing whether to stay where I was and pretend to be asleep, stay and wait for him to come up or go downstairs to him. I stayed awake for a long time, lying in the darkness, ears cocked for the creak of the stairs that would herald him beginning his ascent. But it didn't happen. I knew he was downstairs, but what he was doing, I didn't know, and I didn't want to go and find out.

I awoke to the smell of bacon and Sam walking into the bedroom with a breakfast tray in his hands. I could see a plate with a bacon and egg sandwich on it, a mug of coffee and a single white rose that I knew he must have cut from the bush in the garden that had only come into flower last week.

'I'm sorry babe,' he said as I sat up and he laid the tray across my lap, 'I don't know what I was doing. I'm so sorry I hurt you.'

I didn't want to say that it was ok because it wasn't, but I didn't want to upset him and make him angry again either.

'You were horrible to me,' I said.

'I know, I was stressed out by something that happened at work and I took it out on you. I shouldn't have done that. It wasn't fair of me.'

That was an understatement I thought, picking up my steaming mug and taking a sip.

He sat on the edge of the bed beside me, 'I've never done anything like that before and I swear, I will never do it again. I love you far too much for that.' He brought his hand up to wipe the moisture out of his eye and my heart melted.

'You didn't come up to bed last night?' I asked.

'I didn't think you would want me to. I slept on the sofa instead.'

His eyes went to my pillow where my head had bled again slightly during the night and his hand came up to touch the cut. I couldn't help but flinch as I felt his hand come near me and he pulled back sharply.

'Oh, my love, please don't be afraid of me. I promise you. I will never hurt you like that again.'

I lowered my gaze and placed the mug back onto the tray.

'I know. I'm tired. Do you mind if I go back to sleep?'

Sam stood, 'eat the sandwich first, it'll do you good. Then sleep. I'm off to work shortly, but we'll make up properly when I get home tonight ok?'

I picked up the sandwich, 'ok, see you later,' I said as I took a dutiful bite. The food tasted like cardboard moving around my mouth.

Chapter Forty-Seven

Penny-May

Tuesday May 6th 2015.

Brian dropped me off at the door of Silverwell again. He had tried to talk to me on the way in but I wasn't really feeling very chatty today. I wasn't rude or anything, I don't think I was anyway. I just surfed the internet on my phone and pretended I was busy.

Busy, busy, busy. Always so very busy. A veritable busy bee I am with so much to do.

As if.

I'm bored rigid most of the time and for the last week it has been like cabin fever, stuck within those four walls with nowhere to go and no-one to see.

Sam has been lovely. Waiting on me hand and foot and taking care of me so sweetly. Nothing has been too much trouble for him to do for me. He's even been washing my hair since I can't do it properly. I'm scared I'd open up the cut again. I couldn't even go and see Daniel on Saturday. His personal assistant seems brilliant though. When I spoke to Daniel on the phone and explained that I was too poorly to come and see him, he just said,

'No worries. Joe taking me Zoo. I see penguins!'

I could see him doing his waddling impression around the room and all I wanted was to be there with him. To take him out myself. I'd definitely do it next week though. I'd be well enough next week and Sam would surely let me go.

That was one reason why I insisted on coming for my Zumba class. To show Sam that I was better and able to do it. Besides, if I sat around at home any longer then I would get even fatter and the weight would be even harder to shift. I had to struggle to do up my size ten jeans yesterday and there is no way I can possibly go up to a size twelve. Sam would really hate me then.

I didn't have a training session booked. I told Sam I would wait for Tabitha to come back and it would be better for me to ease myself into exercise gradually. I don't want to undo the healing I've already done. Then I wouldn't be able to take Dan out at the weekend, and I have to see him. I have to make sure that he is as happy with Joe as he seems to be. I wasn't sure what I would say if I bumped into Will after I had promised to stick with him. I was hoping it would be his day off and then I wouldn't have to deal with it. I didn't want to deal with anything, and yet, I needed to be out and see other people, to know they existed beyond my world of Sam and Karadow. It was a weird situation to be in.

I went up to the desk and the same receptionist was there again, a quick glance at her name tag reminded me she was called Kelly.

'Mrs Lambert, good to see you back,' she smiled her painted smile that I knew was reserved for the general public. We all have one of those. The one that upturns the corners of the mouth, shows a row of white teeth, but never touches the eyes. I returned her smile. It didn't reach my eyes either.

'Hello Kelly. I think I'm booked into the Zumba class?'

'Ah, yes. It's in studio one, can you remember the way?'

Her bright red fingernails tapped away on the computer keys, feeding it with the information that would say where I was and who I was seeing so the invoice could be sent on for Sam to pay at the end of the month. There was no way I was going to be able to work with Will anyway. The paper trail would dob me in.

'Yes, I'm fine, thank you.' I smiled again, just to see if I still could. It still didn't reach my eyes.

The Zumba class was a lot harder than I expected it to be. When I had peeked through the window last week, all the participants made it look easy, spinning around in unison and not missing a step. The song was Beyoncé's 'single lady' and I loved that song. Emma and I had always danced around the lounge to it, waving our left hands about. We knew all the moves. This was different though, there was a sequence that was only three steps forward and three steps back and I could not get the hang of it. How can you not get three steps forward and three steps back right? I am thick as well as fat. And I felt stupid in my long sleeved top that I had chosen to cover up the bruising on my wrist. When I collided with the man in front of me because he came back when I went forward, I decided enough was enough. I picked up my things and left the room at the end of the song. I was going to stick with our original moves in future and keep them to myself.

'Hey, Penny-May isn't it?'

I heard a voice from behind me as I walked up the corridor towards the café and turned to see who had called me.

Damn! 'Oh, hi Will, yes, it is.' I was fumbling with the towel, trying to stuff it into my bag as I walked. I hadn't wanted to do it in the studio where everyone was watching me dip out early.

He ran the few feet until he drew level and then fell into step beside me.

'You cancelled your training session. Have you decided to go with Tab then?'

I felt my face flush and looked down at the floor. I felt so guilty and I was already feeling wretched enough.

'It's ok you know,' he said, placing his right hand on my shoulder. 'It's up to you who you see and I really don't mind.'

I couldn't help myself; I buried my head in my towel and burst into tears.

I felt his left hand rest on my other shoulder and it was so gentle and caring. I leant into him and he put his arms around me, holding me while I sobbed into his chest.

'I'm so sorry,' I said, pulling away when I finally managed to stem the flood of tears, 'I must look horrendous.'

'Don't worry about it, you look fine. Just a bit blotchy. Come on, we'll go and get a coffee somewhere quiet and you can tell Uncle Will all about it.'

I wasn't sure I could tell him all about it. He was probably just being nice.

'Oh, no, I couldn't take up your time. Don't you have a client to see?'

He looked at his watch. 'Nope. Not for another hour so you can have my undivided attention.'

I gave in. I liked this man and I had been starved of adult conversation for so long.

'Shall we?' He asked.

I smiled, a small smile, but I was aware that this one did start to reach my eyes and took his proffered arm.

'Ok, but you must promise not to get yourself into trouble by talking to me when you should be working.'

'Moi? Trouble?' he put on a mock horrified face, 'I never get into trouble. Well, I never get caught anyway,' he winked.

. . .

He guided me down a corridor and through a door that said 'staff only'. I held back as he opened the door wider and gestured me inside.

'But that's for staff, I can't go in there,' I said, holding back and shaking my head.

'There's nobody around today and if anyone does come in, I'll say I was trying to get my wicked way with you and led you in here blindfolded.'

I laughed, it felt good to hear that sound coming from my mouth.

'They won't believe that in a million years!'

'Ah, you've rumbled me. I'm wounded.' The twinkle was in his eye again and I followed him into the room. It was a small staff kitchen with a microwave, kettle and under counter fridge along one wall. To the side was a table and four hard back, farmhouse style chairs. He walked over to flick the kettle into life and indicated that I should take one of the seats.

'It's not quite as stylish as the café, but it's nice and quiet when you don't want to be seen by anyone,' he said.

Doing as I was told, I headed for the chair by the wall and facing the door. I wanted to be able to see if anyone was coming and then I figured I could duck down under the table quickly so Will wouldn't get into trouble.

'Tea? Coffee? Milk? Sugar?' he asked, lifting a couple of mismatched flowery mugs from the draining board. 'We even have some Earl Grey if you fancy it.

Although it has been here for a few years, so maybe that's not a good plan.'

'Coffee please, milk, no sugar. I'm not a fan of tea, even fancy tea.'

'I don't blame you. Tea that smells of parma violets just isn't right. Lucy used to love it though.'

'What was she like? Sam doesn't talk about her very much.'

Will's eyes took on a misty glaze as he placed the mug of coffee in front of me.

'She was funny, and sassy. She always saw the good in people and always put them first. She got me out of many a scrape, especially here.'

'I know Sam loved her very much. More than he does me. I don't think I measure up to her standard very well,' I said, placing my hands around my mug.

Will came and sat opposite me, wrapping his own hands around mine.

'Hey, don't sell yourself so short. I'm sure you are very wrong if that's what you think.'

'I dunno, I can't seem to do anything right at the moment.' I took a sip of my drink. It was still hot and scalded the top of my mouth making me spit the offending liquid back into the mug before placing it back onto the table. 'Christ, I can't even drink bloody coffee properly.'

Proper fat drops of water started finding their way out of my eyes and down my cheeks again. I didn't want to cry all over Will a second time, he'd think I was a total mess. Scrabbling around in my handbag I finally managed to find a bundled up piece of tissue and tried to stop the flood that was threatening to break through.

He stood and fetched the kitchen roll from the worktop, 'I think that might work better don't you?' He said with a smile as I reached out to pull off a couple of sheets.

'What's that?' He asked, holding my outstretched wrist. I hadn't noticed my sleeve riding up as I reached my arm out with the yellowing bruise shining for all to see. I snatched my arm back and yanked the sleeve back down.

'Oh, it's nothing, it's just me being clumsy as usual.'

Will took my arm back again and gently rolled up the sleeve to take a closer look at my wrist, turning it over to look at both sides.

'It doesn't look like nothing; you must have been really clumsy to do that. What happened?'

'I...I...I just fell a bit awkward in the garden and hit it on a rock. Honestly it's nothing.'

'Wouldn't that just make one bruise on one side though? This is all the way around, like it's been grabbed and squeezed too hard?'

'Does it?' I tried to look innocent; shocked even. 'I don't know, maybe I hit the other side as I was trying to stand up. I bruise really easily and it looks much worse than it is. It's almost healed.'

I knew I was gabbling and I wasn't sure if he believed me. The look on his face told me that he probably didn't.

'Did someone do this to you Penny-May? Did Sam do it?'

This time I didn't have to feign my shock, 'No! Of course not! Sam would never hurt me.' I pulled my arm away and pulled my sleeve down. 'I have to go. Brian will be waiting outside by now and wondering where I've got to.' Lifting my bag and successfully jamming my things back into it, I moved towards the door.

'I'm sorry,' Will said, standing opposite me, 'I didn't mean to jump to conclusions and of course he wouldn't. I don't know why I said that. Look, come back next week and we can start afresh, yes?'

He looked so distraught at his mistake that I couldn't hold it against him.

'Uh, I'll have to check our calendar, I'm not sure what we're doing.'

He put his hands into the pockets of his tracksuit bottoms, 'Ok, well, I hope I do see you next week. Take care Penny-May.'

I opened the door, turned to him and smiled. 'Thanks, I will.'

Walking down the corridor towards the reception I couldn't help but wonder why Will's first thought about the bruising might be that Sam had caused it.

Chapter Forty-Eight

Penny-May

Wednesday May 7th 2015

'Hi Hun, how you doing?' Emma asked as soon as she answered her phone.

It felt so good to hear her voice, it had been weeks since we last chatted and I was starting to forget how long it had been since we actually met up. A lump started forming in my throat and I swallowed a couple of times to try and get rid of it.

'I'm good, just thinking about you and felt like we needed a catch up.' I could hear the falseness in my voice, so I was sure that she would pick up on it.

'It's been ages! What have you been up to? How's Sam? And Daniel?'

'Oh, everyone's fine, you know how it is. I've just been running around so much sorting stuff that I don't know where the time has gone.'

'Don't I know it; at school all the teachers have had enough and are really looking forward to the summer break. The little brats are totally manic with all the excitement of Easter just gone and breaking up soon. It's an absolute nightmare! I swear the parents think it is a sport to fill them up on chocolate for breakfast, so we have to deal with all their hyperactivity and then they're knackered when they get home and

fall asleep when the sugar crash hits. Hang on a sec— '

I heard a loud pop down the phone line.

'Is that why you've just opened a bottle of wine?'

'Christ yes, I need it tonight. Shame you're not here to share it with me though.' The lump came back and I was struggling to swallow it down a second time.

'I know, I wish I could,' I eventually managed to reply.

'Hey, are you sure you're ok? You sound a bit funny.'

I tried to laugh, 'Oh, yes, don't mind me. I'm just missing my bestie and thinking how much fun we used to have on Friday nights.'

'They were the best, weren't they?'

I nodded, not thinking about the fact that she couldn't see my agreement through the ether.

'You still there?'

'Oh, uh, yes. Sorry. I'm here.'

'Are you sure you're ok?'

I sniffed and a tried to stifle a sob.

'You're not, are you? You're crying. What's up?'

'Nothing,' I replied, 'I'm just being silly and probably hormonal. Do you think I'm fat? I feel fat.'

'Don't be so bloody stupid!' Emma scoffed down the phone, 'If you're fat then I'm a beached whale flapping about on the sand and begging to be put out of my misery.'

'But you haven't seen me for a couple of weeks, I've put on so much weight and

Sam will hate me if I keep putting it on.'

'You can't have put on that much weight in a couple of weeks, it's impossible, especially with the amount of bedroom exercise you get! Not that I'm jealous or anything.'

I smiled at her sarcasm; it was one of the things I missed most about her.

'And Sam won't hate you at all, he loves every single bit of you. Even if there are some small wobbly bits, which I'm totally sure there aren't, it'll give him something more to grab hold of. They're not called love handles for nothing you know.'

A small snigger found its way past the lump as I listened to her, she always made me laugh eventually.

'I haven't got to love handle stage yet thank you very much, more like love knobs.'

'And I'll bet Sam loves playing with your knobs as much as you do his.'

I could almost see her winking at me and I burst out laughing.

'Trust you to take every conversation into the bedroom.'

'Yep, guaranteed. That's because I'm not getting it and you are.'

'I love you Em.'

'I love you too, see you soon? Give me a ring when you're free and we'll do lunch. On you!'

'Definitely, I think Sam is going away in a couple of weeks' time so I'll work something out for then.'

I clicked my phone shut and held it to my chest. I must be wrong about Sam; he was always so gentle and loving. I just needed to be more like Lucy in future and not do anything wrong. It had to be a blip and my fault. I'll be better and stronger. I'll get fit and nail that Zumba routine.

And then he only needs to worry about the knobs that he likes playing with.

Smiling again, I went upstairs, washed my face and changed into clothing that was far sexier than the joggers I'd climbed into when I first came home. Returning to the kitchen, I took a bottle of his favourite red wine out of the wine rack, opened it to let it breathe just the way he liked it and made myself a small vodka and lemonade while I waited for him to arrive. I was going to show him just how sorry I was and how much I loved him.

Chapter Forty-Nine

PENNY-MAY
Monday May 18th 2015

The phone rang and as usual it was right at the bottom of my handbag. Why can you never find the damn thing when it's ringing? I hoped it wasn't Sam. He would get annoyed if I didn't answer straight away and start questioning me about where I was. I finally spotted the purple heart charm that was attached to it and yanked it out to see Rhea's name flashing across the screen. Relieved that I hadn't kept Sam waiting again, I prodded the screen to answer.

'Hi Rhea, what can I do for you?'

'Hey there, I was wondering if you fancied having a gym buddy. Carl said you had started going to Silverwell and I need to get into shape.'

I thought of Rhea's perfect figure and how she didn't, but I kept that to myself. It would be nice to have some female company and someone to laugh with, I wouldn't feel quite so self-conscious if I was with a girlfriend. My conflicting feelings about Will also wouldn't be a problem as I would use the same trainer as Rhea did and surely she wouldn't use him either because whatever the issue was that made Sam not like him, Rhea would also be aware of that and wouldn't like him either. The fact that I liked Will just made my life difficult and this way, the decision would be out of my hands and it wouldn't be my fault if he got upset about it. I'm sure he would understand anyway.

'That would be lovely,' I replied, 'I'll warn you though, I'm not very good at this fitness stuff.'

'Don't worry, I'm not either and I usually lack the motivation to keep going when I'm on my own. The lure of the cakes in the lounge café is far too strong and much tastier.'

I chuckled, 'I know what you mean. It's the lure of the cakes that has made me so fat.'

'My dear, you are so not fat, but there's nothing wrong in keeping fit and healthy. Are you free this afternoon?'

I'd given up keeping a diary, there was no need when you never went anywhere so I leapt at the opportunity of getting away from the house. 'Yes, I'm free all afternoon.'

'That's great, I'll swing by and pick you up about 1:30 shall I? I have to be home by 4:30 when the nanny brings Josh home, but we'll still have plenty of time.'

'Perfect,' I replied, 'looking forward to it.'

As I clicked the phone off, I sat and stared at the screen. I'd been getting on ok with Rhea, and she did sort out all my wedding stuff for me, but we'd only really met up whenever we were on a business meeting with our husbands. This phone call was totally unexpected. I wasn't going to query it though. If it meant that I could get out without troubling Sam or Brian then I was going to grab it. I would just text Sam to let him know where I was going and who with though. Just in case he decided to phone me while I was in the training session. He'll be fine with me going out with Rhea. He trusts her.

. . .

I was stood outside when she pulled up in her BMW convertible. Scarf wrapped around her head and sunglasses on, she looked so much more sophisticated than I did. I jumped in, glad that I didn't have to worry about my short hair getting tangled in the wind.

Not sure it's quite warm enough for the top down yet is it?' I asked, then giggled and pulled my jacket tighter around my neck.

'As long as it's not raining, it's always warm enough for the top down.' Rhea reached inside the glove box and pulled out another pair of sunglasses, 'Here, put these on. Buckle up, I'm going to show you what this baby can do!'

Thrusting it into first gear, the little car shot forward leaving a spray of chippings in its wake. I couldn't help but start to grin as the wind whipped through my hair as we gathered speed.

'This is brilliant!' I cried above the roar of the engine. I raised my arms above my head and let the force of the wind try and take them away.

Rhea was grinning as she glanced towards me, 'That's why we have the top down.'

When we arrived at Silverwell, Kelly was behind the desk again.

'We're here for the gym. We'll go on through,' Rhea said to her without altering her stride and heading towards the gym doors. That was what I should be like I thought as I hastened my step to keep pace with her. I needed to be as confident as she was. Lucy must have been like that as well, although I guess the fact that she used to work here would help her out a bit and I didn't have that knowledge yet. I would though. I would make it my aim to get it.

Swinging open the gym door I was surprised to almost bump straight into Will. I was even more surprised to see Rhea reach up and give him a hug and a peck on the cheek. He then reciprocated with one on hers and a 'Hi Babe, you made it.' I was gobsmacked.

'Of course,' Rhea trilled, 'I said we would, didn't I? Now, where do you want us to start?'

'But... but... aren't we supposed to be seeing Tabitha?' I enquired.

'Oh, no,' Rhea replied, 'I always see Will when I'm here. He's so much better than she is.' She lowered her voice to a conspiratorial whisper. 'Don't worry though, we won't tell Sam or Carl. What they don't know won't hurt them and all that jazz eh?' She tapped her forefinger on the side of her nose to emphasise her words.

'Oh, right, as long as you are ok with that?' I asked, directing my question straight at Will. After the way I had left before I wasn't sure if he would even want to work with me again.

'It's more than fine with me,' he said. His comforting smile radiating into his deep blue eyes. 'Come on girls, warmups and then the treadmill. Let's get those gorgeous bodies pumping shall we!'

Sweating and hurting, I was glad when Will finally called a halt to the session. I picked up my bag and my empty water bottle and started to head towards the main doors but Rhea called me back, 'We're going this way Hun.'

I looked and saw that she was indicating a smaller door at the back of the room, Will was already headed towards it.

'We'll grab a quiet coffee before we head off home,' she said.

I followed her into the corridor which I soon recognised as the one leading to the little kitchenette that Will had taken me to before. I again hesitated outside the door that said, 'Staff only'.

'Are you sure it's ok for us to be in there? Won't you get into trouble if you're found out?'

Will turned and put his arm out to me, gently touching me on my shoulder. 'It's fine, just like it was last time. I'm the only one who uses this room, the other staff prefer the larger staff kitchen behind the café where they can scrounge free cake when Big Boss Helen isn't looking. We never get disturbed in here.'

'Yes, I much prefer it in here to the actual café,' Rhea added, 'Too many prying eyes and ears around for my liking in there.'

'Why would that matter?' I asked as Will closed the door behind us. Rhea was already filling the kettle with fresh water and she flicked it on to boil. It was obvious that she knew her way around in here and was just as comfortable as if she were at home in her own kitchen.

'Well, with the history between Will and Sam, particularly since we lost Lucy, it's better not to give idle tongues any chance to gossip.' She looked across at Will who bowed his head, busying himself with getting the mugs out of the cupboard. His silence seemed to encourage her to continue. 'Carl has also asked me not to see

Will but I can't see why I can't decide for myself who I spend my time with. And

Tabitha is such a 'no pain, no gain' advocate. She's an absolute tyrant.'

She gestured to the table and I took the same seat that I had occupied before. I twiddled nervously with the water bottle I had placed in front of me. The water inside the kettle was at a rolling boil, the indicator on the side jumping up and down as the fluid moved and then a loud click signalled that the required heat had been reached and all the manic movement ceased. Will poured the drinks while Rhea came over to take her own seat beside me.

'Lucy, Will and I used to have such fun in here, especially when Sam was so busy and I can't see why I shouldn't spend time with a good friend. We kind of need each other to help us through our loss.'

Will nodded and placed our drinks on the table before sitting down. 'I miss Lucy so much and it's good to be able to talk about her with someone who loved her almost as much as I did.'

I shook my head. 'But I don't understand why it has to be such a secret from Sam and Carl, or why you're telling me?'

They looked at each other and then Will spoke, Rhea blew into her coffee mug and took a tentative sip.

'I think Sam was always jealous of mine and Lucy's friendship. We had been mates for so long, it was as if we knew what the other one was thinking. He didn't like that so he didn't like her to spend much time with me. Rhea was always able to act as the go between and we'd hide out here sometimes and catch up a bit.'

'It was harder after she lost the baby though,' Rhea said, 'She was so depressed that we couldn't always get her out of the house. When we did, Will was always the one that could get her to smile though. I loved seeing her smile and laugh again. We really thought we were helping to pull her through.'

'She lost a baby. I didn't know that. Sam never told me.'

'Yes, she fell down the stairs. It hurt him a lot too, I think. He never liked to talk about it,' she said.

'How's your arm now?' Will asked, reaching across the table and holding my hand so he could lift up the cuff of my shirt. The yellowing had faded considerably but I still pulled my arm back again and pulled my sleeve back down. I shot an embarrassed look across at Rhea.

'Oh, uh, it's ok now thanks.'

'Will said you fell on it?'

'Yeah, silly me eh? Stumbled in the garden and hit it on a rock.'

'You sound as accident prone as Lucy was,' Rhea continued, 'she was forever tripping over stuff when she was at home. I swear she could trip over a pinhead with ease. And she bruised so easily. It never seemed to take very much for her to be covered in them.'

'Really?'

'Yes,' Will replied, 'I was forever telling her to be more careful.'

'Maybe Sam falls for women he needs to take care of?' I said.

I saw them both glance at each other before Rhea answered. 'Yes, maybe that's it. You need to be more careful though. We don't want you hurting yourself as much as Lucy did.'

'I will.' I picked up my lukewarm coffee and drank it down. It had been an interesting day and one that I would need to think about further.

Chapter Fifty

Sam

Friday May 29th 2015.

Sam walked into his office and slammed the door behind him. The noise it made felt satisfying but it wasn't enough to calm his anger. The document file he was carrying was thrown onto the floor by the window, his briefcase quickly following it.

'Stupid bloody people!' He said to no-one in particular. 'What the fuck do they know about architecture?'

He went back and opened the door, looked into the room beyond, Kate was nowhere to be seen, but Charlotte was. She would do.

'Where's Kate? Get me my coffee now!' He barked at her before turning and slamming the door behind him again, not even bothering to give the assistant time to reply. He saw her jump from the desk before the door closed and was pleased that she had so willingly done as he had asked.

Not like that jumped up pair of nobodies that he had just had a meeting with. What the hell did they know? His plan was perfect for what they wanted to do, there was nothing wrong with the window placements at all. Didn't they realise that he couldn't *just* move them five feet to the right? That would put out all the walls, plumbing and wiring. He was going to have to start all over again *just* because that puny bloke couldn't keep his wife's trap shut.

He heard Charlotte's tentative knock on the door.

'Come in!'

The door opened slowly and she peered around it. He could see the tray in her hand with the cups perfectly aligned and filled.

'Umm, your coffee Mr Lambert. Kate wasn't expecting you back so soon, she's gone to the print room to get those copies done that you asked her to.'

Sam pointed to the table and Charlotte set about putting the coffee items onto the correct coasters.

'I don't need them anymore. Get hold of her and tell her I need her in here now. I have some more work to do.'

'Yes, of course.' She turned and scuttled through the door.

He picked up the espresso and downed it one swallow, the heat searing the back of his throat. The pain wasn't enough to dull his temper like it usually did. The memory of his meeting with that jumped up brat and his fat diva wife whirled around in his mind. How dare they talk to him like he was the hired help. Didn't they know who they were dealing with?

Nobody treated him like that.

Chapter Fifty-One

PENNY-MAY
Friday May 29th 2015

Sam had called me to say that he was leaving work, so I had our evening meal ready to serve and the red wine open to breathe on the counter. A quick check in the lounge mirror made me panic a bit as I realised my mascara and eyeliner had smudged so I nipped upstairs to repair it. Hearing the crunch of the gravel as his car pulled into the driveway, I dropped the make-up back into the drawer and ran downstairs to pour his drink. I had just replaced the bottle onto the worktop as he walked in the house. *Perfect timing Penny-May*, I thought.

'Hi Babe,' I said, handing him the glass and reaching up to give him a kiss on the cheek. He took the drink from my hand and took a large mouthful, swirled it around in his mouth for less than a second and then spat it back into the glass.

'That's disgusting! What the hell have you done to it?' Picking up the bottle he looked at the label.

'God, you're so stupid. Any idiot knows this needs to age for at least a couple more years before it can be drunk. You've just wasted a one hundred pound bottle of wine!'

I didn't know what to say or do. I'd been certain that was the bottle he had got out this morning and said to have it ready for our meal. I was sure he said he was looking forward to drinking it. I must have got it wrong, maybe he didn't mean later today, he meant later later. Much, much later. 'I...I'm so sorry, I must have picked up the wrong one.'

The glass smashed into the sink. The crash as it landed and the flying shards making me flinch as I shrank back towards the staircase.

'Shall I get a different bottle? Are you ready to eat? I can serve if you like?'

'You think I'd trust you to get the right wine after this?' The bottle followed the glass into the sink, but it didn't break this time, he didn't throw it with quite as much force. The red fluid glugged from the mouth and swirled around the plughole, like the blood when I washed my hair following our argument the other day. I reached to grab the oven gloves and bent to take the casserole out of the oven. He walked behind me, bumped into my back so I almost dropped the hot dish. I lifted it quickly onto the hob and closed the oven door with my foot. The atmosphere was charged and I could feel Sam's temper as he stood and watched me ladle the food into two shallow bowls and place them onto the table. There was already fresh, buttered bread at each place setting.

'Would you like anything else?' I asked, indicating for him to sit and eat. I was hoping that his bad mood would subside if he took some time to calm down. He sneered as he pulled his chair out and sat on it. Lifting his fork he pierced a piece of steak and put it into his mouth. I could see him rolling it around his mouth as he chewed. I picked my own fork up, prodded around the bowl and finally speared a piece of potato and put it into my mouth. It tasted ok, but it felt like cardboard and it stuck in my throat as I watched Sam chewing, the sneer still not leaving his face.

I felt the moist lump land on my cheek before I saw him spit it at me. His arm sweeping the contents of the table onto the floor with a crash that made me jump out of my seat. It toppled and joined the rest of the mess on the floor. I wiped the halfchewed piece of animal flesh from my face, walking backwards until I could feel my back against the sink.

'Do you really expect me to eat that shit?' He asked, walking menacingly towards me. 'It tastes like fucking dog food. Do you think that's funny, getting me to eat dog food? After everything I've done for you? Picked you out of the gutter, given you everything you've ever wanted, even paid for that mongol brother of yours and you feed me fucking dog food?'

He was right in front of me now, I could feel the spittle landing on my face as he spoke. His tone low and quiet, enunciating every syllable of every word.

'I didn't Sam, I promise!' I cried, 'I would never do that to you.'

From the corner of my eye, I could see his fist clenching and unclenching, I wanted to run, to get away but I was cornered between the worktops with him towering in front of me. I didn't have a hope of getting past him.

'Please don't hurt me, I'll be better next time, I promise,' I sobbed.

I doubled in pain as his punch landed in my stomach, 'You bet you will,' he replied as he laid a second one to follow the first. Winded and in pain I fell to the floor amongst the shattered glass and pottery and the ruined food. I felt the glass pierce the skin on my knees and arms and I curled into a ball, crying out in pain. 'Please, please don't hurt me.'

I saw the booted kick coming but was powerless to move. I lay there, cowering at his feet and took the blow. It was my penance for upsetting him so much. I must have deserved it.

The punishment stopped. I was scared to move in case it started again and I could still see his feet in front of me. I daren't look up, couldn't antagonise him any more than I already had done. The black boots turned in a crunch of glass and started to walk away.

'This place is a mess. Sort it out.'

I heard the front door slam. I was alone, lying in a sea of beef casserole and broken kitchenware and I still didn't know what I had done. Gingerly, I managed to get to my feet and survey the damage. I had no idea where he'd gone or how long he would be and I couldn't let him come home to this mess. Gritting my teeth against the pain and fighting the urge to be sick, I set about cleaning it up.

I still referred to it as Lucy's study. It stood like a shrine to her memory with everything exactly as she had left it. The cleaner hoovered and dusted it once a week although it never required it really. Once a month would have done. Sam never went in there, never spoke about it and I never asked. He never said it was off limits, that I couldn't go in there, but I usually stayed away from it. The house was big enough anyway, I didn't need to go in there.

I had cleaned everything up downstairs, as well as myself. Soaked in the bath and washed the casserole out of my hair. Wrapped in my fluffy bathrobe, the silence engulfed me as I awaited his return. I felt so alone. Lucy was never as bad as I was, how on earth did I ever think that I could compete with her? I could see the study door from where I was sitting in our bedroom. It was ajar, which was unusual, maybe the cleaner had forgotten to close it earlier on? It would annoy Sam so I went to close it before he came home. Standing with my hand on the door handle however, I felt compelled to enter and curl up in the cosy rocking chair that stood in the corner of the room. There was a pink fluffy cushion in one corner and a matching throw across the back. I picked up the blanket and wrapped it around my shoulders, sitting down into the chair and placing the cushion in the small of my back. The gentle rocking motion combined with the calming, muted colours of the walls soothed my whirling mind and I imagined Lucy sat here, cradling her empty belly after she had so tragically miscarried her baby. I could see Sam coming in and crouching at her feet as he tried to reassure her that everything would be alright, they would try for another and they would make sure the next baby survived and was loved just as much as they had loved the one they had lost. I saw the tears flowing down their cheeks as they tried to come to terms with the tragedy that had befallen their previously untroubled lives.

The tears flowed over my own cheeks, unbidden and without the racking sobs that had accompanied them earlier when I was in the kitchen mopping the floor. This wasn't the ugly crying of before, this was something different, it was the emotion of knowing how hurt they must have been and it would be so much harder to bear than what I was feeling for myself. I couldn't imagine what they must have been through together and me not behaving properly wasn't helping Sam to heal. No wonder he lost his temper with me so often.

I pulled the blanket tighter around me, laid my head back onto the head rest and closed my eyes. I'd just rest here for a couple of minutes, in the quiet of this peaceful room. Just a couple of minutes.

I woke to feel Sam gently lifting me from the chair and carrying me to our bedroom, my head fell naturally onto his shoulder.

'I'm sorry I was bad,' I mumbled.

Sam didn't reply, he placed me into the bed, still wearing my robe, and pulled the covers over me. Kissing me on the forehead he turned and left the room, closing the door quietly behind him.

Chapter Fifty-Two

Penny-May

Monday June 15th 2015

The number on the phone flashed up as 'Joe' so I figured Daniel was calling me again. We had fallen into a routine of him calling me on his PA's work phone every couple of days, usually when Sam was at work, and Daniel would tell me all about everything they had done together. I still felt jealous that Joe spent more time with my brother than I did. I was going to have to get them to come over and see us one day soon.

'Hi Hulk, what's up?' I asked as soon as I clicked the phone to answer.

'Sorry, it's not Dan this time, it's me,' came Joe's voice.

'Oh, no worries, everything ok?'

'We don't know to be honest, Dan isn't doing too well at the moment.'

'What? What's the matter with him?'

Joe's voice sounded stilted and it was beginning to get me worried. 'He hasn't been able to shake that cold off very well and he doesn't seem to be breathing too good. Martha has just called the doctor to come and have a look at him. He said he was on his way.'

'I need to come over, tell Dan I'm on the way.' I was already looking for my jacket and bag, pulling my shoes out of the closet by the front door.

'I'm sure he's going to be ok; I can phone you as soon as the doctor's been.'

'It's not a problem, phone me anyway as soon as you know anything, but I am on my way over. It might take a while to get a lift but tell him I'm coming please?' I heard the note of desperation in my voice, so I guessed Joe did too.

'Of course I will, take it easy and see you when you get here.'

Clicking the phone closed I ran through who could possibly get me over to Oak Tree Lodge at such short notice. Brian was with Sam and Carl and I knew that he couldn't be spared, Emma was working and I didn't want to pull her away from that if it wasn't necessary. Rhea. Maybe I could ask her, we were supposed to be going to the gym again later anyway so hopefully she wouldn't mind running me to check on Daniel instead. She picked up on the first ring.

'You're not pulling out on me now are you? We've nearly got that Zumba routine nailed!'

'I'm really sorry Rhea, but I need a massive favour, please can you help me?'

The happy tone vanished from her voice, 'Are you ok? What's the matter? Are you hurt?'

'Oh, no, I'm fine. It's my brother. He's poorly and they've phoned the doctor to come and see him. I need to get over there and check for myself how he is but I haven't any transport and there's no way I can pull Brian away from Sam today. I've no cash for a taxi and it's too far to walk to get a bus and I've no cash for that either...' I knew I was gabbling but I just couldn't stop myself as the sheer panic of not being able to get to Daniel started to engulf me.

'Hey, slow down and breathe. It's not a problem, I'll be right there.' The phone went dead and I tried to do as she said, a deep breath in followed by an exhale. It sort of worked, but that panicky feeling in my chest didn't disappear. I grabbed my bag and ran out to the driveway to meet her, quickly firing a text to Sam to let him know what had happened, where I was going and who with.

Just as Rhea pulled up and I jumped into the passenger seat, Sam's picture flashed up on the home screen. I answered, expecting him to be as worried as I was,

'What are you doing dragging Rhea out on a fool's errand?' He asked.

'It's not a fool's errand, Daniel's sick.'

'So?'

'Well, I need to see him, he needs me.'

'That's ridiculous, what the hell could you do that his paid for professionals can't?

You'll only get in the way!'

'He's my brother, my family. I have to be there to make sure he's ok.'

Rhea glanced across at me as she drove. The frown on her face told me that she could hear every word he said.

'I'm your family now. You don't have to go running around after him at all. It's probably just a sniffle anyway and those useless fuckwits are worrying you over nothing. Go back inside and get ready for our dinner tonight. I'll tell Rhea not to bother.'

I inhaled deeply. It was going to cost me to go against his wishes but I had to see Daniel. 'No Sam, Rhea's already here and we're halfway to Oak Tree Lodge. If it's nothing, I'll come straight back, I promise.'

Rhea nodded and gave me a thumb's up.

His voice took on an even sharper, clipped tone, 'I'm telling you to go home. Your cabbage of a brother can be looked after by those that I pay to keep him out of your hair. I need you to be ready for my business meeting.'

I was shocked at what he had called Daniel, how could anyone think it was alright to say things like that? There was no going back now.

'I'm sorry, but Dan needs me more tonight. I'll call you when I know what's wrong.'

The dead tone in my ear informed me that Sam had cut off from his end. I heaved a sigh as I dropped my phone back into my handbag.

'You ok, Hun?' Rhea asked.

'I'll be fine when I know how Daniel is. Sam will calm down by the time I get home.'

'We're here,' she replied as she swung into the drive. I gasped as I saw the paramedic car and the ambulance parked outside the front door. Barely waiting for the car to stop, I shucked off my seatbelt and threw open the car door, running across the forecourt.

The front door opened, and a stretcher was being wheeled out through it. Daniel was laying on it, wrapped in blankets and an oxygen mask covering his face. He was pale and listless, barely conscious, his breathing inaudible above the noise of the canister.

'Joe?' I asked as I saw the PA following the stretcher, 'What's happening?'

'Penny-May, I was just about to phone you. He took a sudden turn for the worse and couldn't stop coughing. He could barely get any breath. They think he has pneumonia.'

Daniel was being loaded into the ambulance and I jumped up the steps after him, 'I'm coming too.'

The paramedic looked at Joe for confirmation.

'It's ok, she's his sister,' he told them.

I sat in the chair that was indicated to me and picked up

Daniel's limp and cold hand from the stretcher, 'Hi Hulk, how you doing?'

A lump started to form in my throat when he didn't reply or acknowledge me.

Rhea looked into the doorway, 'I'll follow, you're going to need a lift home again later.'

'You don't need to do that, you've done so much already bringing me here, I can get a taxi home.'

'Don't be silly, you need a friend with you. I'll see you at Treliske.'

Before I could insist that she went home, she vanished and Joe had taken her place.

'I'll follow too,' he said as the doors closed. I heard the siren begin to wail and felt the vehicle begin to move.

Chapter Fifty-Three

PENNY-MAY
Monday June 15th 2015

'Where the fuck have you been?' Sam shouted as I walked in the door. I felt the spittle land on my face, saw the veins pulse on his neck and the tautness of his jawline.

'Dan's really sick, he's in hospital with pneumonia.'

If I thought Sam would calm down once he realised just how sick Daniel was, I was wrong. He was angrier than I had ever seen him before.

His hand shot out and back-handed me across the face and, as my head whipped around with the force of the blow, I wished that I had allowed Rhea to come in with me after all. She had suggested it, almost demanded it, but I'd said it would be fine and that I'd be ok. I wasn't going to be though, I knew that as I stumbled, dropping my handbag and reaching out to grab the wall to keep my balance.

'I don't care about that spastic; he'd be better off dead anyway. He's just a drain on society.'

The punch in my stomach accompanied his heartless words. I doubled over, screamed in pain.

'No, please, I'm sorry, I needed to see him.'

'I needed you here tonight, you knew that. You made me look like a complete idiot when you weren't there for the meeting.'

'The kick took my feet out from under me, causing me to fall to the floor, sprawling at his feet. A second kick and then a third landed in my stomach and chest.

'How dare you humiliate me like that,' he shouted.

'I'm sorry, I won't do it again, I promise.'

'It's too late now, the damage is done.' He reached down and yanked my arm, pulling me onto my knees before pushing me onto my back. He knelt beside me and his hands ripped at my blouse, the buttons breaking from the force.

'You're my wife and you do as I say!'

His hands moved down to my trousers, pulling them off and then my pants followed.

'No, please,' I sobbed, I didn't want this.

'You don't say no to me, you bitch!' He slapped me across the face. I felt him lean over me. The bulge of his penis forcing its way into me, the searing pain as he started to grind his hips as deep as he could into my unwilling body. His hands fumbling across my breasts, kneading my nipples, trying in vain to get them erect.

I closed my eyes. It was pointless to cry again, he would only hurt me more if I did. I lay there and let him do what he wanted, blocking out sensation, blocking out time. When he went rigid I realised that I had been holding my breath and I slowly exhaled. He put his hand on my chin and turned my head to face him, forced a hard, loveless kiss on my lips before pulling out of me.

Putting his head to my ear he whispered, 'You loved that, I could tell. You always were a slut, you asked for it that way.'

I didn't reply. I couldn't. What I wanted to say would make

him angry again so I lay there, choking back the sobs that I wanted to let out.

He stood up and laughed. An evil, guttural laugh that I had never heard him do before.

'You're a mess. Get up and shower before I come back.' With another kick to my shins as he walked past me, he walked out of the front door, closing it firmly behind him.

A few minutes later I heard the car roar down the drive. I pulled myself to a sitting position and leant back against the wall.

Everywhere hurt. I didn't think there was a single place where I didn't feel any pain.

Tears pouring down my cheeks I stood up and made my way upstairs to our bathroom where I did as I was told and took a shower. The water didn't help me to feel clean though, no matter how much I scrubbed, no matter how much I cried through the pain of the scrubbing.

I didn't think I'd ever feel clean again.

Chapter Fifty-Four

Penny-May
Tuesday June 16th 2015

I woke to hear Sam entering the bedroom carrying a breakfast tray and laid it down onto the bed beside me. He pulled the curtains open and I winced in the sudden bright sunlight. As he leaned to kiss me on the forehead, I couldn't help but shrink back into the pillows. He faltered, the smile slipping from his face.

'What's up darling?' He asked, a puzzled look on his face. 'Are you still feeling unwell?'

I nodded and raised a hand to my forehead. 'Um, yes, sorry. I have a bit of a headache.'

'This will sort you out,' he replied, pointing to the tray. Freshly squeezed orange juice and warm croissants either side of a single red rose in an individual vase. He'd even thought to bring some painkillers with him. How romantic. I remembered those heady days when we were first together and he used to do this, when I thought he was the most perfect man ever. How could I have got it so wrong?

I was relieved when he left, it was far too hard to act normally, to pretend that last night hadn't happened. I couldn't understand why going to see Daniel when he was so poorly was so wrong. I mean, Sam was right when he said that Daniel was surrounded by professional carers, maybe I did just get in their way? Maybe they do know more than me and look after Daniel better than I can?

But I can't just walk away and leave him. He hasn't got anyone else to speak for him properly.

Daniel didn't really understand what was happening after they'd died. He'd never known death before.

I'd done my best to prepare him, to tell him that Mum and Dad had been in an accident and they had died and gone to heaven. We were in the kitchen of the family house, surrounded by boxes and my half-hearted packing attempt. The landlord wanted us out at the end of the month. The rain was running down the window, rivulets of water merging with each other, masking the view of the garden and Dad's greenhouse.

Dan had asked if he could visit them, take them some chocolate and crisps with his Hulk DVD so we could all sit and have a sofa picnic while watching it like we always had done on rainy days. He'd thrown such a temper tantrum when I said we couldn't, that heaven was a place we couldn't go to visit and that they couldn't come back to us.

He'd called me stupid. They went out in their car so they could just drive back. We could get a car and go and see them.

He didn't understand.

I'd put the film on anyway. Just let him carry on shouting while I clicked the buttons to get it to start. His shouting became a bit quieter while I got the big bag of crisps and the box of Maltesers from the worktop and tipped them into two bowls, carried them into the lounge and placed them onto the coffee table. He was sobbing when I sat down on the sofa and patted the cushions beside me.

'You gonna come and sit down with me then Matey?' I'd asked, reaching out to pick up a crisp and popping it into my mouth.

'Want Mum to watch.'

The crisp had nearly choked me but I forced it down, picked up another one and put it into my mouth.

'She would if she could, but I'm afraid she can't Dan. She wouldn't mind you watching without her though. If you don't hurry up, you'll miss the crisps, they're your favourite flavour. Smoky bacon.' I hated smoky bacon crisps. I ate another one.

Dan's sobbing became quieter and he sidled over towards the sofa, reaching for the bowl.

'Oh, look, Bruce Banner's about to get gamma rayed! Come on, you're missing the best bit!'

While I kept my attention on the screen, he picked up the bowl and, cradling it, he slowly sat beside me, dipping his hand in to select the biggest crisp he could find. I leant back and put my arm around his back. After a few minutes, he edged closer, snuggled into my side and I curled my arm around him.

I picked up my phone and called the hospital, asking to be put through to Dan's ward.

'I'm Penny-May Lambert, Daniel Meares' sister. How is he?' I asked when the nurse finally came onto the phone.

'Hi there, he's been a bit unsettled and doesn't like wearing the oxygen mask but he is doing ok.'

'I'm sorry, but what does ok mean exactly? Is he any better or is he worse than last night?'

'We think he's responding to treatment and doing a bit better. The consultant will be doing his rounds shortly and we will know more then. Of course, he would find his breathing a lot easier if he would keep the mask on.'

'I see, he can be funny about things like that, he finds it hard to understand that it will make him better. I'll come in and see if I can persuade him.'

'That will help, he is sleeping at the moment and we're going to be doing tests on him this morning though so you may not be able to see much of him if you're coming now?'

I thought of the pain I was in and how much make-up I was going to have to put on to cover the bruising on my face, there was no way I could come straight over.

'That's ok, I'll leave it until this afternoon, but please phone me if anything changes.'

'Of course we will, see you later.'

Clicking the phone off I thought about what I had just said I would do. Sam would be furious if he knew I was going to the hospital, but I guess he can't do any worse to me than what he did last night. I won't tell him beforehand though. I'll go early afternoon and make sure I'm back before he gets home.

Lucy's study door was open as I walked gingerly across the landing. Every step was painful and I held my arm across my front as if that could stop my chest from hurting. I was heading downstairs to make myself a coffee but decided to take another look around instead. The rocking chair looked inviting but I sat at the pure white leather desk chair instead, slowly spinning it around in a circle before stopping, facing the desk. I couldn't help wondering what kind of work she did here. Sam never spoke about how she spent her days, what she did with her time in here. The top of the desk was mostly clear, a forlorn pot of pens stood to one side of the computer monitor whilst the wireless keyboard and mouse were placed dead central, waiting to be clicked into life. It was almost as if a ruler had been used to position them. The cleaner was obviously very precise in her cleaning methods. Or Sam had told her off for not doing it properly before. A humourless shout of mirth escaped my lips. It was only me that he did that too, everyone else thought he was the perfect gentleman.

Only I was bad enough to deserve his wrath.

Feeling like a thief who has snuck into a stranger's dwelling, I opened the top drawer only to find it as neat and pristine as the desk was. Pens, pencils and stationary items all arranged into military order within what looked like a custom made pen tray. No wonder Sam loved her so much if she was this neat, and no wonder I exasperated him so much. I was tempted to mix them up, create some of the havoc that was running around in my mind, but thought better of it. Sam would be annoyed with me if he knew I had done that.

The second drawer was more stationary. Unopened boxes of pens and pencils, felt tip pens, highlighters and packets of erasers shaped like animals; an empty pink fluffy pencil case with 'Princess' emblazoned upon it in an italic, glittery thread. Why does anyone need so many pens?

The third drawer was stiff to open and I had to pull hard on the handle. It felt like something was stopping it from opening and with a final yank, it finally yielded. Something gave a soft thud as it slid off the back of the drawer. I tried to push the drawer back in again but it was now wedged and wouldn't lie flush with the rest of the desk. I couldn't leave it like that, Sam would notice it in an instant and he would be furious that I had been nosing around in here. Cursing my way through the pain I crouched down and tried to fit my hand between the drawers to see what had fallen out. It didn't work, I could feel something flat and hard, but couldn't get the angle right to be able to pull it out. With a lot of fiddling, I managed to lift the drawer off the runners and drag it out revealing a small pile of books neatly stacked at the back with one turned askew to the rest. The culprit that had fallen off the drawer.

I picked up the one that was out of place, '*Bridget Jones' Diary*'. I laughed, she wasn't into highbrow fiction then? Maybe I would have liked her after all, I loved this book. The other books looked like notepads, A5 size with broken spines and dogeared edges.

I opened the first book, a piece of paper fluttered to the floor. I picked it up, one edge jagged as if torn from a notebook. The handwriting scrawled; scratched across the page to be nearly unintelligible:

To whoever finds my diaries, my successor maybe? The cleaner? Please don't let it be Sam, I couldn't bear for him to read what is contained inside.

You, however, must read them and I hope they help you.

I guess that if you have found them, then things aren't going too good for me and that will mean that life as I knew it is over and I don't want to think that I have failed. Sam doesn't know about them, they were always my secret, my way of making sense of my world. The good times and the bad. Don't show them to him, at least not until you have read them and understood why I have done what I have done.

I'm not good at failure.

I'm not ready for everything to end just yet.

And I loved Sam.

Probably too much.

. . .

Lucy xx

Intrigued, I started to turn the pages and read.

Chapter Fifty-Five

Lucy's Diary

Friday 13th November 2009.

I love Friday the thirteenth. I know everyone says it's an unlucky day but as I was born on Friday the thirteenth I consider myself to be exempt from that rule and something good usually happens for me.

It was a normal start to the day. You know, put the make-up on, do the hair, don the black tunic with the pink edging that is supposed to be so stylish for a physio of my expertise to wear. I actually remembered to clip on the shiny silver 'Silverwell Health Club' badge that said *Lucy Barton, Head Physiotherapist* on it, and made my way into work.

The first part of the morning was taken up with Mrs Barrett, full body massage to sort out her back problem. She really needs to lose a bit of weight, that would make a whole lot of difference to her back, but I'm not allowed to tell her that, yes, jelly babies are fattening and no, you shouldn't sit and eat three packets of them while you are waiting for your driver to arrive to take you the three hundred yards from your house to the shop to buy some more. Some people just don't help themselves and expect they can pay their way to good health.

She tips well though, so it's worth keeping my mouth shut and just getting on with rubbing away at the flabby rolls across her lumbar region. Sometimes it's much better to just smile and nod in the appropriate places.

But things got interesting very quickly when Will stuffed up big time. I had been taking my break, Sophie Kinsella's new book, '*Twenties girl*' was starting to get quite interesting and my cup of Earl Grey tea was almost at the perfect temperature to drink when he came running in and slammed the door behind him, barring it as if to stop anyone else from coming in after him. He looked a right mess. His hair was no longer in its neat little pony-tail, his usually snow-white Nikes were covered in mud and there was a large rip in the sleeve of his t shirt. It was quite shocking really. I don't think I've ever seen him so dishevelled. Anyway, he begged me to do him a huge favour so that he didn't get into trouble with Big Boss Helen.

I love Will to bits but he can be such a pain in the backside sometimes. I had to get all stern and severe with him to find out what had happened. He'd only been playing tonsil tennis in the gardening shed with that hunky Drew guy from room twenty-one when he should have been seeing to his own client. Helen would burst a valve if she found out and Will is already on his last warning. Apparently Cowbag Kelly from reception had decided to 'help out' by sending the client for a hot sauna followed by a cold swim while he waited for Will who was '*unavoidably detained*'. In her defence, this is called contrast therapy and is usually good for the muscles so it might have worked but silly Cowbag Kelly didn't know that the client had a muscle strain which was sent into spasm by the rapid change of temperature. Therefore, she's still a silly Cowbag and should stop trying to get ideas above her station.

She's a receptionist, not a physiotherapist. She should leave the physiotherapying to us.

Anyway, I eventually agreed to help him on the proviso of payment of a nice bottle of bubbly later (and I don't mean of the bath sort) and he introduced me to one of the most gorgeous men I have ever met. All muscley and rippley. Very yummy.

And he's rich too. Although he has to be to afford our prices.

I think he is going to be a much better prospect than Jake was. I mean, retail manager my arse! Being left in charge of a covered stall in the local flea market isn't quite what I would call retail manager status. And as for that 'trade fair' he took me on? There was I, expecting the whole shebang of champagne and canapes and all he wanted to do was get his hands on a million boxes of Tamagotchis! He reckoned he was going to sell them for a fiver each and make a killing. Beware Alan Sugar, Jake is out to take your crown in a major takeover bid with his animal keyrings. He gave me a pink one though. It matched my uniform, but how the hell are you supposed to keep those damn things alive? I mean, who has the time to remember to feed and walk a poxy plastic toy????

He reckoned I was too high maintenance for him. High maintenance? Me? Pah! He is just a no hoper, loser that doesn't stand a chance with me. I'm aiming so much higher than him.

Today is definitely my lucky day.

He said his name was Sam Lambert and he was a partner in that big architectural company in the town. Mistral Architectural Services. I've walked past it a few times, it's an amazing building, all glass and angles. Very smart. I could be a part of that.

Oh, the sight and feel of his skin under my fingers as I delved deep into his deltoids and rhomboids. The scent of his aftershave mingled with the oils that glistened in the flickering candlelight and I could just imagine the tight, smooth peaches of his buttocks that were hiding under the towel that snaked around his hips. It was just like being in heaven.

I know he liked me. He asked me for my number but Helen would go mad if she found out that I gave my private details to a paying customer. She says she's worried for our personal safety but I know it's not that. She's just a dried up old spinster who doesn't want us to have any fun. It's either that or she's afraid she's going to be done for running a knocking shop.

They all like me of course, it comes down to whether I like them and if they can afford me. I've learnt a lot since that Jake episode.

There is nothing in the rule book to say that Will can't help me out here and give him my number, accidently like. It doesn't have to be all guns blazing, you know, just drop a piece of paper in plain line of sight with my name and number scribbled across it in large capital letters so that it can't be missed. Something like that would do.

I'm going to make sure Will repays that favour by getting me a date with the delicious Sam Lambert.

I think Mr Lambert might be just perfect.

Chapter Fifty-Six

Lucy's Diary

Saturday 21st November 2009.

Will is most definitely the bestest best friend a girl can possibly have. I may not have got the bubbly that I asked for, although that's really not a surprise. He isn't exactly flush with money at the moment, so I guess I can let him off, but he has only gone and got me in contact with the delectable Sam Lambert.

Oh, I am so excited I can't stop jumping around the room and going

'squeeeee!!!!!!' I've no idea what the neighbours think but I really don't care either.

I've just had a phone call from Sam!

Apparently, he came into the Health club asking for another massage appointment with me on Saturday, but as it was my weekend off he had to see Jessica instead. Oh, I was so annoyed that she had been given him in my absence. It was that silly Cowbag Kelly sticking her nose in where it wasn't wanted again. I know she's got the hots for him herself, so I'll bet she stuck him with Jess just to get herself in with a chance instead of me. It would have been so easy to move my appointments around on Monday to slot him in there somewhere, but no. Apparently, I was fully booked for the whole week.

Lying little Cowbag!

Of course, I'd have been able to slot him in.

Anyway. As he was leaving, Sam booked another exercise session for Wednesday evening with Will and, when he turned up, he was asking all these questions about me. Will couldn't wait to phone me when he clocked off work to let me in on all the gory details. Sam was asking what I was like, what did I do with my spare time, what did I like to eat, where did I like to go and, best of all, whether I was single or dating. Crikey, even if I were still dating Jake there would be no competition there. Jake would be out of that door quick smart cos Sam is so much better than he is.

Of course, Will said I was the greatest girl in the whole wide world and Sam would be a fool to let me slip through his fingers. There was the slight problem about the giving of my private number to strangers and clients, but Will got around that by deciding that Sam wasn't really a stranger anymore as he had been a valued client for so long he was just like a friend really, and he couldn't help it if he had a piece of paper on his desk with my name and number on it in plain view of anybody who cared to look. Will said he had taken Sam over to the desk after the session on the pretence of checking that all his personal details were up to date and made sure that the sheet of paper couldn't be missed. He even made a show of picking it up and putting it down again, all but waving it under Sam's nose. He said he'd done a massive fist pump after Sam left and the paper had vanished with him.

This afternoon, my phone rang with an unknown number. I don't normally answer them, I wait until they leave a message and then call them back if I need to, but after my conversation with Will I decided to be brave and see who it was.

Sam's voice sounded deep and husky as I listened to him introducing himself and asking if I minded him calling me. He is so polite! Jake didn't ask me that when he first phoned me, that was more of a 'Hi Babe, how you doin'?'. I think he was channelling his inner Joey cool character. It was funny at the time, but now it just seems so corny compared to Sam's sophisticated approach.

I played it cool though. Put on my posh, work voice and made sure that I didn't swear even once. 'Of course I don't mind you calling, Sam,' I said. He then apologised for pinching my phone number from Will's desk and he hoped I wouldn't get Will into trouble for it. See, such a gentleman. I assured him that no, it was fine, and I would make sure that Helen didn't find out.

If she does ask, I'll blame it on Cowbag Kelly...

He then asked if I wouldn't mind accompanying him to Pareusi's for a meal one evening. He said he would understand if the answer was no as I didn't know him very well, but he would be honoured if I would allow him to entertain me at the restaurant. He thought we'd got on so well when I sorted out his shoulder that he just knew we would have a wonderful evening.

I played it cool. I ummed and aahed for a bit as I didn't want to seem too eager, but I didn't keep him waiting for very long. I couldn't risk him finishing the call and ending up with nothing could I! So, I agreed, and we have a date booked for tomorrow evening. I mean, he can get into Pareusi's on one night's notice. That's so unheard of. He's even coming to collect me in his car with his driver. He had laughed as he said that I would be perfectly safe as Brian would act as a chaperone.

That means I have just one day to sort out my hair and defuzz everywhere and find something absolutely drop dead gorgeous to wear and I'll have to make sure it doesn't look like I've made too much of an effort. Although this is Pareusi's we're talking about. Is it possible to not make an effort when you're going there?

I'll phone Will and get him over here to give me a hand. He is so good at knowing what to wear to these places. Beats me how he does though, he certainly can't afford to go there by himself.

I'll bet Drew took him. He's got a few pennies tucked away.

Chapter Fifty-Seven

Lucy's Diary

Sunday 22nd November 2009

Oh my, that was just absolutely amazing!

What a night!

What a place!

And oh, What a hunk of a man!

I am so much definitely and awesomely in love!!!!! If I were living in the 1600's I swear I would just swoon, fan fluttering delicately in my hand, with the sheer pleasure that has been this evening. And I would say something like,

'Oh, heaven above. Mr Lambert is such a lovely gentleman. I wonder whether he shall call on me again?'

Sam is perfection.

. . .

Will had raced round to my flat as soon as I told him that the date was on and he helped me pick out a cute little black trouser suit with an electric blue satin camisole top underneath. I felt so sexy in it as the short boxy jacket cinched in at the waist, making the most of my cleavage. I'd thought about having plastic surgery to get them enhanced, but I wasn't brave enough. Also, I couldn't afford it anyway, but it's amazing what a good bra and a cinched in waist can do to a girl's self-esteem. Especially with sky high stilettos. Under Will's watchful eye, I kept my make-up neutral and I was glad that I had been to the hairdresser only last week to have my blonde roots done and the pixie cut put back to its rightful length. When Victoria Beckham had her hair cut this way last year, I had to get it done as well and I totally love it. So stylish.

His driver arrived at seven pm on the dot. I was hiding behind the curtain, trying not to make it twitch in my excitement and saw that Sam was sat in the back. Getting out of the car, he smoothed down his grey suit jacket, adjusted the bunch of flowers that was in his hand and walked up the path towards my block of flats. I saw him sidestep next door's overflowing bins and hoped that he didn't turn around in disgust thinking they were mine, but he didn't. He kept on walking, actually, I think he might have even been nearly skipping, and then I heard the doorbell ring. Not wanting him to think I had been waiting for him, I didn't want to answer the door immediately, so I went to stand behind it, counted to thirty, I might have sped up a bit for the last ten, and then turned the handle, opening the door and smiling brightly.

He smiled as he saw me and held out a bunch of carnations. I know he gave me that cheeky once over that all men think they get away with, but they never do. Shame really that they don't realise we secretly love it when they do that, when they give away their smile of approval they thought they were hiding so well. I could just imagine him thinking 'cha ching' as his eyes swept from my feet to the top of my head. Although that's probably more what

Jake would have thought. Sam would never be so crass, he would have been thinking something much more along the lines of,

'What a gorgeous woman she is.'

Yep, that's definitely what Sam would have thought.

After I had said how gorgeous the flowers were and how did he know they were my favourites? We exchanged pleasantries and he told me how lovely I looked. He held out his arm to escort me to his car. His driver held the door open for me and as I slid into the seat, putting my clutch bag onto my lap, Sam walked around the car to get in the other side. The driver closed the door quietly and I resisted the urge to look back at my neighbour's window. I was sure I had seen the curtains twitch as I walked down the path and skirted the bins. I knew that if I looked at them then I would poke my tongue out in a most unladylike way so I turned myself away from the window, licked my lips before flashing Sam a sexy smile, and asked him how his day had been as the car picked up speed and headed for the restaurant.

The driver held the door open for me again when we arrived. Sam even stopped to thank him and said he would call when we were ready to go home again.

The driver nodded, returned to the driving seat and drove away.

I've never been to Pareusi's before. It's always been well out of my price range. I could get used to it though. The Maître d' called Sam, "Mr Lambert" and he led us to our table himself. We were in a little section at the back of the room, next to the roaring log fire and away from any prying eyes. Not that I would have minded being noticed that much, but it was nice to be alone with him. The waiters were so attentive. Nothing was too much trouble and as soon as the champagne bottle was empty, another one appeared. Sam did that bottle upside down in the silver bucket thing you see on the telly. I never realised it actually happened in real life. It was so cool!

He was attentive too. He asked all about me and was really interested in my life. I even told him about my parents. Well, Mum anyway. As Dad was a total waste of space and never actually around while I was growing up, he doesn't deserve the breath it takes to talk about him. I glossed over him, and my sister, Rebecca. Instead I told him how hard mum had battled with cancer before she died. I never tell anyone about mum, especially someone I barely know. Sam was different though. He understood.

He actually cared.

He also told me about himself. His mum and dad live in Trecase and he sees them whenever he can. He seems quite close to them, although as an only child I guess he would be. No sibling rivalry there. Or falling out over wills. He made me laugh with his antics as a kid though. He got away with murder with his mum. One time, she was out shouting for him for ages while he was hiding in the apple tree outside the back door. When they finally spotted him - a fit of coughing gave him away - he told them he'd been looking for the cat and he couldn't get down again, so his dad had to get the ladder and climb up to get him. Just as they got back onto the ground, the cat came around the corner of the house and meowed at them all. He got sent to his room and grounded for a week for that, but his mum had relented after an hour because he said he was sorry. I can just see his mischievous face, legs in tailored shorts with moss stains on them from climbing in the tree. Bet he had a flat cap like *Just William* did as well. Oh, he would have been so cute. I'd have let him off as well.

The food was cooked to perfection. Not a lot of it on the plate, but it looked really pretty. No runny gravy just sloshed over the top like they do at *The Notoriety*.

I had such a good time. I don't think I've ever met a man so attentive to my every need. Who cared so much that I was enjoying myself.

We had our liqueur coffees as the fire died down to flickering embers. I pointed out the fairies at the back of the fireplace, clinging to the soot before whooshing up the chimney. I said they were watching us for Santa and they were going to tell him that we had been ever so good so he would bring us what we asked for at Christmas. Sam had looked at me a bit weird when I said that, but I explained that mum had always told us that when we were children. He'd smiled then, reaching across the table to hold my hand. It felt so nice. Soft and smooth. Warm and comforting as it settled around mine. I didn't draw mine away. I left it there and smiled back at him, slightly embarrassed at having said that. It was a silly thing to say really. Childish. Not adult and sophisticated like I should have been. But he was lovely, said he thought it was sweet and he wished his parents had said things like that to him.

He slid his arm gently around my waist as he guided me towards the door. Nothing improper, no cheeky bum squeezes like Jake did on our first date. Just a gentle pressure so I knew he was there to protect me. It felt really nice. There was no grabbing me in the back of the car either. He just rested his hand on mine and continued chatting all the way home. I didn't know what to expect when we got there. I mean, was I supposed to ask him in? Would that have been the right thing to do? I didn't want him to think I was easy, but I didn't want to lose him either.

Did I say he was a gentleman? Oh, he most definitely is. He led me to the door, said he wouldn't come in as we both had work the next morning, but he would love to see me again.

He leant in and brushed his lips across mine, his hand smoothed across my cheek as he turned and walked down the path. When he got to the gate, he looked back and waved. I waved back before unlocking the door and walking into the flat.

I don't think I'm going to sleep tonight, I'm far too happy to allow this evening to end.

Chapter Fifty-Eight

Lucy's Diary
Thursday 17th December 2009.

The last few weeks have been absolutely amazing!

Sam and I, oh that sounds so good; Sam and I have been out loads of times. He is so attentive and says that he hates it when I'm not around. Isn't that just the sweetest?

Of course, we are a 'proper' couple now. I know it's been barely a month since our first date but holding out for just a week was hard enough. And it feels so right for us to snuggle up to each other in bed. He's so masterful as well, and passionate. Boy, is he passionate! He totally takes my breath away. Last weekend we barely made it out of the bedroom for the whole two days!

Will laughed when I went into work on Monday with the biggest smile on my face. Said I looked like I'd not only had the cat's cream but all of the dog's bones as well, with plenty of meat on them. He'd given me that cheeky wink he did as he said it so I knew damn well what he was hinting at. It was funny though.

Only he can get away with stuff like that with me, and he knows it.

He's well made up that Sam and I are together. Started calling himself my cupid's arrow and taking all of the credit for our happiness. I nipped out in my lunch hour and bought some of those fairy wings you can get for kids dress ups and gave them to him. The idiot only went prancing off onto the bus at the end of the day wearing them, it was so funny. The other passengers didn't quite know what to make of him and the bus driver's face was an absolute picture while he was checking Will's ticket. I think he was trying not to laugh, but he wasn't succeeding.

Sam's house is perfect. Much better than my poky one room flat. I guess being an architect, he should live in a nice place, but it surprised me that this wasn't the same type of glass box as his offices are. He bought himself an old farmhouse called Karadow in the middle of nowhere and updated it to suit him. Apparently 'Karadow' means 'beloved' in Cornish, he renamed it when he moved in because he loved it so much. When he took me on a tour of it, he said how he had knocked down several internal walls to make the rooms bigger and more suitable for social occasions and it did look lovely. The kitchen was part of the dining area and then it just flowed into a large lounge area and vestibule. I've never been in a house that had a vestibule before. If I'm honest, I'd never even heard of a vestibule before, but that's what Sam called it so it must be right. There is a very ornate newel post at the bottom of the stairs as well. I went to hang my coat on it the first time we went there and Sam took it from me and hung it in the closet instead. See, he's just so thoughtful. His house is very manly though. I'll have to start putting a bit of a feminine touch into it, a few cushions and stuff to break down all that magnolia paint, but I can do that once I move in.

He's not asked me to move in yet, but I know he will. We are virtually inseparable and he hates staying at mine so it makes sense for me to be at his really.

He invited his friends Carl and Rhea over for a meal last night. It was just the four of us and he had hired a catering company so we didn't even have to cook or serve. Or wash the dishes afterwards either. It was a lovely evening where we could talk and relax with a few drinks. Carl is a property developer and Rhea stays at home to look after their utterly gorgeous two-year-old son, Josh. They have a nanny for him as well. Rhea showed me the photo she had on the screensaver on her phone, he has the most beautiful blonde curls and a beaming smile. In the photo he is in her arms and Carl is stood the other side with his arm around them both. Rhea said they were laughing at Josh trying to say the word biscuit but he could only say "bidit" instead. Carl said they'd better not let him loose on eBay.

They make such a lovely family; I hope Sam and I are like that.

I liked Rhea, she was bubbly and fun. Carl couldn't take his eyes off her and I'm sure they were in for an all-night session when they got home. He swung his arm around her shoulders as they left and placed a kiss on the side of her neck. She laughed and batted him off, but I know the signs.

Sam and I certainly made good use of his king-sized bed after they'd gone. He'd sent the help home and put his arms around me as I leant against the worktop, kissing me long and slow before his lips became harder and more forceful. Of course, I was turned on. I've hardly been turned off for the last fortnight so when he turned and picked up the bottle of champagne and a couple of glasses, gave me that suggestive smile that he does just for me, inclined his head towards the stairs and raised his arm to lead the way. I couldn't get up to that bedroom fast enough. It was quite a while before we actually drank any of the bubbles.

It was a delicious dessert though.

Chapter Fifty-Nine

Penny-May

Tuesday June 16th 2015

I love Rhea. She is such a natural mother and has always been so friendly to me. It would have been so easy for her to ignore me and even hate me for trying to take Lucy's place in Sam's heart. And hers. But she never showed any signs of resenting me for being here.

I can just see her and Carl now with a baby Josh. I never knew him at that age, but he's adorable now so he would have been even more so then.

And Lucy is so much in love with Sam. I'm not sure I've ever seen him look at me quite the way she describes his look to her. It must have been love at first sight.

I couldn't help the tear that fell down my cheek and slowly wiped it away with the bunched up tissue I held in my hand.

I looked at it with contempt and threw it into the wastepaper basket. Lucy wouldn't have been sitting here in sloppy joggers, a damp, balled up and ripped soggy tissue in her hand. She would be dressed properly in her Harvey Nic's finest. Fully laundered and ironed handkerchief at hand, ready to place on the end of her pert and cute nose to stop the slightest sniffle should it occur.

And if she was caught out without one? Then she would laugh it off and everyone would adore her for her dotty ways.

Unlike me, and my imperfect, laughable attempt at being anything even remotely as good as her.

Chapter Sixty

Lucy's Diary

Saturday 26th December 2009.

Boxing Day.

I have been spoilt. Christmas was just plain awesome!

The Health Club closed at lunchtime on Thursday which was Christmas Eve and doesn't reopen again until Monday so I'm going to have almost a whole week off. I'm going to spend all of that time with Sam as he has closed Mistral for the whole of the Christmas period. Said that people aren't interested in planning and building new houses during the festive period so he always gives all his staff the whole ten days off so they can spend time with their families and come back in January all refreshed and raring to go.

Will and I went for a quick lunch when we closed up. We exchanged our presents to each other and I gave him a massive hug for giving me a bottle of my favourite perfume, Live by Jennifer Lopez. Actually, I've never really known how to pronounce it. Live as in 'it's alive' or Live as in 'live in a house'?

Whatever it is, it's a gorgeous scent and I love him forever for buying me the biggest bottle they do. I bought him a lovely cashmere scarf which he immediately wrapped around his neck and told me it was perfect for his date with Drew next week. Things seem to be going well between them two, they have progressed from playing tonsil tennis in the shed to a much less risky spending the weekend together in Will's flat. I don't think it will be long before Drew looks to move down here permanently and they get a much nicer flat together. They make such a cute couple.

Sam picked me up after we had finished, he even had his driver drop Will to his home on the way to Karadow as it was on his way. As Will got out of the car, Sam gave him a wrapped present as well. It looked like an expensive watch box but I didn't get a close look at it. I asked Sam what it was but he just laughed and said it was nothing, Will had earned it for introducing him to me. Brian was given the weekend off as well once we had got back. Sam is so thoughtful. Said for Brian to go home and relax, he wouldn't be needed again until at least Monday.

After our evening meal, we cuddled up on the sofa, the log fire slowly burning to embers. Sam gave me a piece of paper and a pen and told me to write down what I wanted for Christmas on it. At first I didn't know what he was on about but I did it anyway and then folded it in half. He gently took it from me and moved over to the fire where he told me to make a wish as he sent it up the chimney with the fairy embers, just like mum used to do for me when I was a child. His compassion took me so much by surprise that I started cry and he held me tight as I said how much I missed her and my sister. It has been so hard not having any family to turn to, I've only really had Will for the last couple of years. Sam said that I didn't have to worry about that anymore, he was my family now and he wasn't ever going to let me go.

It was so romantic with the log fire crackling, casting dancing shadows across the walls as the warmth radiated around us, cocooning us in its embrace making me feel even more secure as I snuggled further into Sam's arms. We made love in front of the fire that night. Not the usual hot, fiery passion that engulfs us and doesn't let go until we are totally satiated, but a slower, more sensual experience where we drank long and deep from each other's bodies. We became intoxicated on each other's taste and smell, each curve and nuance explored and appreciated, each moment savoured and recorded to replay again over and over in our minds.

Afterwards, he told me he loved me.

And that I would always be his.

That means he will always be mine too.

I love that idea.

Christmas Day we woke early and drank Bucks Fizz out of crystal flute glasses while we wrestled with the fresh turkey that Sam insisted we had. He said it wouldn't be a proper Christmas without a real turkey and we managed to get it into the oven without too many mishaps. I used the steamer to get all the veg done. Sam wasn't too keen on the washing up though, said he was too full to be doing any housework, but I soon got the dishwasher going and everywhere spick and span. It was funny when I opened the oven and found the parsnips still in there. Sam had laughed and said it didn't matter, he didn't like parsnips anyway!

He gave me my Christmas presents after lunch was all finished. He'd been teasing me with them all morning, pointing them out under the tree but not letting me poke and prod them. Said it would spoil the surprises if I was allowed to try and guess what they were. They were beautifully gift wrapped, he did admit that he hadn't done the wrapping, he'd got Kate - his PA - to do that, and to help him to choose what to buy me. I don't mind that, it's nice that he was so determined to get the right things for me that he asked for somebody else's help. There was the softest pale pink lambswool jumper, a Mulberry Bayswater handbag in beige. It was huge and definitely the real thing because it had the lock on it. I can fit all my bits and bobs in there no trouble. He even gave me a matching purse for it. Then there was this little oblong box that he was keeping for last. When I opened it, I couldn't believe what I was seeing. There was the most exquisite gold necklace with a single diamond drop pendant on it and a matching pair of earrings which dropped to just above my shoulder, each finishing in another single diamond. They were so beautiful. I've never received such expensive jewellery before.

I said it was too much, I couldn't wear them because I might lose them or break them, but he had smiled and told me not to be so silly and he had taken the necklace from the box and carefully fastened it, kissing the nape of my neck once he had done so. It was perfect.

I was a bit embarrassed then about the presents I had bought for him. They seemed so cheap in comparison to what he had spent on me. I had spent ages in Mark's picking out a jumper and I'd got him a bottle of the aftershave I knew he liked as I had taken note of the bottle of Aramis on his chest of drawers. I did like that smell; it was so him. All dark and woody, so sexy.

He said they were perfect of course. He would because he knows I don't earn very much money, especially compared to him. But I do wish I could have bought him something better. More expensive to show how much I loved him. I made it up to him later though with an extra special massage, where I massaged absolutely everywhere. Very slowly so that he could enjoy every second of it.

Chapter Sixty-One

Lucy's Diary

Sunday January 3rd 2010.

The flat is still the same as when I left it. Although there is a bit more dust everywhere and it needs hoovering. I don't think I feel like doing that today though, it is such a downer to be back here after the last week or so at Sam's. We just fit so right together and it all seems too good to be true. But I guess real life has to come back into play some time. I wish Christmas could last forever though, it was so heavenly just Sam and I in our own little cocoon. Our beloved Karadow love nest.

But it's work tomorrow. Sam has to be at Mistral early to pick up on some architect type stuff that needs sorting out, he did tell me but I can't remember the actual details. It was all about load bearings and planning permissions, that sort of thing. He spent ages on the phone last night to Kate, telling her what he needed for his first meeting in the morning. He said the meeting is at eight so goodness knows what time she is going to have to start work.

Although, she has had the whole of Christmas off so she can't complain.

Actually, he spent so much time on the phone that we were late for our meal at Pareusi's. Sam said we had to have a special night out as it was going to be the last evening of our holiday. It wasn't a problem though. Brian waited patiently for us to be ready and the waiting staff were just as attentive as always. I bet if it had just been me that was late, the table would have been given to someone else. That's the power that Sam has. Everyone accepts everything he does without question. He's an important man and therefore he can't be punished for being late or asking his workers to do more for him. If it weren't for him, they wouldn't get paid, so they have to do what he says. They must like it though or else they wouldn't stay. From what I've seen, he's a brilliant boss. I mean, fancy giving the whole team the whole Christmas off? And he phoned Silverwell to persuade Helen to give me the same amount of time off. Said he would pay them for the extra holiday I would need and he was sure that they wouldn't be inconvenienced that much by me having the time off.

Helen was like a big dollop of putty, all soft and simpery.

See, that's what money can do. That's what I never had growing up. That's why I'm aiming so much higher than the likes of Jake. I'm never going to be poor again. Work is going to be such a pain tomorrow.

Chapter Sixty-Two

LUCY'S DIARY

Monday February 15th 2010.

OMG! OMG! OMG! OMG! OMG! OMG! OH MY ABSOLUTELY,

FLABBERGASTINGLY, I CAN'T BELIEVE THIS HAPPENED TO ME, OH MY FLIPPING GOD!!!!

I am only engaged to be married to Sam Lambert!!!

I can't believe this, it's all happened so fast. We've only been together for three months!!!!

Obviously, yesterday was Valentine's Day and there was no way Sam was going to let it go with just a bunch of red roses. He'd told me to pack a weekend bag and my passport as he was whisking me to Paris for a couple of days. I was supposed to be working, but Sam worked his magic on Helen again and it was sorted. Will was well jel, him and Drew were going to spend a quiet weekend together in Devon. Drew's parents live there and Will was going to meet them for lunch on Saturday for the first time. He was bricking it but it's good that they are getting on so well. I don't feel quite so guilty spending all my time with Sam knowing that Will is all loved up as well. Maybe we could have a double wedding at this rate?

We flew on Saturday morning, business class of course and stayed in a private suite at the *George V Paris.* Oh, it was gorgeous there, gold counterpanes on the beds, room service, and a whole suite to ourselves. A one room travel lodge with a tiny ensuite and piddly plastic pots of UHT milk that you need two of to make a half drinkable cup of tea, this most certainly was not. I mean, it wasn't just a bedroom, with a bed so big it had three sets of pillows all lying side by side in front of the headboard. It had a lounge as well, and a balcony and a massive bathroom with two separate sinks. I've never been anywhere that had his and hers sinks before. The bath as well, oh that bath was just amazing, large enough to fit both of us and standing centrally in the room. We definitely made good use of that when we arrived, complete with the bottle of chilled French champagne that was waiting for us.

We ate in the restaurant that evening. I love it at Pareusi's, but this was something else entirely. Everything was so ornate and immaculate. It was so French. Sam even spoke in fluent French when he was speaking to the waiter. I felt so silly as I couldn't read anything on the menu, but Sam had said it was sweet, he's going to make sure I get some lessons when we get home so I can order for myself in future. He explained all the offerings on the menu and then suggested I have the escargots. When he told me they were snails and I said there was no way I could ever eat slimy things like that, he laughed and said he was only teasing. In the end, he ordered Coq au vin for both of us and it was absolutely delicious.

We went for a walk along the Champs Elysée after we had eaten. It was all lit up and looked like a fairy playground, all sparkly and twinkly. It was cold though, so Sam cuddled me close and we tried to make smoke rings out of our breath as we walked. He was much better at it than I was. I challenged him to make a love heart but he wasn't good enough to do that as well. Just as well really, I'd have never been allowed to forget it if he had achieved it.

That bed was ever so comfy, I've never slept in a bed so big. Or had so much fun in one. It's amazing what a difference it makes when you're not thinking about falling off the edge of it.

I woke up yesterday, Valentine's Day, to knocking on the outer door. Sam was already up and, dressed in a hotel robe, answered it to let in the waiter with our breakfast. A full French breakfast, fresh croissants, butter and jam and lots of freshly brewed coffee. Sam had even remembered that I don't drink much coffee and he delighted in showing me that he had ordered my favourite Earl Grey tea. It seems you could get anything you want in this hotel.

After breakfast we went outside and Sam had arranged for a horse and carriage to be waiting for us to take us on a tour of the city. We even had blankets to keep us nice and warm as we rode. I don't think Sam quite expected the horse to take a dump halfway round the tour if the look on his face was anything to go by. I poked fun at him for it, I mean, what horse doesn't do that? Him being a Country boy should have been used to it. He said it had ruined the moment; he'd wanted it to be perfect. I reached up and kissed him on the lips and told him that it was perfect, the horse taking a dump just added to the memories and then Sam seemed a bit happier as he snuggled me close again.

The tour ended at the Eiffel Tower and we had a table booked in the Michelin starred *Restaurant Le Jules Verne* on the second floor. The view was exquisite once we got to the top. We could see for miles. The weak winter sunshine was struggling to break its way through the clouds, but when it did succeed, it was awesome. I half expected Sam to say he had organised the weather as well, but I think that might be beyond even his control. Maybe God is smiling on us though, telling us this is the right thing to do.

Or mum is.

After our dessert of profiteroles (I didn't like to tell Sam that they should have had a dollop of clotted cream on them) he put his hand in his pocket and pulled out a very tiny box. It was covered in velvet and looked like it opened in the middle. I held my breath, it was so surreal as Sam slowly opened the box to reveal a ring with one glittering, solitary diamond on a gold band.

'Lucy,' he said, 'I love you so much, will you please do me the honour of being my wife?'

I was speechless, he looked so open, I saw his face start to fall as I hesitated,

'I'm sorry,' he said, starting to close the box, 'it's too soon isn't it?'

I reached out and grabbed his hands, 'No, I mean, yes, I mean no, I'm shocked that's all, it's not too soon, I love you so much too. Yes, of course I will marry you!'

He pulled the ring out of the box and placed it on the third finger of my left my hand, before raising it and kissing it tenderly to seal its place.

'This is the Vena amoris, the vein that leads straight to the heart,' he said.

I leaned across the table and kissed him on his lips.

'You are my heart,' I said.

We flew back this morning,; I couldn't stop looking at my ring all the way home. It feels so strange on my hand, its weight heavy with every movement I make, but I'm loving being reminded every time that Sam Lambert is going to marry me. I'm going to be called Lucy Lambert. It sounds much better than Lucy Barton, more sophisticated and grown up.

Lucy Lambert.

Lucy Lambert.

Lucy Lambert.

. . .

I'm going to be Sam Lambert's wife.

When Brian brought us here from the airport, Sam walked me into the flat and he took a glance around at my tiny flat and the contents of it. A couple of pieces that I had managed to get from home before my sister barred me from the house and took everything else for herself and the rest was stuff that I had managed to pick up in charity shops. He said that it wouldn't take long for me to pack, I wouldn't need very much as his house was fully furnished so I could ditch all of the furniture, just bring my clothes and personal bits and pieces.

He's right of course, Mum's old rug and armchair would look ridiculous in his farmhouse amongst all the new white modern furniture he has there.

And this is a new life for me. A new start.

I'm going to be Mrs Lucy Lambert.

And I'm moving in tomorrow.

SQUEEEEE!!!!!

Chapter Sixty-Three

Penny-May

Tuesday June 16th 2015

I looked at the clock on the wall, I had been so engrossed in what I was reading that I hadn't noticed the time moving forward. They sounded so happy and so much in love. I knew that if she had still been alive then I wouldn't have stood a chance with him, their engagement told me that. He went to so much trouble. My hand went to my own ring finger, twiddling my engagement and wedding rings around. Our engagement had been magical too, even if not quite on the same scale as theirs had been. He was certainly one for quick proposals though. The phrase 'marry in haste, repent at leisure' sprang to mind but I pushed the thought away. Look at how Sam and Lucy had been together, the fault had to be mine, I pushed him to it because I wasn't as perfect as she was.

I would have to change.

That thought didn't help me with my situation with Daniel

though, he still needed me and I needed to be there with him. Trusting that Sam would think I was too poorly to go anywhere, which I probably was judging by how much pain my ribs were in, I was sure I still had time to get to the hospital and back before Sam knew I had gone.

I had no money for a taxi, and I couldn't ask Brian to help. My only hope was Rhea.

She arrived within half an hour of my phone call. It had taken me ages to get ready, I was wearing so much make up to hide my swollen face, but it didn't fool her.

'Oh my God, what happened to you?' She asked as she walked into the kitchen while I was gingerly making my way down the stairs. She came across and took my elbow, guiding me to a chair.

'I'm just too clumsy,' I said, 'I'd left my phone downstairs and when it rang, I thought it must have been about Daniel. I ran too fast and tumbled all the way down.' I couldn't look at her while I spoke, 'Does it look that bad?'

'It looks horrendous, you poor love. Did Sam take you to the hospital?'

'No, I asked him not to, I'm sure I'm fine, just a bit battered and bruised.'

'Well, we'll get you looked at while we're there.'

'Honestly, no, I don't want to be any bother, I just want to see how Dan is.

Please, can we just go and see him? I need to be back before Sam gets home.'

'He needs to do something about those stairs if you ask me,' Rhea said, shaking her head and refusing to say anymore. She got my coat and led me to the car, locking the door behind us with my keys.

. . .

We were quiet for the half hour journey to Treliske. I was trying not to cry in pain every time she drove over a pothole, she appeared lost in her own thoughts as she whisked her way around the tight corners and through the narrow Cornish roads. Pirate FM played on the radio and the slight rain spattered on the windshield, just enough to make the windscreen wipers squeak as they forced their way across the glass.

'I'll drop you at the entrance and then go and find a parking space, you don't want to be walking any further than you have to.'

I smiled at her, 'Thank you, that's kind of you.'

'Hmm, I'll come find you when I'm done.'

I made my way to the ward and approached the main desk.

'Can you tell me where Daniel Meares is please? I'm his sister.'

'Oh, he's been asking for you, I'll take you over,' the nurse replied. I could see her glancing at me as we walked but I ignored her look, steadfastly concentrating on how my brother would be.

She led me into a small side room and pointed towards the bed where Daniel was sat, pale and listless but awake and watching a film on the bedside tv. An intravenous drip stood next to the bed and fed fluid into Daniel's arm. Joe in the armchair, head nodding onto his chest and sleeping soundly. 'He's much better this afternoon, I'll leave you to it.' With another glance in my direction, she left the room.

'Hey Hulk, how you doing? You had us worried there for a while.'

Daniel looked at me and I went over to the bed, bending over to kiss him on the forehead. 'Where Penny-May been?'

'I was at home. I came last night but you were very poorly. I'm here now as well and you are looking much better.'

'Me ok, Joe got me chocolate. What matter Penny-May face?'

My hand reached up to touch my cheek. 'Oh, it's nothing, I'll be fine in a few days. What are you watching?'

Daniel started to reply when a spasm of coughing hit him, the little bit of brightness he'd gained vanished in a flash as he struggled to regain control of his breathing. Joe woke with a start and leapt to his feet, 'Hey man, take it easy,' he said, smoothing his hand behind Daniel's back and helping him into a sitting position until the outburst stopped. I tried to help from my side but the pain in my ribs made me wince and stopped me from taking any of Daniel's weight.

'Have you been here all the time?' I asked him. 'Please tell me you've been home.'

'I did go home last night; the nurses kicked me out and said there was nothing I could do. I came back this morning though, I wanted to see how he is. I'm sorry I fell asleep, that's not very professional.'

'It doesn't matter about that, it's great that you came in, you didn't have to.' 'I know, but he's a bit special.'

I smiled and reached out to hold Daniel's hand. 'You don't have to tell me that.'

'Looks like you shouldn't have come in either. What happened to you?'

'Oh, nothing, I fell down the stairs running for the phone. Silly old clumsy me.' I turned and walked to the window where the world was continuing to turn as normal. 'You can take a break if you like, I'll be here for an hour or so before I have to go home.'

'Ok, I'll come back and see how he is this evening. See you later, Mate,' he waved and as he reached the door, he stood aside to let Rhea come in, armed with magazines, sweets, drinks, comics and some felt tip pens.

'Thought I'd bring some refreshments and stuff to do. It can be so boring in these places. You should be sat down,' she said, looking at me sternly and emptying her arms onto the bed.

Daniel made a grab for a can of cola. 'Me thirsty, me like coke.'

'Thanks Rhea, I truly appreciate you being here.'

She sat in the other chair, picked up the edition of Hello magazine and opened the first page, 'Hey, I'd be doing this at home anyway, here I can pretend I'm reading while I'm really checking out the eye candy.' She winked as she indicated a doctor who was just walking past the open door. 'Now, keep an eye on the time, we don't you getting home late.'

Chapter Sixty-Four

LUCY'S DIARY

Sunday 18th April 2010

Everything is so busy! We've set the date for Saturday May 1st. May day.

It's always a special day down here, the end of Winter and the beginning of Spring. A rebirth, the ancient pagan rite of fertility. Of course, most people will be in Padstow dancing around the 'obby 'oss, I've done it myself a few times, great excuse for a knees up and a few drinks. The atmosphere is amazing. Sam thought it would be symbolic to celebrate our nuptials on such an auspicious day. And with most of the tourists away at Padstow, we'll have Trecase to ourselves for once.

It's going to be a Church wedding of course. Sam wouldn't even hear of going to a registry office. He said we're only going to do this once, so it had to be done properly. His mum is so excited. I reckon she's more excited than I am. When we first met, she was a bit stand offish, I thought she was a right snob actually, but she seems to have accepted me now. I think she just didn't want anyone taking her Sam away from her, but I would never do that. I know how important mums are. I know mine would love to be here. She would have cried when she saw me trying on dresses at Belle's Belles. We could have spent the whole day dress shopping, and colour choosing.

Mum always laughed at people wearing hats. She would have had a fascinator instead. I know she would. It would have a big feather on it, that she could tickle people's nose's with as she walked past them. She was a right shortie so she could get away with doing stuff like that. Maggie will wear a hat. I haven't seen it, but she is the type. It's the 'proper' thing to wear a hat so she will definitely get one.

Will has been brilliant at helping me out. Him and Drew took me shopping for the day and we found the perfect dress for me really quickly. It was a bit of a disappointment really, because I was looking forward to trying on lots and lots of dresses, but once I had found that one, it didn't seem right to be trying on any others.

I'm going to have a veil as well. I know I'm not exactly pure and innocent, but I want that moment when Sam lifts it and gazes into my eyes at the altar. It's going to be magical.

Will is giving me away and Rhea is going to be my chief bridesmaid with little Josh as the most delightful pageboy. Carl will be Sam's best man. I'd love a little flower girl as well, but there's no way I can ask my niece to do it. Amelia's five now and would look adorable in a snow-white dress with a yellow plaid sash. That's our colour scheme, the colours of the Cornish tartan. The men are all wearing the Cornish kilts as well. It's Sam's idea. Because of the Mayday thing. Will's not too happy about it, said it's just as well he's not Scottish because there's no way he's going commando under it. Drew on the other hand is quite looking forward to wearing one in his role as chief usher. Said a bit of breeze is good for the soul and he can't wait to get Will alone in them afterwards, easy access he reckoned. I think that was a bit too much information for me!

The reception is going to be in a marquee in the grounds of our farmhouse. Our farmhouse. Still can't get used to calling it that. Sam has pulled in loads of favours to get the wedding and reception organised so quickly. It's amazing what having money can achieve.

It was my hen do last night. Will organised it. Well, he is my best friend in the whole world, so I couldn't have a hen do without him. My secrets have always been safe with him anyway, as his have been with me.

He'd got all these feather boas, feather trimmed cowboy hats and hen do badges from *eBay*, he'd even managed to get bright pink t-shirts printed up saying 'who let the hens out?' Sam had laughed when he read them, said he wished he could go so that he could keep an eye on us as we looked like we were going to get into trouble dressed like that. I promised him I'd be good and that Will and Rhea would look after me. Besides, Sam hired a minibus for the night and Brian was driving us. Brian would never let us get into trouble.

We started at *The Notoriety*. It really doesn't live up to its name, it's not that indecent at all. But the drinks are cheap so it's always a good place to go for pre-drinks. And they do 2-4-1s before 9 o'clock. Absolute bonus. They had a disco too, so we all had a dance to warm us up before we moved onto *The Night Club*. I've always thought it a weird name for a club, I mean, it's not very imaginative is it? Still, at least it says what it is I guess?

Will and Rhea did this amazing jive routine, I always knew that Will was a bit of a mover on the dance floor, but Rhea surprised me. I've met her a few times now with her husband and always got on with her, but last night she was really out to party. I suppose with a two-year-old she doesn't get a chance to go out on her own very much so she was making the most of it.

The girls from work came as well. I thought Helen would be really stuffy and standoffish like she is in work, but she started the evening by saying that she wasn't the boss tonight and what happened on the hen do stayed on the hen do. I'm thinking she doesn't want the story of her trying to snog the DJ getting around the health club. He was quite a hunk though. She has good taste. Although he wasn't having any of it, so I guess he does too.

Cowbag Kelly made me laugh. She was stuck up and snooty all night, kept whispering with Jessica and looking at me as if she wanted me to drop down dead. I know she's jealous of me and Sam. I just kept dancing past her and waving my 'I'm the bride' flag around. Well, if she can't be happy for me then she shouldn't have come with us. I only asked her to be polite because everyone else was invited. I didn't expect her to actually say yes, and I certainly wasn't going to let her sour face spoil my fun.

It was a fantastic night. I can definitely say that I saw my single life out in style. I'd told Will not to get any male strippers or do any funny business because I was a respectable woman now and couldn't be seen doing anything like that. He was really good and did what I asked.

I didn't say not to bring a male blow up doll and perform his own rendition of the looking for some hot stuff song from *The Full Monty* though. He must have been practising that routine for ages in his flat, all that bumping and grinding he was doing was hilarious and perfectly in time with the music. I can see why Drew is with him that's for sure.

I have such a headache today. Brian got us all home by about three o'clock this morning. God bless Brian, he is such an angel. But I'm really not up to very much. Sam was in work but called me about eleven to ask how I was. When I mumbled into the phone and asked him to whisper, he spoke louder saying he had no sympathy for self-inflicted pain. Silly git. I know he was just having a joke but he could have made it quieter. Or better still, come home and got me some water and extra strong paracetamol and then snuggled me close while I slept it off.

He had some work to do today though, said he had to get ahead because of the time he would have to take off for the wedding and the honeymoon.

I'll let him off. He is marrying me after all. He'll be all mine forever then.

Chapter Sixty-Five

Lucy's Diary

Friday 30th April 2010

It's tomorrow.

I'm getting married tomorrow!

I have to pinch myself to believe it's true. I still can't believe that I, Lucy Barton, have managed to snag the most eligible, most handsome, most muscle-bound hunk in the whole of Cornwall.

I mean, me, from the lowliest Council estate on the outskirts of Camborne, with a deadbeat father who I never knew and a wonderful mother who worked her ass off to bring us up. Even then she had to rely on hand outs and hand me downs to make the money last for the whole month instead of a fortnight.

When I left home at twenty and moved to Trecase, I vowed never to live like she did. I would never, ever live in a cold, damp ridden house with mould on the ceiling and creeping down the walls. It used to scare me in the middle of the night as it morphed into monster's faces, coming to smother me if I dared to close my eyes. I would certainly never bring any children up in a world like that. When I have children, they're going to have everything they want. And they will never have to dress in next door's cast offs and then have them sniggering and pointing at them in the school corridor because of what they're wearing.

No, neither I, nor my children, will ever live like that.

I'm staying at Will's tonight. I can't stay at Karadow because Sam is there, and I don't want any bad luck to jinx our future happiness. I didn't want to stay in a hotel either even though Sam offered. I wanted it to be just me and Will. Drew isn't even coming down until the morning.

I've been with the caterers and the wedding planner today, making sure the marquee is ready and decorated just the way we planned it. Sam was there as well. He was so masterful, knew exactly where everything should be and made sure that anything that was in the wrong place was quickly put right. Must be the architect in him, that attention to minute detail. He said he wanted everything to be perfect.

The perfect wedding for the perfect lady in his life.

That's me.

It doesn't sound like me though. I don't think I've ever been perfect, just ask Cowbag Kelly. I'm pretty sure she would love to list a load of my faults. Sam's comments did make me panic a bit, wonder if I'm doing the right thing? I mean, it's been so quick, what if he wakes up one morning and hates me? Regrets what he's done?

I asked Will what he thought when we were having a take-away Chinese for our evening meal tonight. He said I was just being silly. I was bound to be nervous because tomorrow was going to be such a big day, but Sam was totally and utterly in

love with me and he always would be. Then Will put *Runaway Bride* on the DVD and joked that it wasn't too late, I could still do a runner if I wanted to. It was after I said *"I do"* that it would be too late. He thinks he's so funny sometimes. But I can't imagine life without him in it.

It's been lovely spending this time with Will. Since Sam and I became a couple, I've neglected him a bit. We'll have to start going out as a foursome once things settle down a bit. I know Sam will love him just as much as I do once he gets to know him. I mean, they already know each other professionally from the personal training, and it will be brilliant once they get to socialize together.

I always wondered what it would be like to be getting married. I can't make up my mind if I'm excited or scared witless about tomorrow. Obviously, there won't be many people on my side of the Church. Only Will and the guys from work. I'm really missing my family and I'm gutted they won't be there to see me. How can one person have so few family members? I'm only thirty-two, surely there should be more people around that actually care for me?

Sam said he'd make sure some of his clients would be sat on my side to even it up a bit, not make it so obvious that my family is so small. He said his family were mine now. I didn't need anybody else. He would take care of me better than they ever did.

It isn't going to help in the photos though is it.

When the sum total of my family is Will, and he's not even related.

Chapter Sixty-Six

Lucy's Diary

Sunday May 2nd 2010

It's official. I am now Mrs Lucy Lambert.

Yesterday was amazing. It was just like I imagined. A total picture book, fairy tale wedding.

Sam put Brian at my disposal first thing in the morning to take me to the hairdressers and have my make-up done. Not that there was very much to do with my hair, it's too short to do much with. The hairdresser did a very good rough tousle job though, before weaving a silver flowered garland through and around to the back before attaching the veil onto it. My make-up was all neutral. Tracy at Belle's Belles did it for me and she spent ages doing it, but when I looked in the mirror, it looked as if I wasn't wearing any. I knew I was of course, it wasn't *The Emperor's New Clothes* or anything like that. But it was the perfect set of shading to make me look pure and natural. I know, I could never be that, not really, but it's nice to look that way on your wedding day.

My dress was figure hugging to the knee, then flaring out to the floor. The Marilyn Monroe style bodice was covered in sparkling crystals, starting from a large central flower just above my left hip and radiating outwards, across my breasts and spreading down into the skirt to the flounces at the hem. There was just the smallest hint of a train at the back, just enough to sweep the floor. White satin stilettos finished the look and I felt like a real princess.

The white stretch limousine pulled up at Will's door to take us to the church. There were Cornish tartan ribbons on the bonnet and the driver even had tartan bows on the door handles. Rhea and Josh travelled with Will and I in it, Sam had said to get them a car of their own as it was traditional for the bride to ride just with her father, or the man that was giving her away on the journey to the church, but I said that I didn't want that. Will isn't my father, no matter how much I love him, and if she were still alive, it would have been Mum giving me away. I didn't want to be reminded of that on my wedding day, so I said I wanted us all to travel together. It was only about five miles anyway, hardly seemed worth having two cars. He said to leave it with him and he would get something special for all of us.

It was certainly that, and there was champagne in it, chilled with three crystal glasses which the driver poured and handed to us before getting in and driving us away.

Sam turned and faced me as I walked up the aisle on Will's arm. I didn't want the traditional wedding march played, even though Sam had said it should be that piece of music, because I remembered the old school chant of,

'Here comes the bride, all fat and wide, slipped on a banana skin and went for a ride'

. . .

I knew I would be singing that all the way, so I asked for Clarke's Trumpet

Voluntary instead. It was the piece of music that Diana used to meet her Prince at St Pauls' Cathedral. If it was good enough for her, then it was good enough to take me to my Prince as well. Sam thought that was amazing and instructed the organist to make sure he was note perfect.

My hands were so sweaty I was worried I would drop my bouquet, but once I started walking up the aisle and saw Sam at the end, my nerves vanished. All that mattered was me and him.

He didn't take his eyes off me as I walked along the aisle and as we drew together, Will let go and Sam took my other arm'.

'You look beautiful,' he whispered.

I know he meant it; I could see it in his face and in the warm strength of his hand as he gently squeezed mine.

The moment he lifted my veil and tucked it behind my head to fall down my back, I could see all the love in the world in his eyes. And I gave him all that love back. It could have been just the two of us there as the onlookers faded away into the distance. It was just him and me and I love him so much. I couldn't believe he could be in love with me too.

The ceremony was a blur. The vows and the hymns, the organ music and the male voice choir. (Sam had said we needed a choir to make sure the hymns were sung properly, there was nothing worse, he said, than a church full of people just mumbling the words). They sounded heavenly, their voices rising in harmony, echoing through the vault of the tiny church.

Will was in floods of tears of course. He is so emotional. I dread to think what he'll be like at his own wedding. When we went to sign the register, I saw Sam's Dad, Frank, hand him some tissues that Maggie had given him as he left the pew. Will promptly burst into even more tears and blew his nose the loudest I have ever heard anyone blow their nose. I don't know if the church acoustics amplified the sound, but it was the funniest thing I have ever heard. The rest of the congregation thought so too because they all burst out laughing. Even Sam did, after the momentary frown had passed across his brow.

It was a beautiful day. The sun was shining in the cloudless sky and the marquee was a big hit. The atmosphere was amazing with guests all laughing and dancing to the band. Nobody argued at all. I don't think I've ever been to a wedding where at least one punch wasn't thrown or one harsh word spoken. I mean, there's always one member of the family that doesn't get on with someone else isn't there?

Although, as none of my family were there, that might have explained it.

If my sister were there then an argument definitely would have happened.

And it would have been with me.

And that would have ruined my perfect day.

We stayed at Karadow last night. Sam had said about leaving early to go on our honeymoon, but I said it didn't seem right to leave our guests at the first and the biggest party we'd ever thrown. Not to mention the fact that he paid so much money for it, I didn't want to miss a party we'd paid for. Sam kissed me on the forehead and agreed. Said he understood, and we could start our married life the following day instead.

That's today.

When we woke up, he said, 'Good morning Mrs Lambert.'

A delicious thrill ran through me as he said my new name before claiming me as his own in an early sexual romp that was accompanied by the dawn chorus outside the window. After living in town for so long, I'm still amazed by the sound of the birds singing in the garden, it's so much nicer than the traffic and the sound of my neighbours flushing their toilet in the upstairs flat.

We're all packed, and Brian is about to take us to the airport. I don't know where we're going, Sam said it's a surprise, his wedding present to me. I think he has already given me more than enough, but it would be ungrateful to refuse wouldn't it?

I am Mrs Lucy Lambert and I am married to Mr Sam Lambert.

A rich architect, a proper gentleman and the hunkiest Sex God in the world. I am the luckiest woman alive.

Chapter Sixty-Seven

Penny-May

Wednesday June 17th 2015

I thought that too. I felt so lucky to have been picked out by him, I couldn't believe just how lucky I had been. She sounds lovely and they were so happy. I can't understand how she could take her own life in the way she did.

Something must have gone terribly wrong for them. Although it felt like I was snooping into her private life where I shouldn't be, my curiosity won in my inner battle that I really shouldn't be reading this when Sam had obviously not wanted me to know exactly what had happened.

I had a right to know though, didn't I? I couldn't help him if I didn't know what they had gone through and what made her so unhappy.

And I wanted to know why he treated her so much better than he treated me. If I could be as perfect as she was, then I could make him happy again.

Chapter Sixty-Eight

Lucy's Diary

Saturday May 15th 2010.

He only went and brought me to Venice!

This life just can't get any better, Paris to get engaged, Venice for our honeymoon. I can't wait to find out where we will go for our first anniversary. And what about when our first child is born? That will be amazing.

If Sam as a husband is this good, then Sam as a father will be the absolute King of fathers.

Not that I'm pregnant, yet. I think we need to be together as a couple for a year or so first, really cement our love for each other before we have a child. Sam says so too. But I just know that he is going to be a doting father. We're going to be the perfect family. Just like Carl, Rhea and Josh are. I love the way they fit together, always happy and laughing.

Anyway, back to the honeymoon.

Venice is awesome. Our first day here we went for a gondola ride. I was surprised to find out that the gondoliers didn't sing themselves, but Sam had it covered, and we had an accordionist and a singer on board with us. It was beautiful. The sun was setting and with the gentle motion of the boat, sorry, gondola, the operatic musicians, and with Sam's arm around my shoulders, I couldn't imagine that even heaven could be better than where we were right then. I was sad when it ended. But Sam soon cheered me up again once we got back into our suite at the hotel.

Sam always knows what buttons to press to make me happy.

We did venture out every day. We went to Verona to put our signatures on the wall of Juliet's balcony, we climbed the Campanile to get a view of the whole City, we went to the Piazza San Marco and St Mark's Basilica, The Doges Palace and Toro Dell Orologio. We ate gelato. We went on a vaporetto and toured the Grand Canal.

We studied art and we ate food that I had never eaten before.

And we made love. Every morning and every night, and sometimes in the afternoons. Sometimes quick and fast, when time was short before the next excursion and our need for each other couldn't wait until later. And then, when later came, slow and exploratory, savouring every moment just as we'd earlier savoured every morsel of food and drop of drink that was presented to us.

It's been two weeks of heaven that I don't want to end. But we have to go back tomorrow. Sam to his work and I to mine. It's going to be the pits after the excitement, the freedom and the blessed release every time I am in Sam's arms and in his bed.

I love being Mrs Lucy Lambert.

I hope Helen's got my new name badge sorted.

Chapter Sixty-Nine

Lucy's Diary
Friday 27th August 2010.

It was my last day at Silverwell today.

Sam said I didn't need to do it anymore as he could provide anything I wanted. I didn't have to work, he said. He wanted me to stay at home and look after everything here.

Maggie has never worked. She was always the homemaker and always there for Sam when he was growing up. Frank paid for everything, so I guess that's what Sam wants as well.

I've never been without a job. It's going to be a bit weird for a while getting used to not having to go to work, and I won't get to see so much of Will either, or the girls. Even Cowbag Kelly was crying when I handed my work pass in as I left this afternoon. That surprised me. Didn't think she was capable of actual, real emotion.

I know I'm going to enjoy being a homemaker though. And I see a lot of Rhea so she can keep me up to date on all the gossip, and we can go shopping together.

I will be a lady who lunches! I always wondered what it would be like when I spent my break watching those types of women who sat in the health club, sipping lemon water and eating lettuce leaves after their treatments. I can find out now, Rhea and I can be the ones sitting idly watching the world go by.

Sam was funny when he first started mentioning that I should give it all up. He has always asked how many massages I'd done each day, and what kind of treatments. Whether they were male or female. I always thought it was quite cute that he got a teensy bit jealous if I was treating a male client. I used to tease him about it, especially if they were hunky, but I always made sure he knew that he was the hunkiest. He knew I'd never cheat on him of course and we always made mad, passionate love afterwards. He would pin my arms above my head, holding my wrists as he thrust inside me. It was like he was proving his prowess, that he was so much better in bed than anyone else could be. No, I'd never need to cheat on him.

I can't believe how he could be so jealous really, I mean, has he looked at himself in the mirror? No man can compare to him. And he is so much better in bed than anyone else I have ever been with. Those thrusts really hit the spot!

We have so much sex that I really don't need to go with anyone else anyway, Sam is always up for it. He's my studmuffin.

I love eating muffins, so much better than lettuce leaves. I wonder if ladies who lunch can eat muffins instead of lettuce leaves? I really hope so. I'm not going to survive very well on just salad with no dressing.

The girls and Will all clubbed together to get me a gorgeous bouquet of flowers and a silver bracelet as a leaving present. Helen said I could come back to work anytime and that she was very sad to lose me as I was a favourite of the guests.

Just as well Sam didn't hear that bit. He's taking me to Pareusi's this evening for a celebratory meal. He said it was a momentous occasion becoming a lady of leisure and for that reason a double date with Carl and Rhea was required so that Rhea could give me some tips on how to be the perfect housewife. He'd kissed me and laughed then. Afterwards, he said that of course I was the perfect wife already or else he wouldn't have fallen in love with me. Then the kisses got stronger and harder and he lifted me on to the kitchen worktop, the buttons torn off my tunic top, and the zip of my trousers in pieces as he was so desperate to be inside me, the heat of our bodies building to a crescendo until we climaxed together.

When we were finished, he picked up my torn uniform and joked that it was just as well I didn't need to wear it anymore, it might have been a bit awkward trying to explain to Helen what happened to it. I laughed as well. I was intending to put it back into my wardrobe as a sort of memento, but it was a bit pointless now it was ripped. I did take my silver name badge off before Sam put the uniform in the bin though. I was still proud of that. And I wanted to keep the memories that it brought back. After all, we would never have met if I hadn't been working there when Will had messed up.

Sam reckoned I was too sentimental for my own good and slapped my backside, sending me to the shower. He said to dress up tonight, wear my little black dress that he bought for me when we went shopping for a new wardrobe last month. He was so generous. Said I needed a complete clothing overhaul as it must have been ages since I had bought anything new. He's right of course, charity shops have been my usual haunt for any *'new-to-me'* clothing as I could afford to buy much more from them than from the shops Sam took me to. Saying that, the shops Sam took me to I wouldn't have been able to afford to window shop in.

It was an experience shopping without knowing what the price of the garment was. Sam said to be ruthless with my old stuff when we got back home, to either throw them out or send them back to the charity shops they came from. I couldn't throw all of it away though. There's that cardigan Mum made for me when she was giving up smoking. It's hideous and Sam hates it but it reminds me so much of her.

Even if it was too late for her by the time she finally gave up the fags.

You should have done it ten years earlier Mum, you might have stood a fighting chance then.

Anyway, the cardigan is hidden at the back of the drawer under the bed, I'm wearing the little black dress with black stockings as well as silver bracelet. The satin jacket is waiting for me on the bed and I'll carry the stilettos down with me as Sam doesn't like shoes to be worn inside the house.

Our table at Pareusi's is waiting. I think I'll have the crab tonight.

Chapter Seventy

Lucy's Diary

Sunday 21st November 2010.

I have been so foolish.

Sam knows he shouldn't have done it, but it's all my fault. He was just so worried about me that when I got home, he flipped and back-handed me across the face.

He bought me flowers today and has been treating me like his Princess again. He's so very sorry for what he's done. I shouldn't have made him do it, I should have told him what I was doing.

I haven't seen Will for ages. With his work schedule and my not being at Silverwell anymore, we just haven't been able to meet up. Sam keeps me pretty busy running errands and I go out shopping and stuff with Rhea quite a bit, so we haven't been able to meet up properly.

Will phoned me yesterday afternoon though, said he needed to speak to me and wanted to meet up for a drink. He sounded pretty urgent, so I said I would meet him at *The Notoriety* at four and we could have a bite to eat as well.

I was really looking forward to seeing him again, we've never been apart for so long.

Sam had back-to-back meetings all day and Brian was running him around, so I didn't want to bother either of them. I rang for a taxi and didn't think any more about it.

The couple of hours in the pub were fab. Will was excited because he's pretty sure that Drew is about to pop the question and he wanted to get my opinion on how he should react. I mean, as if I was any good at telling Will what to do? He has always been my advisor, not the other way around.

When I arrived, Will held me at arm's length and took a good look at me. He couldn't get over how long my hair had grown since we last met. Sam said he thought my pixie cut was a bit too severe and he wanted to see what I looked like with longer hair, so I've been growing it out. I'm not too sure of it really, I love the pixie cut look and it was so easy to manage, but like Sam said, now that I'm not working anymore, I have more time to get it styled properly. He had a good point there, Rhea introduced me to her stylist and it's gradually coming together.

Will and I eventually decided, after a couple of glasses of wine and a few handfuls of peanuts, that Will would graciously accept his proposal and act all demure and coy and maybe shed just one tear for effect. We knew that wouldn't happen as Will would get all excited and start flapping his arms around and running up and down the room squealing before grabbing Drew and shouting 'Yes!!!' in his ear so loud that it would deafen him, tears running down his cheeks totally unchecked all the time. Will's not very good at hiding his emotions.

We also agreed that yes, I would be his chief bridesmaid/groomsmaid? What is the main supporter of one half of a gay wedding called anyway? Whatever it is, I was gonna be it, for sure. I'll have to look it up though, I can't not know what my title is on the day. If it happens anyway. I've not heard from Will so far today and I daren't try and contact him. I know I'll cry and then he will want to know what's happened and I can't tell him. Not when he's so happy. And Sam has said he's sorry and promised he won't do it again.

Sam phoned me at about seven last night. He sounded really worried because I wasn't at home and he didn't know where I was. I said I was at the bar with Will and everything was fine, I would get a taxi home later, but he told me not to be so silly. He would send Brian for me, but it had to be then because Brian was about to finish work for the day. I tried to say that I didn't mind getting a taxi home later and to send Brian home, he'd had a long day, but Sam was adamant. He said to be waiting outside the pub in ten minutes and the driver would be there for me.

Will came and waited outside with me, we joked that Sam was so desperate to see me because he was really horny, and I was in for the sesh of a lifetime when I got home.

Sam was waiting for me when I walked in the door. The room was lit with just the light of the fire and a couple of standard lamps. I could smell the wood smoke and it looked so romantic, but there was a look on his face that I hadn't seen before. He was standing in front of the staircase and strode towards me. He raised his arm and hit me with the back of his hand across my right cheek. I stumbled and brought my hand up to protect my face as I tasted the blood from the inside of my cheek.

Sam stopped and stood still before reaching out to me, to pull me in and whisper how sorry he was in my ear. His hand caressed my hair, the curls that were starting to form wrapping around his fingers. He looked horrified as tears started to roll down my cheeks and he wiped them away with his thumb.

He said he was sorry. He said that he didn't mean it, he had just been so worried because I wasn't here and he didn't know where I was. He said that I should have told him where I was going, who I was seeing before I went out. He would have given me Brian for the night so he would have known I would be safe.

I said I was with Will; I was always safe with Will but Sam had said to just look at myself. Rolling in drunk like a wanton slut. Who did I think I was? What right did I have to worry him so much?

I said I was sorry and I wouldn't do it again. I didn't think. I figured it would be ok to go for a drink with Will. I didn't mean to make him worry so much. His dad had cancer and I knew he was worried about Frank and the diagnosis so I should have been more thoughtful. I wouldn't do it again.

He said he was sorry. He was so, so sorry. He went and got some ice for my face, gently pressed it against my cheek. Said that should cut down on the bruising. He said not to worry, he would take good care of me. He would show me how sorry he was. He said he only did it because he loved me so much it physically hurt when he came home and found me gone.

He has been so good today. He said I don't have to go out and see anyone if I don't want to. He brought me breakfast in bed and then went out and bought me the biggest bunch of flowers ever. It's Sunday so the florist was shut, but he drove around all the local supermarkets and got me so many roses and freesias and gypsophila that we had to improvise with cut down squash bottles as vases.

He said he was sorry, he should have thought to buy more vases to put the flowers in. I said it didn't matter, the plastic makeshift vases looked cute and rustic.

He said I deserved better than rustic.

I'm staying home today. I don't really feel like going out anywhere and having to hide the bruise with make-up. I'm going to stay here by the fire today. Maybe tomorrow as well. Sam's looking after me so well. Said he'll make dinner tonight as well.

He's going to cook his Bolognese special and then we're going to cuddle up on the sofa and watch one of my favourite films. He doesn't usually like chick flicks, so I know how sorry he is if he's going to do that for me. I think I'm going to go for either *Pretty Woman* or *Legally Blonde*. I might even see if we can watch both. Yes, watching both will definitely cheer me up.

Chapter Seventy-One

Lucy's Diary
16th March 2011

Frank died yesterday.

He refused the last round of chemo when the consultant said it may only give him a few weeks. The time for a total cure was gone. Sam is really upset but he won't show it. After the visit to the doctor Sam shouted at Frank, said he was giving up on his family and that he was being weak and stupid. Frank tried to explain that the pain and the side effects weren't worth it for just a few more weeks. He was dying and Sam had to accept that. I don't think Sam does accept that. He doesn't like it when he thinks people are being weak.

When I said to let it out and he would feel better if he cried, he snapped at me to stop being so silly. What did I know?

After Mum's battle with cancer I know a lot, but I didn't say that to him. I didn't want to make him angrier so I said I was sorry, of course he was right and I went and made us both a cup of tea. He didn't drink his though, he threw the cup straight into the sink, smashing it into tiny little bits. I know I flinched. I took a couple of steps back as well, just in case. But he turned and left the room. He didn't tell me where he was going and I didn't ask. He slammed the door as he left. It was quite a relief to know he had gone out.

Sam was with his dad when he died at his parents' house. Frank had declined to go into the hospice and they had a private nurse there to help Maggie out. I was there as well, but I didn't go into the room at the end. I said my goodbyes earlier. It was too emotional and brought back too many memories of Mum. I sat in the kitchen and waited for it to be over. I made loads of mugs of coffee, but most of them went cold before I drank them.

Sam didn't speak to me when he came out of the bedroom. He gave his mum a hug and let her cry on his shoulder, but he didn't come to me. The doctor came and did the official paperwork so the undertakers could take Frank away and Sam dealt with all of it. Maggie wasn't in any fit state to do anything anyway. He sent me home with Brian in the end, said he was staying with his mum as he couldn't leave her alone. I offered to stay as well but he wouldn't let me. Said, no, he would look after his mum and I was to go home.

Karadow was so quiet. I haven't spent a night alone here before and it was so strange being on my own. It's not even a year since we got married and the silence never used to bother me when I was in my little flat. It bothers me now though. I don't know what the little creaks and noises are. Sam fills the house when he is here, I rattle around it not knowing what to do.

I phoned Will when I got in. I had to speak to someone who would understand what I was going through and Will had always been the one I ran to. We've not seen much of each other lately. I've been busy and Sam likes me home in the evenings. It's much easier to say yes and do what Sam wants. I feel really bad about it though, Will and Drew have set a date for their wedding next

August and I wish I could help him arrange things more. He said I am still his number one choice for best woman, so that's good. I'm sure Sam will be fine with me doing that. Will's my best friend, I've got to support him on the most important day of his life, haven't I?

Chapter Seventy-Two

Penny-May

Wednesday June 17th 2015

By the time Sam came home yesterday, complete with enough flowers to fill a florist shop, I was sat on the sofa watching *Pretty Woman* on the DVD. I've watched it a million times, but it always makes me cry and when Sam and I first fell in love I felt just like Julia Roberts would have done. Although I was never a prostitute. I was skint but never one of those.

And Lucy wasn't either. I couldn't believe he could say those things to her, call her those names when they were so much in love.

Or maybe I could.

He'd even bought some extra vases to put the flowers in. I'd thought that was so sweet and thoughtful last night. After reading some more of Lucy's diary this morning I now know it's because he's been here before. I guess he didn't want to have the cut down squash bottles this time, it had to be the perfect scene.

He laughed when he saw what film I was watching.

'I might have guessed you'd be watching some chick flick rubbish,' he'd said as he started dishing out the Chinese takeaway he'd bought for us. He'd sent me a text saying not to worry about cooking anything, that he would sort it when he got home. He didn't reprimand me for not warming the plates before he got home either, just pulled them out of the cupboard and popped them into the oven for a few minutes.

I'd smiled at him, 'You said to put my feet up and relax, that's just what I'm doing.'

He came over to me, leant over the back of the sofa and kissed me on the top of my head. 'No worries, you need to get better after your fall. You're far too clumsy.'

My fall? I didn't fall. I was hit, and kicked, and forced to have sex? I didn't fall. I'm sure I didn't fall. Did I? It was such a crazy night; I was exhausted and worried about Daniel. Did I fall?

'I guess, silly me,' I said, 'How was your day?'

'Oh, the usual stuff, meetings and more meetings, Old Man Reece is getting more and more doddery. He'll have to retire soon and then I'll be able to run the whole company my way. What have you been up to?'

I didn't say I'd been out with Rhea to see Daniel. I didn't tell him that Daniel was starting to get better. I didn't want to risk *falling* again. Not when it still hurt too much to move. If I did everything right then I wouldn't be in a position to fall again. He'd put me back on that pedestal and I'd never be hurt again.

What he didn't know wouldn't hurt him, or me. I'm sure I didn't fall.

I didn't tell him about the diaries either. I needed to read more of them. They were so in love and I wanted to see why Lucy would want to kill herself when she was so happy.

'Oh, just this really, sitting watching films. Relaxing, just like you told me to.'

'Good girl,' he patted my head and served up the meal. I wasn't very hungry but I ate it anyway.

He didn't ask me how Daniel was. I didn't tell him. We watched *The Fast and The Furious* after we'd eaten. He enjoyed it, I fell asleep with my head on his shoulder, just like I'd always done before.

I snuck into Lucy's office not long after he went to work this morning, picking up reading where I had left off. The wedding was beautiful and the honeymoon. All those places. And all that sex. It made me feel wrong reading about their sex life, how they couldn't keep their hands off each other all the time. It was voyeuristic, a part of their life that I didn't need to know. Or want to. I shouldn't want to. But I didn't just turn the pages and skip over those bits, I needed to know that they were in love, especially after he hit her. He shouldn't have done that. She only went out with her best friend.

It's been too long since I saw Emma and I haven't even told her that Daniel is in hospital. I need to call her. While Sam is at work.

He should have let Lucy help him after his father died instead of pushing her away. She missed her own mother terribly, had been through so much, she really could have helped him to grieve.

Chapter Seventy-Three

Penny-May

Thursday June 18th 2015

'Hey Hun, you ready?' Rhea came in the door just as I was washing the last of my lunch dishes. 'I've spoken to Carl. Sam is out with him on site all afternoon. They've got investors coming over so are going to be wining and dining them. We've got plenty of time to get to the hospital and back without him knowing.'

'You didn't tell Carl anything did you?'

'Relax, no I didn't. He was telling me why he would be late home tonight.'

Joe was playing snap with Daniel when I walked into the ward. I could hear Dan's happy shout from outside the door and when I walked in Joe was laughing,

'No mate, that isn't a pair! It's a cat and a dog. You can't shout snap for that.'

'But Martha got cat and dog and says they right pair of — '

'I don't think it matters what Martha calls them, you need two dogs or two cats, not one of each.'

Joe looked up and saw me, 'Here's your sister now, we'll finish this later.' He picked up the cards and went to make his way out of the room.

'Thanks Joe, it means a lot to me that you're here when I can't be. It's above and beyond what you're employed to do.'

Joe grinned, 'Not a problem, I don't see it as work, it's fun being with him.'

'I can see he's getting better?'

'Yeah, the doc came round earlier, said he should be off the drip and onto tablets by tomorrow, He's also mostly off the additional oxygen now as well. They'll think about discharging him then.'

'That's great.' I turned my attention to Daniel, 'Hey Hulk? How're you doing?' 'How you doin?' replied Dan with an upward tilt of his eyebrows.

Joe blushed, 'Uh, sorry, we've been watching *Friends,* he likes Joey.' He shrugged his shoulders, 'I guess I'll leave now.'

'It's fine, it makes a pleasant change from his Hulk impressions, even if it is slightly creepy coming from my younger brother.'

'I'll come back this evening and keep him company for a couple of hours. Don't worry about him, he's going to be fine.'

After he left the room I sat by the bed. Daniel reached out and held my hand, a silent tear escaped down my cheek.

Why couldn't Sam love him as much as I did?

Chapter Seventy-Four

Lucy's Diary

Thursday August 18th 2011

Sam has been struggling so hard to accept Frank's death, but I gave him some news last night which caught him by surprise, but I know he's delighted. I am too.

I'M PREGNANT!!!!!

I think I'm about three months gone, which will make the baby due in February next year. Will be amazing if it's born on Valentine's day. I've got an appointment with the doctor tomorrow to confirm it, but I'm pretty sure it's right. I've done a few tests, couldn't believe the first one, or the second, so I just had to do a few more to make sure the first ones weren't broken.

We weren't trying for a baby. We had talked about it of course, what married couple doesn't? But Sam had said that the time wasn't right, he was too busy at work and wasn't ready to be a father yet. He still had stuff to do and he wanted to do it all with me, on our own.

He did ask if I'd done it on purpose, but I really didn't. I've thought about it and I remember I was sick for a few days a couple of months ago. I must have brought the pill up when I vomited without knowing it. I really wasn't thinking straight at the time, Sam had been annoyed that I was too ill to go for a work meeting with Carl and Rhea and had tried to make me go. Even got the dress out of the wardrobe for me that he wanted me to wear. He stopped when I ran to the toilet and threw up. Stormed out and went on his own. I was glad of the silence so I could get some sleep and recover.

We made it up the next morning. I woke with him on top of me and he had the biggest hard on, I could hardly refuse an offering that size and since Frank's death, he hasn't been as horny as he was before. He whispered in my ear how sorry he was for storming out the night before and he nibbled my neck, his tongue weaving its way down my body.

Well, let's just say I forgave him quite quickly, and the last thing I was thinking about was whether my contraceptive pill was working. Besides, I've been on them for years, surely just one being thrown up wouldn't make a difference?

Apparently, it does.

And we're so happy about it. I know Sam's been quiet, but I think it will help to heal some of the scars his dad's passing has left.

I hope it's a boy. If it is, we'll call him Francis after his dad. And maybe William as his middle name. Yes, Francis William. He can be called Frankie. And if it's a girl then she can be called Frankie too. She can be his little Princess. I hope it's a boy though. Sam would love a little mini Sam following him around everywhere.

For now though, I'm going to call him Peanut.

My little Peanut who is going to make our family complete.

Hello Peanut, I'm going to be your mummy.

Chapter Seventy-Five

Lucy's Diary

Friday 11th November 2011.

Yes!!! It's a boy!!!

We had the scan yesterday and Peanut is definitely going to be a Frankie William. Well, Sam's not so keen on Frankie, prefers Francis and he hates William but I'm sure he'll come round to them by the time he's born. I'll work on him. When little Frankie arrives Sam will be so used to me calling him by those names that it will just be normal.

Maggie loves the fact that she is going to be a Grandmother. She said she's going to insist on being called 'Glamma' though because she isn't old enough to be a Granny yet. She keeps coming round with baby clothes, I reckon we should have shares in Mon Bébé with how much she has spent in there!

They are so cute though, and so tiny! Those little socks are just to die for and I can't wait to be able to put them over his tiny little toes. I joked that if she wanted to be a proper Granny she would have to take up knitting, but she pooh poohed that idea, said she wasn't ready for the sedentary lifestyle yet and why should she sit for hours making a jumper when she can just go to a shop and buy it?

Mum used to knit. She would sit with her needles clicking away as she watched her soaps on the telly. I should have listened when she wanted to teach me, but it was such an uncool thing to do then. I was having a hard enough time with always wearing the hand me downs, I didn't need people sniggering at me because of that as well.

I might try and learn now though. It would be lovely to dress him in something that isn't mass produced. Something that has some meaning to it and is unique. I know, I'll go into town later today and get some needles and maybe a book so I can learn how to do it. Can't be that hard. I'll have a jumper whipped up by the end of next week.

A baby blue one.

Because it's going to be a boy.

Sam said I can do what I like with the room I've chosen to be the nursery. He said he didn't have time to fuss with any of it so I hired an interior designer and a decorator so it would be done properly. He gave me some names and phone numbers of people he knew through his business and I started ringing around a couple of weeks ago. I liked Robyn the most, she had some gorgeous ideas for how to decorate the room and Rhea came over as well to help me decide on what would be best. We're going for a jungle theme and it's going to be all bright, primary colours with lions, tigers, giraffes, monkeys and elephants, all around the room. Robyn said it would be good to have something that would grow with Frankie. If I had something very babyish, it wouldn't be long before I would need to redo it all and that would be difficult with a growing baby as well.

I reckon Rhea is even more excited than I am. She keeps calling herself Auntie Rhe and saying how much Josh is going to love having a little playmate whenever we go out together. I think she would like a little brother or sister for Josh but apparently Carl isn't so keen. Reckons one is enough and they need to concentrate on giving him the best of everything rather than having to share it all. Rhea reckons it's more because he doesn't like being woken up at night, not that he ever got up when Josh cried. It was either Rhea or the nanny that did that.

Sam said we would get a nanny. He said it would be better for me as I would be able to get back on my feet quicker and wouldn't be so tied to the baby. I don't think we need one though, I want Frankie with me. I don't really think it's the right thing to do to pass them off with other people all the time. I mean, what is the point of having kids if you're going to pay for someone else to raise them?

Maybe I'll go along with the idea for now and just not find anyone suitable when the time comes. Once Frankie is born, Sam will understand that a baby needs to be with its mother, not some stranger.

Anyway, the decorators are booked for tomorrow, they are going to strip the room out, paint it first, then put the murals up and then the furniture goes in. I'm not too fussy about the furniture, I'll leave it to Robyn, but I do want one of those funky rocking chairs with the foot stool. That will be so nice to be able to nurse my baby in and then rock him gently to sleep in my arms. She reckons it will all be ready in the next couple of weeks and then I can spend my time in there doing the little bits like filling the cupboards with his clothes and stuff before he's born. I can't wait to try out that rocking chair.

Chapter Seventy-Six

Lucy's Diary

Monday 28th November 2011

I've lost Frankie.

I miscarried two days ago and I just can't believe it happened.

I told them at the hospital that I had fallen down the stairs, tripped over an electrical wire that was running across the landing from the decorators while they were doing the nursery. Of course, that's a lie. The decorators finished their work a week ago and took all of their equipment with them. There was no wire for me to trip over. There was Sam though.

I find it so hard to admit that I think he pushed me down the stairs. I'm not sure that he did it on purpose though, it must have been an accident. He would never have hurt me this much. I guess that's why it was so easy for the lie to come out. When he called the ambulance crew I was lying in the hallway, it was obvious that I had come down them. It wasn't obvious how it happened and Sam just said I'd tripped.

I'm sure I didn't though. We were at the top of them talking, I was excited because I'd been sat in the rocking chair and felt Frankie moving for the first time, and I had run out of the nursery calling for Sam. He had thought something was wrong so dashed out of his study to see what the matter was. I reached out for his hand and went to place it on my tummy and said for him to say hello to Frankie William. Sam had snatched his hand back and told me not to be so stupid and there was no way on earth that any son of his was going to carry the name of that buttfucker.

I was horrified. I never realised Sam was so homophobic. I said that he should never call anyone that, it was horrible and nasty. Sam had just laughed and said he'd say whatever he wanted to say and if he wanted to call Will a buttfucker, he would.

He was only stating the truth after all. That's what people like them did wasn't it?

I said he was wrong, everyone has a right to live and love whoever they choose, regardless of their gender. They do not deserve to be called hateful names just because a person doesn't feel the same way as we did. I reached out for his hand again and went to put it back on my stomach. I asked him how he would feel in the future if Frankie turned around and told Sam that he was homosexual? I think that's when it happened. He pulled his hand back while raising his other one to slap me. I saw it coming and went to duck the blow, but his sudden movement made me lose my balance. I remember shouting his name as I felt myself falling but all I could hear was him shouting that he would never have a faggot for a son, he would rather not have a son at all. I could feel his spittle land on my cheek as his words swirled around me and I think I felt his hand hit my arm, pushing me towards the open staircase rather than catching me to stop my fall.

I remember the first few steps as I fell, the pain in my arms and chest. I had tried to curl up, protect my stomach, but I couldn't. I screamed and then I must have blacked out for a few seconds because the next thing I remember is waking up on the hallway floor. Sam was walking down the stairs towards me and I remember begging him to call an ambulance. To save our baby.

He kicked me then. Twice. In the stomach.

He said it was no baby of his.

I blacked out properly and woke up with the ambulance crew around me. Sam was holding my hand, saying he was so sorry. That he was in the study and heard me falling down the stairs. He had come running out but it was too late, I was already at the bottom. There was nothing he could do. He was crying and he looked so desperately upset, I believed him. The paramedics believed him and the doctors and nurses believed him when we got to the hospital.

I must have got it wrong. I could feel the pain in my stomach. There was blood all over me. I was screaming that I was pregnant and they had to save my baby. It's probably the drugs they gave me to calm me down and take away the pain. Maybe they cause hallucinations? Alter your memory?

Sam says that it wasn't anyone's fault. It was a tragic accident.

Frankie was dead when he was born. They had to make me go through a normal labour as that was the only way that his body could be removed from mine. He was only 23 weeks. I don't even have a birth certificate. He wasn't 'viable' they said. He never stood a chance. All that is wrong with me is a broken arm and a bruised stomach. It's not fair.

It was somebody's fault.

It was my fault. I didn't protect him.

I'd have made a rotten mother.

Chapter Seventy-Seven

Lucy's Diary

Friday December 16th 2011.

I'm sitting in my rocking chair. Sam doesn't like me coming in here, he says it isn't good for me to be around all this baby stuff. He says I'd feel much better if I got rid of it all. Turned it back into the spare room it once was.

I can't do that though. This is Frankie's room and I feel that he is with me in here.

Rhea and Maggie have both been to see me. To say how sorry they are for me and that I can have another child. It wouldn't happen again. It was an accident.

It wouldn't be my Frankie though would it. And Sam hasn't said anything about us trying again. He says that everything happens for a reason and maybe now just wasn't Frankie's time. Imagine if I hadn't lost it after falling down the stairs? What if it had survived but was disabled? What sort of life would that be for it? Or for us with a damaged child to look after for the rest of its life?

It? He was never an it.

From the moment I knew I was pregnant; he was a living being. He was part of mine and Sam's love for each other. He was a part of us.

I wanted my baby boy.

The weekend before I lost him, I went into Truro and bought myself a teach yourself to knit bundle. The lady in the shop was ever so helpful. When I told her that I wanted to make a jumper for my baby she didn't laugh like Sam had done and told me not to be so stupid. I caught a taxi in that day because Brian was driving Sam around a lot.

The lady asked me if I had ever knitted before and when I said no, and that my mum had died so couldn't teach me now, she pulled out some needles and a ball of wool and taught me there and then how to cast on and do the plain stitch. She also told me to maybe start with a patchwork blanket, she said it would be better if I learnt on something basic rather than something as complicated as a jumper. I made a whole square while I was there and was ever so pleased with myself.

Sam said it looked rubbish when I showed him. Said even a beggar off the street wouldn't be seen with anything like that.

He was right of course. I made a few more squares but they were all different sizes, and I kept dropping stitches so they left little ladders like when there's a run in your stockings.

I'm rubbish. Can't even knit a simple square so how the hell did I think I could ever be a good mother? Can't even keep him safe inside me. Why didn't I take more care on the stairs? I should have seen that wire, stepped over it. The decorator shouldn't have left it there really. Sam said he was going to speak with him, make sure he knew what he had done and make him pay for his negligence.

Sam has been so lovely since I came home from hospital. He's been waiting on me all the time, nothing is too much trouble. He took a few days off last week to look after me himself but I said that I was fine now and he needed to go back. Brian's wife has popped in and out every hour or so to check on me at Sam's insistence.

She has also been making my lunch and cups of earl grey tea.

She's lovely, but she keeps looking at me in that *I'm so sorry for you* way. I don't want her to feel sorry for me. I want her to shout at me. To yell about how stupid I was to be so reckless with my poor baby. That actually, he was probably better off now because I would have been a rotten mother.

Sam says we need to get away for a few days. That I need to get away from here in order to get better properly. He says that Christmas in Paris will brighten me up again. Get me back to my normal cheery self. He's booked the flights and the hotel. Not the same one as last time. He said it was fully booked and he couldn't get a late booking for over the festive period. He said that the one we are going to is quite nice though. He said it will be good for me to see a different hotel anyway. Bring back the explorer spirit that he fell in love with. He still closes Mistral for the ten days but he said we can only go for the long weekend that Christmas falls on.

I don't care though. I don't want to go away. It's too much hassle.

I just want to stay here in my rocking chair.

Where I felt my baby boy move.

While he still lived.

Chapter Seventy-Eight

Lucy's Diary

Wednesday February 15th 2012

I got so many roses yesterday. I know Sam was expecting me to be really excited about them all, and I did try to be, but I just wasn't.

I feel so ungrateful, I mean, he has been trying so hard to make me happy since we lost Frankie. I just don't think I will ever be happy again. How can I be happy when my little boy was supposed to be in my arms next month?

Paris was nice. It was cold and it was lovely to sit in front of the fire and be waited on after walking the chilly streets, but the excitement of our engagement wasn't there. The pretend smoke rings he was making with his breath as we stood under the Eiffel Tower just wasn't very funny this time. It was boring. We held hands as we went up to the restaurant. We ate the same meals and drank the same drinks. But it wasn't magical this time. It was boring.

He bought me a diamond ring for my Christmas present. It reminded me of the last time he had given me a ring in Paris and it made me cry. I was so happy then. I think Sam was a bit annoyed that I didn't 'snap out' of my sadness. I think he thought that a holiday, an expensive present and getting away from the house would be enough to make me forget what had happened. But it will take much more than that.

I was glad when we got back home and he went back to work. Even though it was in his study because the office wasn't open yet, I didn't have to put on that false smile for him all the time.

Sam hasn't said anything else about dismantling the nursery. I still can't bear for anything to be taken out of here. I can't just wipe Frankie's memory out of the house like a piece of old rubbish, even if Sam can. I have another reason for not wanting it redecorated though. I keep my diaries hidden in here. He doesn't know about them. I've never told him I write them because I need them to be just for me. They are my haven, and my truth. I don't think he would like to read my truth. My imperfections.

I told Rhea.

I told her that he hit me sometimes.

I told her that I deserved most of them because I didn't do what he told me to do, or because I did something stupid to upset him.

I told her he was still struggling to accept his father's death. That he still hadn't cried for him, let alone for our baby.

I told her that I couldn't remember tripping over any wire at the top of the stairs.

I told her that I felt so alone. That I had no-one to help me.

She told me that I shouldn't accept it, that I should find some help and get out. I should go to the police and tell them he pushed me down the stairs.

I told her I couldn't do that. I had no proof. I was probably wrong anyway. It must have been the drugs making me hallucinate.

I told her I had nowhere else to go.

I told her I still loved Sam and he had promised he would change.

He hadn't hit me once in the three months since I lost Frankie.

He told me he wouldn't hit me again.

I told her it was going to be ok; it will be.

She told me to be careful. To come to her if he did it again.

I made her promise not to tell anyone, not even Carl. Sam would be furious if his friend found out.

She hugged me close as I cried.

She promised it would all be ok.

I'm sure she's right. He's trying so hard.

Chapter Seventy-Nine

PENNY-MAY

Friday June 19th 2015

Oh my goodness, that poor, poor woman!

And so confused. I can't believe that Sam would do that, push her down the stairs and then kick her. I mean, he could have killed her! It must have been the drugs that she was on. He would never be that vicious.

Would he?

I know he's done it to me, but he loved Lucy. I'm just her replacement. And a pretty poor one at that.

I closed the diary and held it on my lap, gently stroking the leather cover with my fingertips. As much as I wanted to, I couldn't read anymore today, I needed to process what I had just found out.

Rhea knew. She knew that Sam had hit Lucy and she didn't tell me. She didn't do anything to help her. What kind of a friend is that? She should have got her out of there, should have saved her from him.

But he didn't hit her again. Lucy told her that she was safe now, that Sam was sorry and full of regret and he was. He took her on holiday and treated her lovely again.

Just like he has been with me for the last few days.

He still hasn't asked how Daniel is, and I haven't told him I'm still going to see him every day. Rhea is taking me again shortly and she will make sure I'm back before he comes home and finds me gone.

Does she suspect that he did this to me? Is she trying to help me the way she couldn't help Lucy? Does Will know as well? Is that what all the gym talks are about?

The thoughts inside my head were churning around and around, going over and over themselves in their desperation to find an answer.

I stood up and replaced the diary in its hiding place. I couldn't think anymore.

He called Will a 'Buttfucker'. Does he really think that? How can anyone in today's society think like that?

He said a disabled son would be 'damaged'. Is that how he sees Daniel? Is that why he won't have anything to do with him? Because he's not perfect? I brought my fist down onto the desktop. My brother isn't damaged! He is the most wonderful, funny, loving human being I have ever known. He just needs a little bit of help and to be loved back. That's all he asks for.

And a never-ending supply of *Hulk* memorabilia.

I smiled. I'd get Rhea to run into the toy shop on the way to the hospital and pick up an action figure shaped like his hero. He'd love that.

'Hey Dan, how are you doing today?'

I was delighted to see him sitting in the chair beside his bed without any tubes attached to him.

'I've got you a present.'

'Yay! How you doin' Penny-May? Me want present please.' He got up and came to me, not his usual barrel roll which I was quite pleased about because of my still sore ribcage, but a slow walk and his arms held out to take the carrier bag from my hands. Eagerly, he delved inside and pulled out the toy *Hulk* figure, ripping it out of the box and then handing it to me to uncurl the plastic tags that anchored it to the cardboard base. It had moveable arms and legs and the first pose Daniel put it into was arms above its head and then thrusting it towards my face.

'You wouldn't like me when I'm angry!' He laughed, the pleasure of such a small gift putting colour back into his wan cheeks. I couldn't help but laugh with him.

'Oh, save me, save me!' called Rhea as she walked into the room behind me, 'there's a monster on the loose!'

A look of puzzlement crossed Daniel's face, 'Hulk not monster, he hero!'

'I wasn't talking about the Hulk,' she replied, 'I was talking about you! Look at you up and about on your feet already.'

'Me better. Hulk make me better.'

'I think it might have been the doctors and nurses that made you better,' I said as a male nurse came into the room.

'No, he Hulk, but never gets angry in the hospital. That's why he never go green.'

The nurse started to blush, 'Ah, sorry about that. It seemed like a good idea when we were trying to get him to keep the mask on.'

'It's ok,' I said, 'if it works don't knock it is my motto when it comes to dealing with our Daniel.'

'He's doing so well now that we're going to be sending him home tomorrow. Can you arrange some transport? Should be sometime after the consultant rounds in the morning so around mid-day?'

I looked at Rhea and she nodded.

'Yes, I can give you a lift here and then we can both take him back to Oak Tree Lodge.'

'Are you sure? I can see if Joe can do it. You've done so much for us already.'

A frown flicked across her face, 'Of course I'm sure, I wouldn't offer if I wasn't. It's the least I can do. I'll make sure Carl takes Sam out somewhere and that you get back home in time too.'

'Thank you. You are too good to me.' She knew. I was sure of it.

Chapter Eighty

Lucy's Diary

Thursday 19th April 2012

Sam slapped me today. It was only a little slap and he said he was sorry as soon as he did it. He was just angry that I had been speaking to Will on the phone and I had sounded happier than he had made me in months. He said I was wrong to do that, to make him feel bad when I did that.

I haven't spoken to Will in ages. He texts me every few days, but if Sam is home I usually text back and say that it's not convenient for him to call me at that time. I still find it hard to accept Sam's feelings for Will just because he's gay. That isn't fair. But it's not worth the sour looks and sarcastic comments I get whenever Will's name is mentioned.

I didn't realise Sam had come home early. It was only lunchtime and I thought he was at work when my mobile rang so I answered it. It felt so good to hear Will on the other end. He was excited about the wedding plans and wanted to know when I was going to be able to get over to tell him what I was going to wear and of course, it was part of my duties to arrange his stag night wasn't it? He wanted the full works, including the male stripper, and he had found some numbers for me to ring around so that I could organise it all for him. He said he had found them out for my hen night until I had forbidden him from hiring any. I laughed and said he could always make use of the blow-up doll again if I couldn't get anyone to do it. He replied that it was too late for that, 'Dick' had died a while ago after Drew had got a bit too exuberant with him whilst experimenting with a rather pointed cucumber. Apparently, Dick had gone with a blast and had really enjoyed the experience.

It was as I was crying with laughter at this image that I turned to see Sam standing in the nursery doorway. His face was red and his fists were clenching. I stopped laughing and told Will I had to go. I would call him later to arrange a meet up.

Sam was really angry. He shouted that I shouldn't go behind his back calling strange men. Wasn't he good enough for me? I told him he was being silly and that Will would never be anywhere near what he meant to me. Will was just a friend, nothing more. I tried to walk past him out of the room, asking him if he would like me to make him some lunch but he grabbed my arm and held me still. He said it hadn't sounded like I was just talking to a friend. What kind of friends talk about male blow up dolls called Dick?

Coming from Sam, this gave me the giggles again. I couldn't help it. The image that Will had started to describe came into my mind and made me laugh, but Sam thought I was laughing at him. He raised his hand and slapped me across the face.

"To wipe the smile off it," he said, before turning and slamming back into his study.

It's been so long since he last hit me that I wasn't expecting it. I should have seen the signs, the clenching fists were always a give-away, but he promised me he wouldn't do it again.

Later, when he was calmer and came out to find me, he apologised. Said he didn't mean to do it and that he was jealous of the friendship I had with that man. He knew he shouldn't be jealous but he just wanted me to laugh at things he did the way I had been laughing at Will when he came up the stairs.

I didn't say anything about the fact that he had slapped me when I had been laughing at something he said. I said I was sorry I'd upset him. That I wouldn't do it again. We were just excited about Will's upcoming wedding and stag night. I asked if I could still go. I promised I would be good and that he could come too. It would be good for us to get out and have some fun together, even if it was with Will.

Sam said he would think about it. I hope he says yes. I really want to go.

Chapter Eighty-One

Lucy's Diary

Sunday 29th July 2012

It was Will and Drew's stag night last night. They decided it was silly to have separate ones because they shared the same friends. They tried taking the names out of a hat to decide which friends were to go to which do, but that didn't work.

I was the only woman there. It was touch and go as to whether Sam would let me, but he has been trying so hard to be nice to me again. I said it would look funny if I didn't go, that people would wonder where I was, whether I was ok? It was so rare that we went out anywhere these days. I felt as if I was becoming a hermit. I begged him to let me go.

Sam came too. That was the deal. He didn't trust all those men around me, especially when they were drinking. He said it could turn nasty and I could get hurt.

He can talk, he wears the T shirt.

I wasn't able to do any of the party arranging though. The way he acted with me just talking about blow up dolls was bad enough. I figured it would be better if I didn't antagonise him further by researching and booking some hunky male strippers, even if they were for someone else.

I told Will that I still wasn't up to it after losing Frankie. He said he understood, but I don't think he did really. I think he was a bit hurt that with all this time on my hands I couldn't do that one simple thing for him. And I know I could have done it while Sam was at work but he checks my computer history. He told me ages ago that if I had nothing to hide then I didn't have any reason to put a password on my computer, so I took it off. It was easier than to argue.

I have to be careful about what I research though. The other day I was bored and aimlessly browsing, flicking from screen to screen and looking at the mum sites, reading the forums about miscarriage and baby loss. It helps to know I'm not the only one who has been stupid and lost their baby. My finger slipped on the mouse and I accidentally clicked on an advert for Viagra. I clicked it straight off again but didn't realise it would show up in my history. When he saw it, he asked me who I was buying it for because it certainly wasn't him. There was no way he was ever going to be one of those sad, dickless, fuckwits that couldn't get it up.

I explained what had happened and that I hadn't bought anything from there, I hadn't even stayed on the page once I realised what it was. He said he believed me.

He had to really, I bought everything on my credit card because he never gave me cash to spend. He knew everything I bought from the statements and he could check online whenever he wanted to.

He proved to me that he was still virile. It was fine though. I'd rather that than when he used to hit me. The bruises aren't so visible afterwards and I can block out the pain, be compliant and go through the motions. He never has figured out the difference when I fake it.

I'm such a good actress.

Sam didn't enjoy the stag do. He stood at the bar most of the night, watching and brooding. He did buy a couple of rounds for all the party goers and a bottle of champagne for Will and Drew, so I know he tried. I was the only one who noticed his distance. Everyone else there thought he was the bees knees for being so generous, told me how lucky I was to snag a man like him. Sam had laughed and said he was the lucky one, then kissing me, tongues and all, in full view of everyone. Announcing his claim on me, warning everyone else off with his actions.

He didn't have to do that. It made me embarrassed and the focus of attention when I shouldn't have been. I don't like it when people focus on me anymore, it makes me anxious, wary of what will happen later. I laughed it off and said we were both lucky, we were the perfect couple, just like Will and Drew were.

I only wanted to deflect the attention but I realised my mistake as soon as I said it. Sam didn't like being compared to them. Sam would never like being compared to them. He didn't say anything, but I saw the fist clench, the jaw tighten as he turned and ordered himself a whisky from the bar.

I went up to him and said I was sorry, that I didn't mean anything by it. I put my arms around him and told him how special he was and how much I loved him. That he was much more of a man than anyone else in the room. I leaned in and kissed him on his cheek, whispered in his ear that I would make it up to him later when we were alone and he could show me just what a real man could do. He held my arm and looked into my eyes, the lights and the smoke from the stage billowed around him, blurring my vision as he continued to search, to see if I was lying. I must be getting better at hiding it. He released me, snaking his arm around my back to pull me into him, forcing his groin into mine where I could feel his semi-hardness. He said he was looking forward to it.

When he released me, I took a glass of champagne from the bar and, saluting him with a wink over the rim of the flute glass, I took a sip, followed by another. I was going to need the alcohol.

We left when the strippers came on stage. Although he was quite partial to watching a female stripper, there was no way Sam was going to sit through a male striptease performance, so I suggested he call Brian to wait at the front door while I said goodbye to Will and Drew. He told me not to take too long about it, he didn't want to be kept waiting. I quickly explained to the couple that Sam had an early meeting so we had to leave and that I would call them in the week. They were enjoying the display on stage so I was able to slip away without any fuss and got to the door just as Brian turned up in the Audi.

When we got home, Sam insisted on a striptease of his own. Of course I obliged, I gave him the works and it wasn't so bad. The alcohol helped. I didn't feel as self-conscious as I would have without it. Maybe I should take up drinking more? It might help to lessen the pain I feel every day.

We had sex again this morning. He said he was still turned on by my performance the night before and was I sure that I hadn't learnt all that by giving my old customers extras on the massage table? He said I must have learnt it somewhere, I must have lied to him, but at least he was the one that was benefitting now and that I could do it for him more often.

I cried when he left the room and went for his run. I came into the nursery, curled up in my rocking chair and hugged Frankie's teddy so tight. I don't know what to do. When he's being nice, the man I fell in love with, I know that I am still in love. But when he's angry...

Maybe it is me? Maybe I do make the silly mistakes that he chastises me for?

I must do. It must be me and my big mouth that never thinks before it speaks. I must try harder, do what he wants and then he will love me again like he used to.

I can see him leaning on the gate to do his stretches before he comes in. I'll be better today. I'll be the Lucy he first met and fell in love with.

Chapter Eighty-Two

Lucy's Diary

Saturday 26th August 2012.

Will and Drew got married today.

I was Will's best woman, I told Sam that I really wanted to do it and, as I've been so good lately, he let me walk my best friend up the aisle to his soul mate.

It was a beautiful service. I've never been to a gay wedding before so didn't know what to expect, but it was so romantic, just like mine and Sam's was. I was crying by the time they got to say their vows. They had written their own and they were so special, so personal. You could see how much love there was between the two of them. It seems a lifetime ago they were first making out in the gardening shed at Silverwell. I suppose it was a lifetime ago. It was the day I met Sam and my life has changed completely since then.

The reception was held at Silverwell. Helen let them have it for free so they only had to pay for the food. Even the chef and the waitresses all chipped their time in for nothing. They said it was their wedding presents to the happy couple which was so sweet. Sam and I gave them their honeymoon. A week in Paris. It was a cheaper hotel than any of the ones we had stayed in, but it was still nice. Sam said it was about being there that mattered and it wasn't about how much the room had cost. I wanted to pay for a meal at the *Restaurant Le Jules Verne,* but Sam wasn't having any of it. He said the hotel and the flights were enough of a present and I didn't want to push it. I couldn't pay for it myself. Although Sam doesn't usually mind what I put on the credit card, he checks the statements and I know he would have been angry if he saw that I had purchased their restaurant bill. I don't have any cash of course. I pay for everything by card.

I felt incredibly brave doing my best woman's speech. I didn't think I could do it. I was shaking so much. It's been such a long time since I stood up and spoke to that many people at once. I used to have to give presentations when I was at university, it didn't bother me then. I quite liked the experience, the adrenaline it gave me as I knew everyone was listening to what I had to say. The feeling of achievement when I finished and everyone applauded.

Sam was watching me all the way through and I stuttered a bit to start. I spoke about how Will and I had met and how he had looked after me after my mum had died. How he had been the best friend a girl could ever have. How he had even been the one to introduce me to my own gorgeous husband. Without Will my life would have been so very different and so empty of the love I received from both of them. Will had blown me a kiss as I said that which was so sweet. I wished that he hadn't though, I know Sam saw it. I saw his jaw clench again, but he didn't ball his fist. He looked down and twirled the stem of his wine glass instead, the red liquid swirling in time with his actions. I waited until he looked up and smiled at him, I hoped he would let it go. Will was no sexual competition to him, never had been. I am safer with Will than with any other male, but I think Sam is jealous of our friendship, of what we have shared. Things that Sam could never share with me. I had been getting braver but I started to stutter again until Sam smiled back, raised his glass to me and took a drink.

I relaxed and said that Drew was very lucky to have Will in his life, that Will would stand by him through all the good times and the bad, just like he had for me. I wished them all the luck and love in the world and may they always be as happy together as they were today.

I didn't say that I wished them as happy a life as Sam and I had. I couldn't wish that on them.

We stayed for the first half of the evening do. Will grabbed me for a slow dance and then Sam and I danced a couple more. He held me tightly, whispered in my ear that he loved me and how much he was reminded of our own wedding when I was stood up at the top table. How he had missed hearing my laughter and that it was good to hear it again. He wanted me to laugh more often and he would be better, he would make it all up to me. I told him I would love that.

When we got home, he opened one of his special bottles of champagne. The ones he usually saved for important dinner parties. He said I was the most important person in his life. I deserved the best.

As we sat in the lounge and drank the bubbles, he kissed me slowly, gradually undressing me as our passion for each other grew to an unbearable need. He dripped some of the champagne over my breasts and then licked it off, teasing me all the time, awakening a need in me I'd forgotten I possessed. As the passion took over and we came together, I screamed his name, clung to him with all the power I had, succumbed to the fireworks that were shooting through my body.

He's asleep now. I watched him for a while, lying naked beside him and gently tracing circles across his chest with my pale pink acrylic nails. I could feel it rise and fall with every breath he took and it felt so nice. So gentle.

This was the Sam I had fallen in love with.

Please let this Sam stay.

Chapter Eighty-Three

Lucy's Diary

Wednesday 10th October 2012

I have found that nice Sam only visits when I don't mention Will. Now that he is married, Sam says that I shouldn't bother them anymore, they don't need me interfering with their new lives. He says they've moved on and I shouldn't be a part of it, I would only get in their way. Like Will should have done when we got married. Sam really doesn't like Will. I don't think he will ever change his mind, it's like he only sees that Will is gay and can't see the man behind that.

I asked him once why he didn't like gay men and he replied that they weren't real men. They weren't natural. Well, of course that's just poppycock and I didn't know what to say. It's too weird to even think that anyone thought that way. I mean, how can Will and Drew not be real men? They have dicks and they quite obviously make each other happy so what's not to be real? I didn't say this to Sam though, it would have made him angry and I try my best not to do that. Anyway, he had turned his back on me and walked out of the room and I know that means conversation closed. I don't dare follow him and ask him to continue with his reasoning.

Will has been texting me though. I can't reply because Sam checks my phone every night to make sure that I'm not talking to anyone who he thinks might not be suitable for me. He'll tell me off if he finds out I reply to Will's messages. He reckons that if I just ignore them then Will won't send anymore, he'll get the message and move on. He reckons Will is a parasite and only trying to keep in contact with me because of our money and contacts. It was ok for me to be his friend when I was just a physio but I have a new life now and I don't need him holding me back.

I don't know what he's holding me back from though. I only ever leave the house when I'm with Sam or when he lets me have a 'girly shopping day' in Truro with Rhea.

We do that about once a month. I spend lots of money on clothes and shoes while we're there, even though I don't have anywhere to wear them. Sam gets annoyed if I'm not dressed smart when he comes home from work and I swear he comes home early sometimes to catch me out. Find me lazing around in my joggers and then he calls me a lazy harlot, and a council house wallah. Just because that is where I come from, he says, doesn't mean I have to go back there and show off my slum roots. I know we were poor, but mum always made sure that the house we lived in was clean and tidy. I know we always wore second or third hand clothes, but they were never torn or dirty. Mum made sure we didn't live in a slum. It hurts when he says stuff like that, almost as bad as the slaps do.

I need to speak to Will before he decides to come round here and check up on me. That will make Sam even angrier because he will say that I invited Will over, even when I haven't. Sam will be lovely while Will is here, but I will pay for it after he's gone.

I asked Sam if I could have a membership at Silverwell so that

I could get back into shape, like I was before Frankie. I have let myself go a bit, I mean, I have never been over nine stone before, and Sam has commented that I'm getting fat. Heaven knows what he will do to me if I hit nine and a half stone. He wasn't having any of it though. He said that the staff wouldn't treat me properly if I went back as a client, they would be too familiar. I suppose he's right, although I was hoping to be able to see my old friends again. Even Cowbag Kelly would be a welcome change from these four walls. I never ever thought that I would voluntarily want to see her again, but everything has changed now, and I am so lonely.

Sam said he would change the nursery into a gym for me, that it was about time it was changed but I said that I didn't want that to happen. I felt that it was my space where I could be calm and be still when I needed to. I didn't tell him that it was really because I didn't want him to find my hiding place for my diaries. I'm surprised he hasn't pushed it though. He doesn't normally do anything I ask if he thinks something else should be done. Maybe he is still grieving Frankie after all? He never speaks of his dad's death, or of how much he misses him, never speaks of any of it and I'm pretty damn sure he's never cried for him, so is it the same with his son?

He never goes into the nursery and most of the time he ignores it. He knows I spend a lot of time in there when I'm home alone. I curl up in my rocking chair and read a book. I know he sneers at my choice of chick lit, says it's not literary enough for him and I should try bettering myself, but I don't care. I enjoy them, and why is it so wrong to want to see a happy ending? Just because I can't have one doesn't mean I can't live somebody else's.

He comes home early sometimes and he knows where I am but he shouts up the stairs to summon me. Calls me down to speak to him, listen to him talk about his day and tell me our plans for the evening. That's why I can't wear joggers during the day. I have to be dressed nice and wearing a full face of make-up for when he comes home unexpectedly. When he used to catch me out, he would call me slovenly and lazy and not fit to be his wife. Sometimes I'd also get a slap for my laziness and I'd be sent to shower and change and make myself more respectable. He would follow me into the bedroom then, pick out the clothes that he thought I should wear and I would end up prancing around the house in clothes more suited to a meal at Pareusi's than sitting in front of the fire watching a film. I've learnt now though. I buy clothes that are smart but comfortable so he can't tell me off so easily.

I don't need to give him any excuses.

I wonder if Rhea can get a message to Will for me. It's risky because she might tell Carl and then he would tell Sam, but I can't think of any other way. She's got a membership for the health club and could give it to him when she goes to her aerobics class.

I'll speak to her tomorrow and see if she can do it for me. She keeps asking if I'm ok, how did I get the bruises and stuff. I've told her that I was wrong about Sam hitting me, it was the grief of losing the baby that had me all mixed up. She said she understands and that she is there for me. I don't know if she believes me though.

I just need to stop Will coming over and getting me into more trouble.

Chapter Eighty-Four

Penny-May
Saturday June 20th 2015

Rhea definitely knew.

And that more than probably means she knows Sam is hurting me too.

I hid the diaries again, the sadness in them was too much for me today. She was so unhappy and yet she still loved him so much. How can that be? How can she forgive him when he has hurt her so much?

I shook my head as I pushed the drawer closed, I knew how that could be. Wasn't I in exactly the same situation?

I tried to recall when I had last spoken to Emma. Our girly nights that we had planned had never happened, there was always a reason why it wasn't suitable, it wasn't convenient. He told me that part of my life was over, I had him and my new friends now, so I didn't need her anymore. That she had moved on with her new flatmate and wasn't interested in me. I had let him do that to me because I loved him. Because I didn't want to be hit because of it.

Picking up my phone, I scrolled through, I'd call her now while I could, tell her we needed to meet up for a drink sometime. I couldn't find her name though, I scrolled up and down through the list, but I wasn't missing it in my haste. It was gone, no messages, no call logs, no contact details. They had all been deleted and I knew I hadn't done it. I also realised that was why she hadn't called me. He had blocked her number so she couldn't get through.

The anger burnt in my chest as my jumbled thoughts recalled Sam's attitude to Daniel, my '*spastic*' brother. I had fought for him before and I would not leave him now because a controlling bully was telling me I had to.

I just had to figure out a way to do it.

I was trapped though, I had no money, no transport and no friends left. Nobody I could call to come and help me.

Except maybe Rhea. Lucy had trusted her.

Rhea had been good to me so far, could I do the same?

'You ready to go get the Hulkster then?' Rhea came into the kitchen as I was picking up my handbag from the table.

'Yes, I think so,' I replied, 'we need to get a move on though, I need to be home before Sam gets back.'

'Oh, it's ok, I've told Carl to take him out for a drink after they have finished their meeting.'

I inhaled sharply and looked at her.

'Don't panic, I haven't said anything about the hospital. I said you needed cheering up after your fall the other day and that I was taking you for a girly shopping day In Truro. You text Sam and tell him that so our story sticks and he'll be none the wiser.'

I nodded, 'I'll do that in the car. Thank you.'

'No problem, now, let's get out of here and spring that brother of yours out of the clink.'

'Was Lucy as clumsy as I am?'

We were in the car, my curiosity about the extent of Rhea's knowledge coupled with needing to know for sure if I could trust her making me ask questions in a way that wouldn't reveal the diaries. I didn't think she knew about them and I didn't want her to know until I was totally sure that she would be on my side.

'Why do you ask that?'

'Oh, I was just wondering if there were any similarities between me and her. I mean, wouldn't Sam go for the same kind of woman for his wife?'

'She was a bit of klutz at times. Sam used to say she could trip over a pinhead if it was lying on the floor. She always bruised really easily, half the time she didn't even know how she got them.'

I could see her hands, fingers drumming on the steering wheel and she looked straight ahead, eyes flicking to the side mirror with a concentration that I didn't remember her usually doing while she drove. Normally, she was relaxed and carefree with one hand resting on the gear stick, the other just holding the wheel lightly as the power assisted steering took most of the strain of the tight corners on the narrow Cornish roads.

'Your bruising has gone down now, you're looking a lot better,' she said, flicking the screen wash and wipers on to clear the dust from the windscreen.

'I'm feeling much better and make up hides the worst of it.'

'That's what Lucy used to say too, she always wore long sleeved tops as well.

Like you do.'

'I thought it would get chilly later, always need to be prepared.' The phrase reminded me of the first time Sam took me out to that business dinner and getting the iPad the next day. I never used it now, didn't even know where it was. Probably still in the desk at work, maybe Michelle was using it now she was back from her maternity leave?

'She used to say that too.' Rhea glanced across at me and caught my eye. 'Seems like you are quite similar.'

We swung through the hospital gates in silence and she parked the car as near to the front entrance as she could.

'We'll go in and get him, then if you wait at the pick-up point, I'll bring the car round to you. We don't need to be walking any further than we have to with him.'

'Thank you, you're so good to me.'

She reached out and put her hand on my arm as I leant down to get my bag from the footwell.

'That's what friends are for. We help each other when we're in trouble. I'm always here for you, you know.'

The lump was back in my throat, stopping my words from tumbling out so I nodded, opened the door and stepped out into the blazing sunshine.

It wasn't going to get chilly while we were out. We both knew that.

Chapter Eighty-Five

Lucy's Diary
Wednesday 19th December 2012

I'm pregnant again and I really don't know what to do.

I want to keep my baby, there's no doubt about that, but I know Sam doesn't want children. He's going to be upset and blame me for getting pregnant on purpose.

I did of course, well, sort of. I desperately wanted a baby so I haven't been quite as good at taking my pills as I should have been. I might have missed a few here and there although I always made sure that I took them properly at weekends when Sam was around so that if it happened and I did get pregnant, I could say that he had seen me taking them. Now that it has happened, I'm not so sure that he will believe me. He doesn't like believing me. Says I'll say anything to get myself out of trouble.

He might be right there. He's caught me out a few times when I've lied about something, but I have learnt to tell the truth. He's taught me well because it always hurts less to own up than it does to try and wriggle my way out of my punishment. He punishes me more then. And he takes longer to say sorry afterwards.

That's why I can't tell him about this baby. If he finds out about it, he will be ever so angry and I know that I can't lie about being good with my contraception because he will see through it easily and then, well, I don't want to think about what he will do.

I can't lose another baby; it would kill me.

I don't even think it's safe to see the doctor. Sam is bound to find out that I made an appointment and I can't trust Brian. If I ask him to take me anywhere, he always asks Sam if it's ok for him to take me. I know that Sam is his boss and Brian's job is actually to drive him around, but on the days that he's not needed and he's just hanging around here, tinkering with random bits and bobs, you'd have thought I could just nip out somewhere without any hassle.

Even getting a taxi or sitting in the waiting room of the surgery is risky. Somebody who knows Sam is bound to see me and tittle tattle on me to him. That's the trouble with living in a small town, nothing is private. There's no place anywhere that you can be inconspicuous and not seen. Everybody knows Sam. He's such an '*upstanding member of the community*' what with all the charities he donates to and the '*good works*' that he's done. Christ, when I can get out into town, I can't even sneeze without some busybody asking him if I'm alright. Then he phones me and asks what I'm doing and where I'm going and who I'm with. He asks me the same questions again when he gets home and God help me if I give an answer different to what I said earlier.

So I can't go to the doctor. I can't get help from anyone.

It was a stroke of luck that I could buy the pregnancy test yesterday. Rhea and I went to do our Christmas shopping and Brian had dropped us off in the car park by Tesco's. When he'd gone, I said that I needed half an hour on my own so that I could buy Rhea her Christmas present and she said that was fine because she still needed to get mine as well. We arranged to meet up again at the coffee shop an hour later, Rhea had said we should phone when we were done but I didn't want to do that because Sam would ask why she was phoning me when we were supposed to be together, so I said not to worry, an hour would be plenty and either one of us could just wait over a latte if the other was a bit late.

I went straight over to Boots and bought myself a test kit and then to the ladies and did it straight away. I had to throw all the stuff away afterwards though, I couldn't risk anyone finding any of it. Especially as it was positive.

I think I'm about six weeks gone. I'm two weeks late and Sam was really horny last month. He didn't need to force me either, he took the time to make sure I was ready and just as horny as he was. I like it when he does that, takes me back to when we first fell in love and couldn't keep our hands off each other. I know he pulled in a really big deal and he is always more considerate to me when a contract is signed and sealed. I get wined and dined at Pareusi's and he buys me jewellery and the florist delivers a big bunch of roses and lilies. I can relax when they arrive. He's a bit stressed and -teasy while the deal is going through and I have to be extra careful not to upset him, but once I get the flowers, I know I'm in for a good few weeks, sometimes a good couple of months.

He's still in a lovely mood at the moment. I know he's got something planned for us for Christmas and he keeps hinting that I'm going to absolutely love my present, it's going to be an extra special surprise.

I'm not going to ruin it. I've got another couple of months before I start to show so I can hide it for a while until I figure out what to do. Maybe my surprise is that he does want a baby after all? I know Maggie has been hinting quite loudly that it's about time she became a grandmother and isn't it time we tried again?

She blames me of course, even told me a few months ago that it was wrong of me to deny Sam his chance of fatherhood.

Stupid bitch!

He didn't correct her, didn't stand up for me. Just said he was sure that I would let him know when I was ready to chance it again. I was upset at the time when he didn't say it was him that was saying no, but maybe it was because he was planning to tell me he had changed his mind?

I'll cross my fingers that this is what he's going to do, but I'm still going to stay quiet for now.

I can't risk doing anything else.

I'm not going to lose this baby too.

Chapter Eighty-Six

Lucy's Diary

Thursday 10th January 2013.

Sam doesn't want a baby, that's not what my surprise was.

He took me on a holiday to Lapland and we spent Christmas Day snuggled under fur blankets on the back of a sled pulled by real reindeer. It was magical and he was right, I loved it. So did he.

We were back to how we were before, and he was such a gentleman again. So loving and considerate, nothing was too much trouble for him. He made sure I had everything I wanted.

He said he was sorry for everything he had done to me in the past, but it was in the past now. He would never hurt me again.

He said it was because he had been stressed about work, and worried about how his mother was coping since his dad had died. I think she's been fine, she's off gallivanting all over the place these days, but I didn't say that of course. I nodded and said that I understood and forgave him.

I asked him if he had thought about having another baby but

he was adamant that he didn't. He said he needed to concentrate on just me and Maggie at the moment. When we had a kid, he wanted to be able to spend time with him, be a proper father to his son and bring him up properly. He didn't want to be a part-time father.

I left it there, I said I understood and that maybe one day, he would let me know when he was ready to try again.

I still don't know what to do about my little Peanut mark two.

I don't even have a nursery anymore. That was the other bit of my Christmas surprise.

Sam had it redecorated while we were away and it's now my study/reading room.

He said he didn't think it was doing me any good to be surrounded by all that baby gear all the time and as all I did in there was read anyway, it made sense to have it redone.

It does look lovely. The decorator has done it out in soft pinks and purples with a white desk under the window and a brand spanking new computer on it and a spinny white leather office chair in front of it. There are a couple of white bookcases along the back wall stuffed full of my favourite books and a load of new bestsellers waiting for me to dive into them. He must have made the sales assistants in *Waterstones* incredibly happy when he put that order in.

My rocking chair is still in there as well. He didn't ditch that one. And there is a big squishy sofa as well, all covered in extra squishy cushions and fur throws across the back.

'Just right for snuggling under on these cold winter days,' he said to me when I walked over and picked one of the blankets up to feel its softness.

I told him it was lovely. It was ever so thoughtful of him to go to all that trouble and that I didn't deserve any of it.

We christened the sofa then. He sat down and pulled me on top of him so I could feel how turned on he was and he asked me to ride him. I did as I was asked, and I enjoyed it. But my mind couldn't stop thinking about what it meant.

I couldn't tell him about the baby. This was definitely proof that he didn't want any children.

At all.

Chapter Eighty-Seven

Lucy's Diary

Wednesday 23rd January 2013.

Rhea said she's worried about me. I can see why. I try hard but I'm hardly the life and soul of the party these days.

She came around a couple of days ago and said she'd been talking to Will and they thought I was depressed.

She had some news for me though, I think it's good, but it might be a bit awkward. Apparently, Rebecca has been in touch with Will and she wants to see me again. It's been so long that I sometimes even forget that I have a sister these days. She had to go through Will as she didn't know how to contact me. The last she heard was that I had moved in with Will but that was so long ago she thought I may have moved far away by now. She couldn't believe it when he told her I was still in Trecase and I was married to Sam. Not that she knew who he was, obviously. She doesn't move in the right circles for him.

Will had phoned Rhea to pass the message on, he didn't want me to get into trouble if he contacted me direct, but he knew how much I missed my family. I think they believe that's the reason why I'm depressed, it's because of the rift.

I'll let them continue to think that. It keeps them away from the truth while I try and figure out what I'm going to do.

I haven't told Sam about the baby. I know I'm going to have to, it won't be long before I begin to show and there's no way I'll be able to keep it a secret then.

He's not going to like it. Maggie was around for dinner the other night and she asked me in front of him when I was going to give Sam a baby. As if it was me that was holding up the process. She had put on her caring voice, and said, ever so sincerely, that I shouldn't mourn the baby I had lost forever and that having another one would help me to get over it. I just mumbled that I was fine and that we would when the time was right.

As usual, Sam didn't stand up for me. I swear he can't bear for her to know that it's him that's saying no. Him that doesn't want any children, or even a child. All he said was that he didn't think I was ready for that discussion and how I had asked for him to change the nursery into a study for me so I could move forward with things that I wanted to do. Lying bastard.

He made me sound so selfish and she looked at me like I was the dirt on the bottom of her shoe.

I desperately wanted to tell her the truth. That would shut her up. She's always going on about how brilliant he is and how caring and sensitive he is. How he's the perfect son and the only thing missing in our little family is having the perfect grandchild to dote on now that Frank has gone.

I couldn't do that though. The price would be too much to bear, especially as I now have Peanut number two to protect. I said that, for now, I needed the space to work a few things out and when we were ready to start again, it could always be turned back into a nursery. It would be nice to have it different from when it was done for Frankie, it would be a new beginning.

Sam had reached over and squeezed my hand. Maggie had commented how it was nice that we were still so much in love and that Sam protected and cared for me so much, particularly when I was denying him something that would make him so happy. Sam had squeezed my hand harder then.

It wasn't reassurance. It was a warning.

I agreed with her, I said that I didn't deserve a husband as good as Sam was to me and that I was sure I would be better soon. I would sort myself out to be a better wife to him.

Sam gave another tiny squeeze and then patted the back of my hand as he withdrew his to continue to eat his meal.

I asked Rhea if she would drive me to meet Rebecca but I didn't want Sam to know. I said I didn't want him worrying about me getting upset if it didn't work out so I said to arrange something in Truro and say we were shopping. I needed her cooperation so that my alibi worked and Brian didn't go tittle tattling to Sam about where I went. She agreed so quickly that I'm sure her and Will have talked about us and the reason why they think I don't speak to him anymore.

Why I can't speak to Will anymore.

That's a point, maybe Will could meet us in Truro as well? I don't know why I haven't thought of that before. I'm sure Rhea will be ok with it. I'll ask her tomorrow.

Chapter Eighty-Eight

Penny-May
Monday June 22nd 2015

I was horrified at what I was reading. She was in such a terrible position and he wasn't standing up for her at all.

I thought it was just me that Maggie hated because I wasn't Lucy, but it wasn't that at all. All Maggie was concerned about was her perfect little boy being treated right and his wife giving him the child Maggie assumed he wanted.

Well, she was a bitch, and he was a bastard for treating Lucy that way.

It wasn't right that Lucy had got herself pregnant without telling him though. She shouldn't have done that, especially suspecting what he had done to her before. If he had done that.

Surely, no man would have his wife so desperately scared that she would hide her pregnancy from him in case he killed her baby. That is just too far-fetched to believe.

But he beat and forced himself on me. As much as I wanted to say she was, at best, exaggerating his brutality, didn't I have the bruises to know, deep down, that she was telling the truth?

Chapter Eighty-Nine

Lucy's Diary

Monday 4th February 2013.

I'm three months pregnant now. I so want to be a good mum to Peanut number two.

But how can I be when her father doesn't want her? I've decided she is a girl this time. I feel different than I did when I had Frankie. This has to be a girl. I'm going to call her Billie.

If I get to keep her safe.

I met up with Rebecca this morning. Rhea set up the meeting and came with me into Truro. She left me outside the coffee shop though, sent me in on my own to meet my sister while she went shopping with Will.

Oh, it was good to see him again. He gave me the biggest hug and I burst into tears. I almost didn't go into the coffee shop because of it, I wanted to be with Will and meeting Rebecca was going to be scary. We parted on such a big argument. I couldn't see how that could be overcome.

It was though. I was wary when she came in. I had planned to be calm and sophisticated, not let her see how much she had hurt me when she told me to leave and never come back, but when she walked in I started crying again and it was her turn to give me a hug instead of Will. I'm sure if I hadn't just had the reunion with him ten minutes before I would have been fine, but I was so emotional I couldn't help it.

The pregnancy hormones didn't help either. That's it, I'll blame those. It's all little Billie's fault.

I told Rebecca about her. I wasn't going to, but I need to talk to someone about it

or else I'm going to go insane. I told Rebecca about Frankie too. She was sorry that she hadn't been there for me. She said she didn't know how I coped with losing my baby so tragically. I didn't tell her I think Sam pushed me though. I definitely didn't tell her I think he kicked me as well. I'm still not sure I can believe it and it would be so wrong of me to tell lies, to blacken his name to my family when they haven't even met yet.

Will he ever meet her? I don't know. We haven't set a date for her to meet him. I need time to get my head around being in contact with her again first, and he'll be angry at me for sneaking around so I'll keep her to myself for a while I think. I'm sure she understands.

I did tell her that he doesn't want another baby and that he will be angry with me for falling pregnant again. I even said about how upset I was when he converted the nursery into an office. That told me he didn't want another baby.

I can't tell him about Billie. He'll go mad. I don't like making him mad.

I think I probably told her too much. I could see that she didn't understand. I mean, how could anyone understand about a husband who hits his wife? Or about the wife that can't leave him? Because he wouldn't let me go. He would find me. And where would I go anyway? I'm useless without him. He's told me that so many times. I can't survive without him. He'd come and find me. He'd make sure I paid for running away. He'd make sure I never ran away again.

Anyway, I have nowhere to go.

And no money to run with.

He's seen to that.

So, I didn't tell her all of it. I told her we were very much in love, but he was fragile following the death of his father and the loss of Frankie as well. I said he felt guilty about Frankie's miscarriage, that he felt he hadn't protected me well enough. He didn't stop me from falling down those stairs.

I do love him. Well, nice Sam anyway. I don't even like nasty Sam let alone love him, but I'm sure if I'm better, then nice Sam will come out to play more often.

But he won't be nice when he finds out about Billie.

As much as I enjoyed spending time with Rebecca and Will today, they can't help me.

There's no way out of it, I'm going to have to tell Sam.

But not today.

I can't face it today.

I need to keep my baby safe for at least one more day.

Chapter Ninety

Lucy's Diary

Wednesday 27th February 2013.

I felt her kick last week.

I was just summoning up enough courage to tell Sam about her when I felt her kick and I couldn't do it. It was as if she was telling me not to. Telling me to keep her a secret for just a little while longer. I'm only just starting to get a bit rounded and he hasn't noticed anything yet, even when we've been having sex. I never say no to him, even when I don't fancy it. He'd only take me anyway so I may as well just get on with it and hope that he doesn't take very long. Better to go through the motions. Sometimes I enjoy it though, it's not all bad, especially when he takes the time to make sure I'm properly up for it.

I'd decided that I would soften him up a bit before telling him, or should I say harden him up a bit? He's always a lot more agreeable after a good sex session. I should say love-making session, he prefers it when I say we are making love. Only people who don't love each other and are just doing it for the physical release have sex, he says.

We mostly have sex these days. Or he does.

Anyway, I ordered in his favourite meal, got the caterers to bring it round and leave me instructions for how to cook it and then they left so it would only be the two of us. I wore his favourite sexy outfit, short skirt and see through chiffon blouse. Luckily, it's quite loose on the belly, so that he can get his hands up underneath it easily and play with my tits, unfettered by an annoying brassiere. I felt like a right tart but if it got him in the right mood for my beautiful bombshell then it would be worth the embarrassment.

He couldn't believe it when he walked in the door and saw me and what I had done for him. I could see him start to go hard right through his suit trousers and as I slowly removed his tie and kissed him on the corner of his mouth, I felt him get even harder.

He asked what he had done to deserve me, asked if he'd forgotten an anniversary? I just said it was an in between birthday present because I knew I hadn't been much fun lately and I wanted us to get back to how we used to be.

He didn't argue with me over that point. He ate the food and we had sex on the rug in front of the roaring fire. I made sure I did all the things that he loved me to do to him, licked him hard and then teased him mercilessly as I rode him really slowly until he flipped me over and took me fast and hard, pounding into me and bringing me to orgasm at the same time as he did. Collapsing beside me and stroking my face as we lay together, spent and happy while the dwindling fire cast its flickering glow over our bodies.

I'd almost forgotten how good it felt to be snuggled up to him in the aftermath of an amazing love-making session. How horny he could make me when he was kind and considerate. When I was being the perfect wife. The subservient, perfect wife that was waiting at home, ready to do his bidding.

I wondered if we could be like this again. Could we really go back to when we first met?

That was when I felt the first kick. The fluttering sensation that was just like little bubbles bursting in my womb. At first, I thought it might be the aftershocks of the orgasm and then I realised that the orgasm must have woken her, made her move and remind me she was there.

And then he said he loved it when it was just the two of us, that we should do this more often. He loved it when I made the effort and he was pleased I was getting back to my old self again, I'd gotten over the baby thing and moved forward, ready to continue our old life where we'd left off.

And I felt the bubbles moving again.

And I started to cry. When he asked me why I was crying I said it was because I loved him so much and I was sorry I had been so horrible to him over the last year.

Then he forgave me. He said it didn't matter what I had done because I was better now, everything could go back to being normal again.

He forgave me.

I can't tell him about Billie.

Chapter Ninety-One

Lucy's Diary

Friday 1st March 2013.

I can't do this anymore.

Sam is going to notice my growing belly soon and after I chickened out of telling him last week there's no way I can admit to him now that I am four months pregnant.

We've had sex every day since I made him that meal and massive love-making session. He's going to work every day happy and coming home horny, and while I enjoy it, I know that it is built on a lie and it's a lie that is going to hurt me when it comes out.

Billie has made her presence felt more often too. I often feel those little flutters that remind me she is here. She needs to be protected.

What can I do when both the people I love need me and want me in such very different ways?

Sam can fend for himself. Billie can't. But I can't provide for her on my own and Sam will never let me keep her.

I only have one choice. I have to go where he can't get to us and if I can't have her in this life then I'll make sure I have her and my Frankie in the next.

I've written Sam a note.

I've told him that I don't hold any grudges, but I just can't live this way anymore.

I hope he doesn't grieve for too long. Although will he be grieving for me or the loss of his perfect married life?

If you are reading this, I hope he has treated you better than he did me.

I hope you don't make the same mistakes as I did, and that he has learnt his own lessons through my leaving the way I am.

Maybe you are a better wife than me anyway? It wouldn't be hard to do that. I made a rubbish wife in the end, far too far from the perfection he craves. I hope you are better than me, stronger than me.

Because I have to go and take the coward's way out. I just can't face what tomorrow will bring if I stay.

I wish you well.

Love

Lucy. x

Chapter Ninety-Two

Penny-May

Monday June 22nd 2015

Tears slid unbidden down my cheek as I closed the diary after the last entry. She was so unhappy and confused. All she wanted was to keep her baby safe and when she realised she couldn't do that because he would get so angry, she had to take her own life.

And he had raped her too. She didn't say it, but I could read it in-between the lines. When she said she didn't enjoy the sex, that it was better to just let him get on with it.

That's not the behaviour of gentleman, that's the actions of a monster.

The monster that I was married to.

I knew now it wasn't me that was the problem. There was nothing wrong with me. It was him who was evil and sadistic.

Slumping back into the spinny white chair, hugging the book to my chest I realised that I was now in exactly the same position that she was. Ok, I wasn't pregnant, but I had Daniel and he needed my protection. If Sam could do all of that to Lucy to get his own way, then I fully believed he could do anything to get Daniel out of the picture.

I couldn't get away though. I had no money and nowhere to go. No family. Nobody to help me. I wasn't even sure now if Rhea had been aware of Lucy's plight at the time. Just how much did Rhea know? I could run away, but he would know I couldn't leave my brother. Sam would always find me through him. No matter how far I travelled, it was going to be impossible to hide with a Hulk loving Down's Syndrome man who loved to talk to everyone.

I'm just as stuck as she was, and I can't even do what she did because I can't take Daniel with me like she did. And I'm too much of a coward. She was much braver than I am.

Carefully replacing the diary back into the desk, I closed the drawer and left the room. I needed to walk, and I needed to think.

The fields behind the house were just coming into bloom. Blood red poppies danced in the early summer breeze, the backdrop of the sea providing a sharp blue contrast. Shielding my eyes against the sun I tried to see where the ocean ended and the sky began, the far horizon remained invisible, mocking my need for it to tell me what to do.

There were people here today. There always was when the poppies came into flower. They came armed with their cameras, all trying to take photographs that would adorn their perfect face-book pages later. It was a beautiful day for it.

I couldn't enjoy it though, not like that couple over there, laughing as they tried to get their little girl to pose amongst the willowy flowers just long enough for them to get the perfect shot. She wasn't doing as they wanted though. Every time the mother put her down in the middle of them, she would run straight out again and cling onto her mother's legs, thumb in her mouth. The father tried coaxing her too, but it still didn't work. After about fifteen minutes, the mother hoiked her up onto her hip and walked in herself, started twirling amongst the flowers while he clicked away. The photos were going to be amazing. I just knew it. This was what Lucy had dreamed of. The perfect family group having fun on a sunny day, making the most of the love they had for each other.

And if she couldn't have it? I understood why she had taken her life.

I couldn't let him get away with it, I couldn't let him do the same to me as he had done to her. I wanted that happy family life too and while Sam was still walking the streets, I could never have it.

Decision made, I pulled my phone out of my pocket and dialled Rhea's number.

Chapter Ninety-Three

Penny-May

Tuesday June 23rd 2015

Silverwell Health Club was bathed in sunlight and there was a yoga class being taught on the lawn to the side of the building. Everyone looked so content as they performed their moves a few seconds after those of the lithe female instructor. Maybe I should have tried that instead of Zumba? It looked so much simpler and not half as energetic.

'Where are you, Hun?' Rhea asked, bringing me out of my daydream.

'Huh? Oh, nowhere really. I was just thinking how much easier yoga is compared to Zumba.'

'Don't you believe it!' She nodded towards the group who were now moving into a position which consisted of their backsides in the air while they rested on their fore arms. 'That's just the beginner's class, you have to be a right contortionist to get to the advanced level. Come on, Will's waiting for us in our usual place.'

Removing my sunglasses as we entered the building and walking right past

Cowbag Kelly without even saying hello now that I knew what she had been like with Lucy, I followed Rhea into the small staff room where Will came and gave me a hug as soon as we entered. It felt so nice to have his arms around me. The sensation of human contact with no hidden agenda, no hidden meaning. Not wanting anything in return or expecting it to lead anywhere. I returned his embrace, inhaled the faint scent of ginger from his shower gel and drew strength from his easy companionship. 'Shall we take these outside?' Rhea asked, picking up the tray of coffees that Will had already made.

'Yes, let's,' Will replied, patting my back gently as he let me go and turned to face her. 'There's a lovely, secluded spot next to the potting shed where the guests never go.'

I smiled as I remembered Lucy's words about what Will had got up to in the potting shed with Drew. It would be interesting to see where their love affair had begun.

He led the way as she carried the drinks and I followed, replacing my sunglasses as we re-entered the glare of the sun.

The potting shed was just that. A small timber shed, about four metres square with a window on the left-hand side of the padlocked door. There was an equally small, paved area in front of it on which stood a rough timber bench set with a closed umbrella poking through the hole in the centre and anchored into a wrought iron parasol base underneath. Will reached out and unfurled it, forcing the clip over the final couple of inches until it clicked into place. He then sat on one side and indicated that we should sit on the other.

'I was surprised to get your call wanting to meet us here,' Rhea said as she sipped her coffee, 'I thought you'd be resting now that Daniel is home again.'

'Yes,' chipped in Will, 'luckily, I've got some free time this afternoon, my client cancelled because of the weather. Although I'd have passed her over to Tabitha with

some excuse anyway when I knew you were coming.'

'So, what's up?' Rhea asked.

'I was thinking about Lucy and how she died,' I replied, 'she must have been terribly unhappy to do what she did. Was there really no-one that could help her?'

I watched them closely. Rhea and Will looked across the table at each other and simultaneously dropped their glances. Will put his hands around his mug and appeared to be contemplating it deeply. Rhea started running her finger around the top of hers as if it was a wine glass she was trying to make sing.

After a few minutes of silence while I looked from one to the other, Will eventually spoke.

'It was such a difficult time and we tried so hard to be there for her. She had lost the baby she desperately wanted and blamed herself for it. She withdrew into herself. It was really hard to get her to talk to us about anything. And Sam; Well— '

I saw him look at Rhea and as they exchanged glances, she nodded slightly before continuing the endless circling of her mug.

'— Sam could be difficult.'

Rhea snorted, her finger stopping its circling as she raised her hand, thrusting it in front of her in anger.

'Difficult? That's one way of putting it! I'd be tempted to use different terminology.'

'What do you mean?' I asked.

She removed her own sunglasses and looked straight at me.

'He monitored her phone calls, who she saw, where she went. She couldn't move without him knowing about it.'

'And he wouldn't let her talk to me at all,' Will said, 'Rhea had to act as a go between and it was always difficult for us to actually meet up. There was no way I could phone her. He would have hit the roof.'

'Much like he does with you,' Rhea said, 'we helped her as much as we could.'

'Just like we're trying to help you now,' said Will. 'He hits you as well doesn't he?'

I couldn't maintain their eye contact any longer, my gaze dropped to my hands, clasped together on the table. My coffee so far untouched. I nodded, Rhea reached over and grabbed my hands and squeezed reassuringly.

'We're here for you, when you want us to be,' she said.

'I found Lucy's diaries,' a hiccup escaped from my throat, 'I thought it was all my fault but I'm married to a monster and I don't know what to do.' I tried to stop the tears. I was so tired of crying all the time, but it was pointless. It was as if my eyes had developed their own lakes and they had reached bursting point. 'How can he do that stuff to us?'

'We thought he was doing the same to you as he was to her,' Will said. 'You don't have to put up with it though. You can get out.'

I shook my head, 'I can't. I have nowhere to go and no money to do it with. Besides, he would find me and God only knows what he would do to me then. I have Daniel as well. Even if I could hide, there's no way I could ever give him up.' The tears were in full flow now, 'I'm totally trapped.'

'You could report him to the police?' Will said.

'They wouldn't believe me. Everyone loves him. He's the perfect, upstanding gentleman of the town, donates to every cause going, helps old ladies across the street and even designed the new police headquarters. No,' I shook my head, 'they'd say I was lying and he would be so angry. I was lucky last time; I wouldn't survive if I made him that angry again.'

Rhea held me as I sobbed against her shoulder, rubbing my back as if I were a child.

'It's ok,' she said in her gentle, soothing tone, 'We'll sort something out. We'll get you out of there, we promise.'

'Yes,' agreed Will, 'just sit tight and be good. Don't give him any reason to be angry with you.'

'I'll try, but it's not that easy if he's had a stressful day at work.'

'Then I'll phone you tonight, I'll make some excuse for a chat, I'll sound off about Josh doing something at school. If Sam's angry, you ask me if the teacher told Josh off. If I hear you say that, I'm calling the cops and sending them right over, have you got that.'

I nodded, 'Thank you. You're so kind to me.'

'Nonsense,' Will said, 'he's a bastard and you deserve so much better. Now, dry your eyes Honeybun, there's a better life a'comin' and we are going to make sure you get it!' He handed me a screwed-up handkerchief from the pocket of his tracksuit trousers, 'One day I'll remember to keep a clean one of these just for you.'

I loved Will. He always had a way of making me smile.

Chapter Ninety-Four

Penny-May

Wednesday June 24th 2015

'We're going to Truro to do some shopping. I've told Sam I'm treating you to lunch out and he has told me to make sure you buy lots of clothes to cheer yourself up after your fall the other day. I'm going to pick you up in twenty minutes, ok?'

'Uh— ok. I guess I'll see you soon then.'

I clicked the phone closed and checked my face in the mirror.

Sam had been lovely last night. When Rhea telephoned to check on me I didn't have to say our code words. Thank God! Sam had phoned before he left Mistral and said he was bringing a curry home for us so all I had to do was warm some plates. He said I deserved some pampering after all I had been through the last couple of weeks.

I didn't really like curry very much, but that didn't matter. I had learnt to like whatever he decided I should eat. I warmed the plates to the perfect temperature, his cutlery too which I wrapped into a cotton napkin to keep them warm until it was time for our meal.

After we had eaten, he ran me a hot bubble bath, surrounded it with candles and opened some champagne. I was in there for ages, until the water was stone cold. When I got out and dried myself off, I saw that the bedroom was lit softly by the bedside lights and the duvet turned down enticingly. I slid between the cotton sheets and pulled the duvet up under my chin.

'Feeling better?' he said as he entered the room.

I nodded, 'Much better thank you.' I was expecting him to slide in beside me, to demand his conjugal rights as my husband. There was usually a price to pay for him being so nice.

'I'll leave you to sleep, I've got some paperwork to do and it will be a late one for me. Night night.' He leant over and kissed me on the forehead.

'Oh, ok, night night.' I replied.

This Sam was perfect, I knew what Lucy meant when she wished that this Sam would stay.

Chapter Ninety-Five

Penny-May
Thursday June 25th 2015

Rhea pulled up in her convertible BMW, the sun was shining and she had the top down again. I settled myself into the passenger seat and clicked the seatbelt into place.

'We're meeting Will in town,' she said, 'he's looking forward to not having to make the coffee for once. He said he'll wait for us in *The Wood Shack*, but we're buying.'

'I'll bet he is, I don't think we've ever made him one at the gym, have we?'

'No, but he's got to be useful for something hasn't he?' She quickly looked across at me as we accelerated down the road, turning back to concentrate on the twists and turns of the narrow streets.

I laughed in reply, it was so nice to be out and about and care-free, if only for a short while.

. . .

The Wood Shack was a relatively new coffee shop on the outskirts of Truro. Will was waiting outside and gave me a hug when we got to the door. The café was true to the beginning of its name in that the décor was all wood, but it was very tastefully done. Nothing ramshackle about it at all. It wasn't large, I quickly counted just eight tables inside. In front of each of the two windows that were set either side of the door was a beer barrel table with a couple of leather bucket chairs. Two larger, wooden bench style booths lined each side wall and a further two wooden tables that each sat four people stood in the middle of the room. A glass topped counter that seemed awash with every type of cake you could possibly ask for was set towards the rear of the café and separated the room from the preparation area beyond.

There was a couple sat in one window, holding hands across the table and staring into each other's eyes, a single plate with just crumbs left upon it, but with two forks. In contrast, a second couple sat in the opposite window, empty plates in front of each of them and coffees going cold on the table, while they scrolled through the screen on their mobile phones. I felt myself give a cynical smile, the opposite ends of the lives of lovers as told through the mirrored lens of the coffee shop door.

The rest of the tables were empty bar the farthest booth at which sat a slim, brown-haired woman with a toddler on her lap. They were playing peek-a-boo with the woman putting a paper napkin over her daughters head and the child laughing as she pulled it off to see her mother's laughing face again. Rhea led the way through the room with Will behind her and I followed him. The woman looked up and pointed at us, saying something to her daughter. She smiled and stood up; the girl was put on the ground where she started to run towards Rhea.

'Auntie Rhe!' she called, the excitement showing as she bundled into Rhea.

'Hey sweetheart, look who else is here,' she put the girl down and stepped aside so she could see who was next in line for a hug.

'Uncle Will!' Again, she barrelled in for another hug and then looked expectantly around, 'Where's Uncle Drew?'

'He's busy today,' Will said as he crouched down to hold her at her level, 'but we've brought someone else for you to meet. This is Penny-May.'

I had stopped walking by now, I didn't know what was going on and felt totally out of place in this scenario. They had obviously already arranged to meet this lady here and not told me.

'Do you want to say hello?' Will continued to ask the girl. She shook her head, popped her thumb in her mouth and buried her head in his shoulder.

'Silly Billy,' said Will, 'We all love Penny-May, and I promise she doesn't bite.'

'Don't worry about it,' I said to him, smiling to hide my distracted thoughts, 'It's always scary meeting new people.'

I looked across to the table where Rhea was now talking quietly with the woman at the table. I stood back awkwardly, confused thoughts running through my head as I tried to make sense of why we were here.

Rhea looked over and beckoned me to the table, 'I need to introduce you. I'm sorry we didn't tell you about this Pen, but we weren't totally sure she would come.

Penny-May— '

She held her left hand out to me as I approached, her right hand reaching out to the lady's. I saw Will stand with the child anchored firmly onto his hip. Abstractedly I thought how brilliant a father he would be, maybe she was an illicit lover of his?

'— This is Lucy and her daughter, Billie.'

Chapter Ninety-Six

PENNY-MAY

Thursday June 25th 2015

'Lucy?' I asked, my mind awash with so many questions that I needed answering but I was so shocked I couldn't ask any of them, 'You can't be!'

The woman nodded and reached out her hand to me, leading me into the booth so I could sit down before my knees crumpled beneath me.

'I'm Lucy, although people call me Mandy these days. Mandy Shaw. That's my daughter Billie Shaw. Or should I say mine and Sam's daughter? Rhea told me you found my diaries.'

'You didn't die?'

'In a way I did. Lucy died. She had to or else he would have killed both me and Billie. I couldn't let him do that. I had to find a way to keep us both safe and so far away from him that he would never find us.'

'But, I don't understand? Everyone said you were dead.' I

swivelled my head to face Rhea and Will, 'You both said she was dead! You lied to me.' I pointed at Billie,

'She called you Aunty and Uncle?'

They both looked to the floor, Will placed the child on the floor and she toddled over to her mother who picked her up and placed a kiss on the top of Billie's head as she settled her onto her lap.

'I'm sorry, we had no choice. We couldn't let him find them,' Rhea answered.

'We didn't know ourselves for quite a while after she left,' added Will, 'I could have throttled her myself when she finally contacted me just before Billie was born. I couldn't believe she would do that to me after all we had been through. But when she told me what he had done to her I understood. I didn't approve, but I understood.'

'You two need to talk,' said Rhea, 'we'll go and get the drinks ordered and keep Billie occupied. Come on Billie Boo, let's go choose some cake!' She bent down and expertly plucked the child out of her mother's arms.

'Choc'late cake?'

'Yes, but don't tell Mummy,' Rhea said in a conspiratorial whisper.

Billie raised her forefinger and placed it in front of her lips.

'That's right,' said Will, beginning to giggle, 'Sshhh, it's a secret.'

They walked to the counter, Billie's laughter echoing behind them.

I turned my head away from the threesome and faced Lucy.

'How could you let everyone think you were dead?'

She looked down and started fiddling with the napkin that had been discarded following the peek-a-boo game, twisting the corner over her forefinger again and again.

'I didn't want to. It was the last thing I wanted to do but I couldn't think how else I could escape.'

'But to fake your own suicide? Lie to everyone around you? I can't believe you could do that!'

'He would have killed me eventually. And he would have killed Billie too, just like he did my Frankie.'

I sat there. Looking at her. Taking in the home dyed chestnut brown hair, the glasses perched on her nose, the fuller figure hidden under a shapeless pair of denim dungarees that she wore over a cotton check shirt. She wasn't the designer dressed, slender blonde who should have been a model, who I had seen in the photos.

She was different.

She was totally not how I imagined she would be.

Her gaze flicked across to land on the tableau at the counter; her daughter laughing at something Will had whispered into her ear.

'I did it for her,' Lucy said.

'She's beautiful,' I picked up the pepper grinder and started tapping it gently on the table, watching the little flecks of black land in a minute dust cloud of its own. I needed to focus on something tangible rather than the tumbling thoughts that were racing around my head.

'How did you do it? You said in your diary that you had nowhere to go, no money, nothing? How did you escape?'

'My sister Rebecca came to my rescue. She gave me her spare room to hide out in for a while and then we moved even further West where nobody knew us. She helped me to get a new identity through some mates of hers. Ironically, the same mates we fell out over after Mum's funeral. I thought they were bad news. They would be the ruin of us and I didn't want any of that. I wanted the perfect life and the perfect man.' She reached across and took the grinder out of my hands, placed it onto the table. 'Funny how situations can be misread, impressions of people based on their looks and station in life can be so wrong. Once you get beneath that superficial exterior and pull back the curtain that's hiding the rotten core of their being, you realise that it's how they behave when they aren't being watched that is the most important, not the façade they hide behind.'

'But didn't he call her? Look for you there?'

'The Police came and told her I was presumed to be dead. They thought I had committed suicide but they couldn't find my body. I was upstairs hiding at the time and I was so scared that one of them would come upstairs and start nosing around like they do in the murder mysteries on the telly.' She stopped speaking and raised her head to look me in the eye. 'They didn't though, they were only in the house for about half an hour and they both left together. Rebecca played the grieving sister like a pro. I didn't know she was that good an actress. She should have been on the stage.' Her wry smile emerged again, a delicate up tilt of one side of her mouth. It was quite beautiful and as she did it, I could see the Lucy who had looked back at me from the photographs hidden in the sideboard drawer.

'Sam never knew I was back in contact with Rebecca. He knew that I had been so evil to her at Mum's funeral that I was never going to speak to her again. I'd told her that she was a loser, stuck in a dead-beat town with a dead-end job and no hoper mates who would drag her down with them.' Her smile dropped, her gaze lowered to the table and she slumped back a little on the bench seat. 'I said she was just like Mum and would always live from pay packet to pay packet with never enough money left at the end of the month. She had no desire to better herself. She had no spunk. God I hate that word now, Rebecca has more spunk than I have ever seen a woman possess. I even said she was a waste of space if she wasn't going to bother to do anything with her life.' Lucy picked up a clean serviette from the pile on the table and wiped her eyes.

'I didn't mean any of it of course. I was hurting from losing Mum. I was angry because we couldn't afford to do some special holidays when we knew she was dying. Angry because we couldn't give her the round the clock nursing care she needed in her last few days. Hell, we couldn't even afford a proper wake! The neighbours took pity on us because we were so poor and they all chipped in with bits and bobs of buffet food in the local pub. I took it all out on my sister and I really shouldn't have done that.'

'We all do things we regret when we are grieving,' I said, leaning over and holding her hands as they started picking pieces off the napkin and piling them up in front of her.

'We talked it through and she understood. She was there for me every step of the way. By the time Billie was born, I was living in Penzance and everyone knew me as Mandy. She doesn't have a father's name on her birth certificate and I've been working mainly cash in hand in a local café and as a barmaid in a tiny village pub. I couldn't have done any of it without Rebecca's help.'

The silent couple by the door stood up. She picked up her handbag, dropped her phone inside and, slinging the strap over her shoulder headed for the door. He followed meekly behind, just catching the door before it closed behind her as he was trying to slip his own phone into the back pocket of his black denim jeans. The other couple watched them and I saw them laugh and lean across the table for a quick kiss. I'll bet they thought they would never be like that, never be so distant to each other. They would love each other forever. Lucy and I had thought that too. He said something that I couldn't hear and pointed towards the door. She nodded in agreement as they stood up and followed the previous couple through the door. Once outside, he threw his arm around her shoulders and pulled her in tight for another kiss. Her arm circled his back and she slipped her hand into his rear pocket where it rested against his buttock as they walked away from the café.

'Young love eh? Ain't it brilliant?' Lucy asked as I realised she had also been watching the two couple's movements.

'The beginning and the end of the relationship?' I replied.

'Something like that. I only hope their break-ups are better than ours.' She straightened and leant forward over the table again.

'But we haven't gotten you out of there yet have we.' It was more of a statement than a question. 'You have to leave; you know that right?'

I nodded. 'Yes, I do. But I don't have anywhere to go and I have my brother Daniel to consider. I can't just vanish from his life. The last few years have been hard enough on him with Sam stopping me from seeing very much of him. We can't just vanish. He would always know to look for the Down's syndrome man that loves The Hulk.'

'That's why I'm here now. Rhea and Will have told me all about you and how worried they have been. I had hoped that when he found you, he would remember how he treated me and that you would be fine. I'm really sorry he's not.'

'Not as sorry as I am.'

'That was crass of me, I didn't mean to upset you. I don't want you to be hurt any more than you have been. This needs to stop now.'

I nodded again. 'But how can we stop him.'

She indicated across the room to Rhea and Will who were sitting at another table with a very chocolate smeared child between them.

'We've been talking and we have a plan. It means you have to go back there tonight and don't do anything to antagonise him.'

She must have seen the look on my face at her words and she

interpreted them correctly, 'I know, sometimes that's easier said than done, but listen to our idea and see what you think.'

'Ok, I'll listen. I guess I haven't got anything to lose.'

Chapter Ninety-Seven

Penny-May

Thursday June 25th 2015

Sam was still at work when Rhea dropped me back to Karadow. We dumped the shopping bags we had bought for our cover story in the bedroom and arranged for her to call me again at ten pm. If I was at all worried about Sam's behaviour, I was to ask if Josh had been told off at school again.

When she called, Sam answered my phone for me but handed it over when he knew for certain who it was on the other end. It was something he had been doing more and more often, as if he didn't believe the name that flashed up on the screen when it rang. I thanked him for giving it to me and Rhea went straight into a girly shopping related chat. I didn't need to say the code words. Despite his mistrust of my phone, he was calm tonight and back to being the nice Sam that Lucy and I had both loved.

He poured me a second glass of wine while I chatted with Rhea and sat on the sofa beside me, throwing his arm around my shoulder. I knew he could hear every word she said, so I kept the call chatty and happy. We didn't speak for long, Sam mentioned how late it was and how he had to get up early in the morning. She had laughed down the phone when she heard that.

'Ok,' she said, 'Tell him I'll let him get his beauty sleep and I will take you out for lunch tomorrow. You can have the pleasure of hearing me whinge about Josh's school antics over a smoked salmon bagel.'

I didn't have to relay the message, he took the phone from me and replied direct to her,

'Cheeky mare! I'll get Carl to sort you out for that comment. Look after her for me won't you? She's still quite fragile.'

I couldn't hear her reply as he moved away but he was smiling when he clicked the call off. He was in a good mood.

Chapter Ninety-Eight

Penny-May

Friday June 26th 2015

He brought me breakfast in bed again this morning.

'You don't have to let Rhea bully you into going out if you'd rather rest in bed and get your strength back you know. Shall I call her and tell her you're not up to it today? You've been out quite a bit over the last few days and you don't want to overdo it,' he said.

I knew exactly what Rhea would think if Sam told her not to come for me, she would have the police out here on a 999 emergency.

'Oh no, it's fine,' I replied, 'It does me good to get out and get a bit of exercise and fresh air. We won't stay out long.'

'Well, make sure you don't, I need you back to full health as soon as possible.'

'I will, I promise.'

He leant down and kissed me on the forehead, then moving down to a longer, deeper kiss on the mouth. It had been almost two weeks since he raped me and, judging by this kiss, he wouldn't wait much longer before he expected sex again. The thought of ever having sex again with anyone made me inwardly shudder. The thought of doing it with Sam was abhorrent.

I had to get out. Any doubts I had about Lucy's plan were extinguished as I imagined what the future may hold if I stayed.

'Be good, love you,' he said as he patted my cheek and walked towards the open door.

'I will— love you too.'

Those last words stuck in my throat, but I managed to grind them out. He expected me to say them. For me not to would draw him back into the room again and I needed him to go.

Ten minutes later I heard the front door shut, followed shortly by a screech of tyres on the gravel driveway.

Half an hour after that I called Mistral and asked Kate to put me through to Sam. I wanted to make sure he was there. If I'd phoned his mobile, he could be anywhere, inside the house spying on me, on the way back because he'd forgotten something. I couldn't take the risk, I needed to know he was where he was supposed to be so I could do what I had to do and get out of there safely.

She put me straight through.

'Hey Babe, what's wrong? I've just got in, is everything ok?'

'Yes, everything is fine here. I just wanted to say thank you for being so nice to me while I've been poorly. I've really loved the care and consideration you've given me.'

'Oh, you don't need to do that, you deserve to be pampered. If you're feeling better you can pay me back later if you like.'

I knew the glint in his eye that would accompany those words, the kind of payment he would require.

'Maybe, you never know your luck.'

He chuckled down the line, 'Well, that's given me something to look forward to.'

I grimaced; thank God we weren't on FaceTime.

'Anyway, I thought I'd get you a special present while I'm out today, I've been thinking and I know the perfect gift. It's going to be a secret for now though. And you'll never guess what it is.'

'Unwrapping you would be the perfect gift for me.'

'You'll have to wait and see. Now, get back to work, I have to get your surprise sorted. No peeking, you'll ruin it. See you later!'

I clicked the call off before he could reply. I know Lucy said Rebecca should have been an actress. I needed an Oscar for that performance.

Rhea would be here in an hour and I had loads to do before she arrived.

I quickly grabbed an overnight bag from the cupboard and put some old clothes in it to tide me over for a couple of days. I wasn't coming back here again tonight. I didn't know if I would ever be back.

I then moved over to the study and took Lucy's diaries from their hiding place in the desk. I made sure that I put the drawers back as they should be. If Sam came back unexpectedly, I didn't want him to think anything suspicious was going on.

With the diaries safely stowed away in a shopping bag and both bags hidden under a bush the other side of the drive, I waited outside. I breathed a sigh of relief as Rhea pulled up, jumped out of the car and hugged me.

'You all ready?'

I nodded, a lump in my throat threatening to choke me if I spoke too soon.

'I'll get my other bag. I hid it behind the bushes in case Sam came home and saw it.'

'Quickly then, I don't want to hang around too long.'

I grabbed the bag and she threw it onto the back seat.

'Have you got the diaries?''

'Yes,' I patted the bag that was now on my lap as I sat on the front seat.

'Then let's get our asses out of here!' She jumped in the driver's seat, put her foot down on the accelerator and we shot out of the drive in a cloud of gravel. 'Arrivederci!' she shouted as we flew out of the gate.

'Dyw genes, Karadow.' I whispered as the house vanished behind us.

'What's that?' Rhea asked.

'Goodbye in Cornish. Sam taught me a few phrases over the years. This one seems fitting.'

She reached across and patted my thigh. 'It'll be alright, you're safe now. Lucy is with Will and they are going to meet us there.'

I nodded, the tears starting to flow unchecked.

They were waiting right where Rhea said they would be, outside *The Wood Shack.*

Lucy wearing her dungarees again, but with a flowered cotton shirt underneath this time. Will as dapper as ever in a pair of chinos and a pale blue polo shirt. Worn with the collar up, of course.

I clutched the shopping bag to my chest as I approached them, Will engulfed me in one of his bear hugs while Lucy stood back. I could see she was nervous. This was going to be hard for her, she had so much more to lose than I did.

'Have you got them?' She asked.

'Yes, they're all in here,' I replied.

She stood up straight, pulled her shoulders back and started walking towards the building opposite.

'Then let's get this over with, shall we?'

I nodded and fell into step behind her, Rhea holding my hand. Will, caught napping, sprinted in front of us and held Lucy's hand. I saw her squeeze it tight as she looked across at him and smiled.

We entered the building and she went straight up to the desk, looking at the man behind the protective glass shield.

'My name is Lucy Lambert. My maiden name was Lucy Barton. I was reported missing, presumed dead two years ago. It was assumed I had committed suicide.' She held her hand out for me to stand next to her. 'This is Penny-May Lambert. We want to report our husband, Samuel Lambert, for sexual and domestic abuse, rape and attempted murder.'

The policeman looked across at me and I nodded.

'Wait there,' he said, 'I'll get someone to come out to you.'

Chapter Ninety-Nine

Sam

Friday June 26th 2015

Sam was working at his drawing board when the office door opened and he heard footsteps behind him. Turning to see who had rudely interrupted him without knocking he was surprised to see two men entering, one in chinos and a white, open necked shirt, the other in a police uniform. Kate was scuttling behind them looking shocked and confused.

'I'm sorry Mr Lambert,' she said, 'they just walked right past me, they wouldn't stop when I asked them what they wanted.'

'It's ok, Kate, you can go.' Sam stood from his desk as she quickly left the room, closing the door behind her.

'Gentlemen, this is unexpected. What can I do for you?'

The first policeman stepped forward and showed his badge, 'I'm Detective

Sergeant Rowe and this is Police Constable Taylor. Are you Samuel Lambert?'

'Yes, that's me?'

'And are you married to Lucy Lambert?'

Sam took a sharp intake of breath at hearing her name, 'I was, but she died. What is this about? Have you found her body?' He sat on the armchair, shock at the idea that he could finally get closure taking the strength out of him.

'And are you married to Penny-May Lambert?'

'Yes, has something happened to her? What is going on?'

'We'd like you to come with us if you would Sir, we have some questions we'd like to ask you.'

'I don't understand. Why do I have to come with you? Can't you tell me what's going on here? Now?'

'I'm afraid not. You have to come with us please and we will answer your questions down at the station.'

Sam stood and started to clench and unclench his fists. Who the hell did this upstart think he was?

'I'm not going anywhere until you tell me why you want to speak to me.'

'If you don't come with us of your own accord Mr Lambert, we can arrest you and take you in that way if you would prefer.' He nodded towards the door. 'I'm sure you would rather not walk out of here in handcuffs?'

'Arrest me? I haven't done anything?' Sam was growing more confused by the second. Images flashed across his mind as he tried to piece together what was happening here but he couldn't pinpoint anything that would have led the police to his office.

'If you would like to come with us please?' DS Rowe held his arm out towards the door while his colleague started to walk further into the room, around the side of Sam so that he could follow him out of the room. Sam watched his movements, realising that he had no choice but to do as the officers asked.

'Will this take long? I have an important meeting this afternoon that I have to be back for.'

DS Rowe smiled, 'I'm sure your secretary can rearrange it for you.'

'Fine,' Sam replied, 'but I'll be talking to the Chief Constable about this inconvenience. We are good friends.'

'I'm sure you will Mr Lambert, but in the meantime, would you mind?' Again, he indicated towards the door but more forcefully this time. He walked over and opened it, the PC walking directly behind Sam and gently touching Sam's back with his hand to start him moving.

Sam looked at him, his fist clenched tight as it hung by his side, 'You don't need to push me, I'm going,' he replied, taking one step forward.

DS Rowe smiled, 'Thank you. The car is downstairs by the front door.'

Kate, Charlotte and Michelle busied themselves at their computers as the trio left, one policeman each side of Sam. They entered the lift, the officers standing slightly behind Sam so they could see him at all times. Sam's confusion growing as he was marched through the glass fronted foyer, past the reception desk and the milling employees who were not as discreet as his secretaries. Instead of busying themselves, they stopped and stared at the sight of the senior partner being led out of the building and into the waiting police car that was parked right outside the front door.

Sam knew that as soon as he was out of earshot, the rumours and the chatter would start. And he didn't have any idea why he was being subjected to this ordeal. He would make these two pay for their insolence. What on earth could it be that meant he was being treated like this?

As they drove out of the town Sam decided to try and question them again,

'Are we not going to Trecase station? Surely that's closest?'

DS Rowe turned in his seat, 'No, we're going to Truro.'

'For God's sake, this is getting more ridiculous by the minute. I've got a business to run.'

Neither policeman spoke. Sam slumped back into the seat and stared out of the window. He was obviously not going to get any answers out of these two imbeciles, he'd wait until he got there and then demand they let him know what was going on.

The car pulled up to the back of the police station. DS Rowe got out of the passenger seat and opened the rear door for Sam to get out. As he stood up and stretched to ease some of the kinks from the uncomfortable ride, Sam heard voices behind him and turned to see a group of four people walking past the entrance to the car park.

'Penny-May? Rhea?' He shouted, starting to walk towards the entrance, 'Will?' he didn't recognise the fourth individual although she looked familiar, he had to get closer.

PC Taylor stood in front of him while DS Rowe put a restraining hand on Sam's arm making him stop. The group turned to face him.

'You can't go down there I'm afraid, please come this way.'

The brown-haired woman removed her glasses and swept her hair away from her face.

'Lucy?' Sam's face went white, 'It can't b__ ' He tried to shake the detectives hand free from his arm but it had turned into a vice like grip, the constable now gripping the other arm as they turned him and began to frogmarch him inside. 'Let me go! I want to see my wife!'

DS Rowe pushed him through the open door and slammed it shut behind them. 'She doesn't want to see you mate. Neither of them do. Now, let's get you checked in, shall we? We've got a lot of paperwork to do and, based on the evidence those two women have given us, you're not going to be seeing them again for a very long time. Do you have a lawyer?'

As he continued to read Sam his rights and formally arrest him, the realisation of his situation finally began to filter through his mind. How can Lucy have survived? Why did she do that? Why didn't she come home? They can't have gone to the police about him. How can they do that after everything he's done for them?

He removed his belt and tie and emptied his pockets in a daze, not really listening to what he was being told. He would wake up in a minute, this was a nightmare that would soon stop.

'Gareth Millen,' Sam finally said, 'My lawyer is called Gareth Millen.'

The detective nodded as he pushed Sam into a cell, 'You're going to need him,' he replied as he shut the door and the lock clicked into place.

Sam sat on the hard bed and the door grill was slid closed. An open toilet and sink beside it. A single blanket and bare pillow the only other things in the room. He had been in here for hours already. They said it was taking a while to get hold of Gareth and he would just have to wait until he got there before they could take him for questioning.

His thoughts revolved around the charges that had been read out to him: domestic abuse; rape; grievous bodily harm; attempted murder. It was ridiculous. All he had done was what they deserved. He had to bring them into line when they misbehaved, when they didn't do what they were supposed to do. Attempted murder was a ridiculous charge anyway, he had never wanted to kill them. He did now though. He could quite easily put his hands right around their scrawny little necks and squeeze them so tight...

He looked down at his hands, opened and shut them,

clenched them into fists, stood and thrust one of them straight into the wall. The pain shot through his arm and he shook his hand to ease it. Clenching and unclenching his fingers as he did so. It didn't release the same tension as when he hit a person. The pent-up frustration was still inside him, bursting to get out.

He sat down on the bed and put his head into his hands, memories flooding into his mind; Lucy's shocked face after he slapped her because she was late home; Penny-May pleading with him to stop as he punched her; Lucy on the floor at the bottom of the stairs as his boot went into her swollen stomach; Penny-May's tears after he had beaten and had sex with her in the kitchen. Is that what they were saying was rape? It wasn't rape. She was his wife; how could they say it was rape?

You couldn't rape your own wife.

Could you?

She was lying on the floor, begging him to get off her, to let her go. The sexual desire and adrenaline that was coursing through his veins was too strong, he had to have her, had to show her who was the boss, who was the one who made the decisions. She'd shut up after he entered though so she must have enjoyed it. Those tears were fake. Women cried for everything, how was he supposed to know whether they were for good or bad reasons?

He stood and started pacing the pitifully few steps the bare cell could afford him. He wasn't getting out of there.

It was his word against theirs and how could he say he'd never hit them when he knew he had? They would have evidence of the fall that made Lucy lose the baby. Maybe she hadn't believed him after all about the wire across the top of the stairs? That push had been so satisfying at the time. He hadn't wanted a brat hanging around, getting in the way. She shouldn't have got pregnant, never have tried to trick him into becoming a father. It had only taken a slight push. She was so fat it didn't take that much to overbalance her. The kicks were just to make sure and they felt so good at the time. She deserved them.

His mother would be devastated. He couldn't bear to see the pity in her eyes, or the condemnation. The gossip in the office would be rife by now too. Surely they would never believe that he could abuse those two sluts that he had been foolish enough to fall in love with...to marry even. They were his wives. He could do what he liked with them. Couldn't he?

The thoughts continued to whirl around his mind. Ricocheting back and forth like the squash ball that he couldn't quite catch. Couldn't quite pin down. He wanted to scream and cry.

He wanted his mother's arms around him, telling him it was going to be ok and that he was a good boy. The nasty people had got it all wrong and he was going to be alright.

The ball stopped its incessant clattering inside his head as he finally realised that it wouldn't be ok. He was going to prison and he would be there for a very long time.

He took off his shirt and wrapped it around the automatic closure on the back of the door, buttoning it to make sure it stayed there. Climbing onto the toilet he pulled both sleeves together and wrapped them around his neck, tying them together under his chin.

He couldn't spend the rest of his life in a prison cell.

Placing one foot out into the air, he bent his standing knee a little and forced himself to jump.

The darkness came quickly as his body swung back against the door.

Chapter One Hundred

Penny-May

Friday June 26th 2015

Rebecca's kitchen was typical council house style. The same two up two down with a small back yard that can be seen on any council estate in Cornwall. Café nets hung from a mid-height pole with the proverbial cactus plant in the centre of the windowsill. Kettle and toaster in pride of place on the worktop, gas slot in cooker with a tea towel draped over the oven door handle. We were sat shoulder to shoulder around the tiny wooden table in the corner of the room, not speaking, each holding our hands round gone cold coffee mugs, when we heard the knock on the door. We looked at each other. None of us wanting to go and find out that they had let him free to come and find us. It wouldn't take him long, not now he knew that Lucy was alive. Did they tell him about Billie? Was her life in danger now as well?

After a pause, another knock and Rebecca rose from her seat.

'I'll go,' she said, her voice so quiet we could barely hear it.

A minute later she came back into the room leading the detective who had spoken to us at the station and a uniformed PC.

They weren't smiling.

Lucy reached over and squeezed my hand. I held onto hers and wouldn't let it go again.

'I'm really sorry,' DS Rowe said as my heart sank even further. *Nice one Penny-May, you can't even report him without messing it up. Now he's going to come and slaughter you for putting him through this.*

'You've had to let the bastard go? How the hell did he wriggle out of this one?' Will asked, standing up and starting to pace the room. 'You've got more than enough proof to charge him surely? He should be locked up and never let out again after what he's done!'

'No, it's not that. I'm afraid he passed away an hour or so ago.'

'What?' I cried, raising my head to look the detective in the eye, 'He can't have, he was fit and well.'

'There isn't any nice way to say this so I'll get straight to it. He used his shirt to hang himself in his cell.'

Will stopped his pacing and leant on the worktop for support, Lucy and I looked at each other, shock mirrored on both of our faces.

'I thought it was impossible to do that now, I thought you had monitoring and stuff__' Rhea asked.

'We do, for those who we think are a suicide risk. He wasn't one of those. He had been banging and shouting at the door, demanding to see his lawyer. He went quiet and the last time he was checked he was told he would have to wait until the lawyer arrived. Nobody had any idea he would do that.'

Lucy whispered, 'And he's really gone? He's definitely dead?'

'Yes.'

I screamed. I didn't even know why I was screaming. This high-pitched wail was coming out of my mouth and I couldn't stop it, no matter how hard I tried, the noise engulfed me and was all I could hear. I felt arms being placed around me, hugging me, trying to protect me from all that was happening. Eventually, I heard murmurings in my ear, I felt Lucy's hair against my cheek as she cradled me to her, pulling my head down onto her shoulder and stifling my screams as they turned into sobs.

'It's over,' she said, 'it's really over. He'll never hurt you again.'

'What will happen to me?' She asked once I had calmed enough. 'Will I be prosecuted for wasting police time?'

'Technically you should be,' DS Rowe replied, 'but I can't really see the CPS taking action in your case. We have enough evidence to show why you vanished the way you did. There is no reason to believe you acted maliciously, or that you may be inclined to repeat it. Are you?'

She shook her head, 'No, I want to be me again.'

He started to make his way to the front door, the PC following, 'We'll be in touch if there is anything else.'

'Thank you, officer,' replied Rebecca as she showed them out.

'I can't believe it,' Will said to the silent room.

None of us had the strength to reply.

Epilogue

PENNY-MAY

Sunday June 26th 2016

It's been a year already. A whole year without worrying if I am saying the wrong thing, moving the wrong way, wearing the wrong clothes, opening the wrong bottle of wine. I've stopped flinching every time I hear a car door slam and changed my name back to Penny-May Meares as soon as I could. There wasn't much paperwork to do, apparently, I was never married to him properly. The ceremony wasn't legal over here and he knew it. That's why he would never let me fill in any forms or have my own credit card. His lawyer told me that when he was sorting out Sam's affairs. He had told Sam that too, before we went through the sham of a ceremony.

Everything went to Lucy as officially she was still the next of kin, she was still married to him and he'd never bothered to change his will.

Maggie was heartbroken. I almost felt sorry for the old bat. Almost. She didn't deserve to go through that, but she was still an old bat. Lucy is more kind-hearted than I am because she lets Maggie see her granddaughter. I don't think I would, but I guess Lucy had a much better relationship with her mother-in-law than I did. Maybe? At the beginning? They are trying anyway. Lucy has told me it's hard with the spectre of Sam hanging over them. Maggie finds it hard to believe all the things her son did. To her he was the perfect, model son. To imagine him as the monster he was must be more heart-breaking than just losing him. She's also lost the image and the relationship she had nurtured for all of his life.

But she's still an old bat.

Lucy sold Karadow. Neither of us wanted to live in it anymore and it didn't take very long to sell. It was a beautiful house and I hope the new owners can exorcise the demons from it. They are a young couple with two little children. Their whole lives in front of them. They looked so happy to get their dream house. I remember when that was me.

Although I wasn't entitled to anything, Lucy split the house sale and gave me half of the proceeds. I used it to buy myself a three-bedroom cottage in Trecase and Daniel now lives with me. We've planted another pear tree, but I really need to learn how to cook 'crumbly pie' like Martha does or Danny is going to disown me. He still gets The Hulk and Joey mixed up but it's cute and I love everything about it.

Emma eventually forgave me for not keeping in contact with her. I turned up on her doorstep after we left Rebecca's house and told her everything. She gave me a right old telling off for not coming to her earlier. I'm still not sure she totally understands why I couldn't come to her at the time, but she was glad that I did in the end. She has moved into my house as well and it's bliss having both my brother and my best friend with me all the time. I don't like being on my own or going out alone. But I'm getting better. I will get better.

Lucy used her money to buy her and Billie a house. It's bigger than mine, but she has set up her own physiotherapy practice there. Will has left Silverwell and is working with her as a partner concentrating on sport rehabilitation. They make a great team. Everyone goes there. She thought at first it would be strange with people blaming her for faking her death, but it's been quite the opposite. She was so well loved that, once they got over the initial shock, she was sought out and told how sorry everyone was for her. The story was in the local news for weeks.

Rhea is amazing. I can never thank her enough for getting me out of that house. She had so much to lose. Carl took ages to believe that his best friend could do what he did to Lucy and me. He and Rhea had so many arguments over why she kept it all a secret from him, but eventually he realised it was because she knew he would confront Sam or tell him that Lucy was in hiding and where. It was a risk she simply could not take.

It was so hard trying to be perfect because there are no shades to perfection. No levels to suggest how far you have to go to get there, or how narrow that pedestal is when you stand upon it.

Do we ever actually stand on it? Or is it our perception of what a perfect life is that brings us crashing down when we realise we don't match up to it?

If there's one thing that both Lucy and I have realised, it's that we don't want to be perfect, have the perfect life or find the perfect love.

We don't want to hide behind the curtain.

We just want to be ourselves and be perfectly imperfect.

Printed in Great Britain
by Amazon

45994536R00233